Pokémon® Mystery Dungeon

GINJI'S RESCUE TEAM

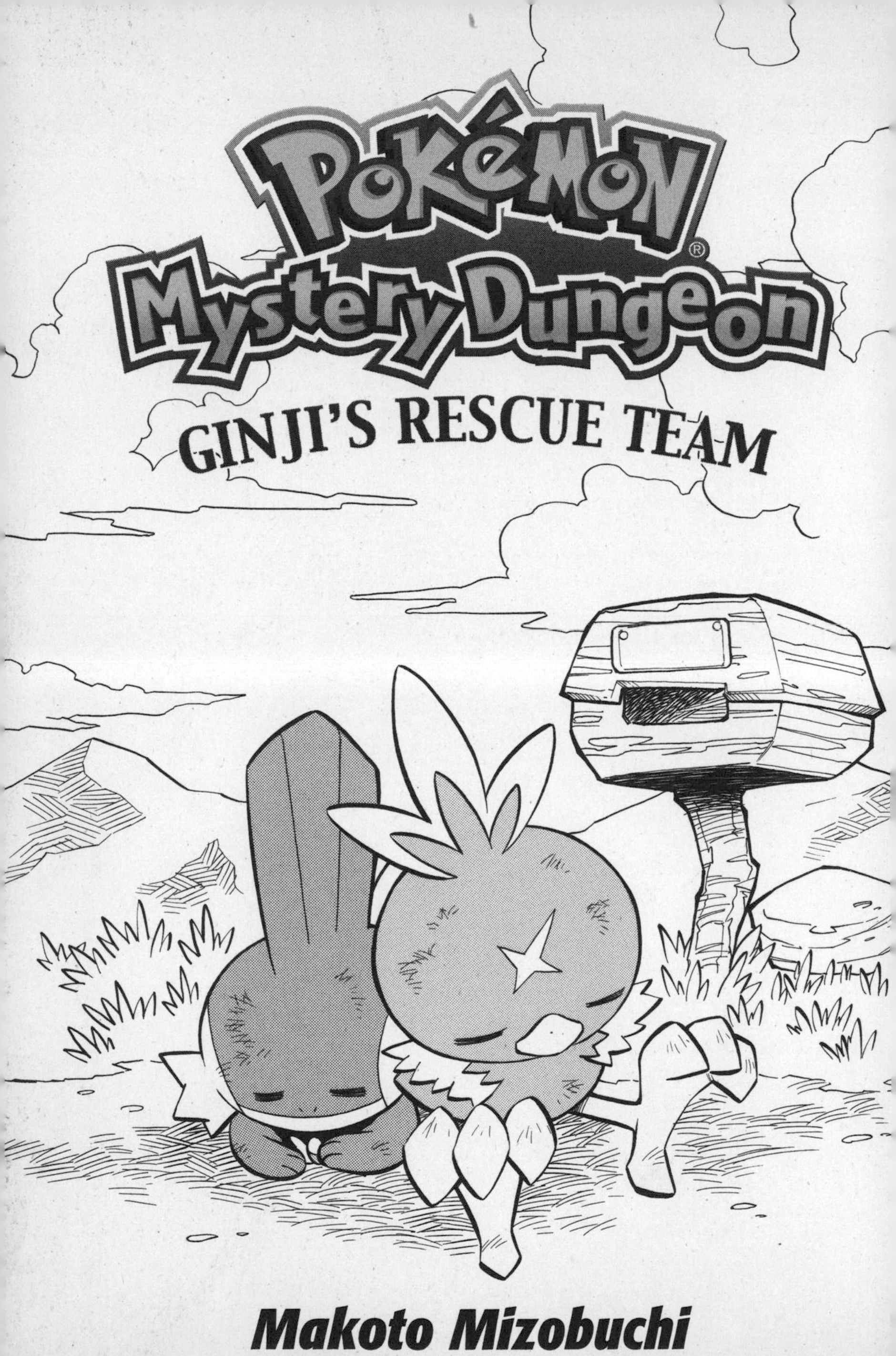

Makoto Mizobuchi

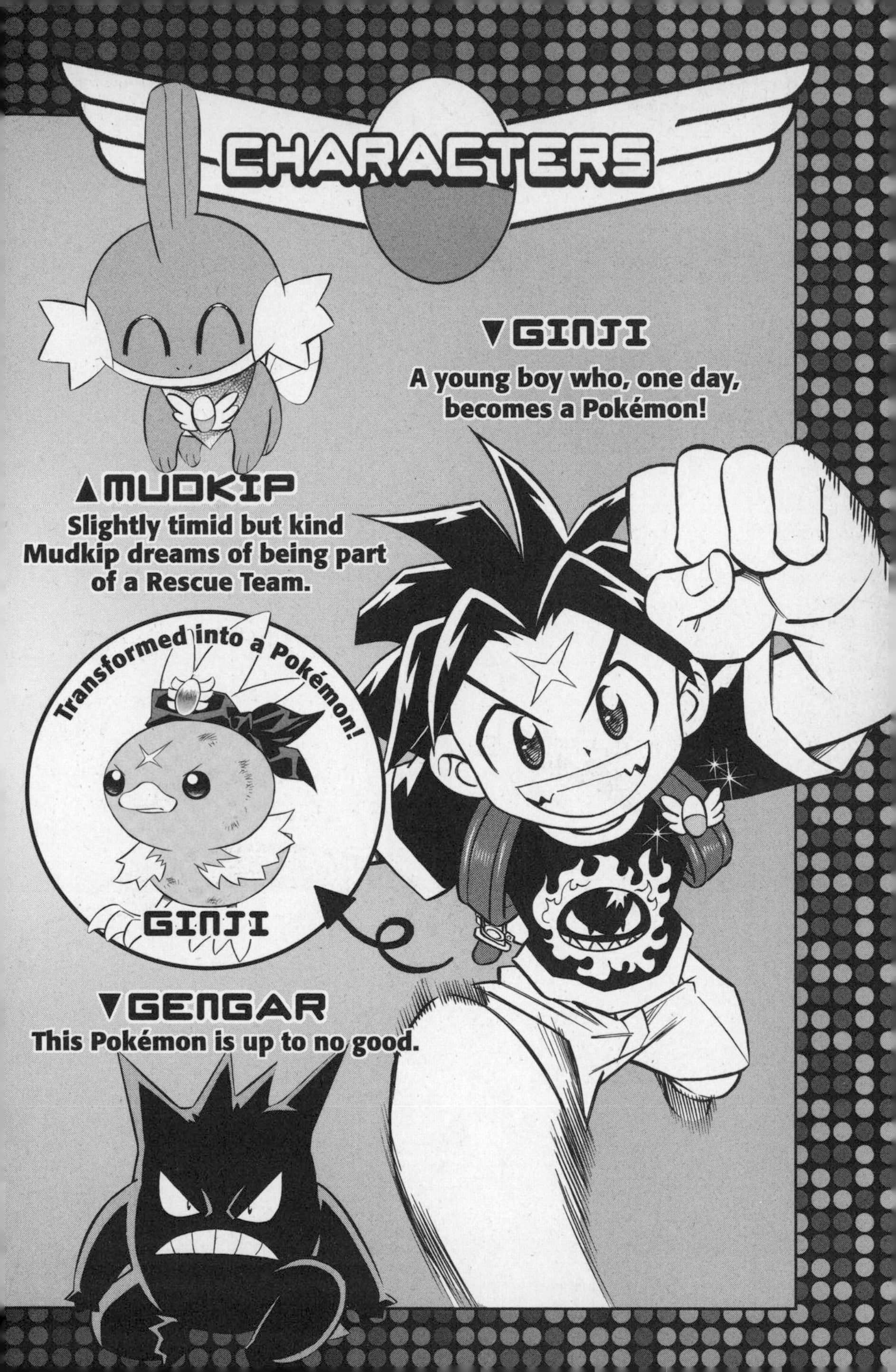
CHARACTERS
▼GINJI
A young boy who, one day, becomes a Pokémon!
▲MUDKIP
Slightly timid but kind Mudkip dreams of being part of a Rescue Team.
Transformed into a Pokémon!
GINJI
▼GENGAR
This Pokémon is up to no good.

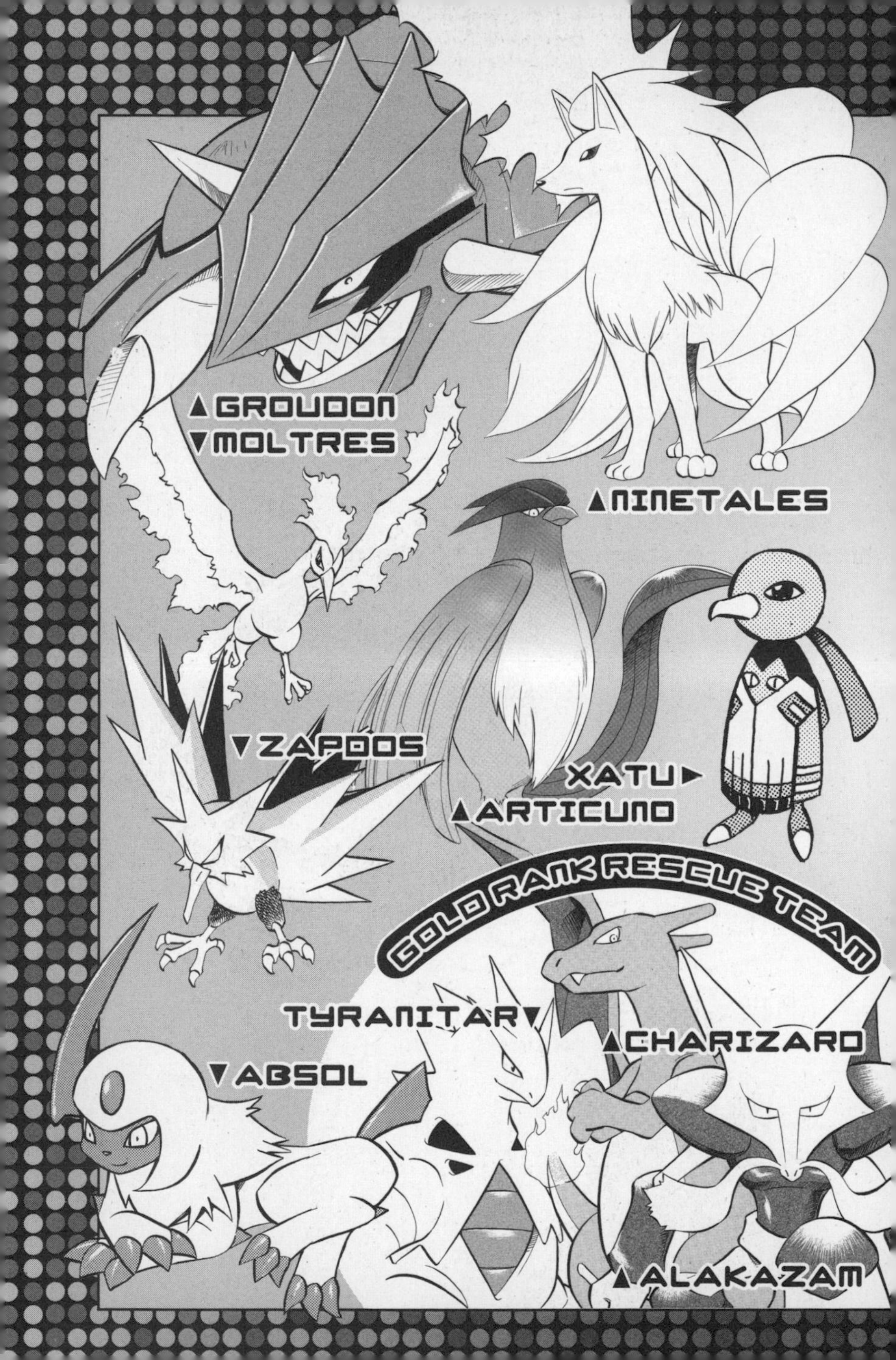
▲GROUDON
▼MOLTRES
▲NINETALES
▼ZAPDOS
XATU▶
▲ARTICUNO
GOLD RANK RESCUE TEAM
TYRANITAR▼
▲CHARIZARD
▼ABSOL
▲ALAKAZAM

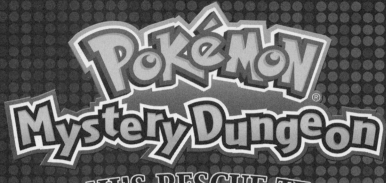

Pokémon® Mystery Dungeon

Ginji's Rescue Team

VIZ Kids Edition

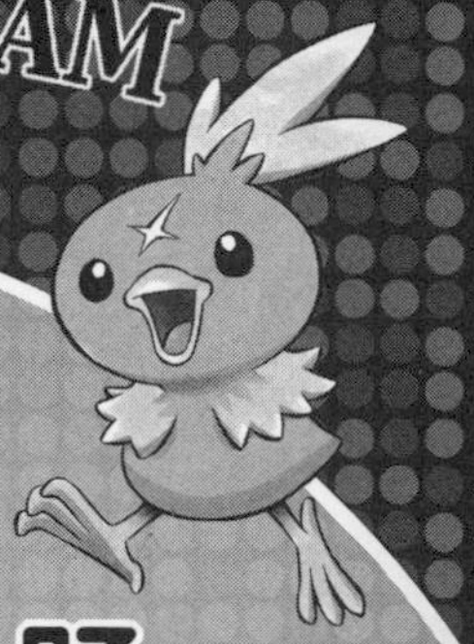

Contents

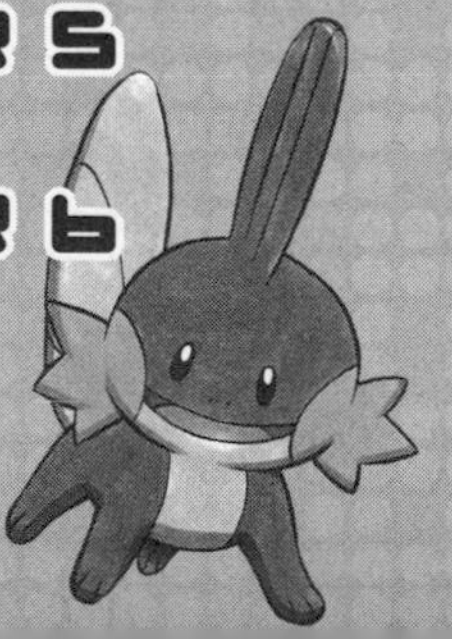

Chapter One

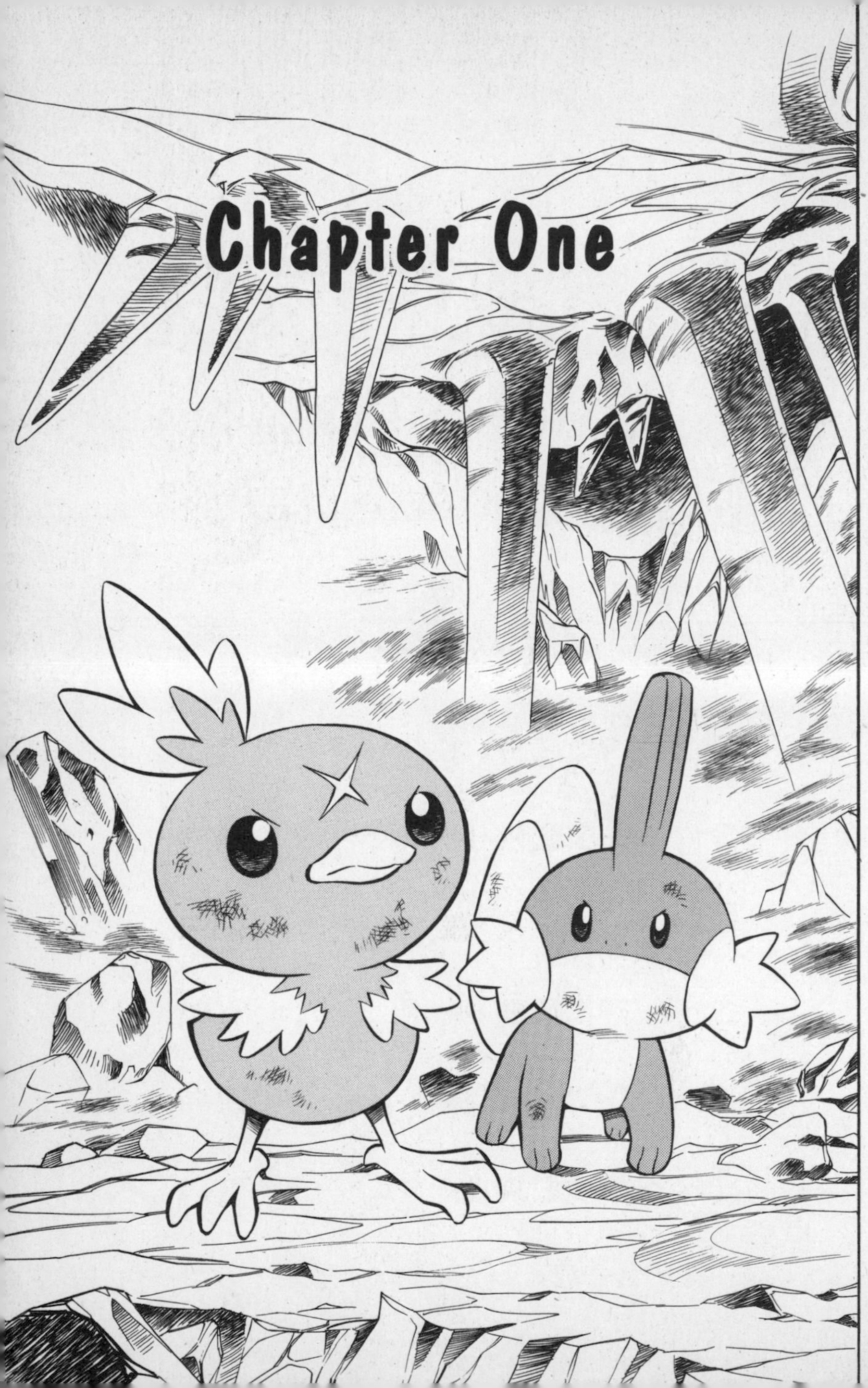

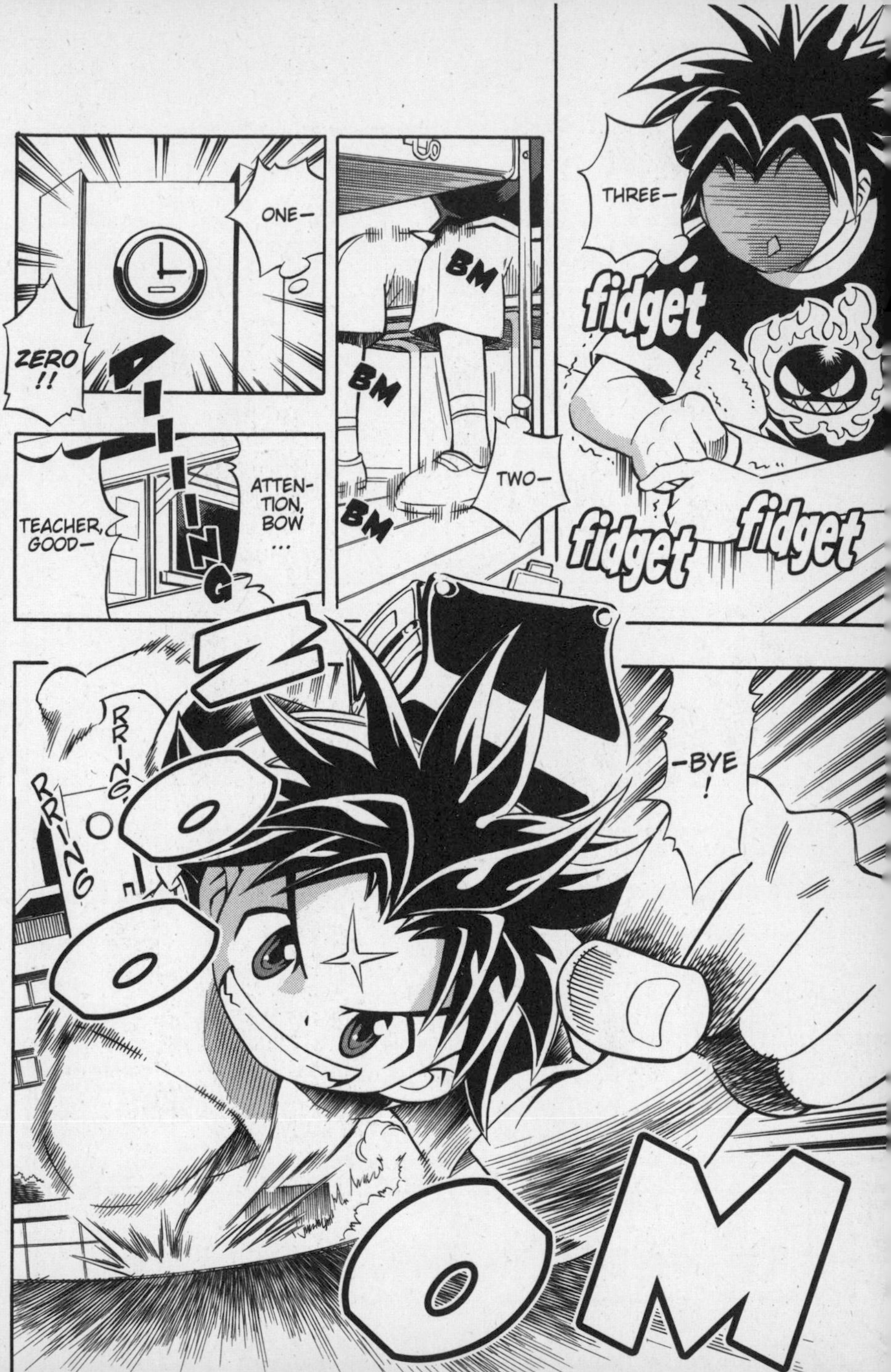
THREE—
fidget
fidget
fidget
BM
BM
BM
TWO—
ONE—
ZERO!!
DIIING
ATTENTION, BOW...
TEACHER, GOOD—
-BYE!
RRING, RRING
ZOOOOOM

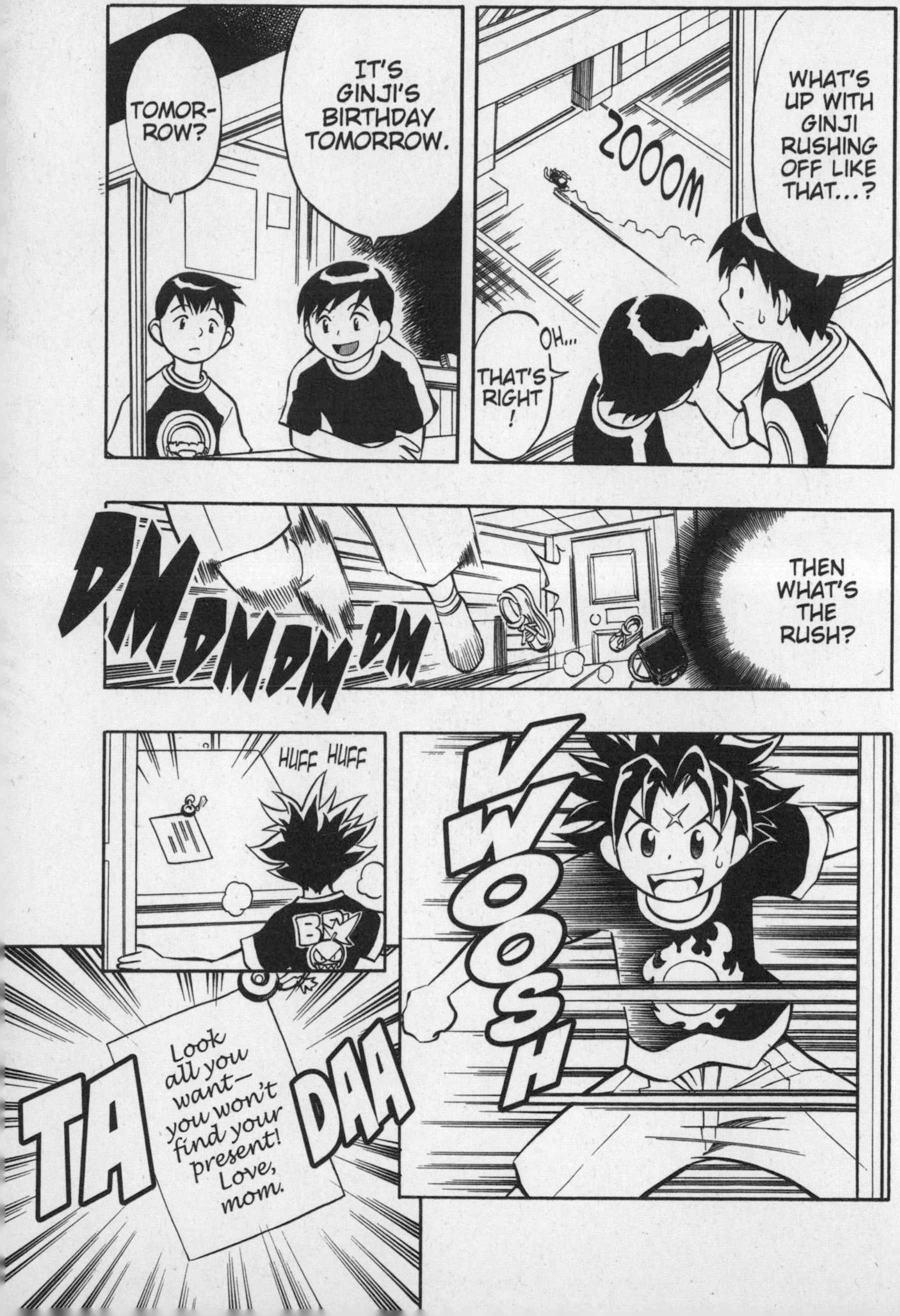
WHAT'S UP WITH GINJI RUSHING OFF LIKE THAT...?
ZOOOM
OH... THAT'S RIGHT!
IT'S GINJI'S BIRTHDAY TOMORROW.
TOMOR-ROW?
THEN WHAT'S THE RUSH?
DM DMDMDM DM
WOOOSH
HUFF HUFF
TA DAA
Look all you want—you won't find your present! Love, mom.

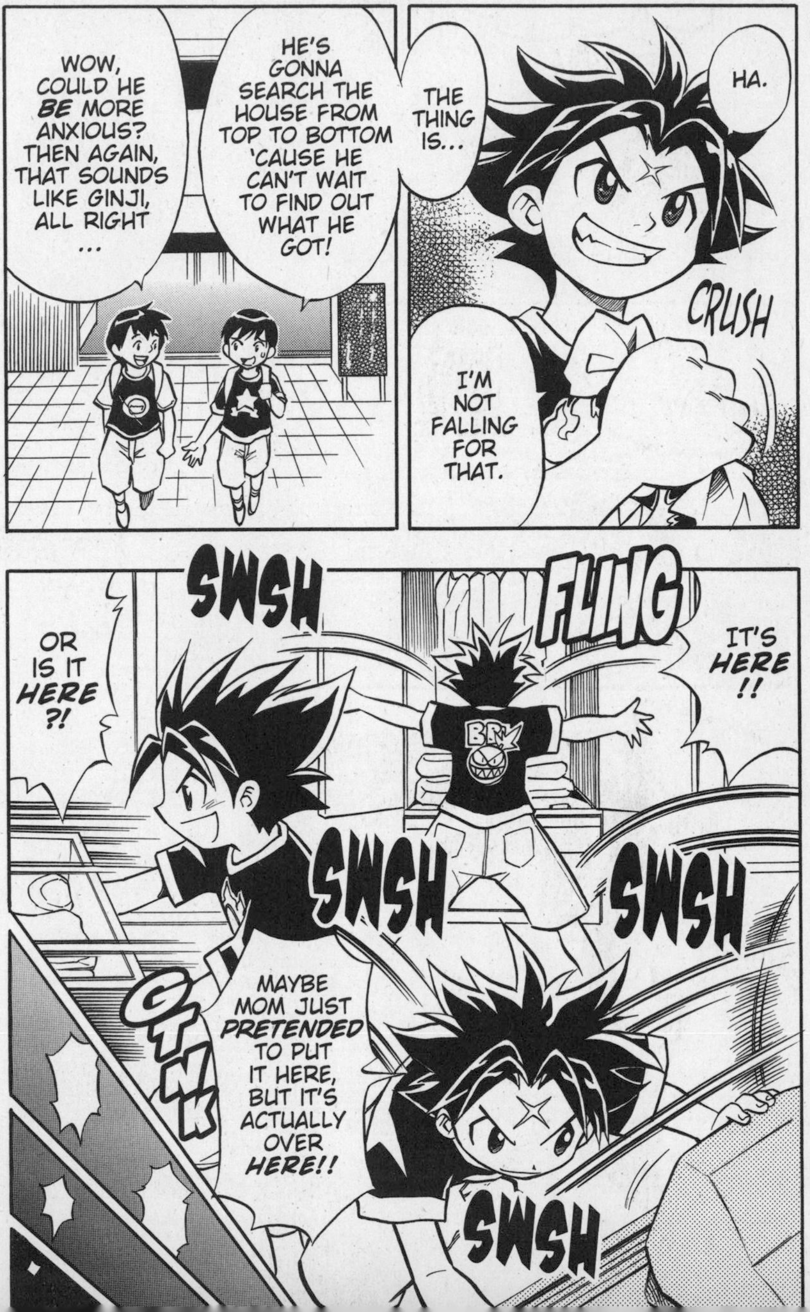
HA.
THE THING IS...
CRUSH
I'M NOT FALLING FOR THAT.
HE'S GONNA SEARCH THE HOUSE FROM TOP TO BOTTOM 'CAUSE HE CAN'T WAIT TO FIND OUT WHAT HE GOT!
WOW, COULD HE *BE* MORE ANXIOUS? THEN AGAIN, THAT SOUNDS LIKE GINJI, ALL RIGHT ...
IT'S *HERE* !!
FLING
SWSH
OR IS IT *HERE* ?!
SWSH
SWSH
MAYBE MOM JUST *PRETENDED* TO PUT IT HERE, BUT IT'S ACTUALLY OVER *HERE!!*
GTNK
SWSH

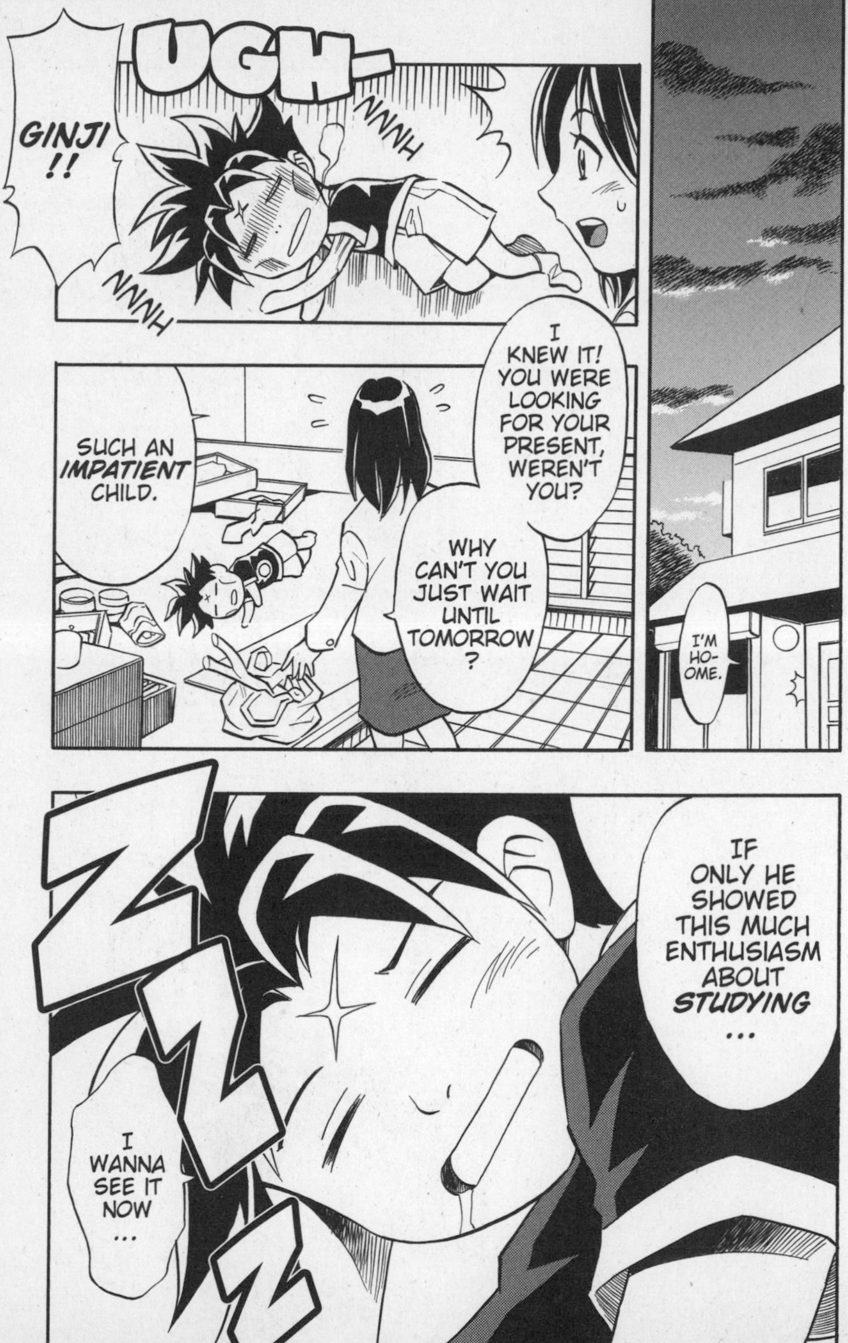

I'M HO-OME.
UGH-
NNNH
GINJI!!
NNNH
I KNEW IT! YOU WERE LOOKING FOR YOUR PRESENT, WEREN'T YOU?
WHY CAN'T YOU JUST WAIT UNTIL TOMORROW?
SUCH AN *IMPATIENT* CHILD.
IF ONLY HE SHOWED THIS MUCH ENTHUSIASM ABOUT *STUDYING*...
ZZZ
I WANNA SEE IT NOW...

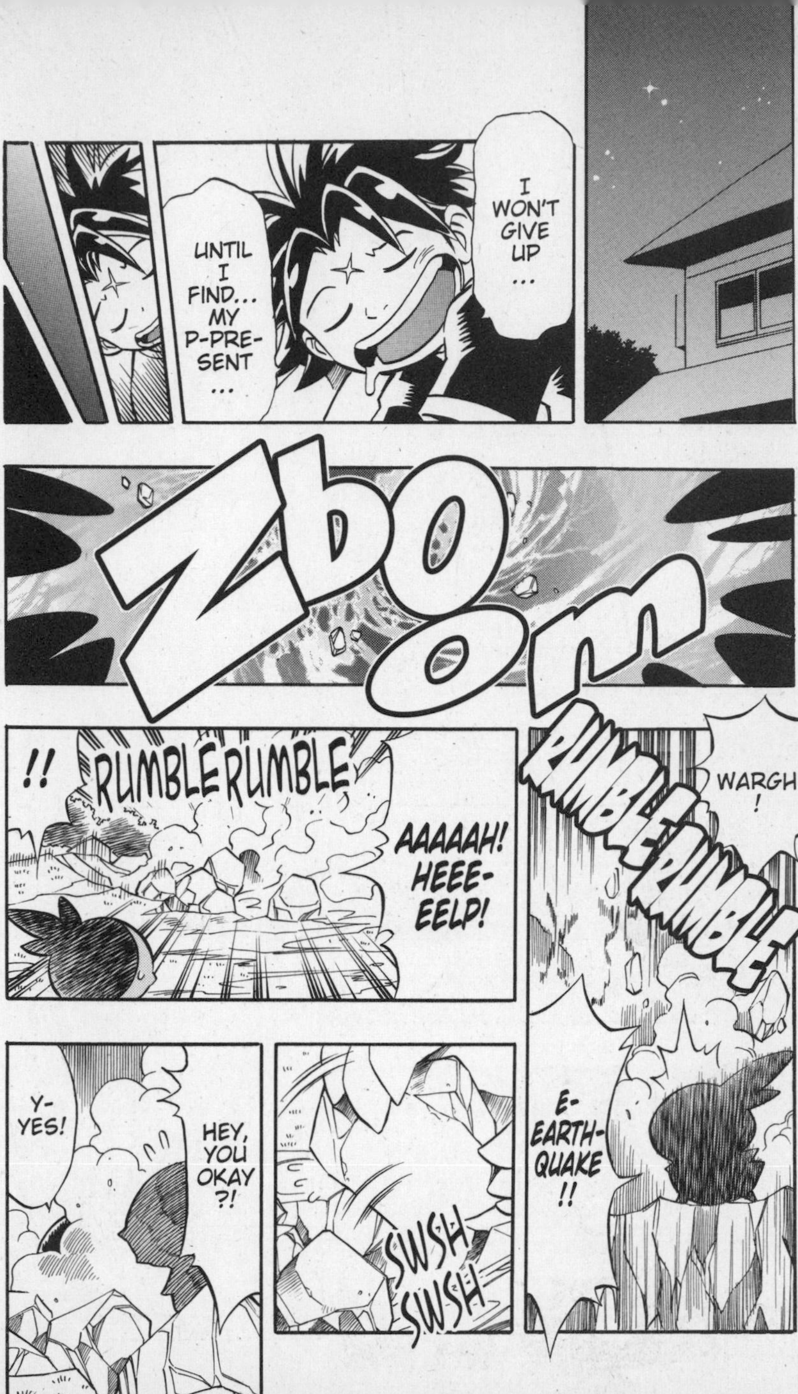
I WON'T GIVE UP ...
UNTIL I FIND... MY P-PRESENT ...
ZBOOM
WARGH!
RUMBLE RUMBLE
E-EARTHQUAKE!!
!!
RUMBLE RUMBLE
AAAAAH! HEEE-EELP!
SWSH SWSH
HEY, YOU OKAY?!
Y-YES!

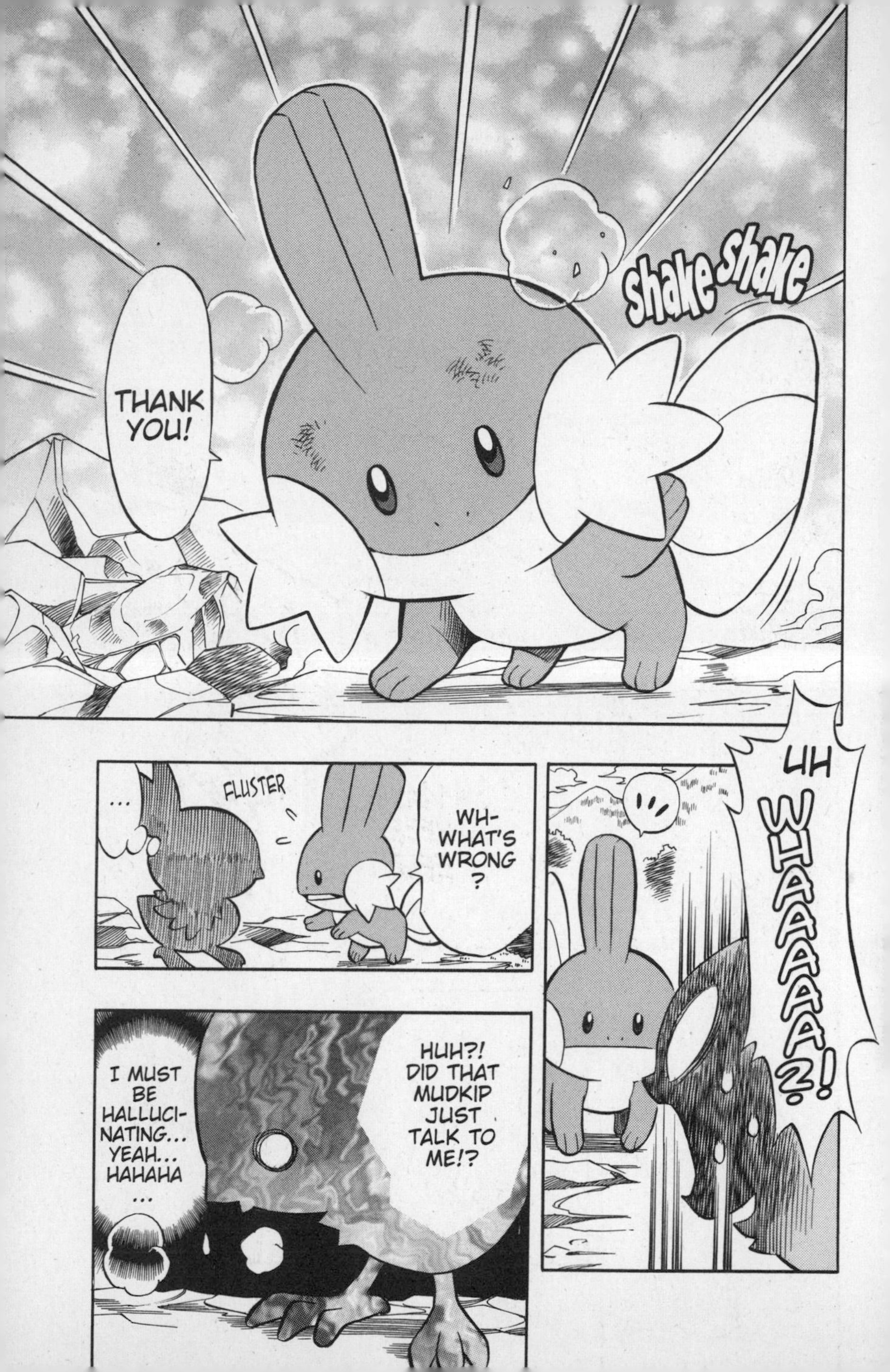
shake shake
THANK YOU!
UH WHAAAAAA?!
FLUSTER
WH-WHAT'S WRONG?
...
HUH?! DID THAT MUDKIP JUST TALK TO ME!?
I MUST BE HALLUCINATING... YEAH... HAHAHA ...

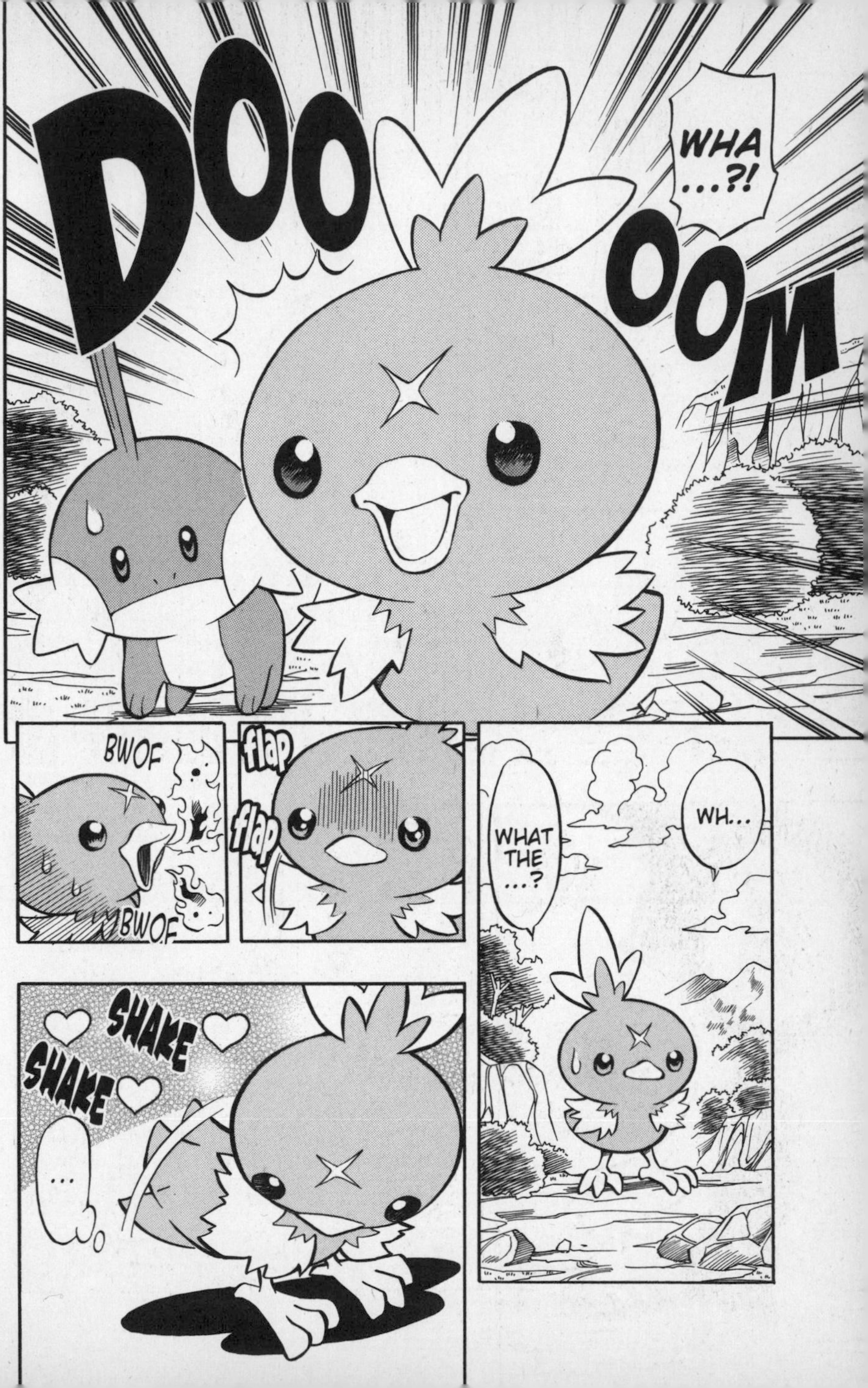
WHA ...?!
DOO
OOM
WH...
WHAT THE ...?
flap
flap
BWOF
BWOF
SHAKE
SHAKE
...

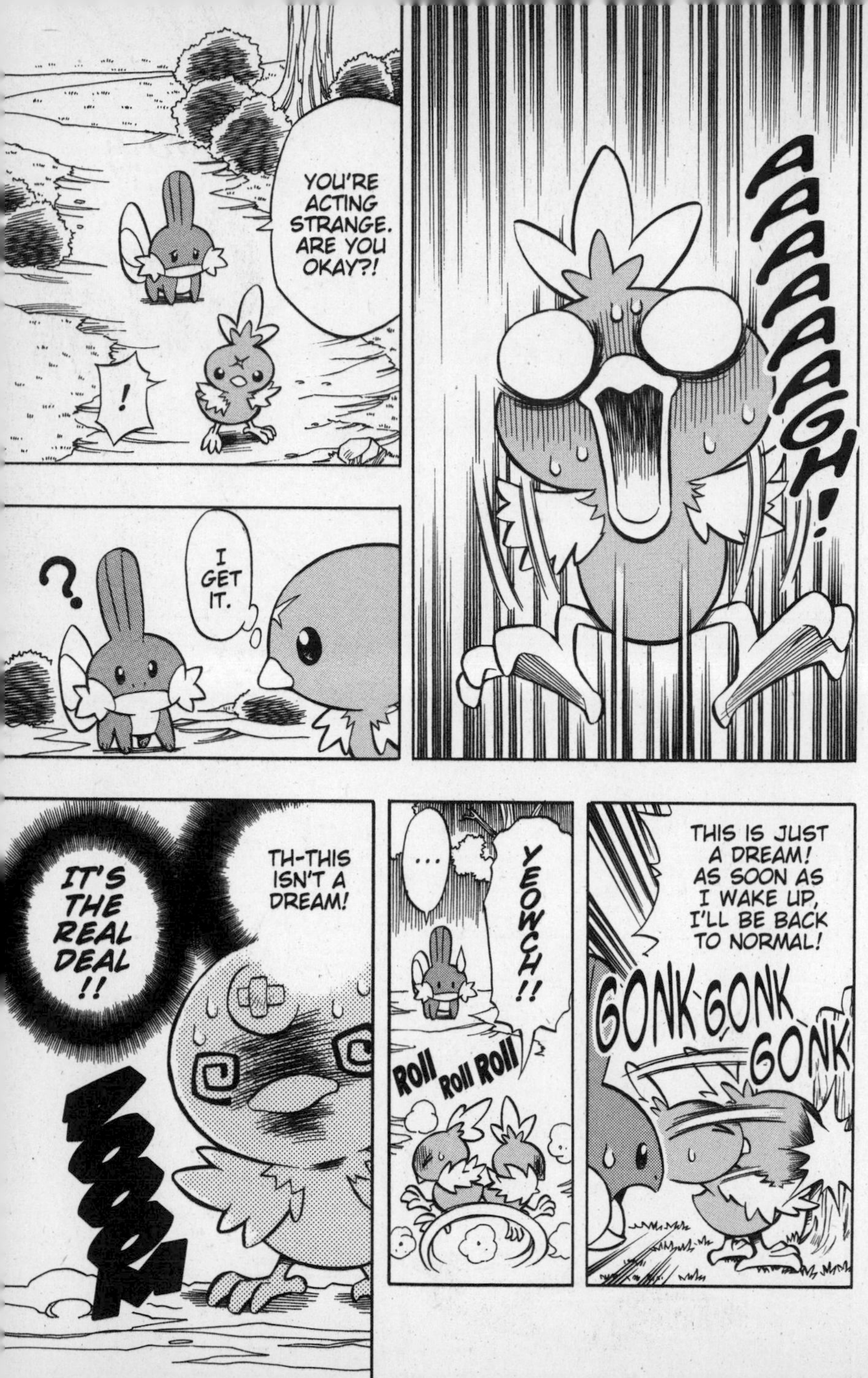
AAAAAAAGH!
YOU'RE ACTING STRANGE. ARE YOU OKAY?!
!
I GET IT.
?
THIS IS JUST A DREAM! AS SOON AS I WAKE UP, I'LL BE BACK TO NORMAL!
GONK GONK GONK
...
YEOWCH!!
Roll Roll Roll
TH-THIS ISN'T A DREAM!
IT'S THE REAL DEAL!!

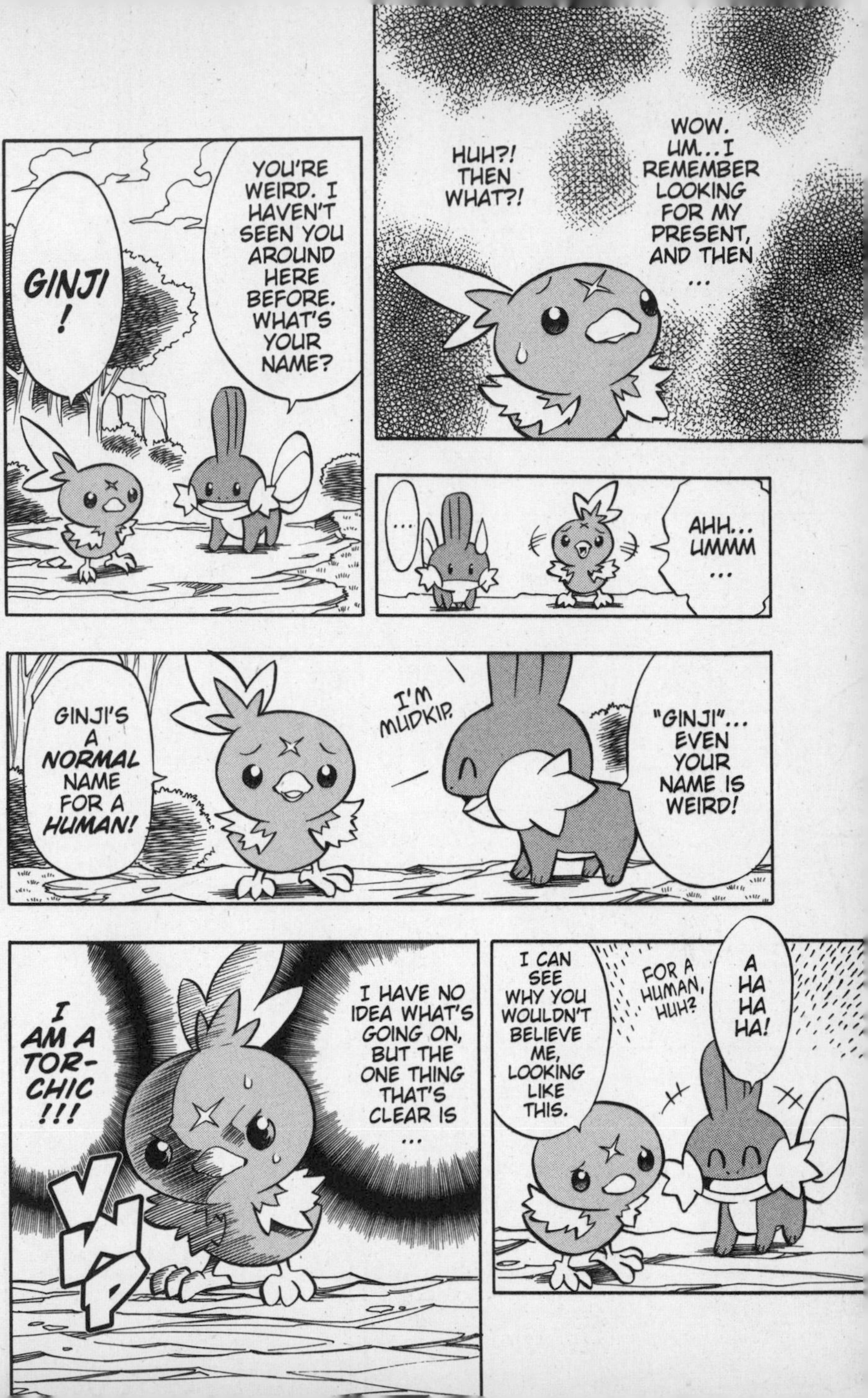
WOW. UM...I REMEMBER LOOKING FOR MY PRESENT, AND THEN ...
HUH?! THEN WHAT?!
AHH... UMMM ...
...
YOU'RE WEIRD. I HAVEN'T SEEN YOU AROUND HERE BEFORE. WHAT'S YOUR NAME?
GINJI !
"GINJI"... EVEN YOUR NAME IS WEIRD!
I'M MUDKIP.
GINJI'S A NORMAL NAME FOR A HUMAN!
A HA HA HA!
FOR A HUMAN, HUH?
I CAN SEE WHY YOU WOULDN'T BELIEVE ME, LOOKING LIKE THIS.
I HAVE NO IDEA WHAT'S GOING ON, BUT THE ONE THING THAT'S CLEAR IS ...
I AM A TOR-CHIC !!!
VP

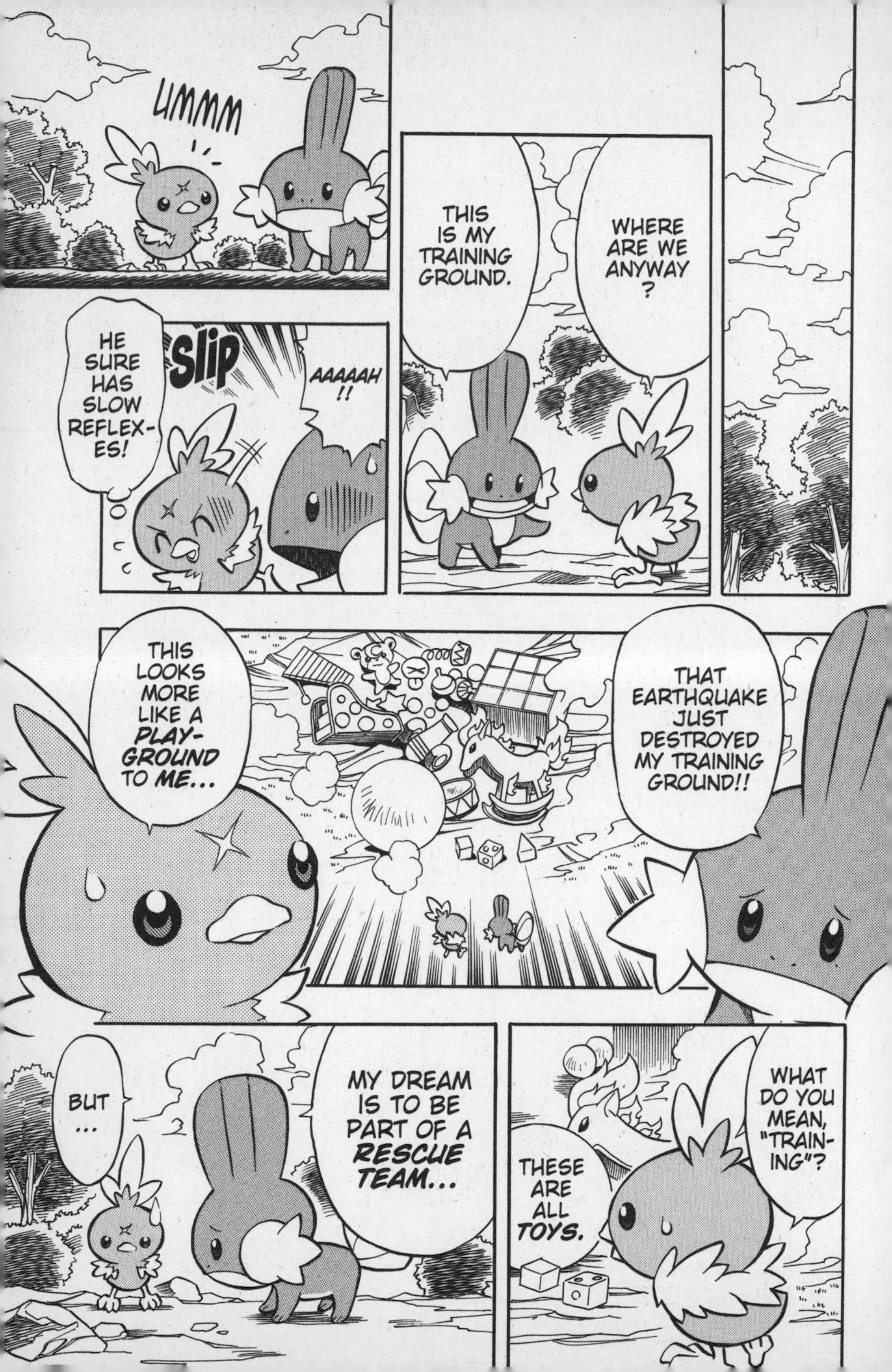
WHERE ARE WE ANYWAY?
THIS IS MY TRAINING GROUND.
UMMM
AAAAAH!!
SLIP
HE SURE HAS SLOW REFLEXES!
THAT EARTHQUAKE JUST DESTROYED MY TRAINING GROUND!!
THIS LOOKS MORE LIKE A PLAYGROUND TO ME...
WHAT DO YOU MEAN, "TRAINING"?
THESE ARE ALL TOYS.
MY DREAM IS TO BE PART OF A RESCUE TEAM...
BUT...

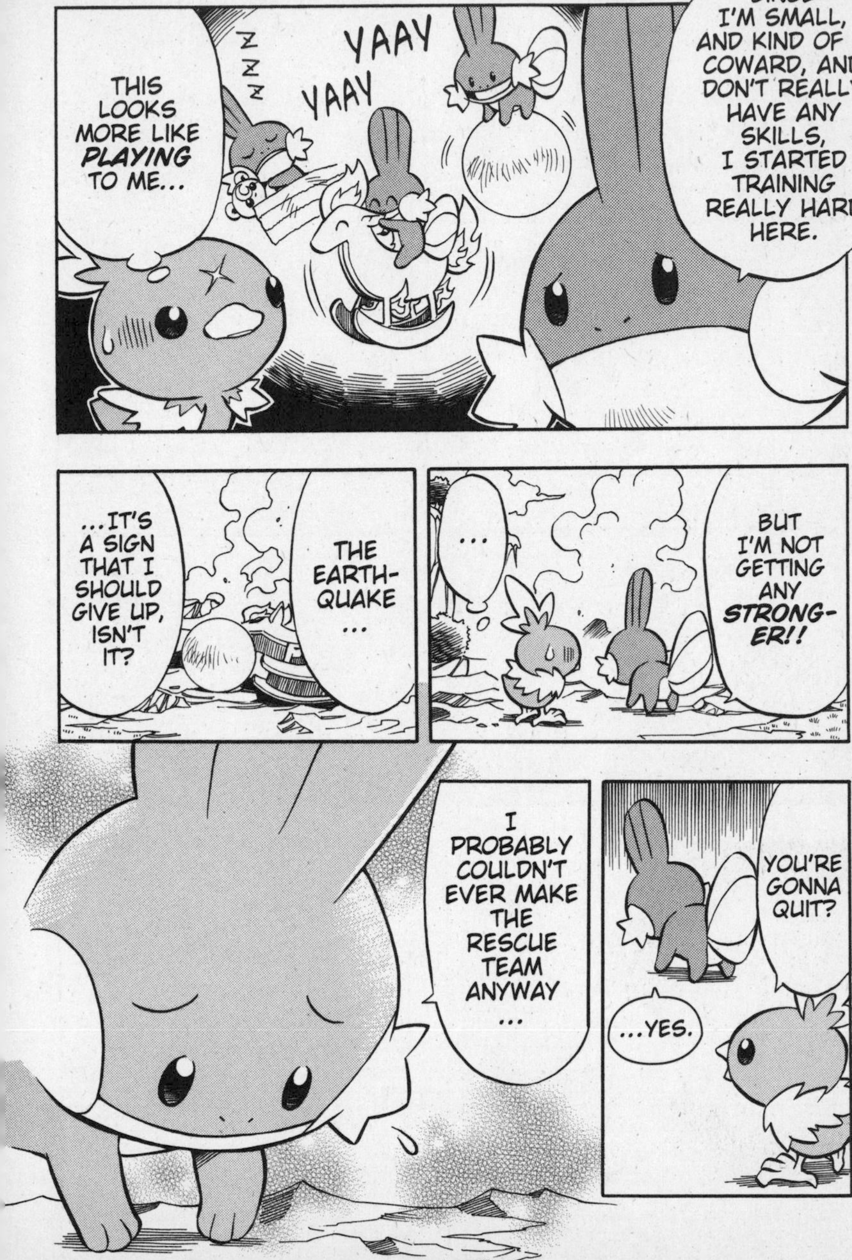
SINCE I'M SMALL, AND KIND OF A COWARD, AND DON'T REALLY HAVE ANY SKILLS, I STARTED TRAINING REALLY HARD HERE.
YAAY
YAAY
ZZZ
THIS LOOKS MORE LIKE PLAYING TO ME...
BUT I'M NOT GETTING ANY STRONGER!!
...
THE EARTHQUAKE...
...IT'S A SIGN THAT I SHOULD GIVE UP, ISN'T IT?
YOU'RE GONNA QUIT?
...YES.
I PROBABLY COULDN'T EVER MAKE THE RESCUE TEAM ANYWAY...

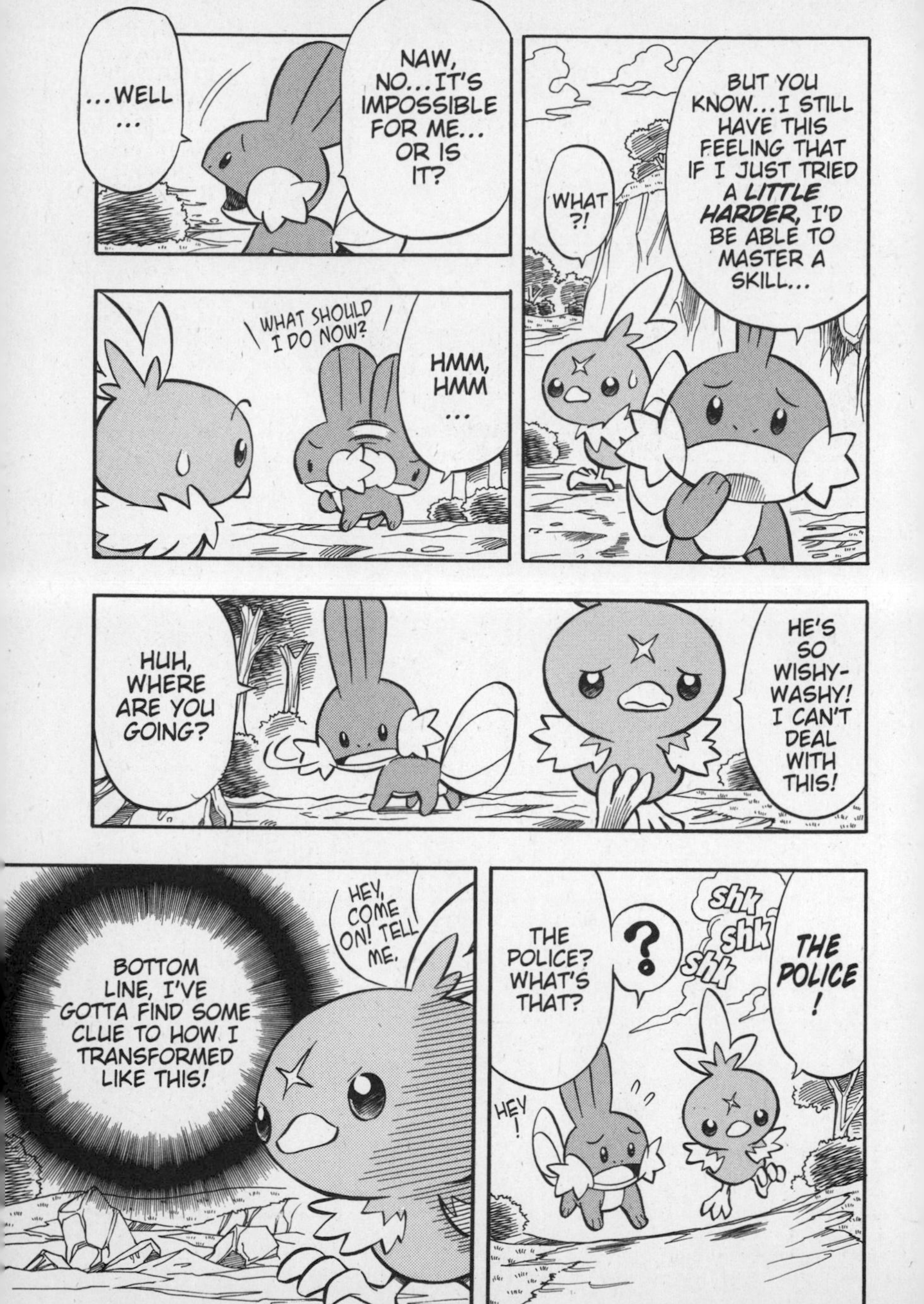
BUT YOU KNOW...I STILL HAVE THIS FEELING THAT IF I JUST TRIED A **LITTLE HARDER,** I'D BE ABLE TO MASTER A SKILL...
WHAT ?!
NAW, NO...IT'S IMPOSSIBLE FOR ME... OR IS IT?
...WELL ...
HMM, HMM ...
WHAT SHOULD I DO NOW?
HE'S SO WISHY-WASHY! I CAN'T DEAL WITH THIS!
HUH, WHERE ARE YOU GOING?
THE POLICE !
SHK SHK SHK
?
THE POLICE? WHAT'S THAT?
HEY !
HEY, COME ON! TELL ME.
BOTTOM LINE, I'VE GOTTA FIND SOME CLUE TO HOW I TRANSFORMED LIKE THIS!

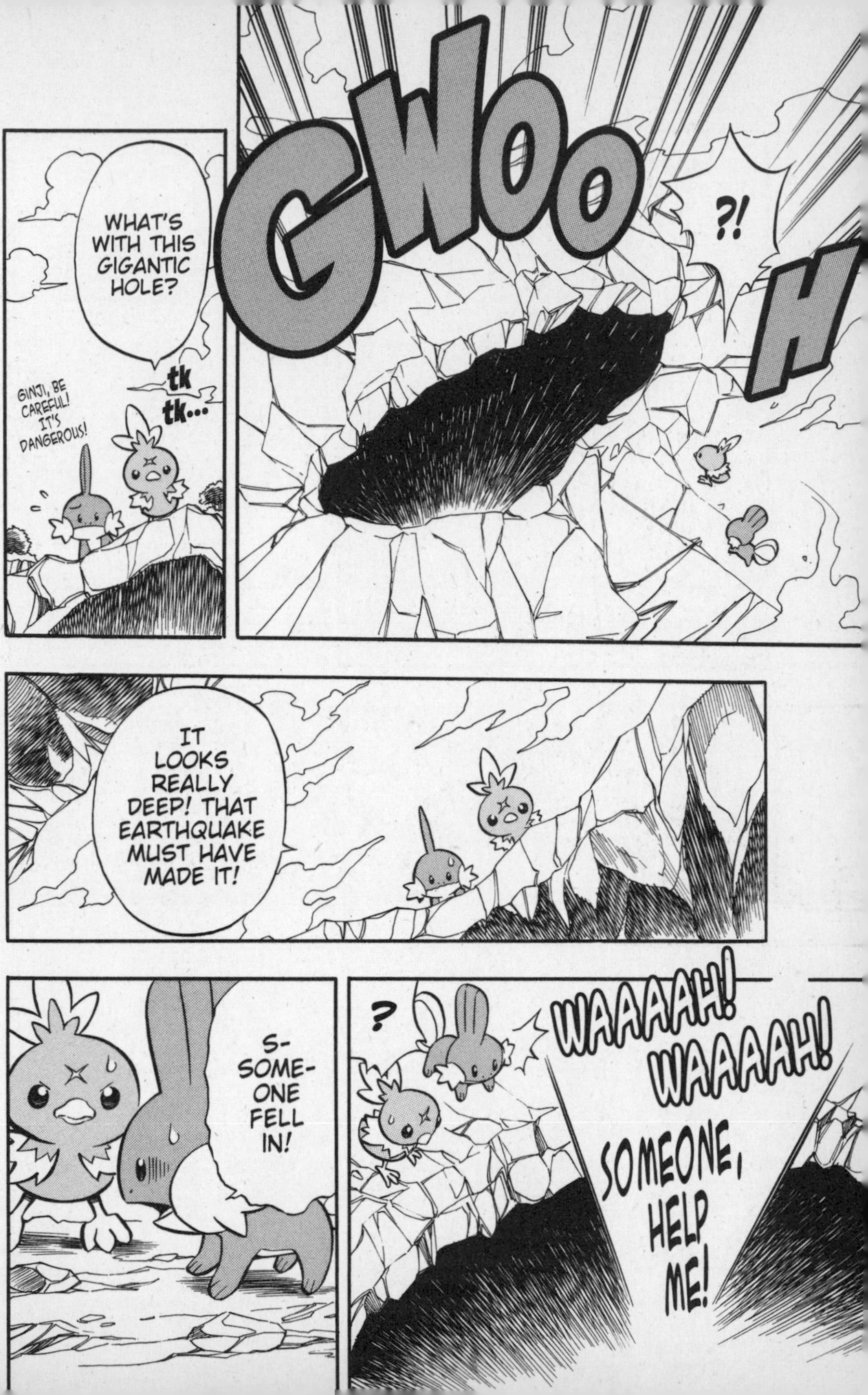
GWOOH
?!
WHAT'S WITH THIS GIGANTIC HOLE?
tk tk...
GINJI, BE CAREFUL! IT'S DANGEROUS!
IT LOOKS REALLY DEEP! THAT EARTHQUAKE MUST HAVE MADE IT!
?
WAAAAH! WAAAAH!
SOMEONE, HELP ME!
S-SOMEONE FELL IN!

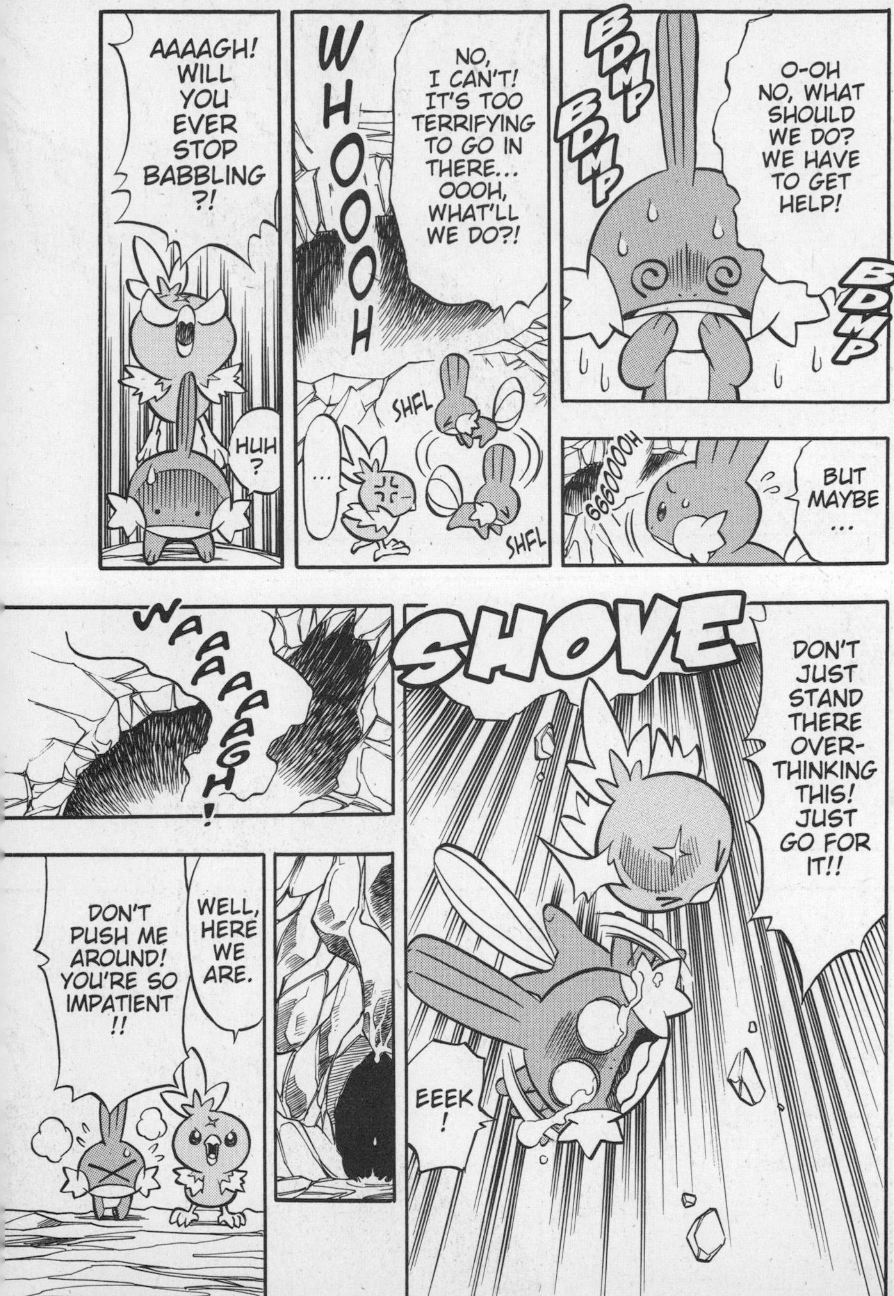
BDMP
BDMP
O-OH NO, WHAT SHOULD WE DO? WE HAVE TO GET HELP!
BDMP
BUT MAYBE ...
GGGOOOOOH
WHOOOOH
NO, I CAN'T! IT'S TOO TERRIFYING TO GO IN THERE... OOOH, WHAT'LL WE DO?!
SHFL
...
SHFL
AAAAGH! WILL YOU EVER STOP BABBLING ?!
HUH ?
SHOVE
DON'T JUST STAND THERE OVER-THINKING THIS! JUST GO FOR IT!!
EEEK !
WAAAAAAGH!
WELL, HERE WE ARE.
DON'T PUSH ME AROUND! YOU'RE SO IMPATIENT !!

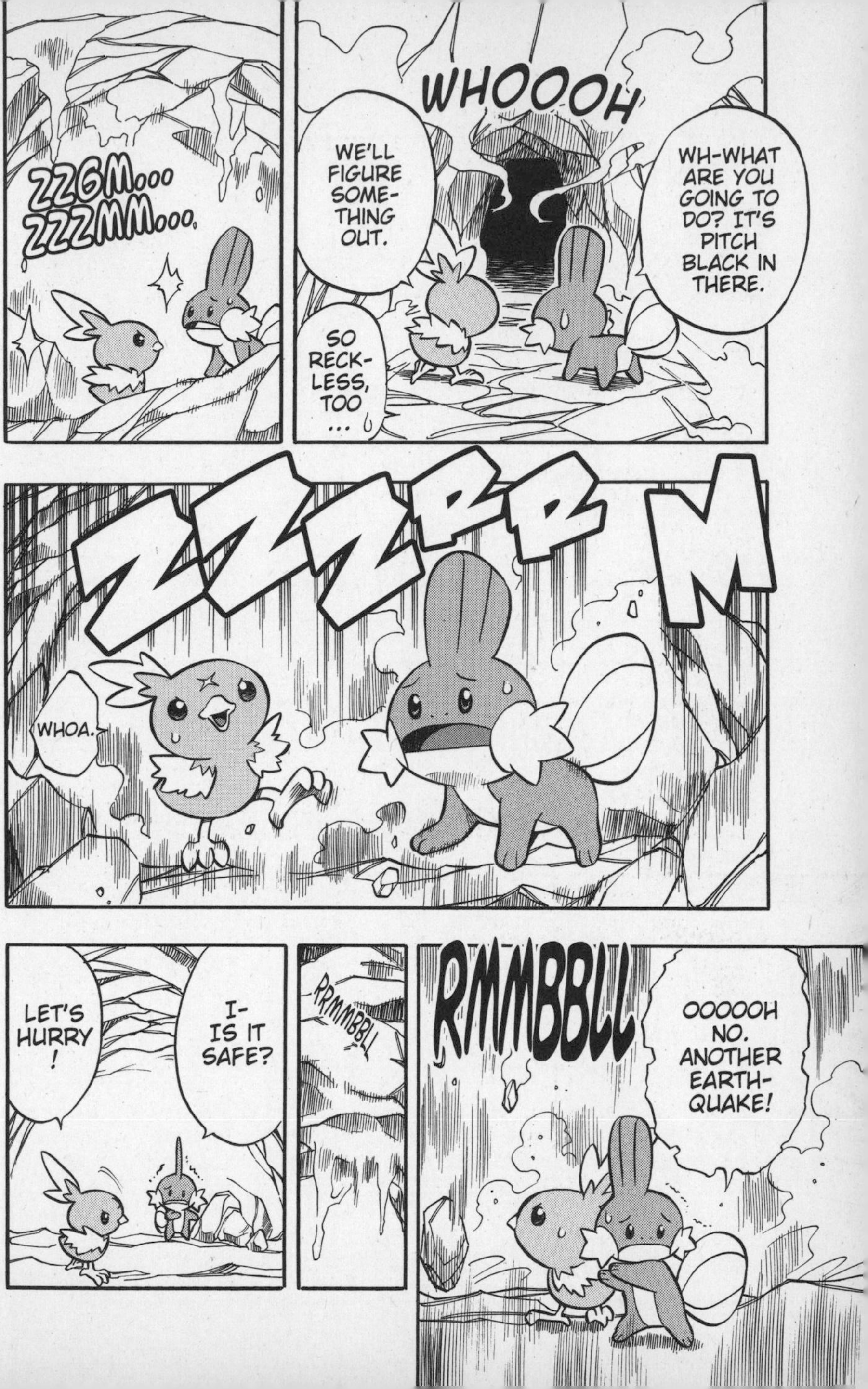
WHOOOH
WH-WHAT ARE YOU GOING TO DO? IT'S PITCH BLACK IN THERE.
WE'LL FIGURE SOMETHING OUT.
SO RECKLESS, TOO...
ZZGMooo ZZZMMooo.
ZZZRRM
WHOA.
RMMBBLL
OOOOOH NO. ANOTHER EARTHQUAKE!
RRMMBBLL
I- IS IT SAFE?
LET'S HURRY!

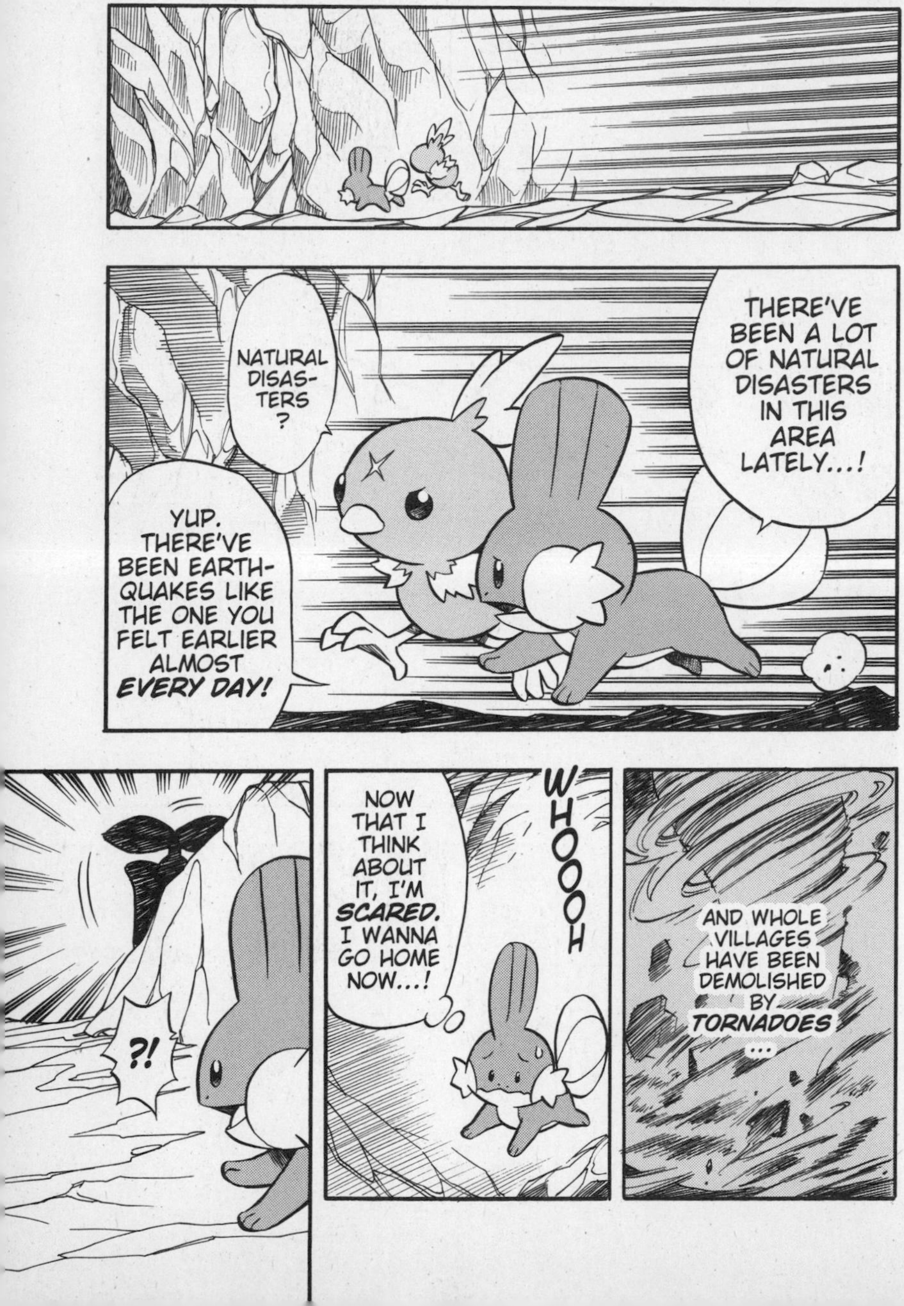
THERE'VE BEEN A LOT OF NATURAL DISASTERS IN THIS AREA LATELY...!
NATURAL DISASTERS?
YUP. THERE'VE BEEN EARTHQUAKES LIKE THE ONE YOU FELT EARLIER ALMOST EVERY DAY!
AND WHOLE VILLAGES HAVE BEEN DEMOLISHED BY TORNADOES ...
WHOOOOH
NOW THAT I THINK ABOUT IT, I'M SCARED. I WANNA GO HOME NOW...!
?!

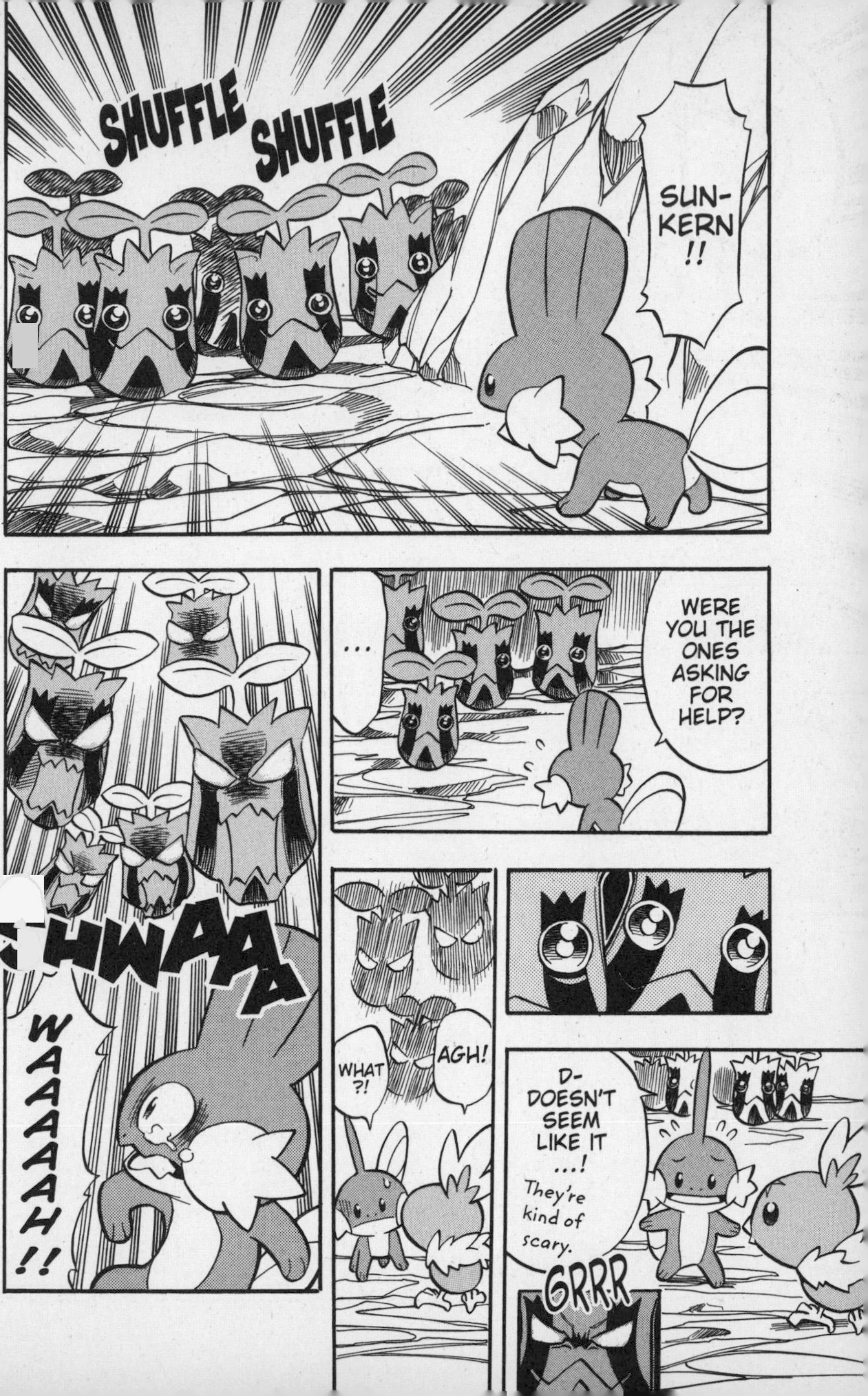

SUN-KERN!!
SHUFFLE SHUFFLE
WERE YOU THE ONES ASKING FOR HELP?
...
AGH!
WHAT?!
D-DOESN'T SEEM LIKE IT...!
They're kind of scary.
GRRR
SHWAA
WAAAAAAAH!!

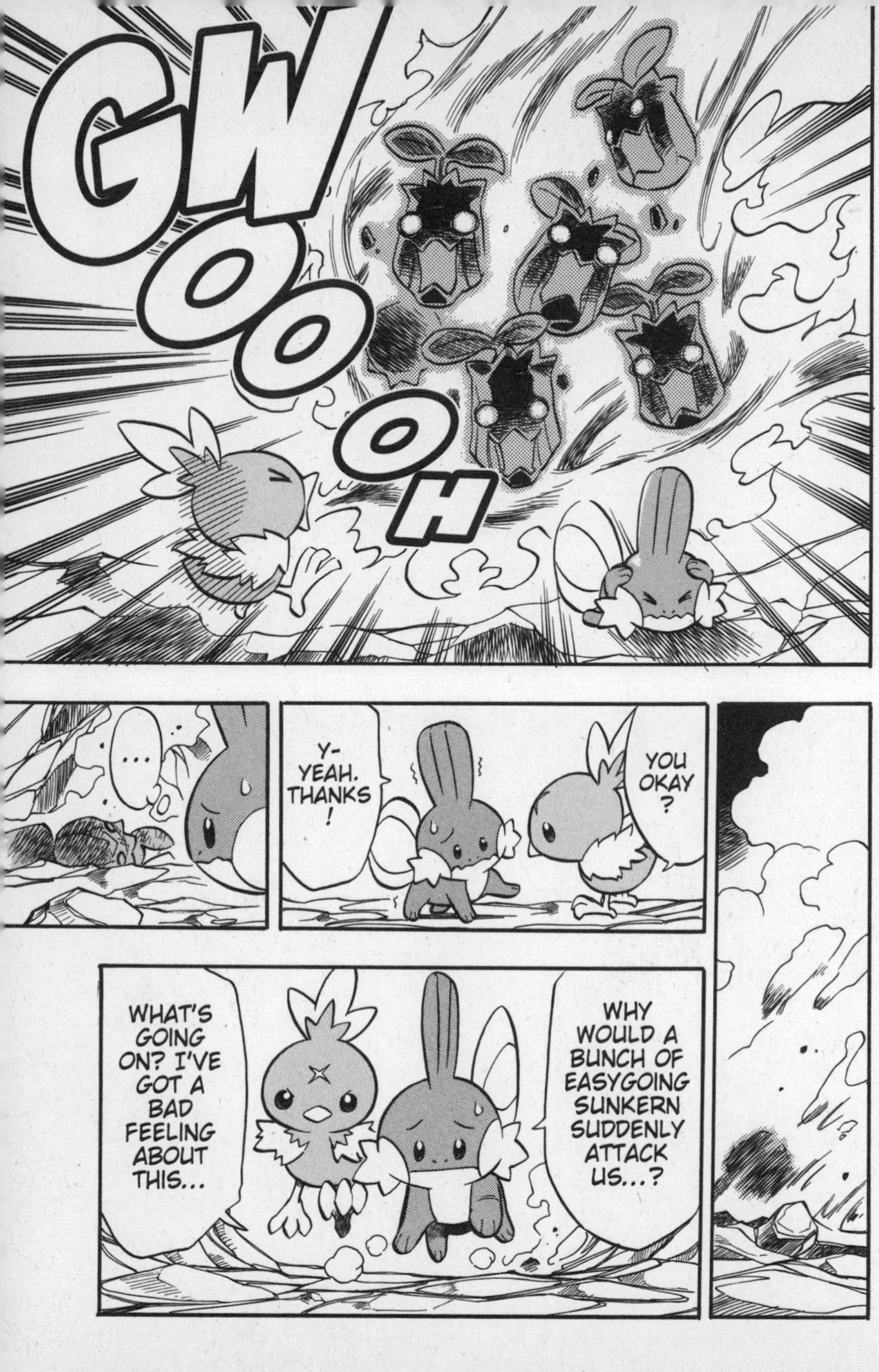
GWOOOOH
YOU OKAY?
Y-YEAH. THANKS!
...
WHY WOULD A BUNCH OF EASYGOING SUNKERN SUDDENLY ATTACK US...?
WHAT'S GOING ON? I'VE GOT A BAD FEELING ABOUT THIS...

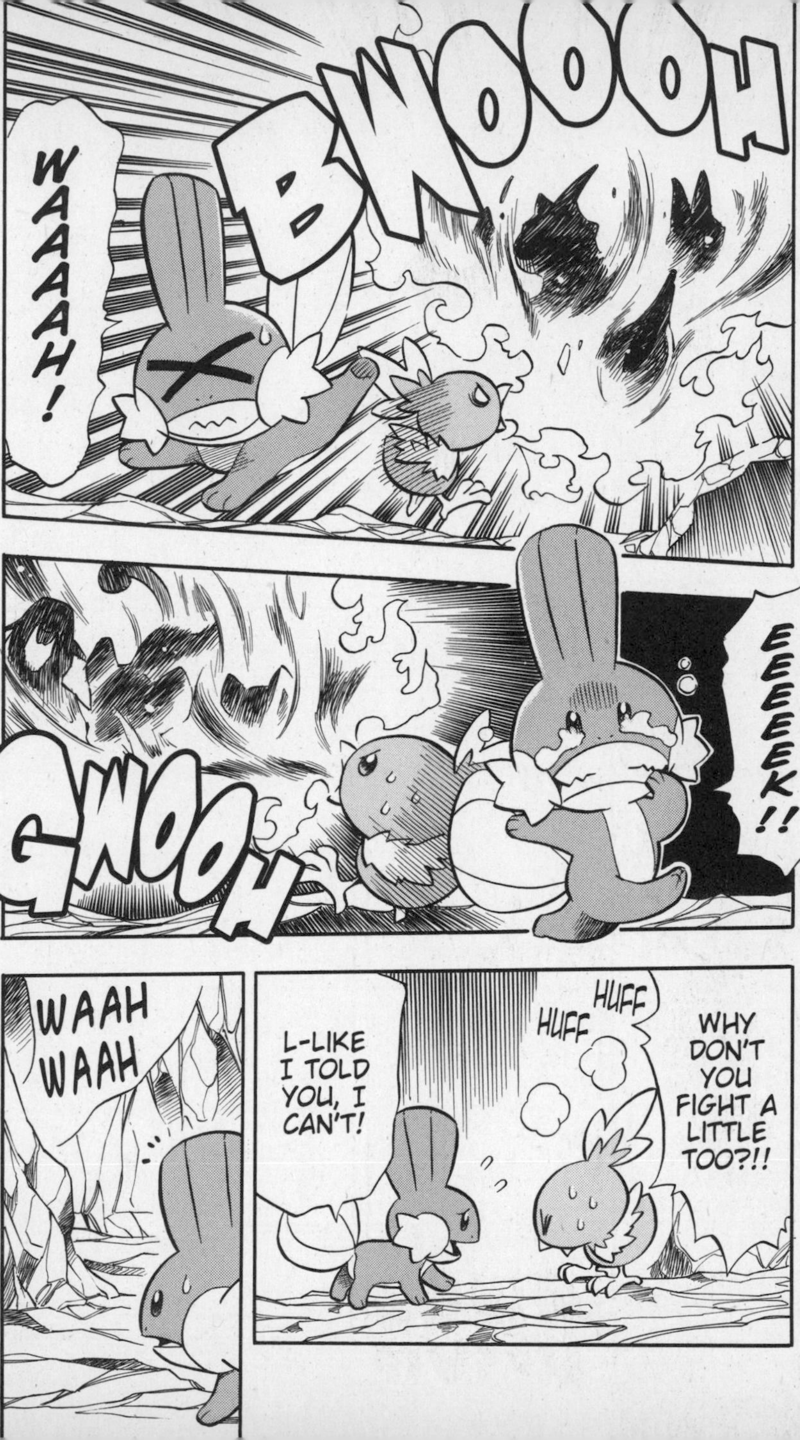
BWOOOH
WAAAAAH!
EEEEEEK!!
GWOOOH
WHY DON'T YOU FIGHT A LITTLE TOO?!!
HUFF HUFF
L-LIKE I TOLD YOU, I CAN'T!
WAAH WAAH
...

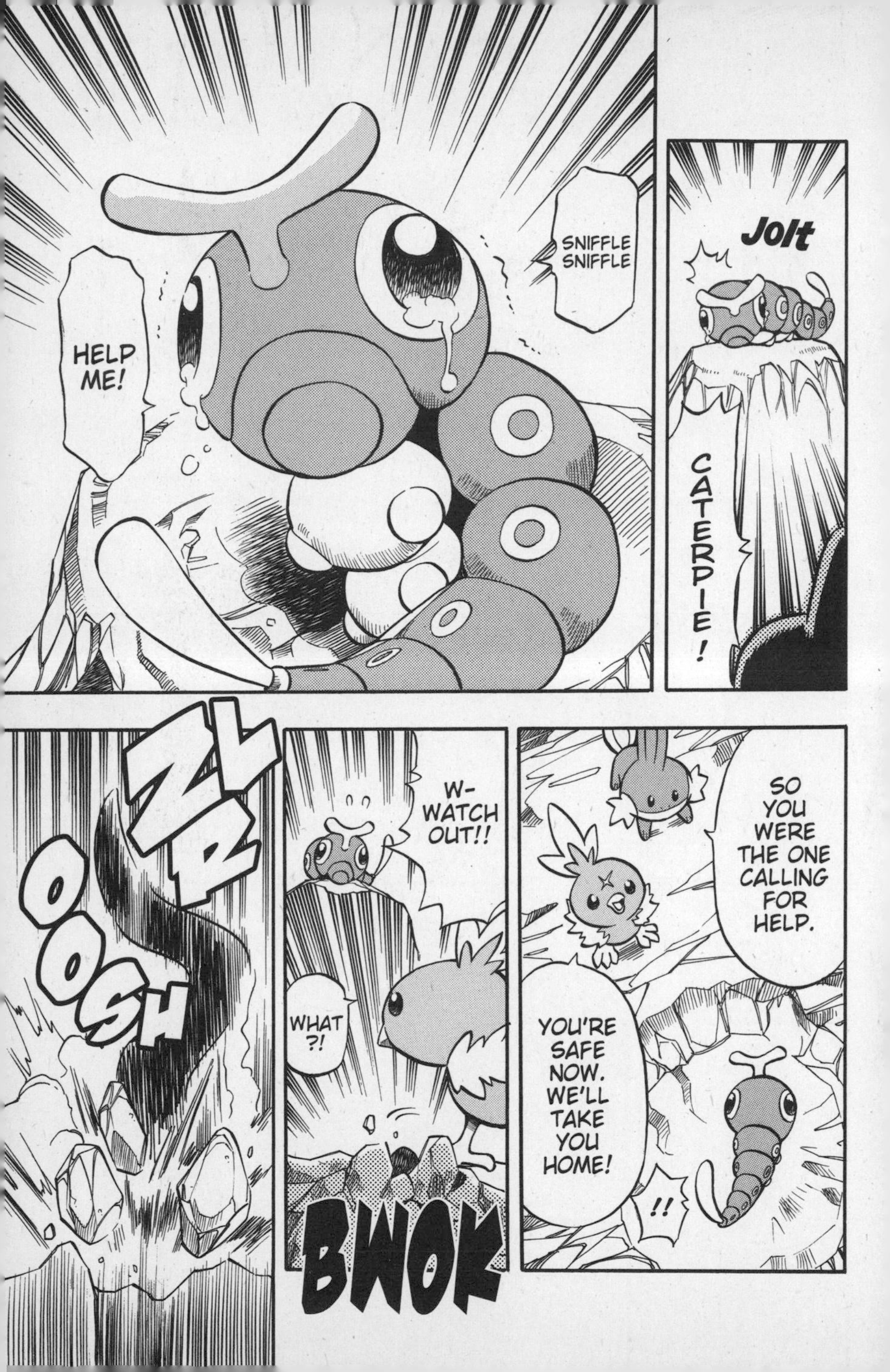
Jolt
CATERPIE!
SNIFFLE SNIFFLE
HELP ME!
SO YOU WERE THE ONE CALLING FOR HELP.
YOU'RE SAFE NOW. WE'LL TAKE YOU HOME!
!!
W-WATCH OUT!!
WHAT?!
BWOK
OOOSH

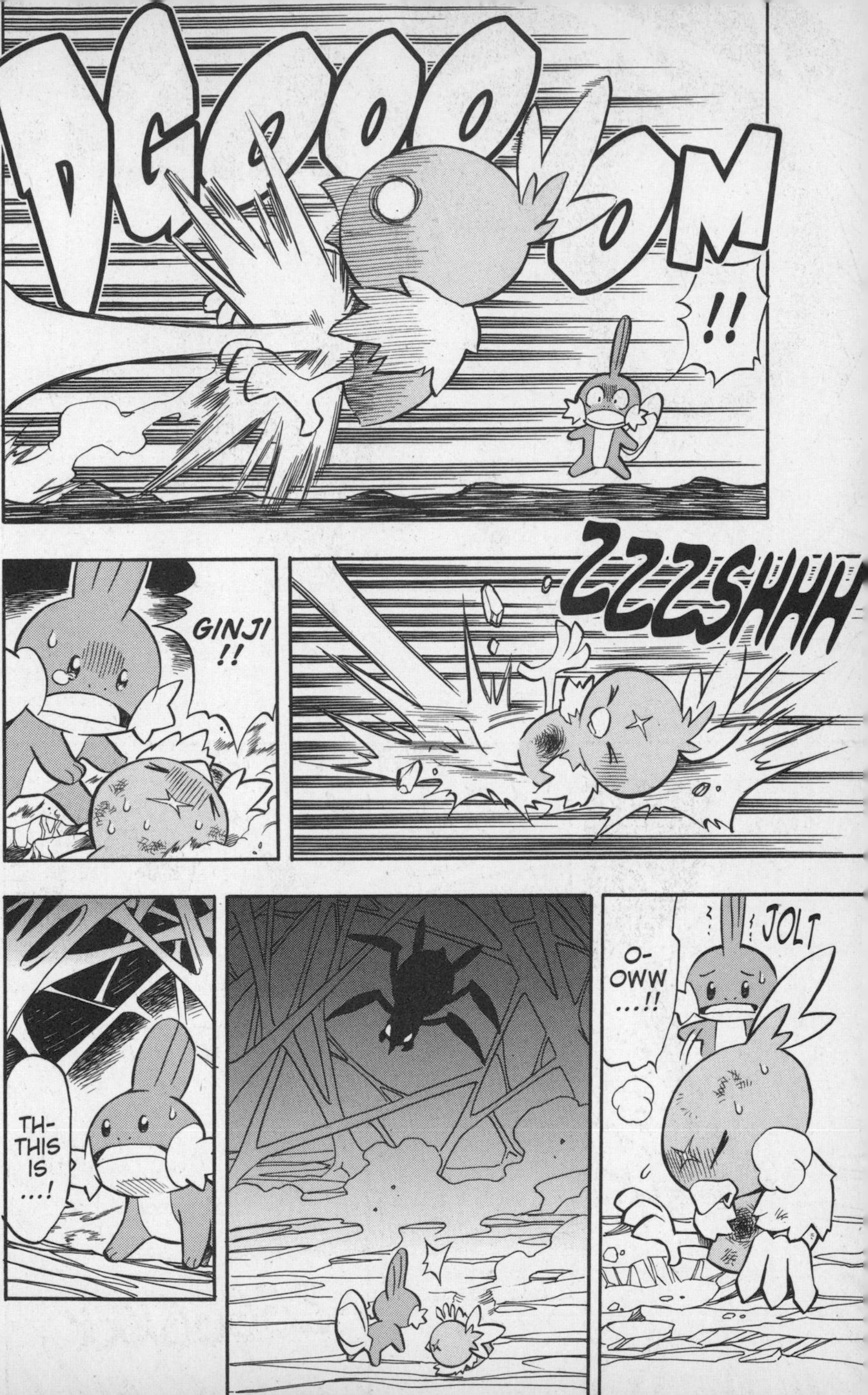
DGOOOOM
!!
ZZZSHHH
GINJI !!
JOLT
O-OWW ...!!
TH-THIS IS ...!

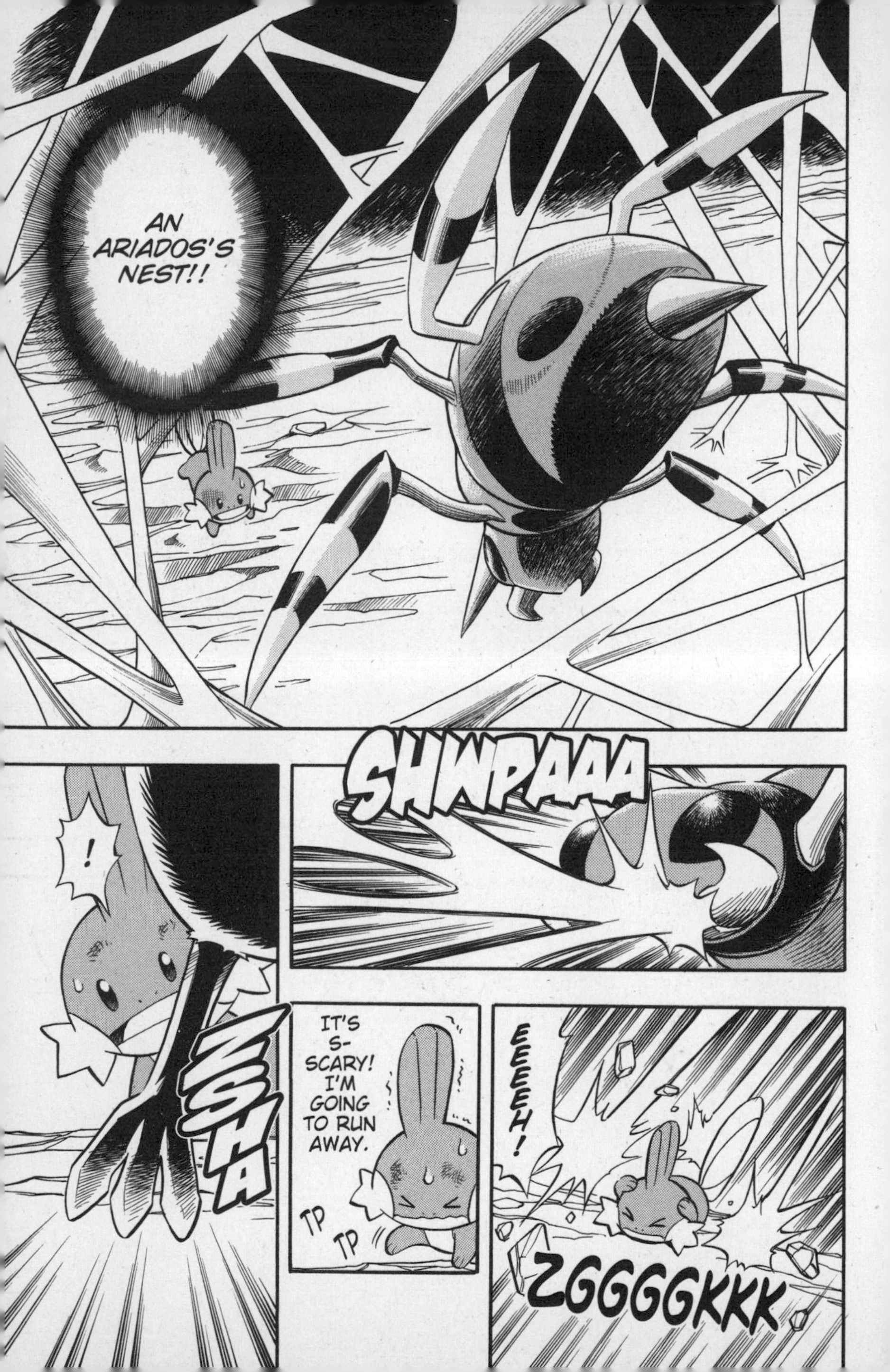
AN ARIADOS'S NEST!!
SHWPAAA
EEEEH!
ZGGGGKKK
IT'S S-SCARY! I'M GOING TO RUN AWAY.
TP TP
!
WSHA

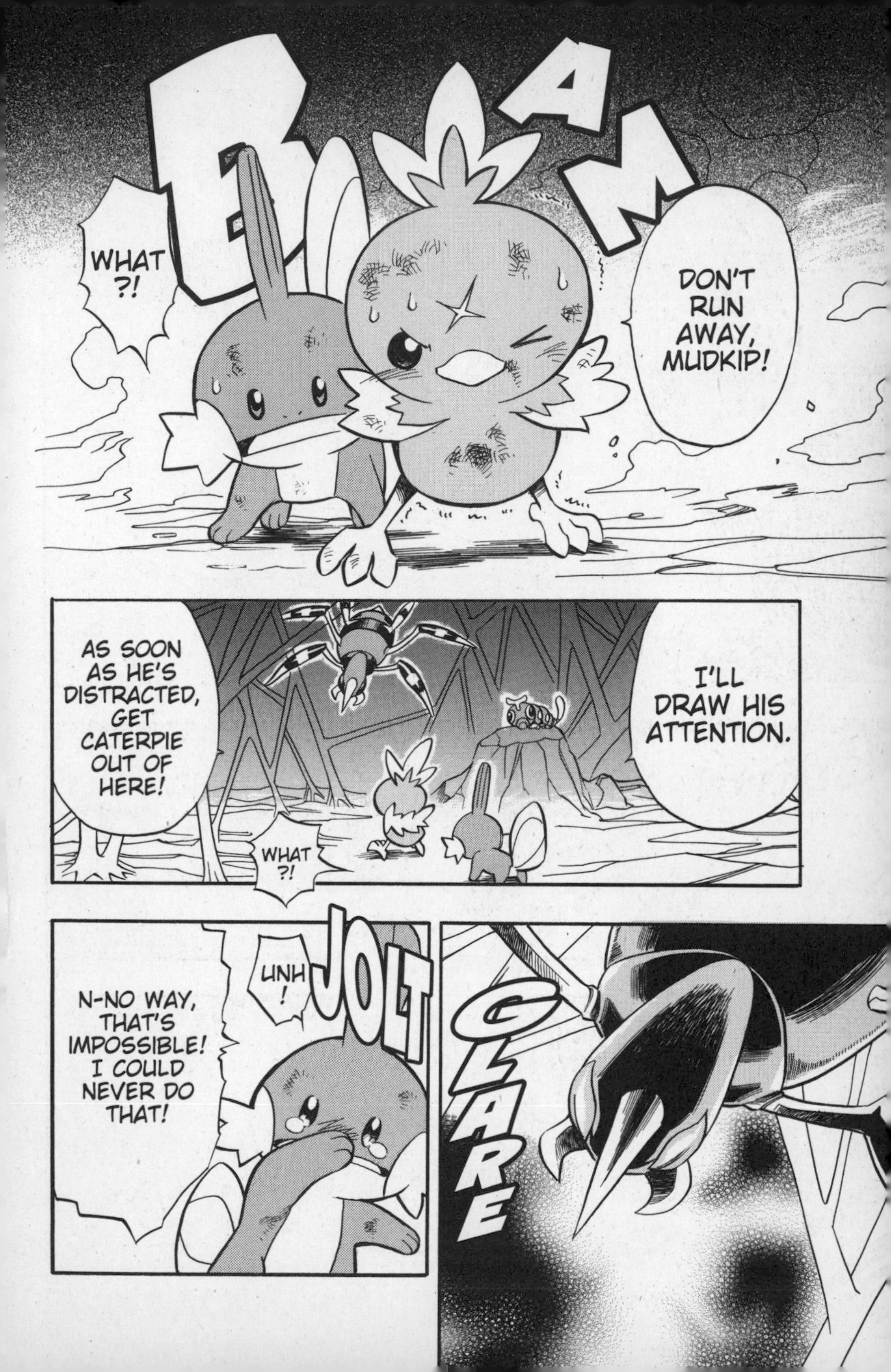
BAM
DON'T RUN AWAY, MUDKIP!
WHAT ?!
I'LL DRAW HIS ATTENTION.
AS SOON AS HE'S DISTRACTED, GET CATERPIE OUT OF HERE!
WHAT ?!
GLARE
JOLT
UNH !
N-NO WAY, THAT'S IMPOSSIBLE! I COULD NEVER DO THAT!

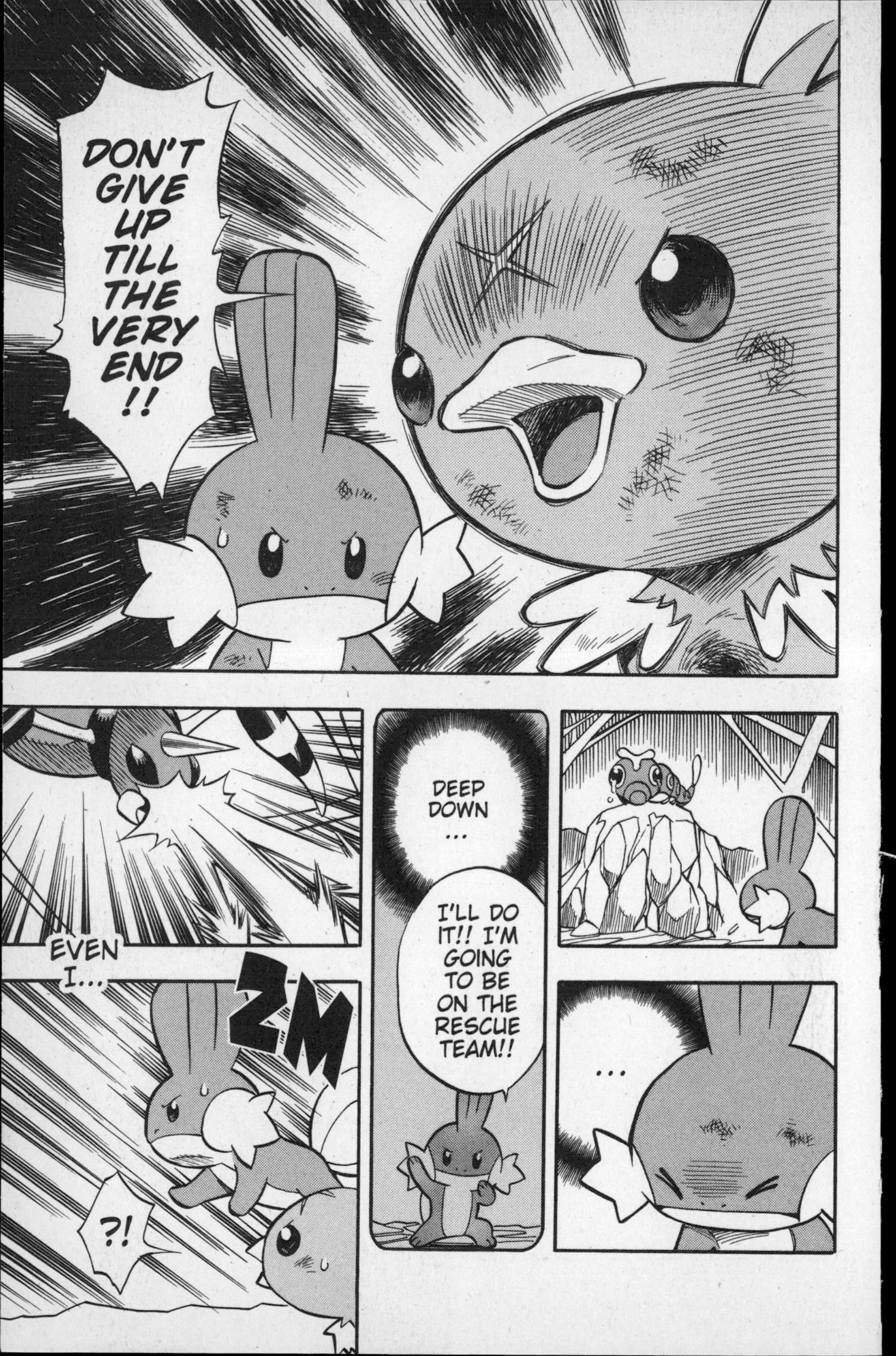
DON'T GIVE UP TILL THE VERY END!!
...
DEEP DOWN ...
I'LL DO IT!! I'M GOING TO BE ON THE RESCUE TEAM!!
EVEN I...
ZM
?!

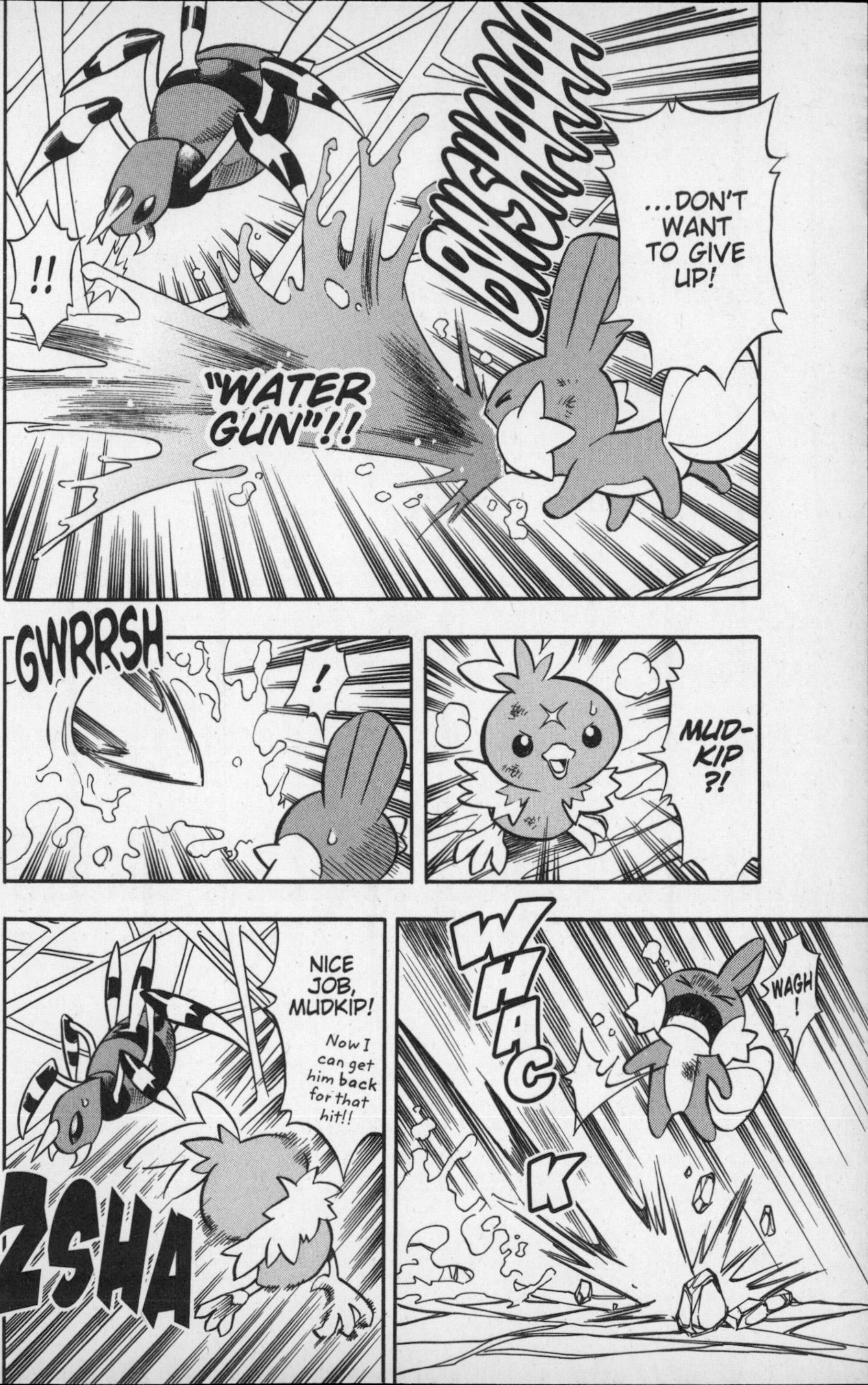
...DON'T WANT TO GIVE UP!
!!
"WATER GUN"!!
MUD-KIP ?!
GWRRSH
!
WHACK
WAGH !
NICE JOB, MUDKIP!
Now I can get him back for that hit!!
ZSHA

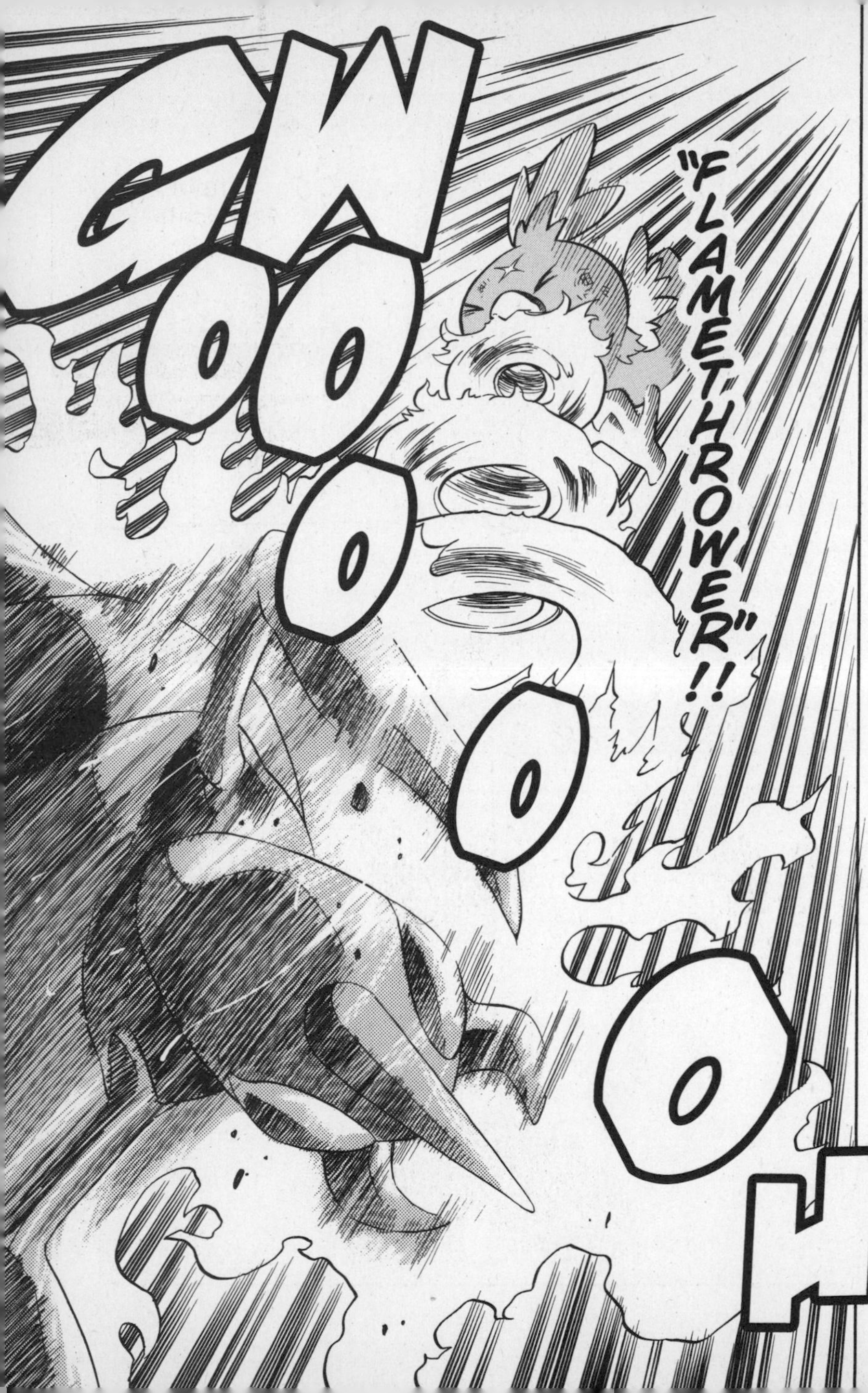
"FLAMETHROWER"!!
GWOOOOOH

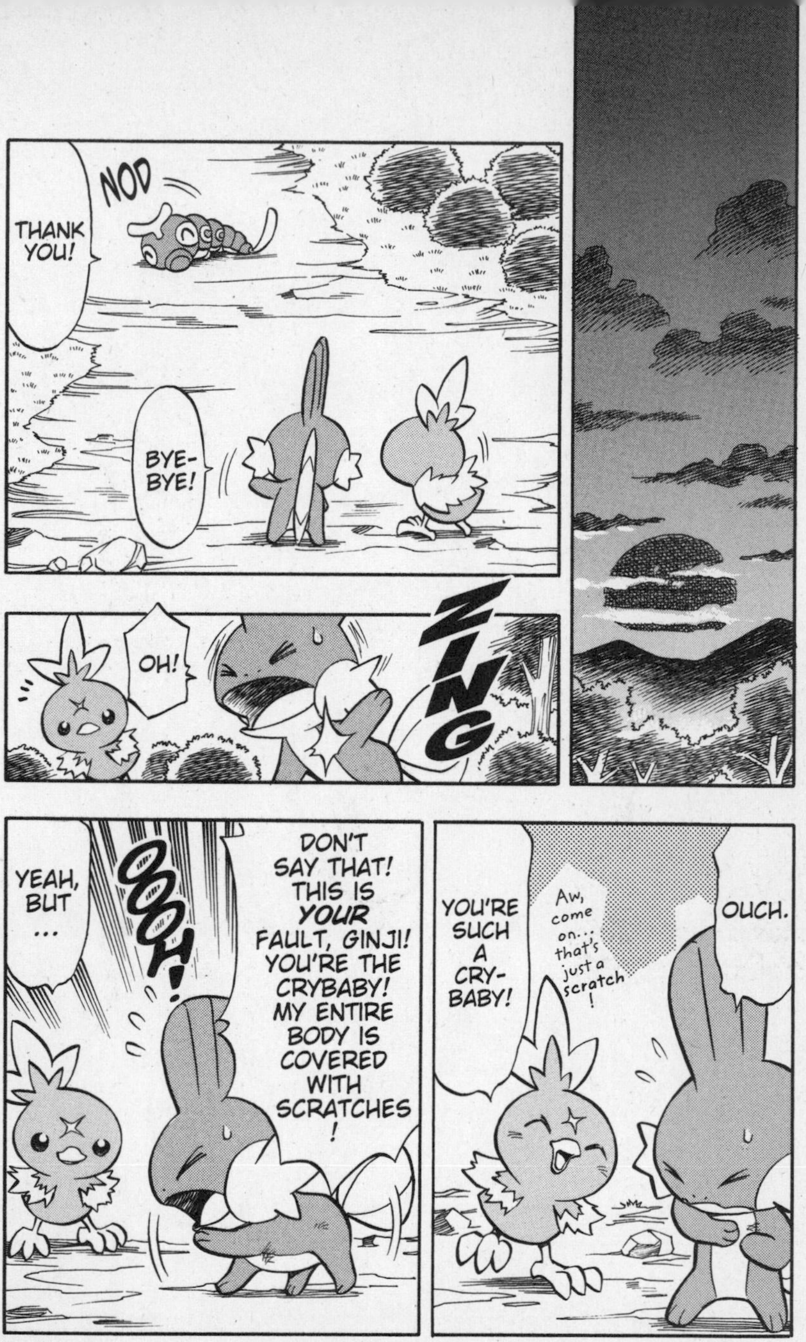
NOD
THANK YOU!
BYE-BYE!
ZING
OH!
OUCH.
Aw, come on... that's just a scratch!
YOU'RE SUCH A CRY-BABY!
DON'T SAY THAT! THIS IS *YOUR* FAULT, GINJI! YOU'RE THE CRYBABY! MY ENTIRE BODY IS COVERED WITH SCRATCHES!
OOOH!
YEAH, BUT ...

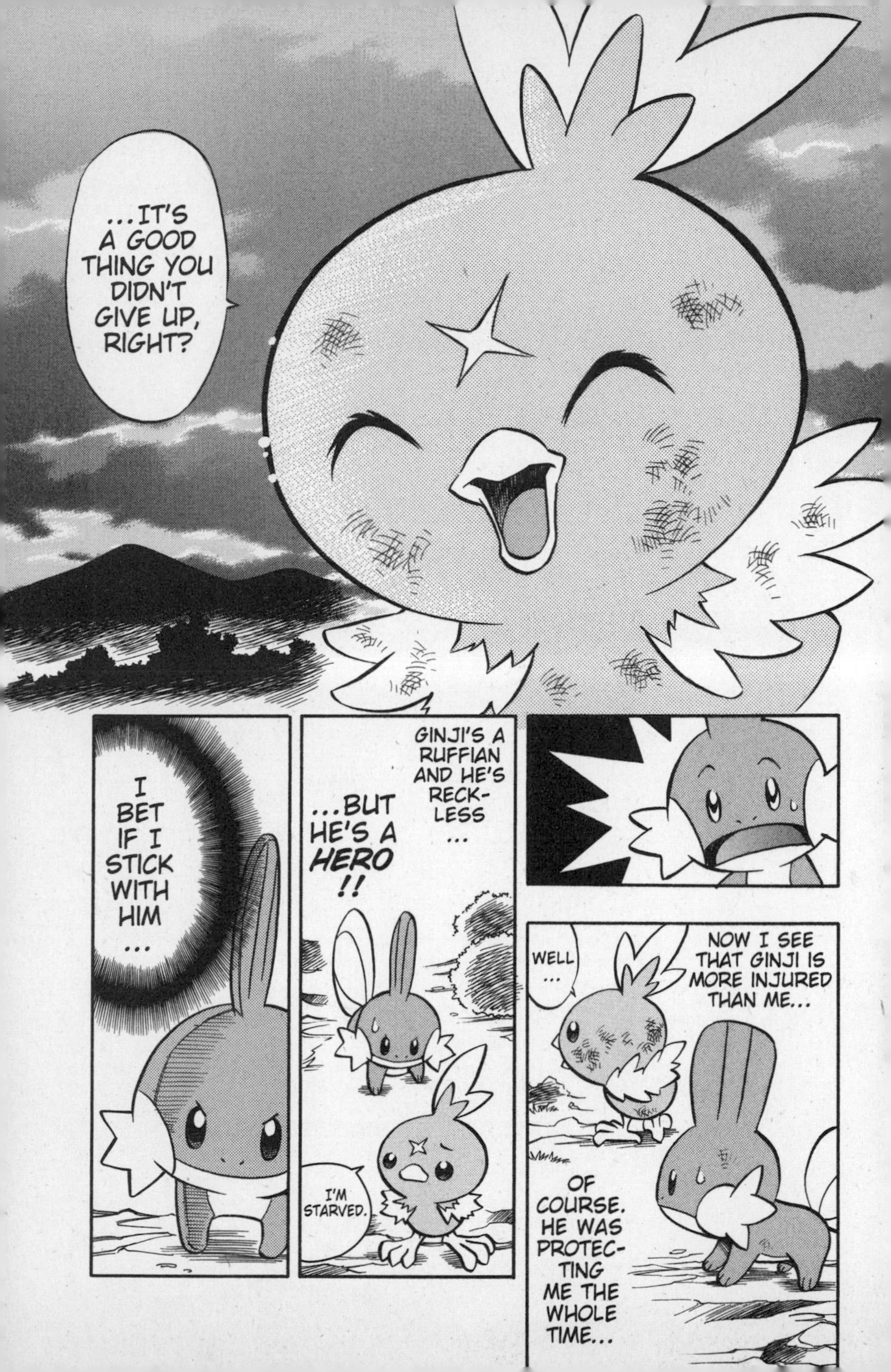
...IT'S A GOOD THING YOU DIDN'T GIVE UP, RIGHT?
NOW I SEE THAT GINJI IS MORE INJURED THAN ME...
WELL...
OF COURSE. HE WAS PROTECTING ME THE WHOLE TIME...
GINJI'S A RUFFIAN AND HE'S RECKLESS...
...BUT HE'S A *HERO*!!
I'M STARVED.
I BET IF I STICK WITH HIM...

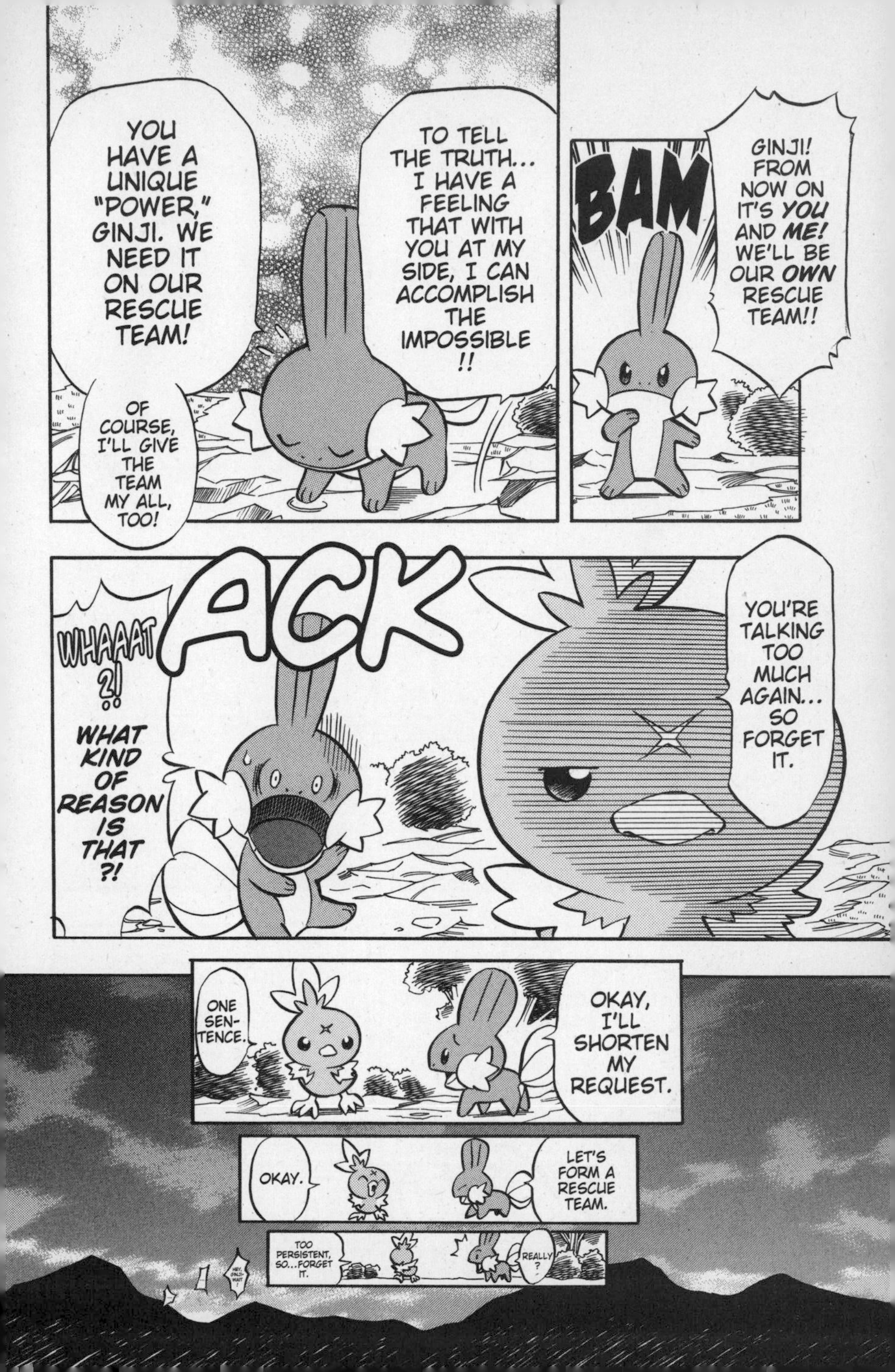
BAM
GINJI! FROM NOW ON IT'S *YOU* AND *ME!* WE'LL BE OUR *OWN* RESCUE TEAM!!
TO TELL THE TRUTH... I HAVE A FEELING THAT WITH YOU AT MY SIDE, I CAN ACCOMPLISH THE IMPOSSIBLE!!
YOU HAVE A UNIQUE "POWER," GINJI. WE NEED IT ON OUR RESCUE TEAM!
OF COURSE, I'LL GIVE THE TEAM MY ALL, TOO!
YOU'RE TALKING TOO MUCH AGAIN... SO FORGET IT.
ACK
WHAAAT?!
WHAT KIND OF REASON IS THAT?!
OKAY, I'LL SHORTEN MY REQUEST.
ONE SEN-TENCE.
LET'S FORM A RESCUE TEAM.
OKAY.
REALLY?
TOO PERSISTENT, SO...FORGET IT.
HEY, GINJI- WAIT!

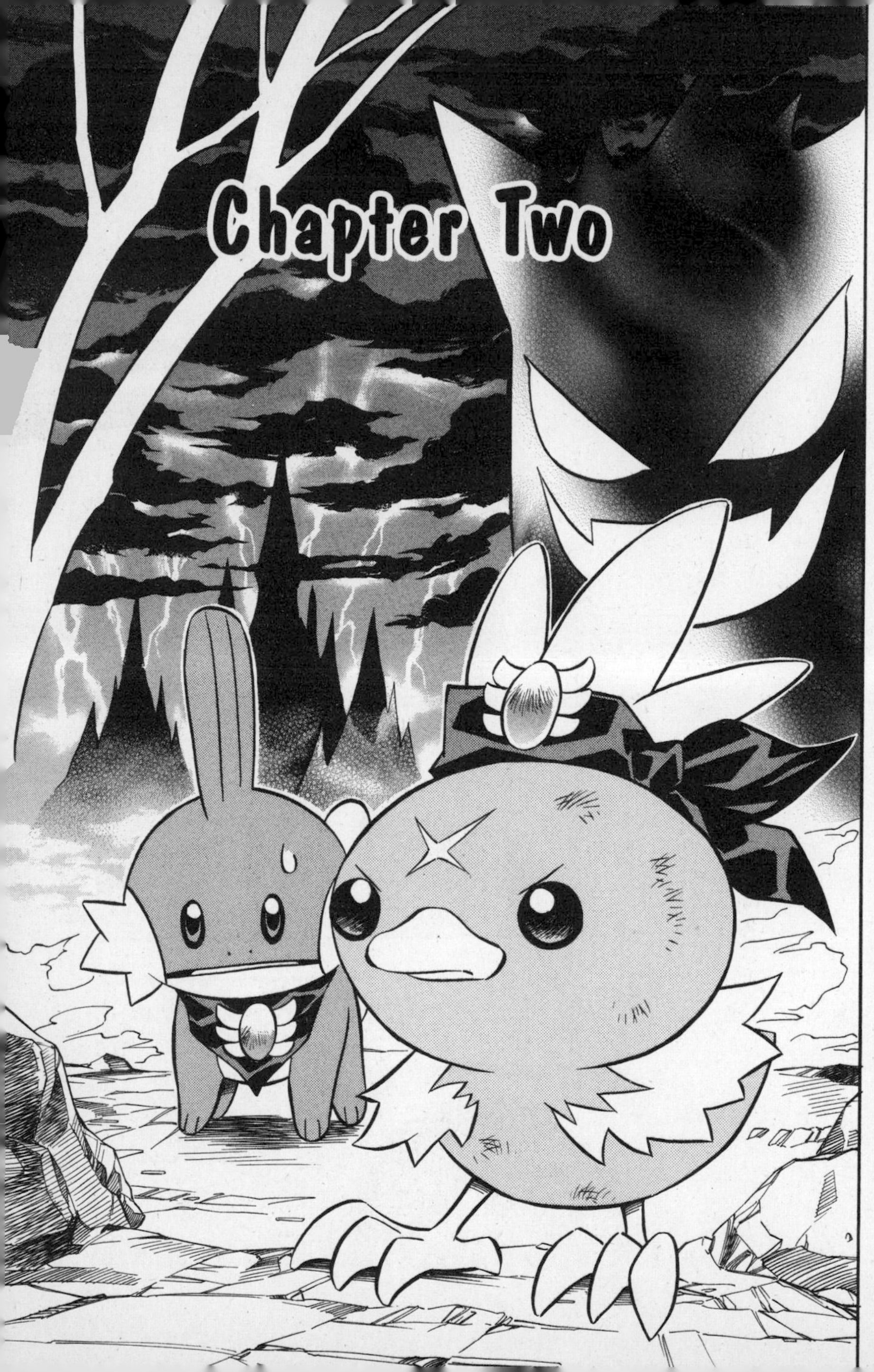
Chapter Two

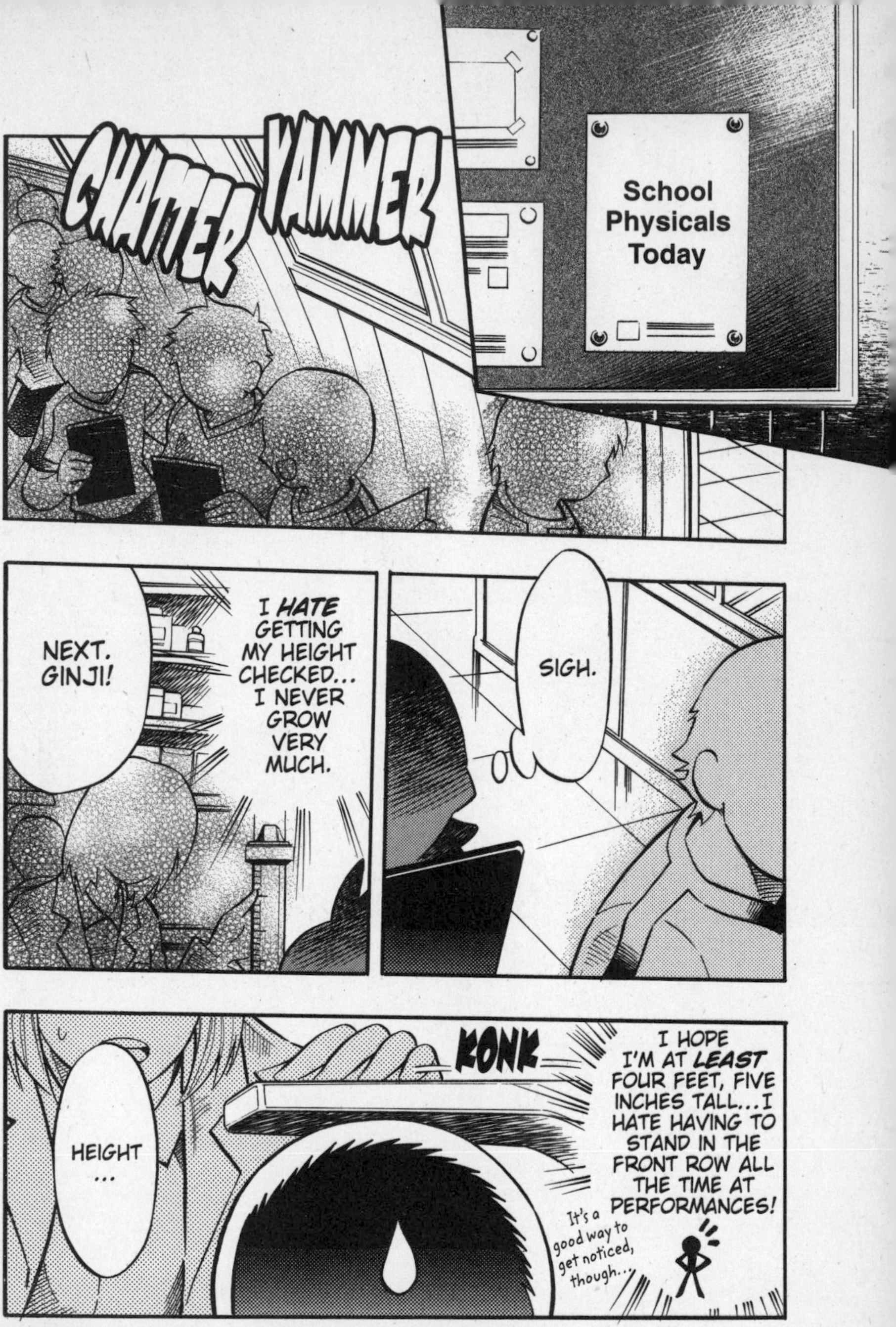
School Physicals Today
YAMMER
CHATTER
SIGH.
I *HATE* GETTING MY HEIGHT CHECKED... I NEVER GROW VERY MUCH.
NEXT. GINJI!
I HOPE I'M AT *LEAST* FOUR FEET, FIVE INCHES TALL... I HATE HAVING TO STAND IN THE FRONT ROW ALL THE TIME AT PERFORMANCES!
It's a good way to get noticed, though...
KONK
HEIGHT...

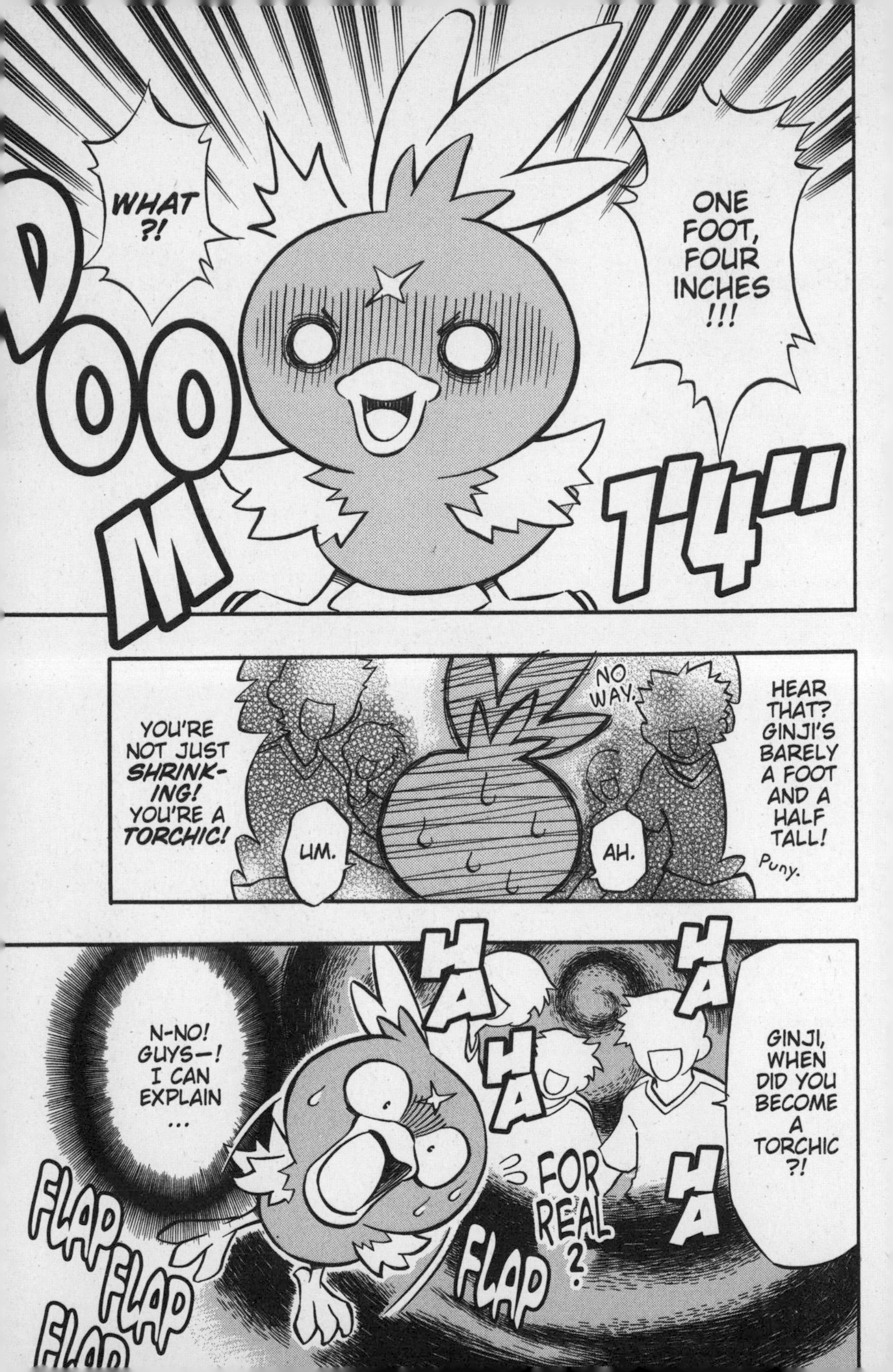
1'4"
ONE FOOT, FOUR INCHES!!!
WHAT?!
DOOM
HEAR THAT? GINJI'S BARELY A FOOT AND A HALF TALL!
Puny.
NO WAY.
AH.
YOU'RE NOT JUST *SHRINKING!* YOU'RE A *TORCHIC!*
UM.
HA HA
GINJI, WHEN DID YOU BECOME A TORCHIC?!
HA HA
HA HA
FOR REAL?
N-NO! GUYS—! I CAN EXPLAIN...
FLAP
FLAP FLAP FLAP

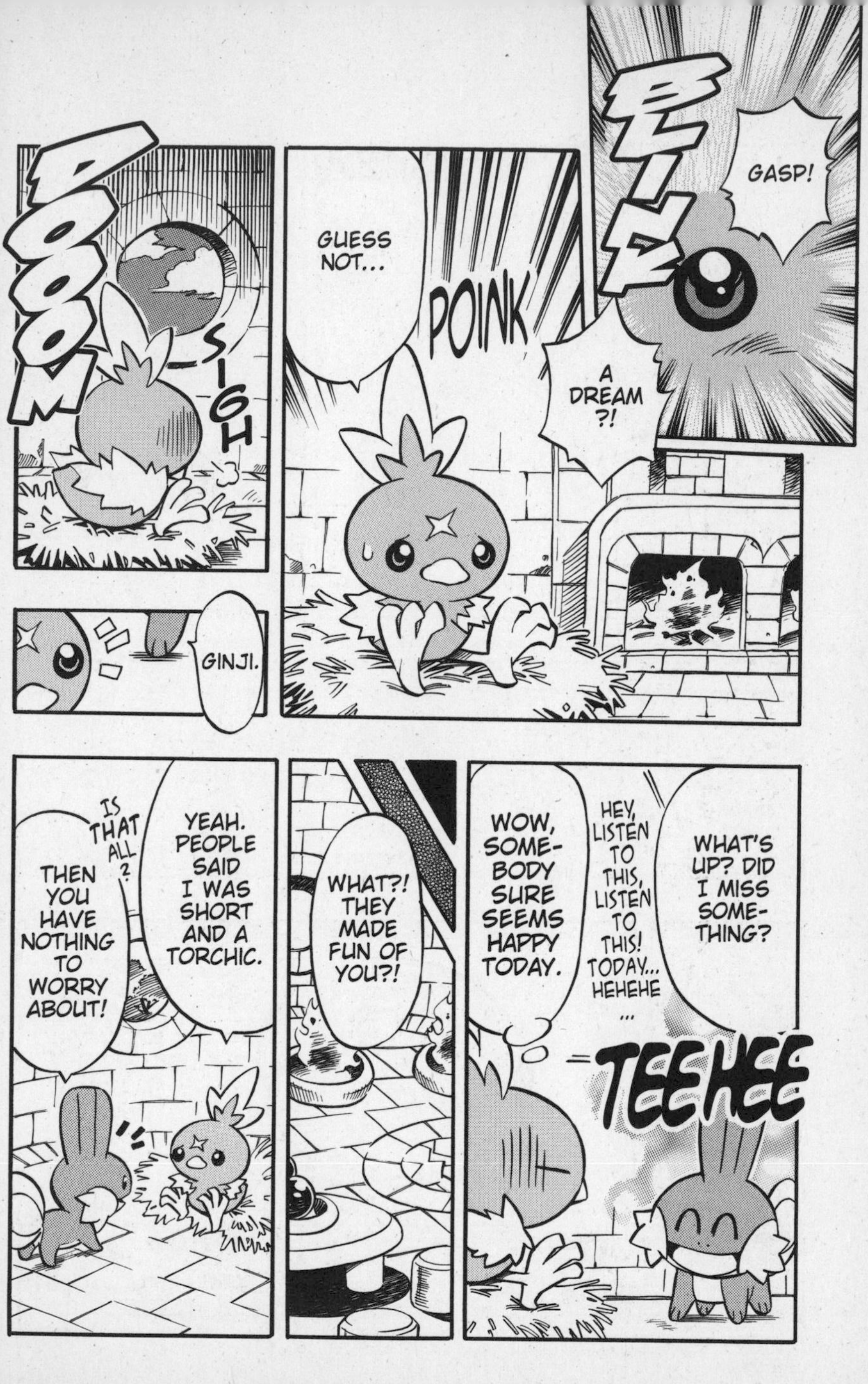
GASP!
A DREAM ?!
POINK
GUESS NOT...
DOOOOM
SIGH
GINJI.
WHAT'S UP? DID I MISS SOME-THING?
HEY, LISTEN TO THIS, LISTEN TO THIS! TODAY... HEHEHE ...
WOW, SOME-BODY SURE SEEMS HAPPY TODAY.
TEEHEE
WHAT?! THEY MADE FUN OF YOU?!
YEAH. PEOPLE SAID I WAS SHORT AND A TORCHIC.
IS THAT ALL ?
THEN YOU HAVE NOTHING TO WORRY ABOUT!

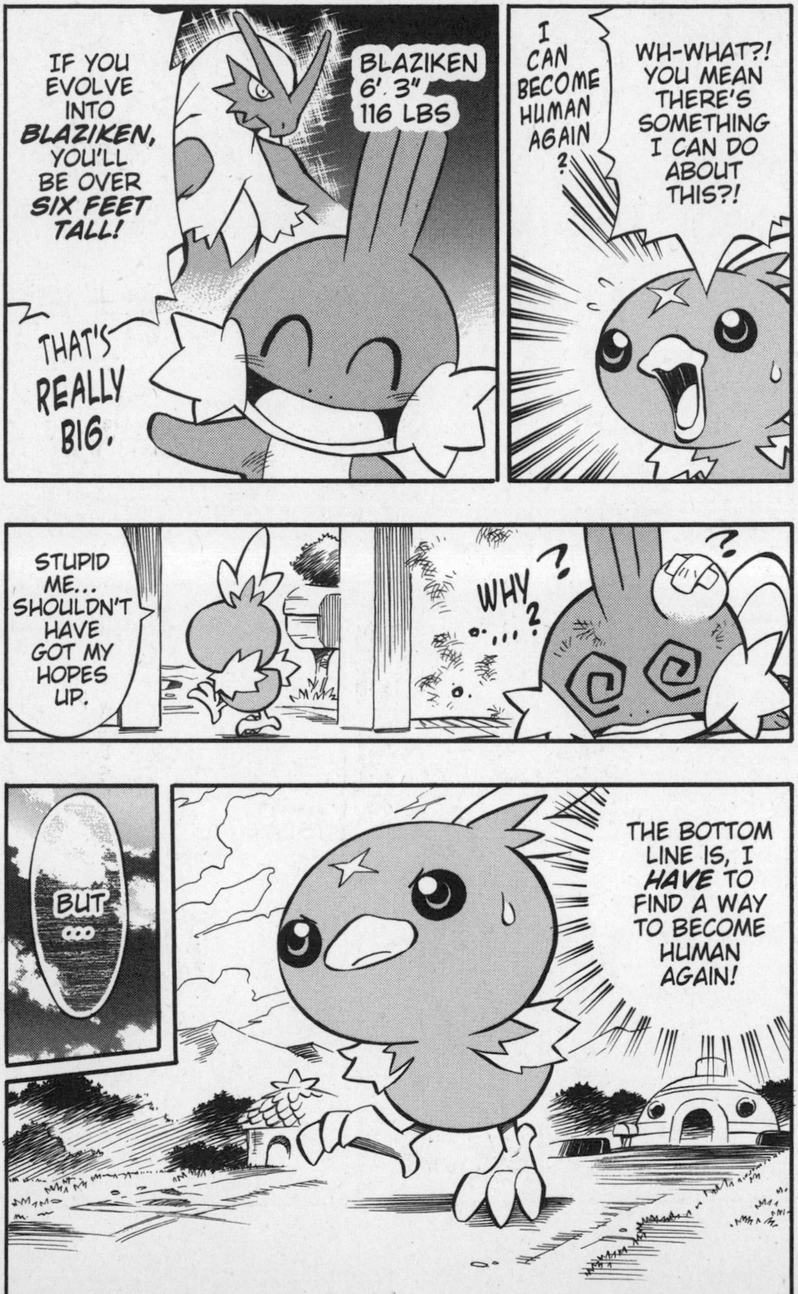
WH-WHAT?! YOU MEAN THERE'S SOMETHING I CAN DO ABOUT THIS?!
I CAN BECOME HUMAN AGAIN?
BLAZIKEN 6' 3" 116 LBS
IF YOU EVOLVE INTO BLAZIKEN, YOU'LL BE OVER SIX FEET TALL!
THAT'S REALLY BIG.
WHY?
...
STUPID ME... SHOULDN'T HAVE GOT MY HOPES UP.
THE BOTTOM LINE IS, I HAVE TO FIND A WAY TO BECOME HUMAN AGAIN!
BUT...

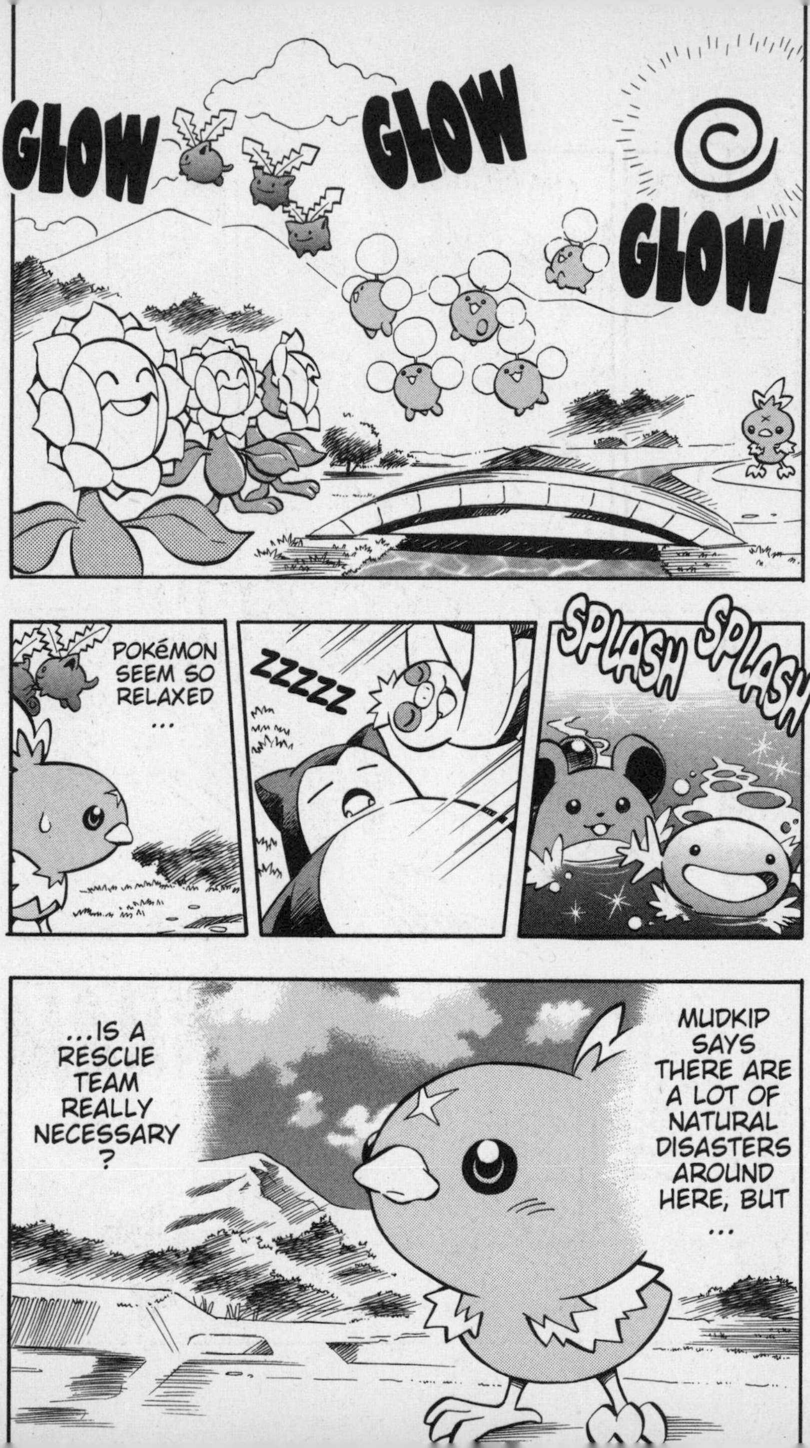
GLOW
GLOW
GLOW
SPLASH SPLASH
ZZZZZ
POKéMON SEEM SO RELAXED ...
MUDKIP SAYS THERE ARE A LOT OF NATURAL DISASTERS AROUND HERE, BUT ...
...IS A RESCUE TEAM REALLY NECESSARY ?

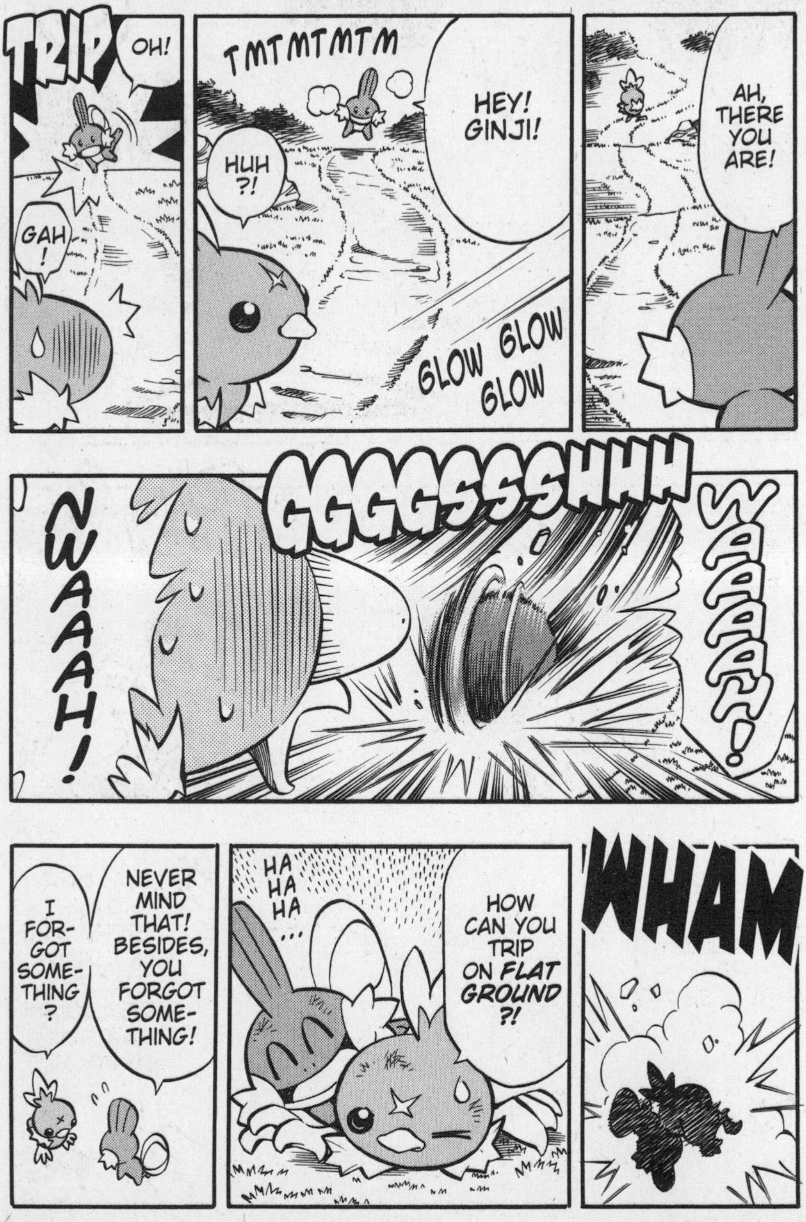
AH, THERE YOU ARE!
HEY! GINJI!
TMTMTMTM
HUH?!
GLOW GLOW GLOW GLOW
OH!
TRIP
GAH!
WAAAAAH!
GGGGSSSHHH
NWAAAAH!
WHAM
HOW CAN YOU TRIP ON *FLAT GROUND*?!
HA HA HA...
NEVER MIND THAT! BESIDES, YOU FORGOT SOME-THING!
I FOR-GOT SOME-THING?

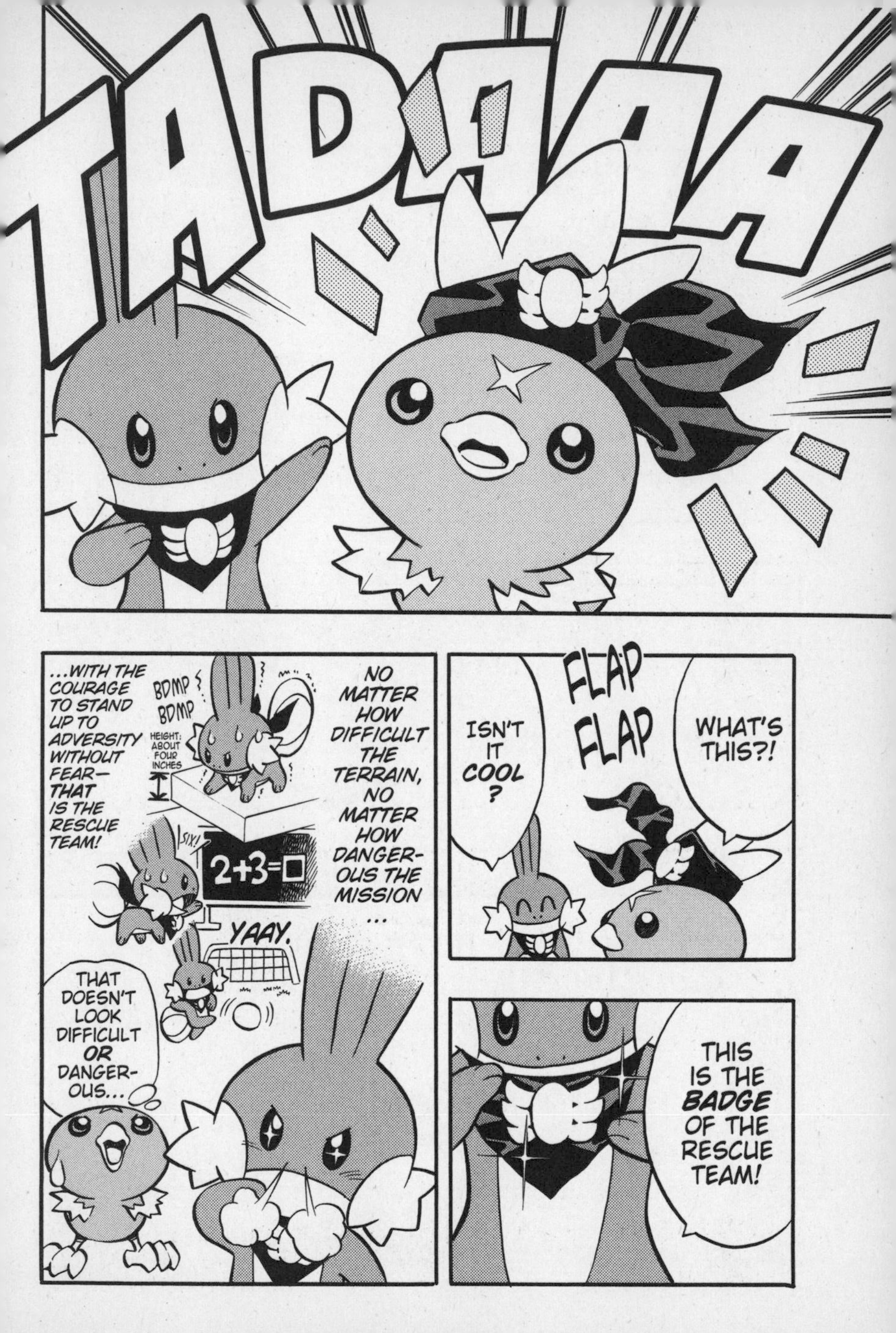
TADAAA
WHAT'S THIS?!
FLAP FLAP
ISN'T IT COOL?
THIS IS THE BADGE OF THE RESCUE TEAM!
NO MATTER HOW DIFFICULT THE TERRAIN, NO MATTER HOW DANGEROUS THE MISSION...
...WITH THE COURAGE TO STAND UP TO ADVERSITY WITHOUT FEAR—THAT IS THE RESCUE TEAM!
BDMP BDMP
HEIGHT: ABOUT FOUR INCHES
SIX!
2+3=□
YAAY.
THAT DOESN'T LOOK DIFFICULT OR DANGEROUS...

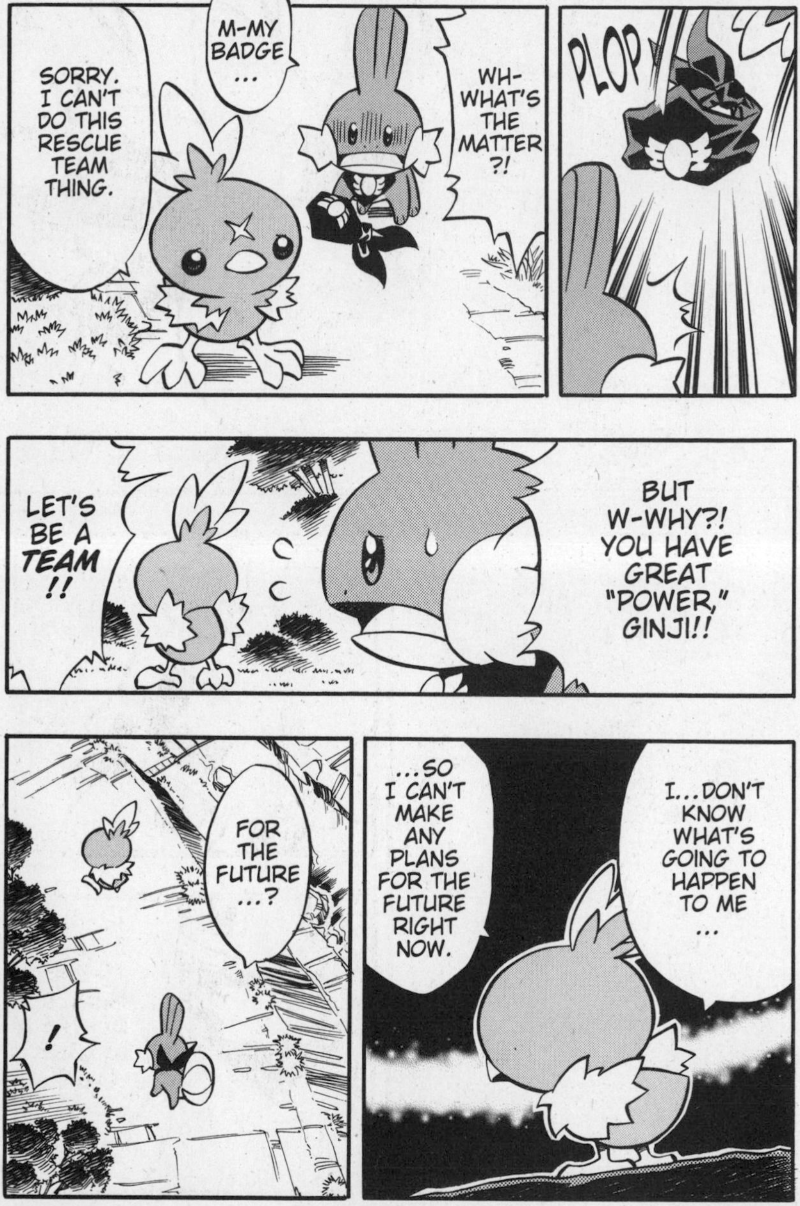
PLOP
WH-WHAT'S THE MATTER?!
M-MY BADGE...
SORRY. I CAN'T DO THIS RESCUE TEAM THING.
BUT W-WHY?! YOU HAVE GREAT "POWER," GINJI!!
LET'S BE A TEAM!!
I...DON'T KNOW WHAT'S GOING TO HAPPEN TO ME...
...SO I CAN'T MAKE ANY PLANS FOR THE FUTURE RIGHT NOW.
FOR THE FUTURE...?
!

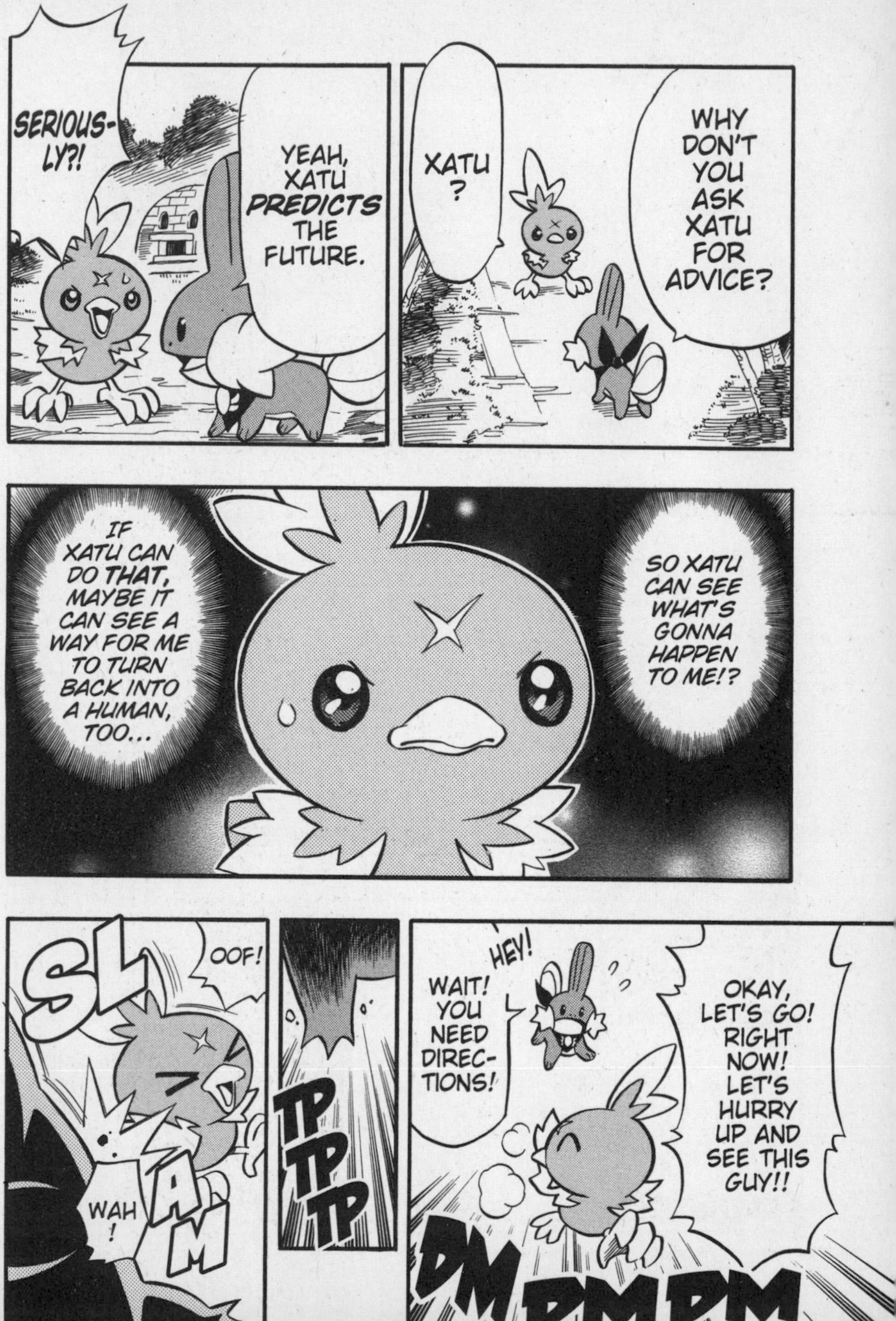

WHY DON'T YOU ASK XATU FOR ADVICE?
XATU?
YEAH, XATU PREDICTS THE FUTURE.
SERIOUS-LY?!
SO XATU CAN SEE WHAT'S GONNA HAPPEN TO ME!?
IF XATU CAN DO THAT, MAYBE IT CAN SEE A WAY FOR ME TO TURN BACK INTO A HUMAN, TOO...
OKAY, LET'S GO! RIGHT NOW! LET'S HURRY UP AND SEE THIS GUY!!
HEY!
WAIT! YOU NEED DIREC-TIONS!
DM DM DM
TP TP TP
OOF!
SLAM
WAH!

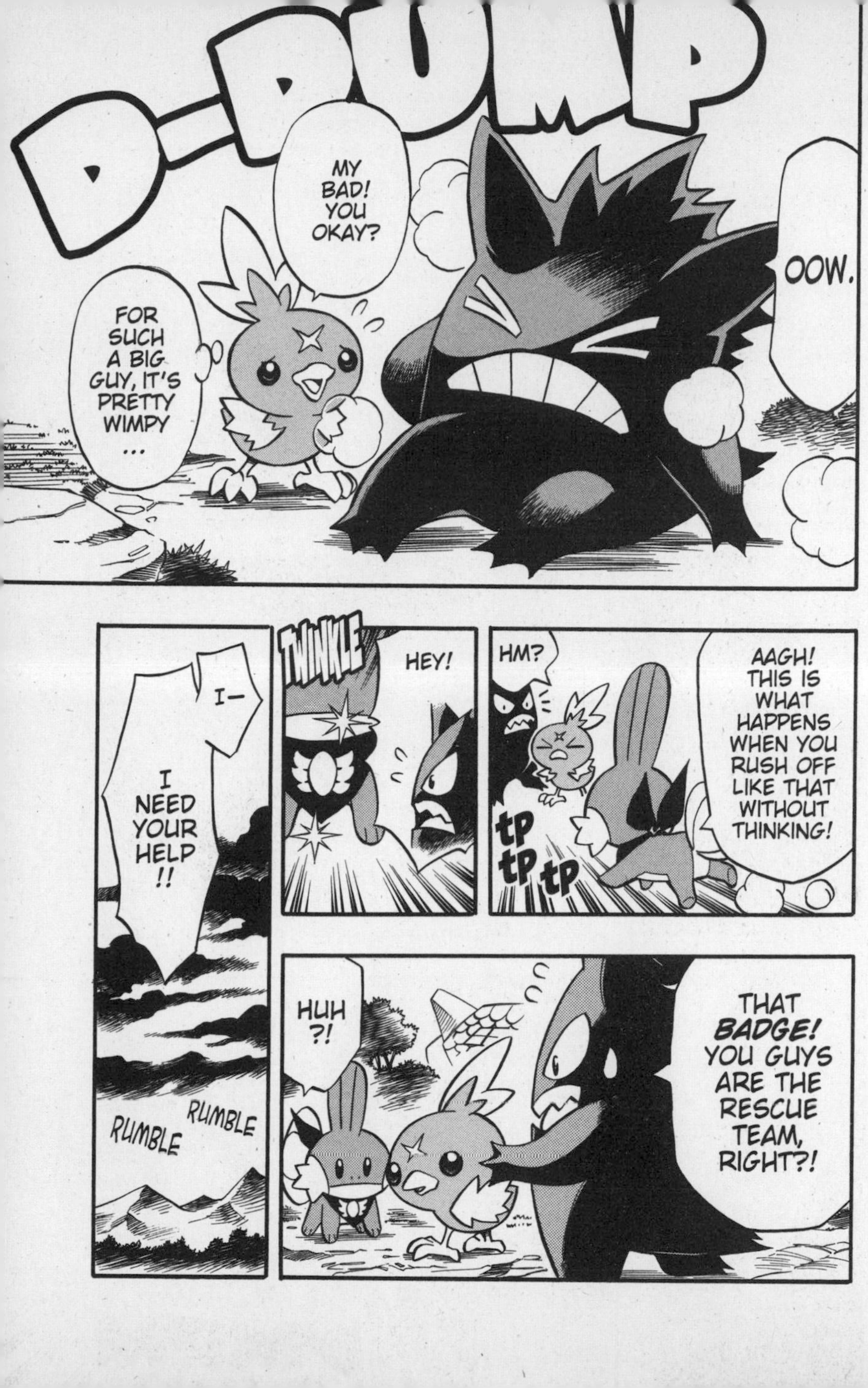
D-DUMP
OOW.
MY BAD! YOU OKAY?
FOR SUCH A BIG GUY, IT'S PRETTY WIMPY ...
AAGH! THIS IS WHAT HAPPENS WHEN YOU RUSH OFF LIKE THAT WITHOUT THINKING!
HM?
tp tp tp
HEY!
TWINKLE
THAT *BADGE!* YOU GUYS ARE THE RESCUE TEAM, RIGHT?!
HUH ?!
I—
I NEED YOUR HELP !!
RUMBLE
RUMBLE

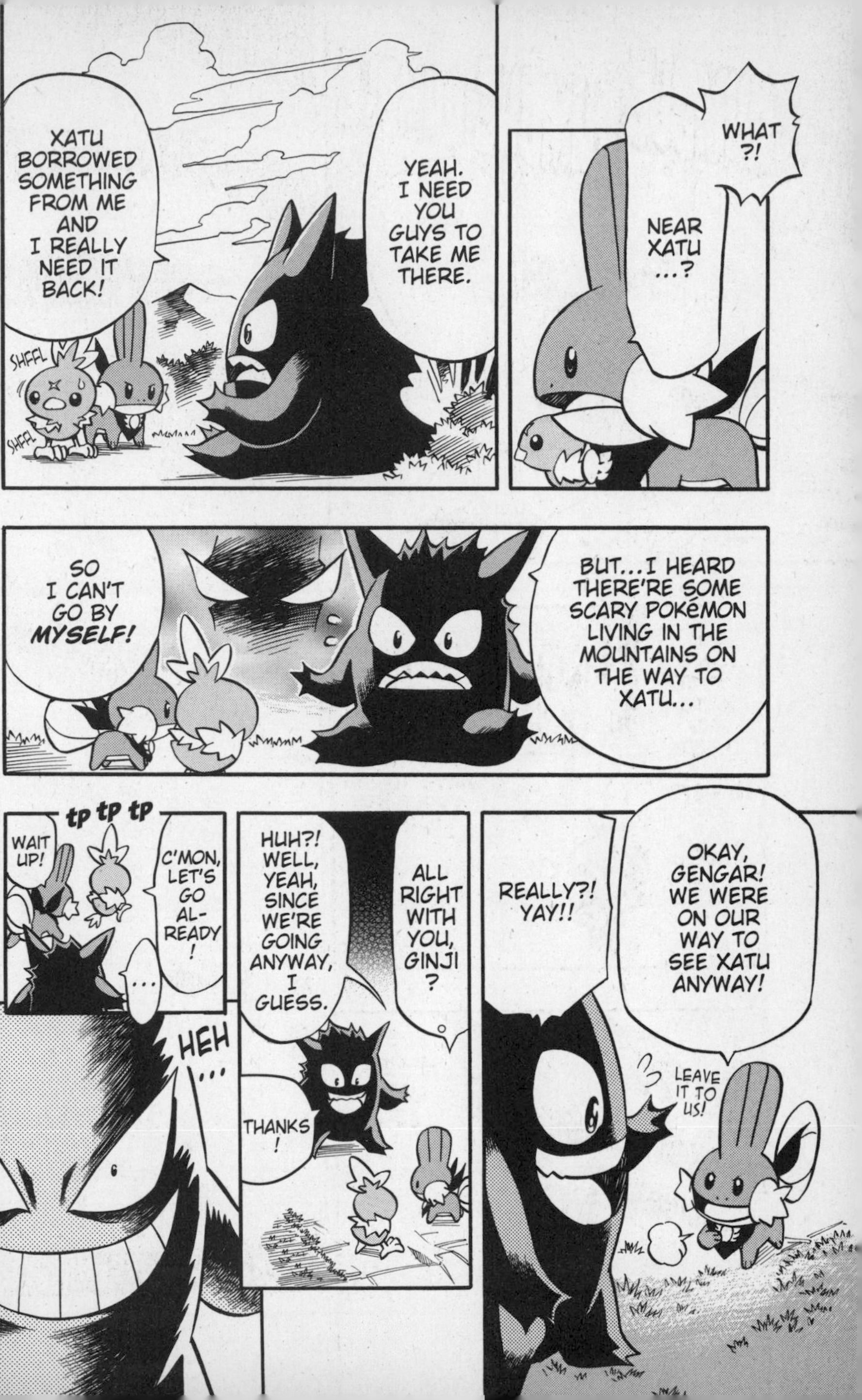
WHAT?!
NEAR XATU...?
YEAH. I NEED YOU GUYS TO TAKE ME THERE.
XATU BORROWED SOMETHING FROM ME AND I REALLY NEED IT BACK!
SHFFL
SHFFL
BUT...I HEARD THERE'RE SOME SCARY POKéMON LIVING IN THE MOUNTAINS ON THE WAY TO XATU...
SO I CAN'T GO BY **MYSELF!**
OKAY, GENGAR! WE WERE ON OUR WAY TO SEE XATU ANYWAY!
LEAVE IT TO US!
REALLY?! YAY!!
ALL RIGHT WITH YOU, GINJI?
HUH?! WELL, YEAH, SINCE WE'RE GOING ANYWAY, I GUESS.
THANKS!
tp tp tp
C'MON, LET'S GO AL-READY!
WAIT UP!
...
HEH...

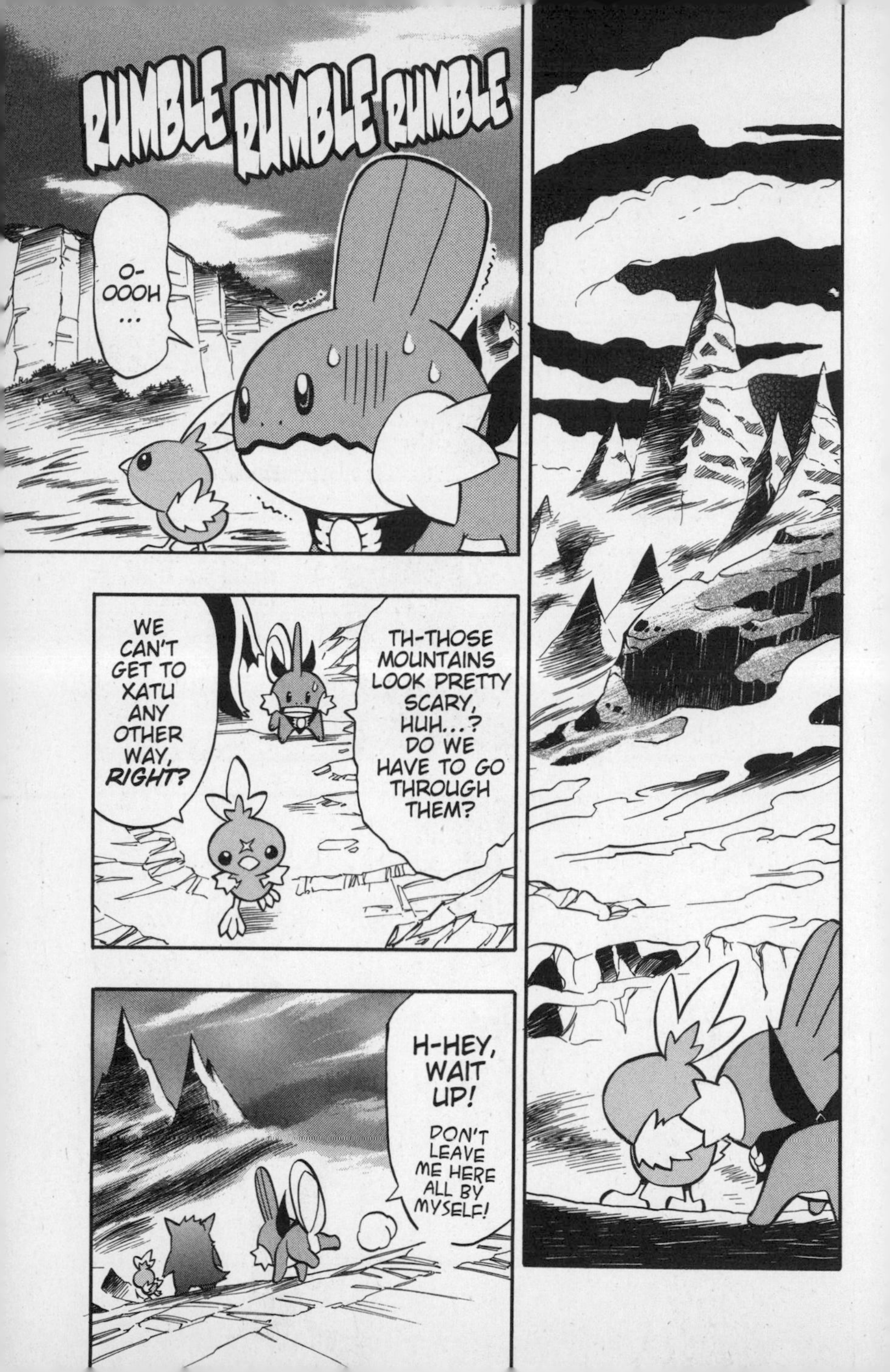
RUMBLE RUMBLE RUMBLE
O-OOOH ...
TH-THOSE MOUNTAINS LOOK PRETTY SCARY, HUH...? DO WE HAVE TO GO THROUGH THEM?
WE CAN'T GET TO XATU ANY OTHER WAY, *RIGHT?*
H-HEY, WAIT UP!
DON'T LEAVE ME HERE ALL BY MYSELF!

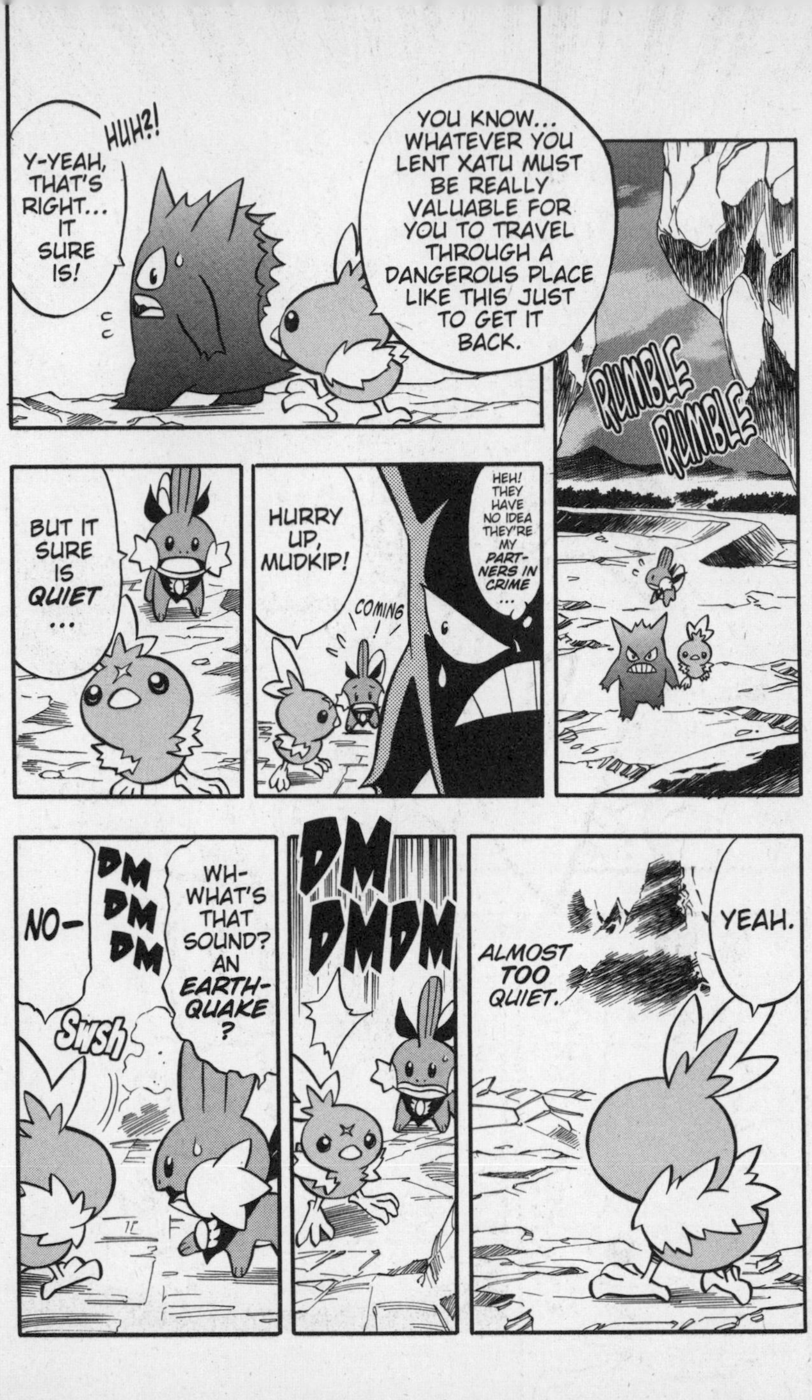
RUMBLE RUMBLE
YOU KNOW... WHATEVER YOU LENT XATU MUST BE REALLY VALUABLE FOR YOU TO TRAVEL THROUGH A DANGEROUS PLACE LIKE THIS JUST TO GET IT BACK.
HUH?!
Y-YEAH, THAT'S RIGHT... IT SURE IS!
HEH! THEY HAVE NO IDEA THEY'RE MY PARTNERS IN CRIME...
HURRY UP, MUDKIP!
COMING!
BUT IT SURE IS QUIET...
YEAH.
ALMOST TOO QUIET.
DM DMDM
WH-WHAT'S THAT SOUND? AN EARTHQUAKE?
DM DM DM
NO-
Swsh

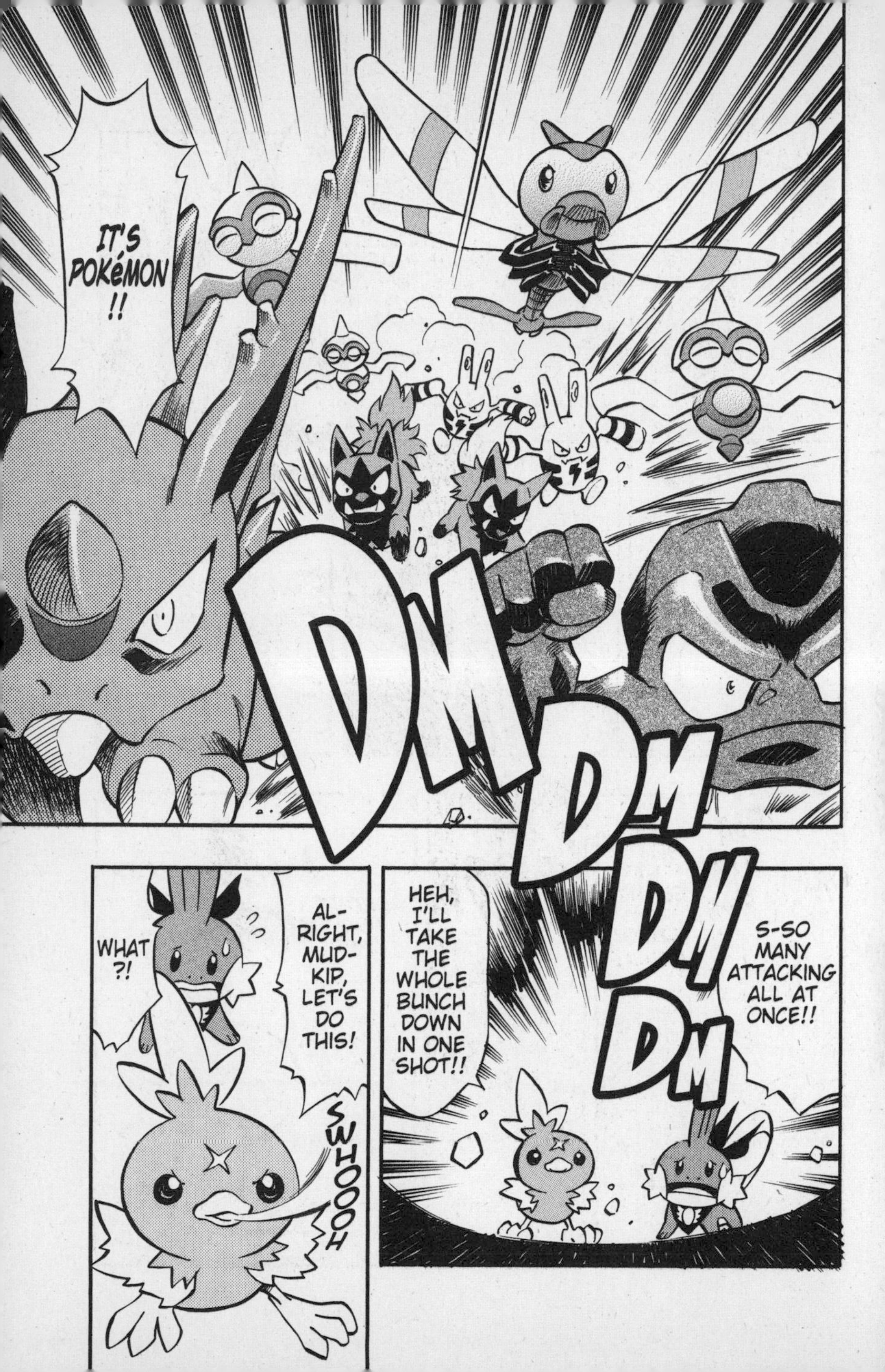
IT'S POKéMON!!
DM DM DM DM
S-SO MANY ATTACKING ALL AT ONCE!!
HEH, I'LL TAKE THE WHOLE BUNCH DOWN IN ONE SHOT!!
ALRIGHT, MUDKIP, LET'S DO THIS!
WHAT?!
SWHOOOOH

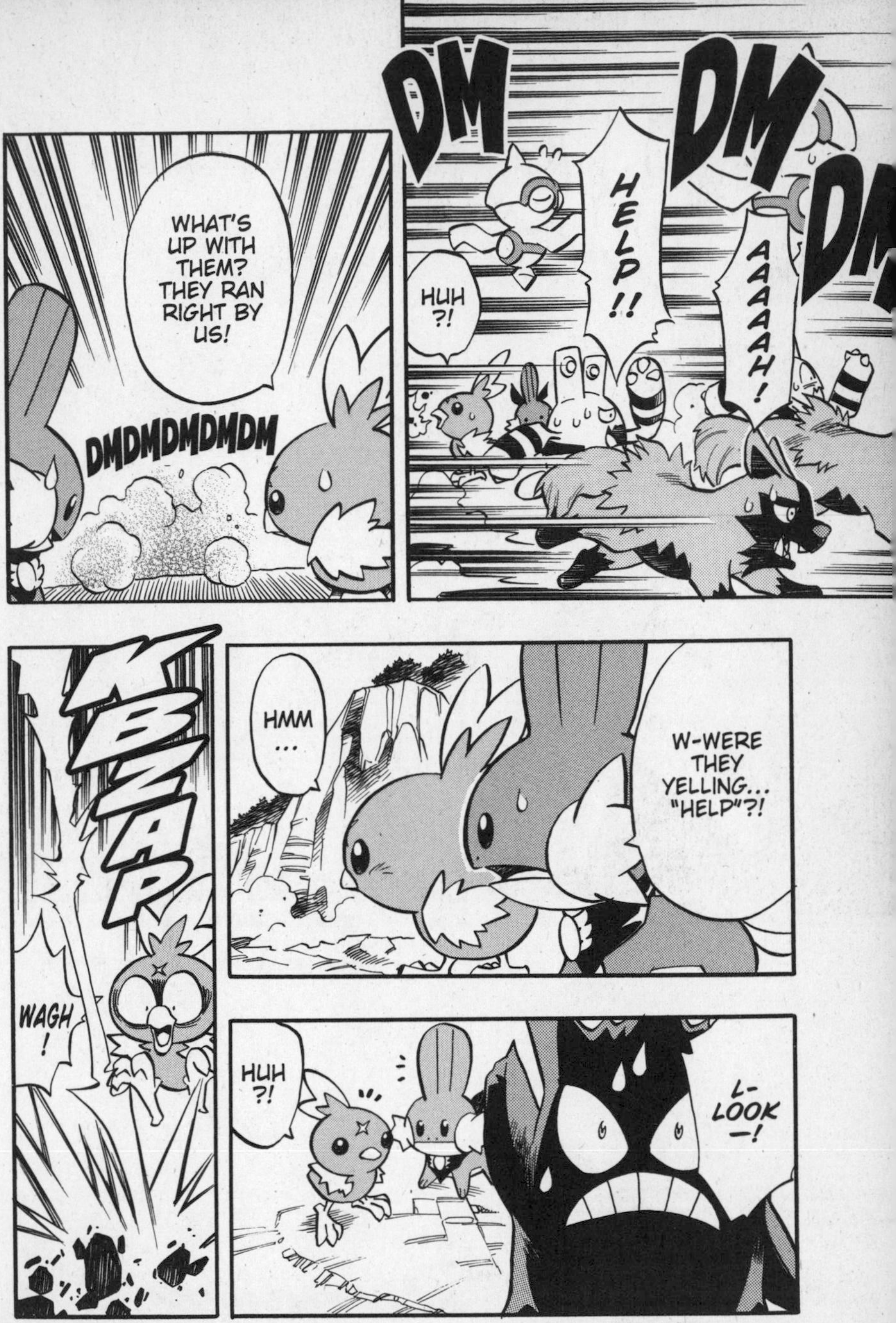
DM DM DM
AAAAAH!
HELP!!
HUH?!
WHAT'S UP WITH THEM? THEY RAN RIGHT BY US!
DMDMDMDMDM
W-WERE THEY YELLING... "HELP"?!
HMM...
L-LOOK—!
HUH?!
KBZAP
WAGH!

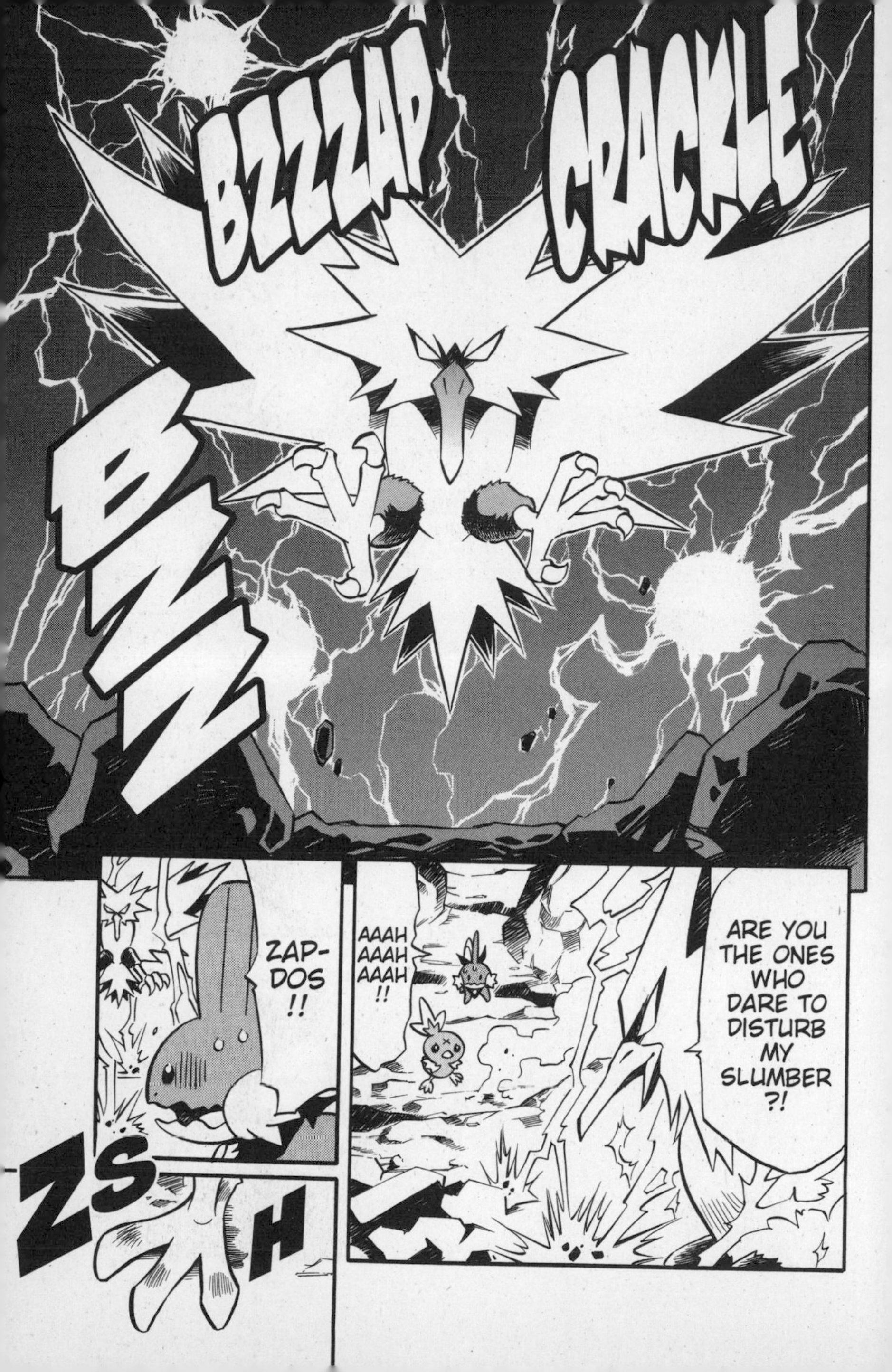
CRACKLE
BZZZAP
BZZZ
ARE YOU THE ONES WHO DARE TO DISTURB MY SLUMBER?!
AAAH AAAH AAAH!!
ZAP-DOS!!
ZSH

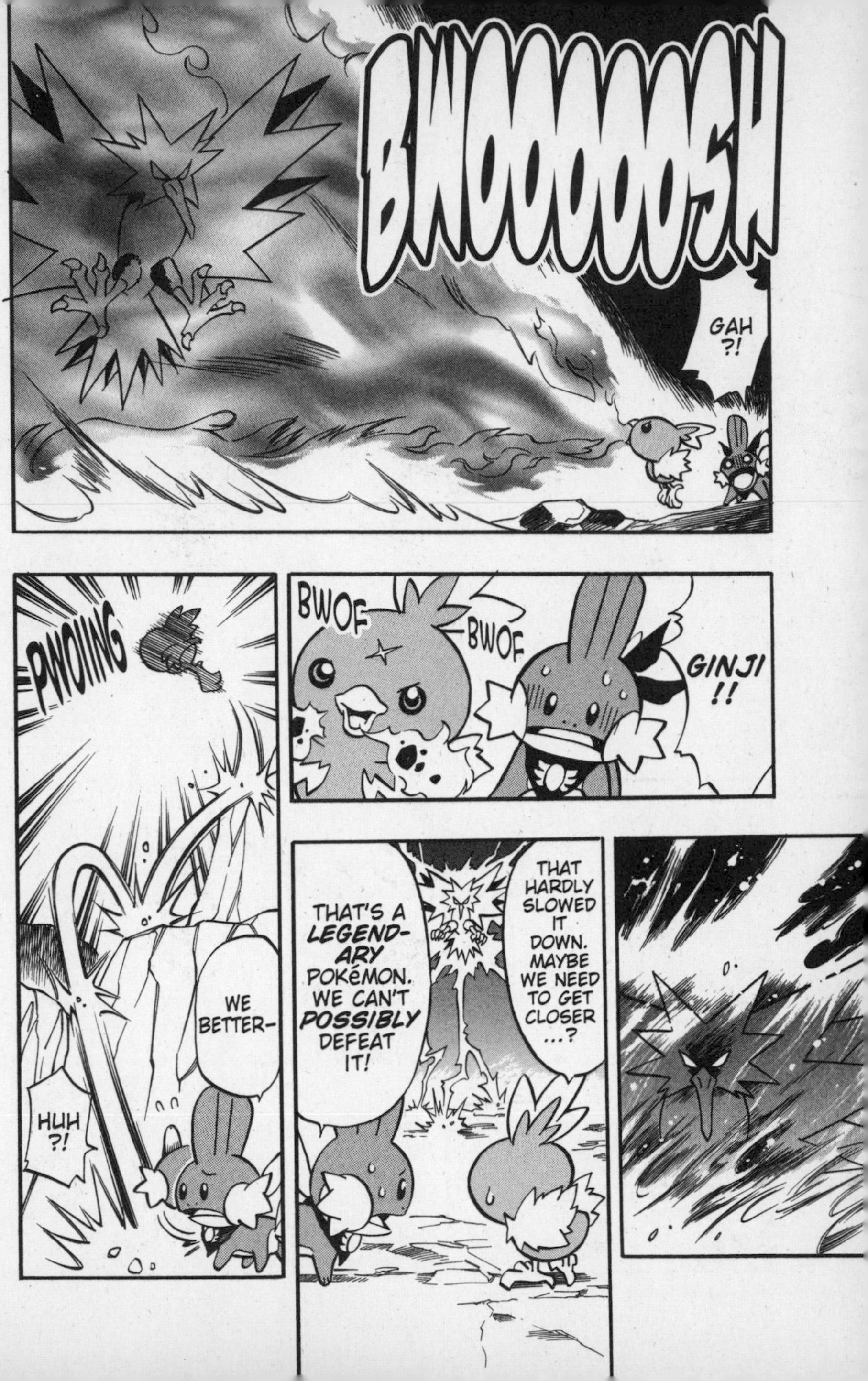
BHOOOOOOSH
GAH ?!
GINJI !!
BWOF
BWOF
THAT HARDLY SLOWED IT DOWN. MAYBE WE NEED TO GET CLOSER ...?
THAT'S A *LEGENDARY* POKéMON. WE CAN'T *POSSIBLY* DEFEAT IT!
PWOIING
WE BETTER-
HUH ?!

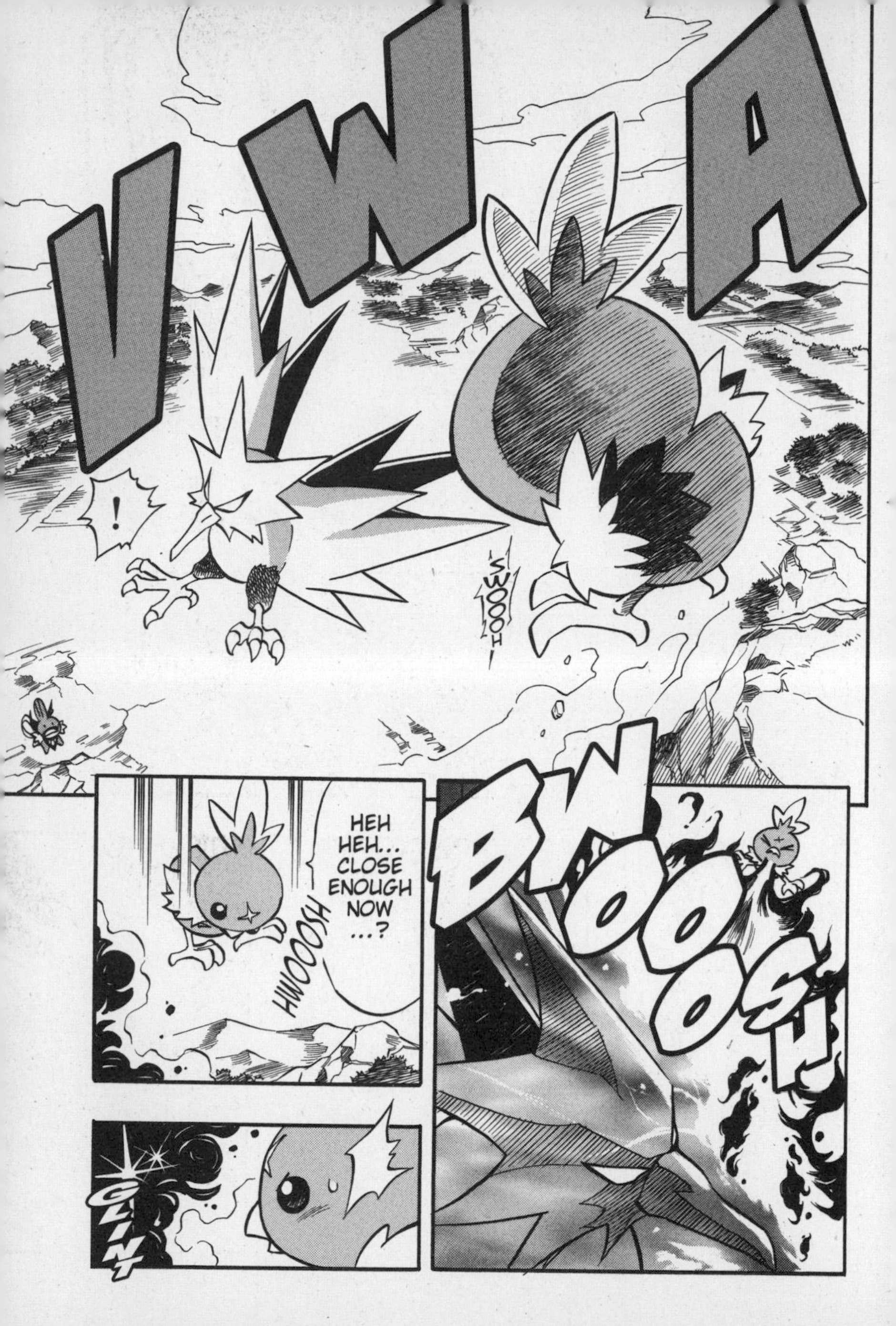
VWA
SWOOOH
!
BWOOOSH
HEH HEH... CLOSE ENOUGH NOW ...?
HWOOOSH
GLINT

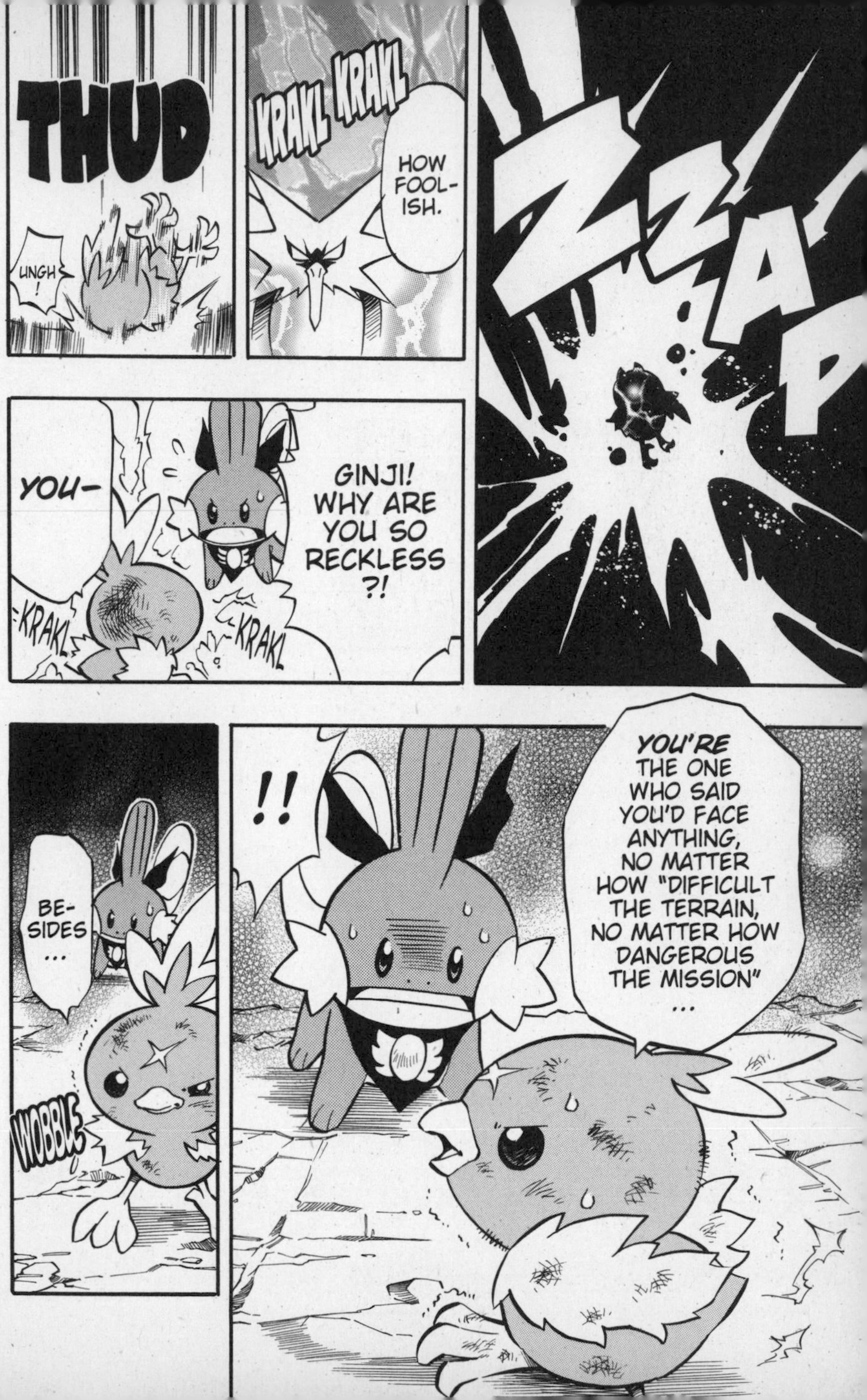
ZZAP
KRAKL KRAKL
HOW FOOL-ISH.
THUD
UNGH!
GINJI! WHY ARE YOU SO RECKLESS?!
YOU-
KRAKL
KRAKL
YOU'RE THE ONE WHO SAID YOU'D FACE ANYTHING, NO MATTER HOW "DIFFICULT THE TERRAIN, NO MATTER HOW DANGEROUS THE MISSION"...
!!
BE-SIDES...
WOBBLE

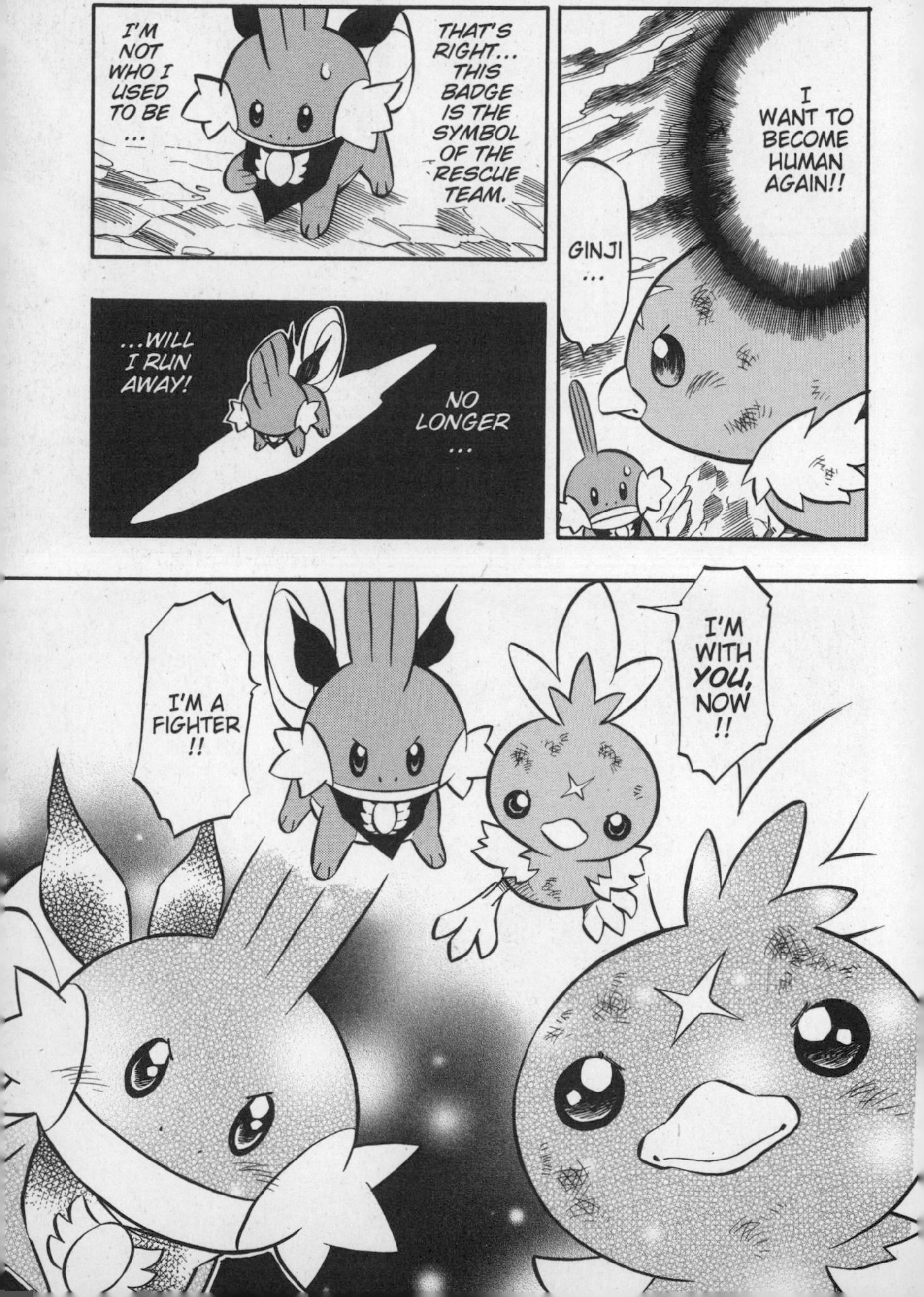
I WANT TO BECOME HUMAN AGAIN!!
GINJI ...
THAT'S RIGHT... THIS BADGE IS THE SYMBOL OF THE RESCUE TEAM.
I'M NOT WHO I USED TO BE ...
NO LONGER ...
...WILL I RUN AWAY!
I'M WITH *YOU*, NOW !!
I'M A FIGHTER !!

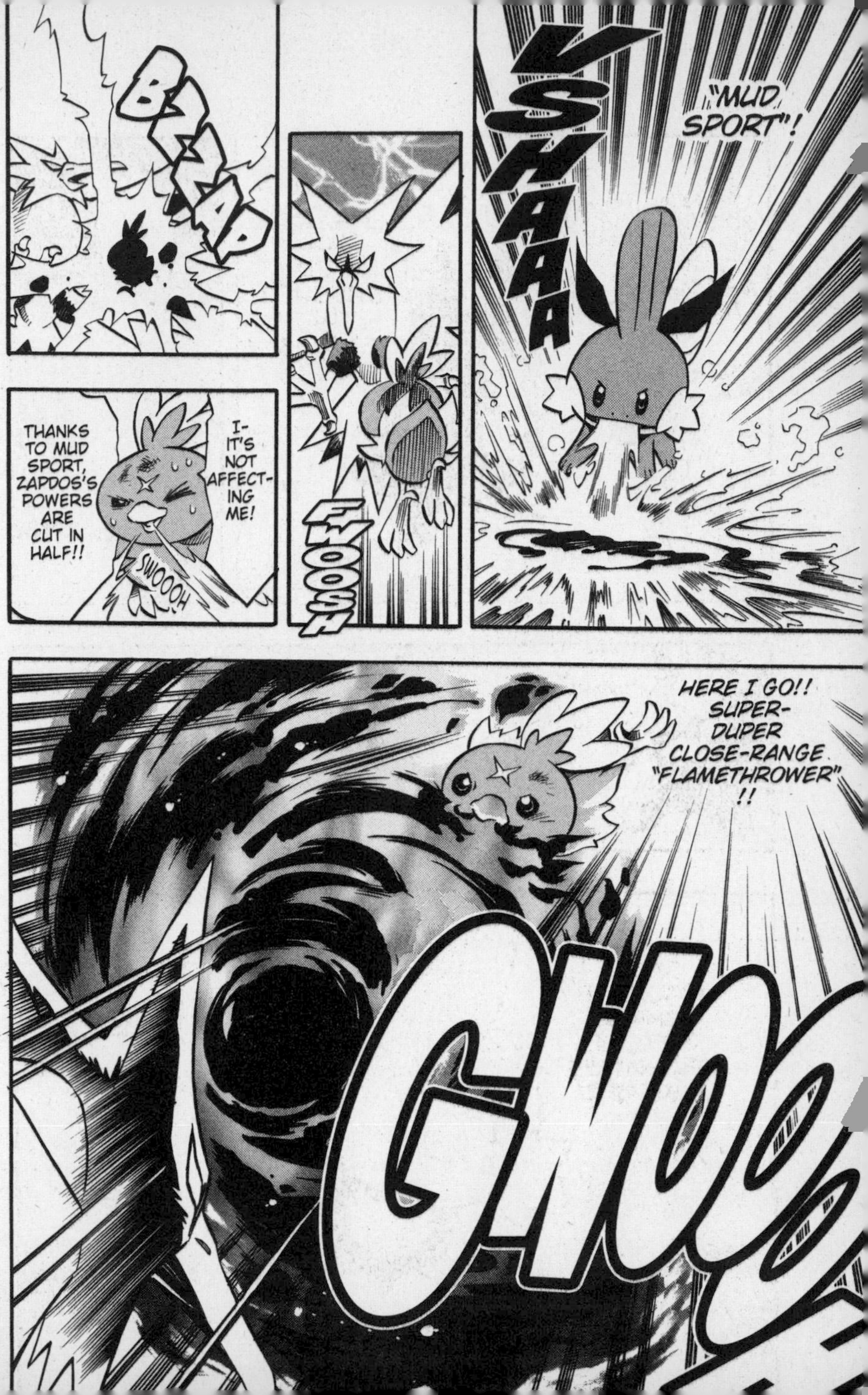
VSHAAAA
"MUD SPORT"!
FWOOSH
BZZAP
I- IT'S NOT AFFECTING ME!
THANKS TO MUD SPORT, ZAPDOS'S POWERS ARE CUT IN HALF!!
SWOOOH
HERE I GO!! SUPER-DUPER CLOSE-RANGE "FLAMETHROWER"!!
GHO

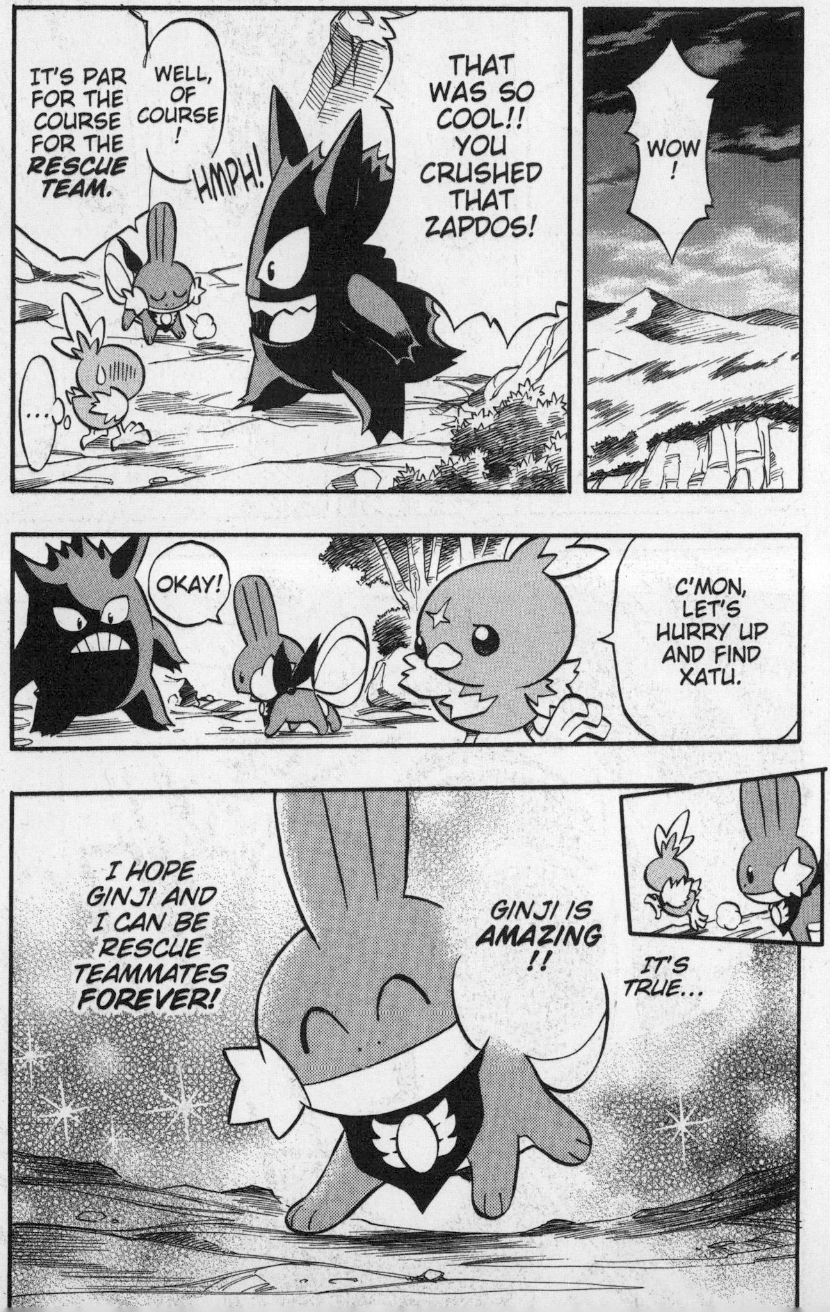

WOW!
THAT WAS SO COOL!! YOU CRUSHED THAT ZAPDOS!
HMPH!
WELL, OF COURSE!
IT'S PAR FOR THE COURSE FOR THE RESCUE TEAM.
....
C'MON, LET'S HURRY UP AND FIND XATU.
OKAY!
IT'S TRUE...
GINJI IS AMAZING!!
I HOPE GINJI AND I CAN BE RESCUE TEAMMATES FOREVER!

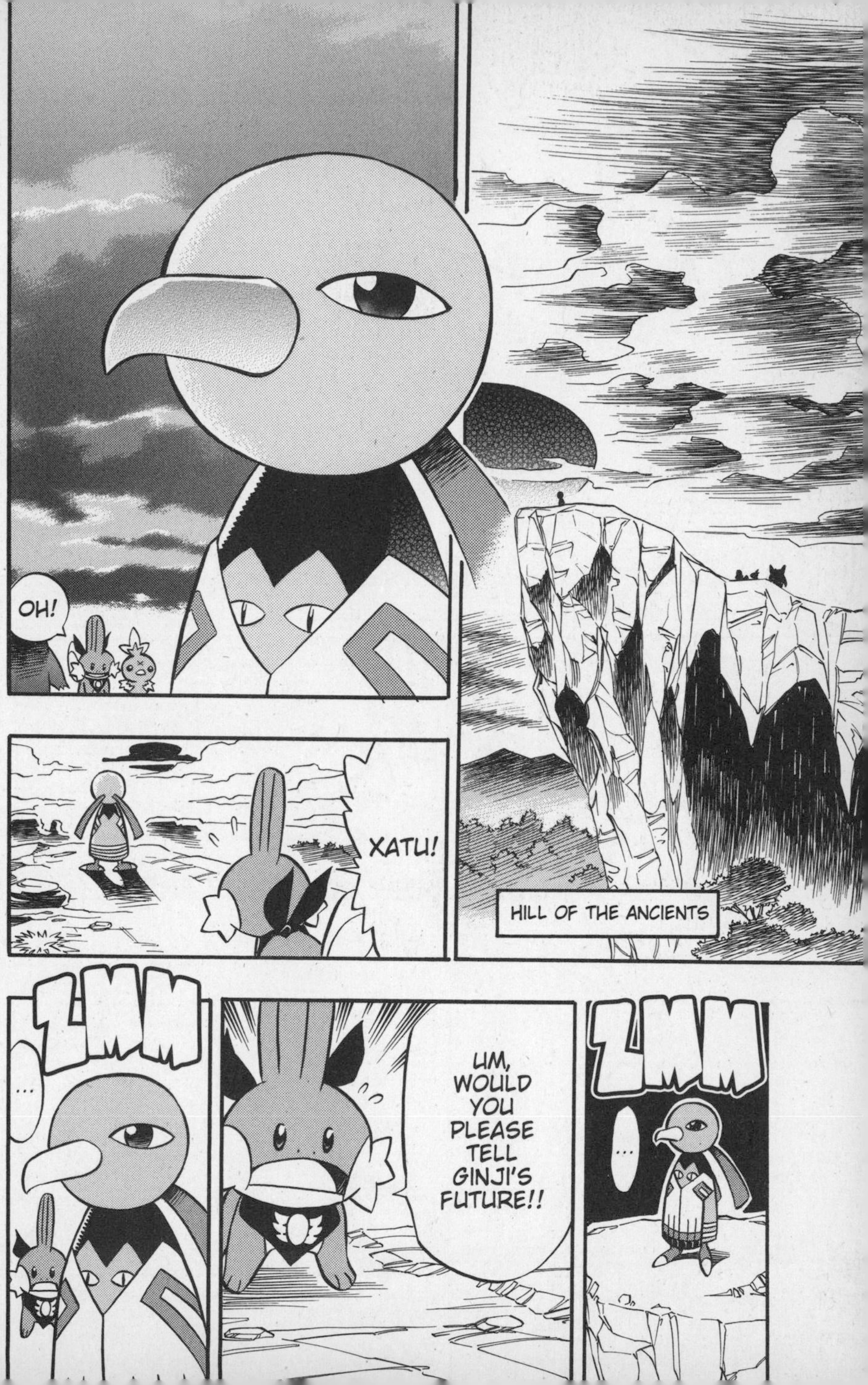
HILL OF THE ANCIENTS
OH!
XATU!
ZMM
...
UM, WOULD YOU PLEASE TELL GINJI'S FUTURE!!
ZMM
...

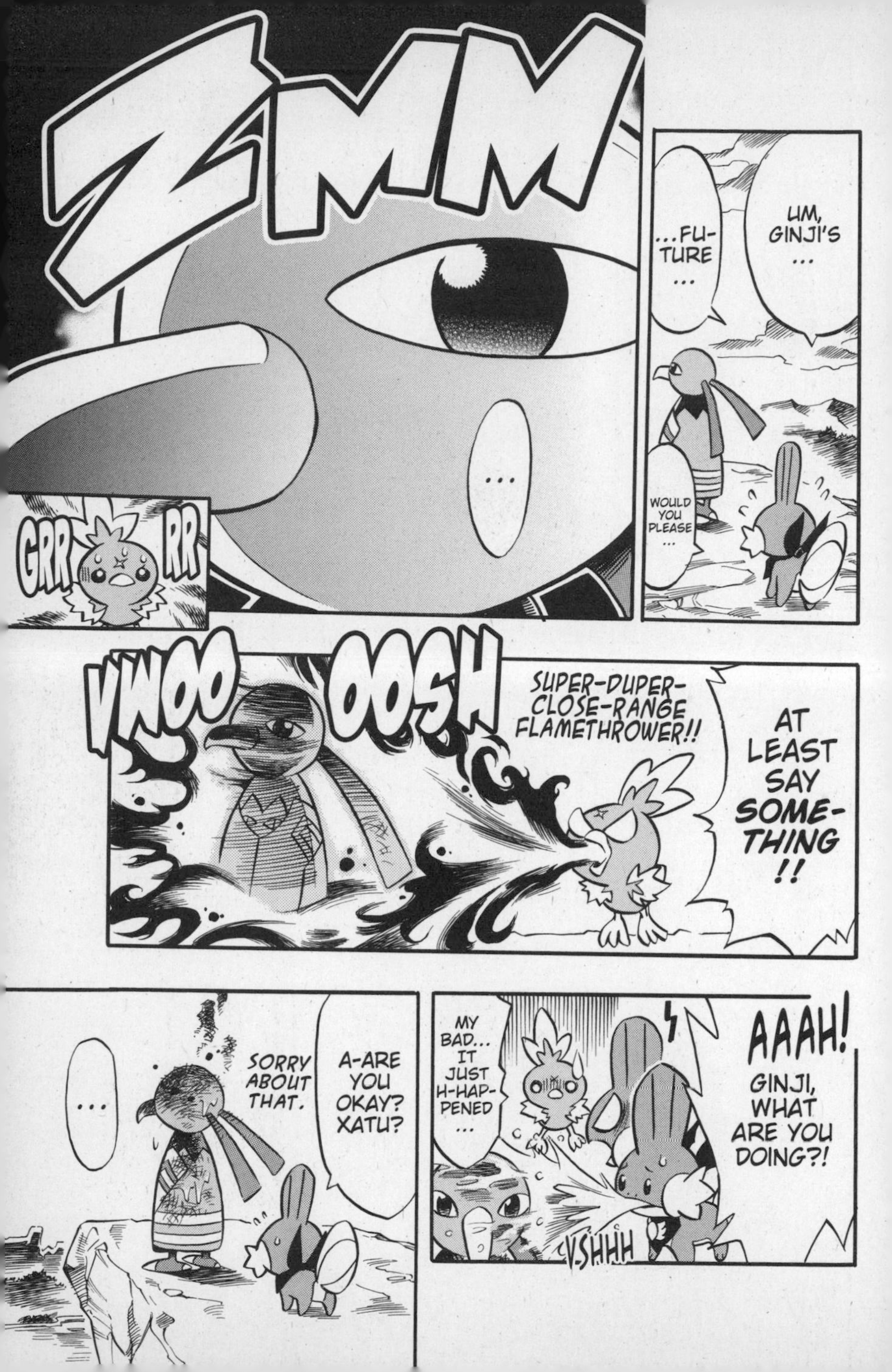
UM, GINJI'S ...
...FU-TURE ...
WOULD YOU PLEASE ...
ZMM
...
GRR RR
AT LEAST SAY SOMETHING!!
SUPER-DUPER-CLOSE-RANGE FLAMETHROWER!!
VWOO OOSH
AAAH!
GINJI, WHAT ARE YOU DOING?!
MY BAD... IT JUST H-HAPPENED ...
V-SHHH
A-ARE YOU OKAY? XATU?
SORRY ABOUT THAT.
...

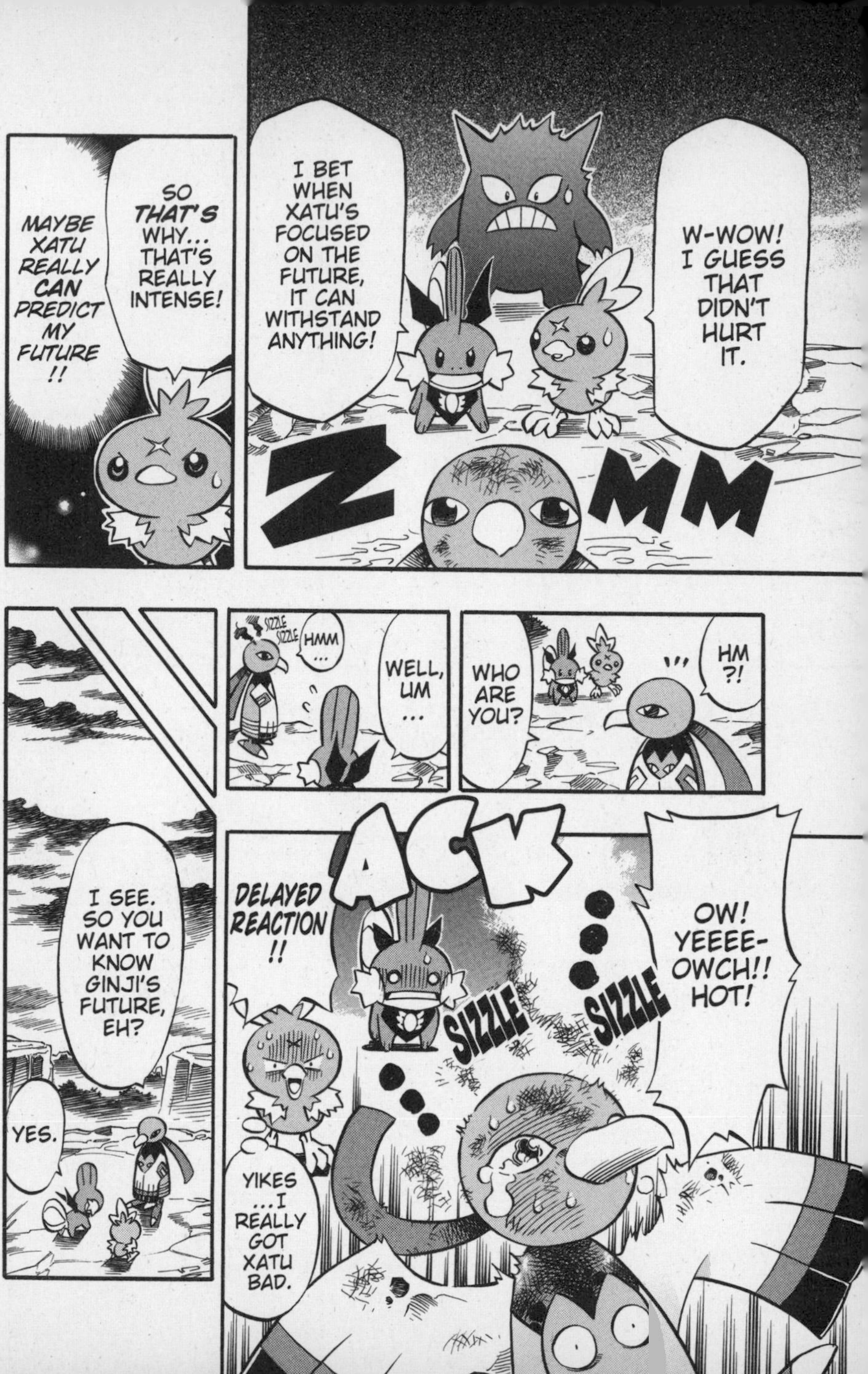
W-WOW! I GUESS THAT DIDN'T HURT IT.
I BET WHEN XATU'S FOCUSED ON THE FUTURE, IT CAN WITHSTAND ANYTHING!
ZOMM
SO THAT'S WHY... THAT'S REALLY INTENSE!
MAYBE XATU REALLY CAN PREDICT MY FUTURE!!
HM?!
WHO ARE YOU?
SIZZLE SIZZLE
HMM...
WELL, UM...
OW! YEEEE-OWCH!! HOT!
ACK
DELAYED REACTION!!
SIZZLE
SIZZLE
YIKES...I REALLY GOT XATU BAD.
I SEE. SO YOU WANT TO KNOW GINJI'S FUTURE, EH?
YES.

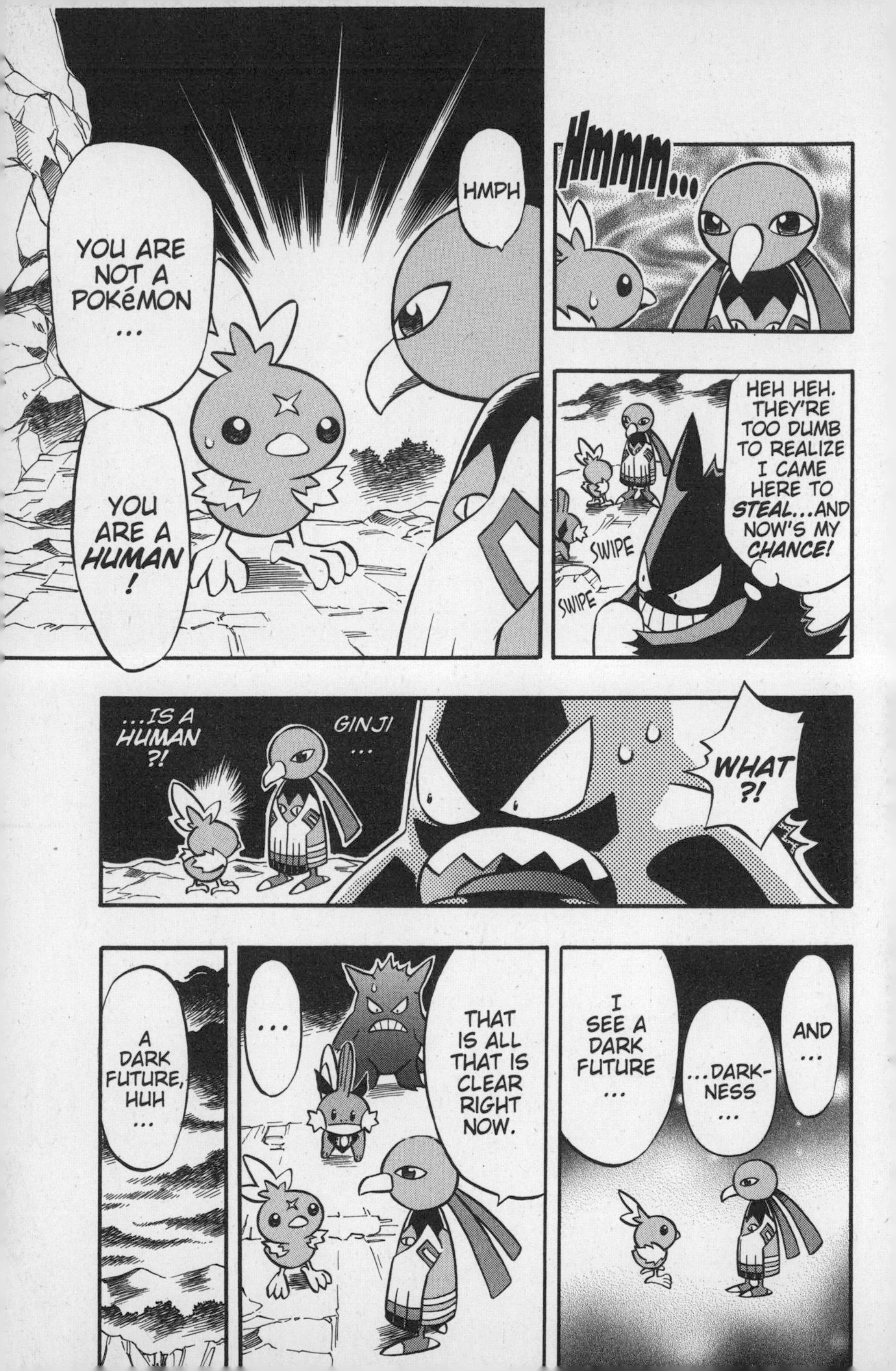
HMMMM...
HEH HEH. THEY'RE TOO DUMB TO REALIZE I CAME HERE TO STEAL...AND NOW'S MY CHANCE!
SWIPE
SWIPE
HMPH
YOU ARE NOT A POKéMON ...
YOU ARE A HUMAN !
WHAT ?!
GINJI ...
...IS A HUMAN ?!
AND ...
...DARK-NESS ...
I SEE A DARK FUTURE ...
THAT IS ALL THAT IS CLEAR RIGHT NOW.
...
A DARK FUTURE, HUH ...

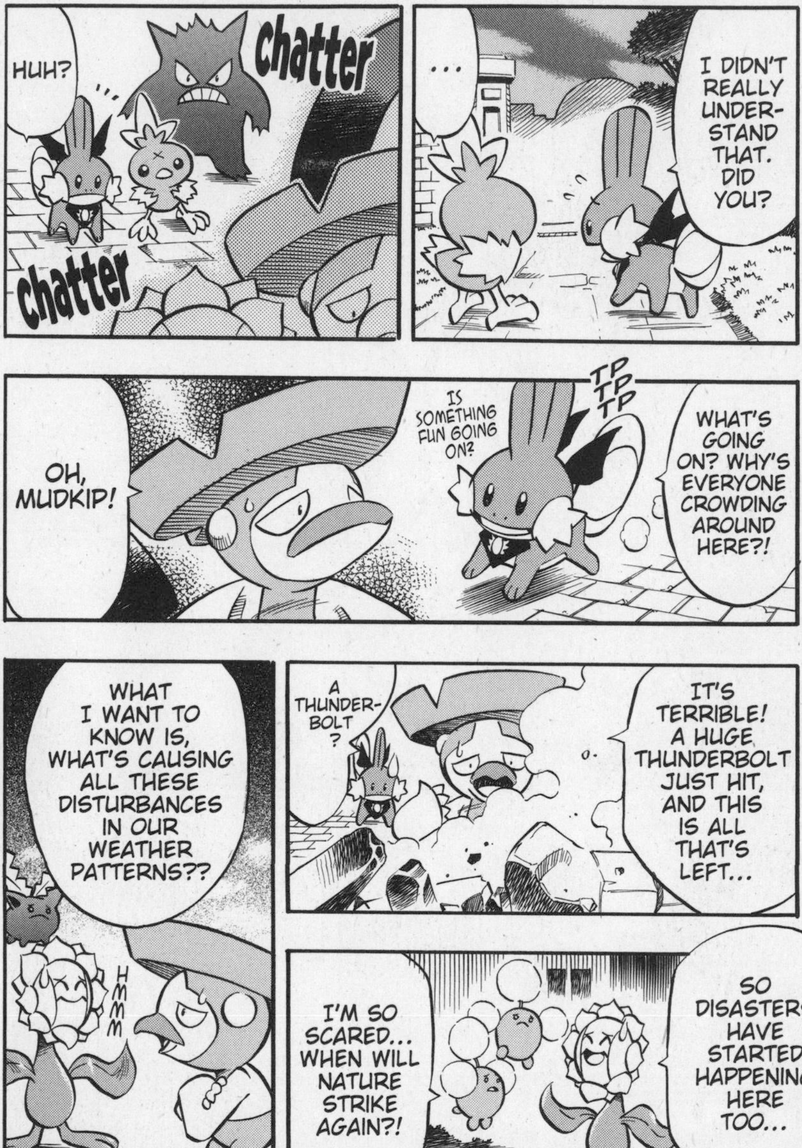
I DIDN'T REALLY UNDER-STAND THAT. DID YOU?
...
chatter
HUH?
chatter
WHAT'S GOING ON? WHY'S EVERYONE CROWDING AROUND HERE?!
TP TP TP
IS SOMETHING FUN GOING ON?
OH, MUDKIP!
IT'S TERRIBLE! A HUGE THUNDERBOLT JUST HIT, AND THIS IS ALL THAT'S LEFT...
A THUNDER-BOLT?
SO DISASTERS HAVE STARTED HAPPENING HERE TOO...
I'M SO SCARED... WHEN WILL NATURE STRIKE AGAIN?!
WHAT I WANT TO KNOW IS, WHAT'S CAUSING ALL THESE DISTURBANCES IN OUR WEATHER PATTERNS??
HMMM

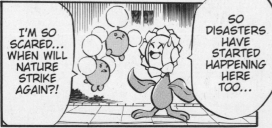

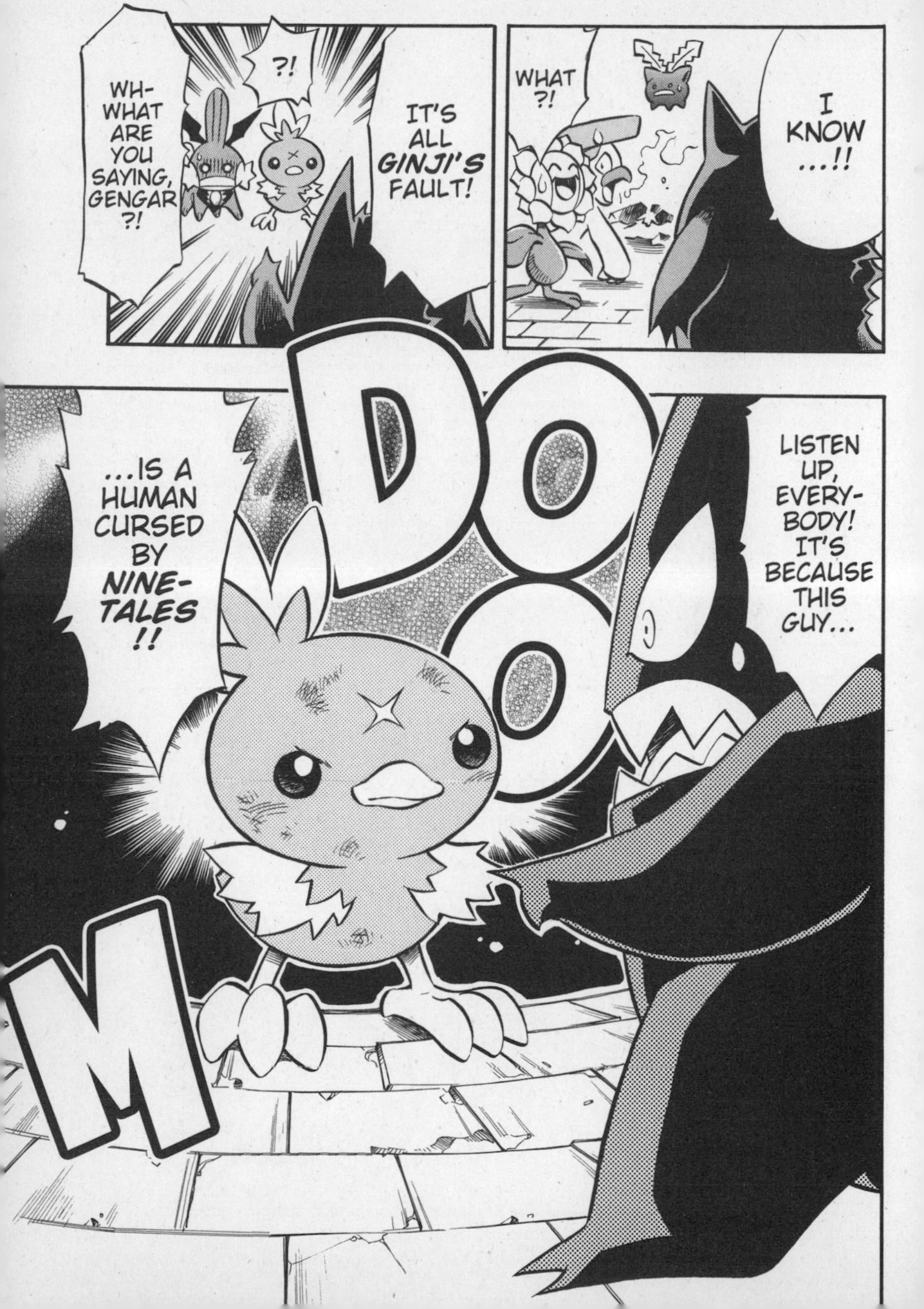
I KNOW ...!!
WHAT ?!
IT'S ALL GINJI'S FAULT!
?!
WH-WHAT ARE YOU SAYING, GENGAR ?!
LISTEN UP, EVERYBODY! IT'S BECAUSE THIS GUY...
DOOM
...IS A HUMAN CURSED BY NINE-TALES !!

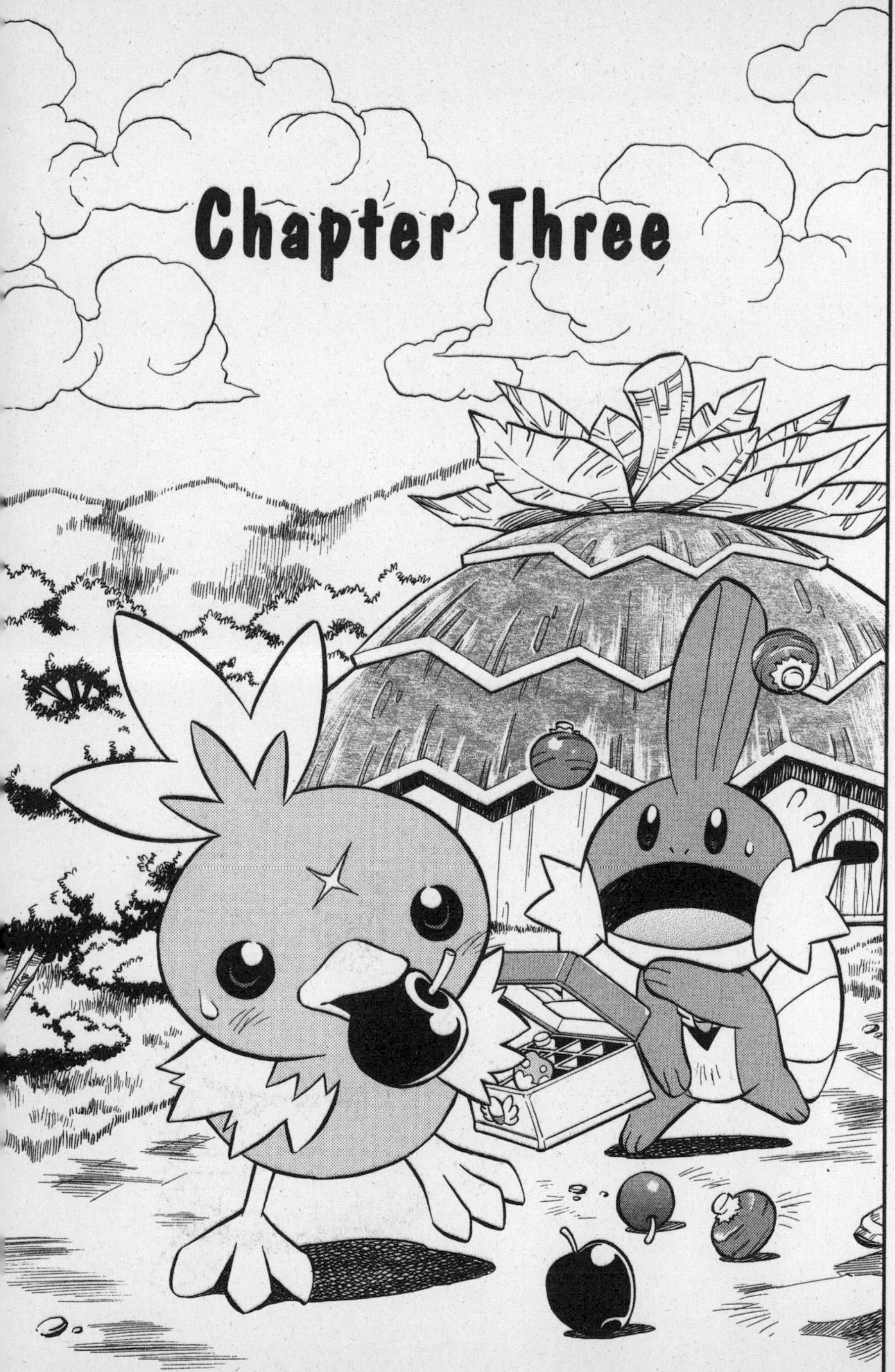
Chapter Three

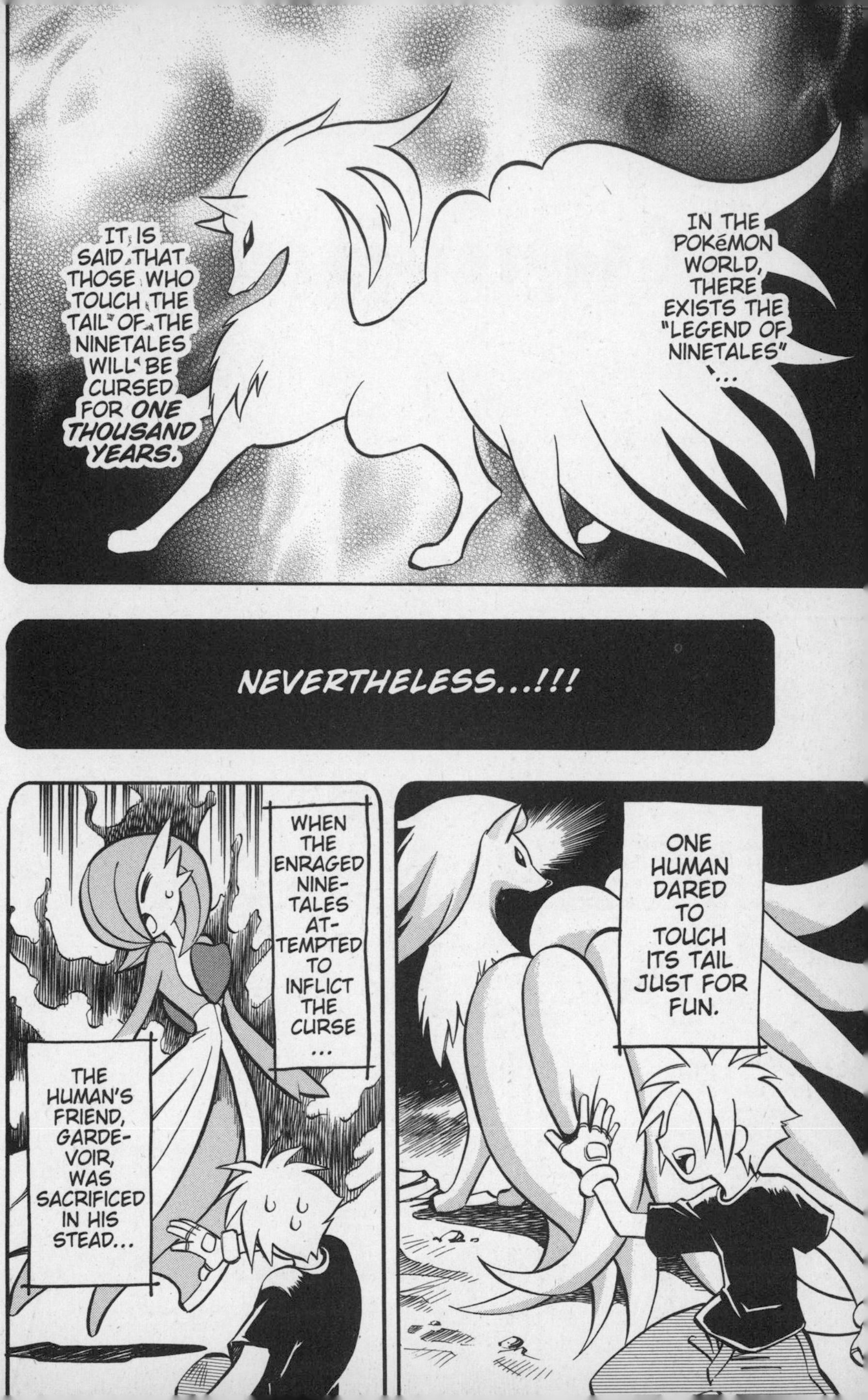
IN THE POKéMON WORLD, THERE EXISTS THE "LEGEND OF NINETALES"...
IT IS SAID THAT THOSE WHO TOUCH THE TAIL OF THE NINETALES WILL BE CURSED FOR ONE THOUSAND YEARS.
NEVERTHELESS...!!!
ONE HUMAN DARED TO TOUCH ITS TAIL JUST FOR FUN.
WHEN THE ENRAGED NINE-TALES AT-TEMPTED TO INFLICT THE CURSE...
THE HUMAN'S FRIEND, GARDE-VOIR, WAS SACRIFICED IN HIS STEAD...

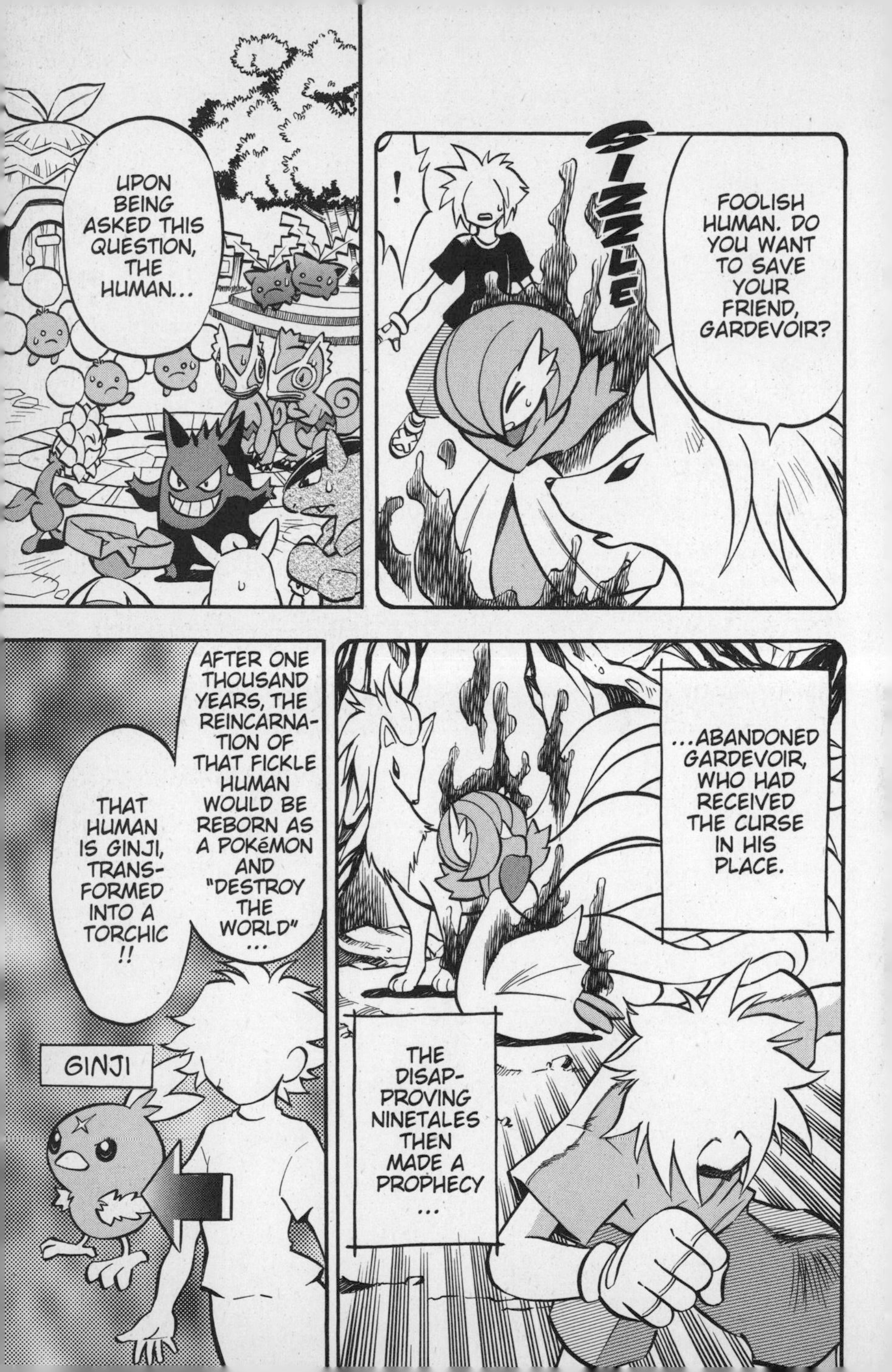
SIZZLE
FOOLISH HUMAN. DO YOU WANT TO SAVE YOUR FRIEND, GARDEVOIR?
!
UPON BEING ASKED THIS QUESTION, THE HUMAN...
...ABANDONED GARDEVOIR, WHO HAD RECEIVED THE CURSE IN HIS PLACE.
THE DISAPPROVING NINETALES THEN MADE A PROPHECY...
AFTER ONE THOUSAND YEARS, THE REINCARNATION OF THAT FICKLE HUMAN WOULD BE REBORN AS A POKéMON AND "DESTROY THE WORLD"...
THAT HUMAN IS GINJI, TRANSFORMED INTO A TORCHIC!!
GINJI

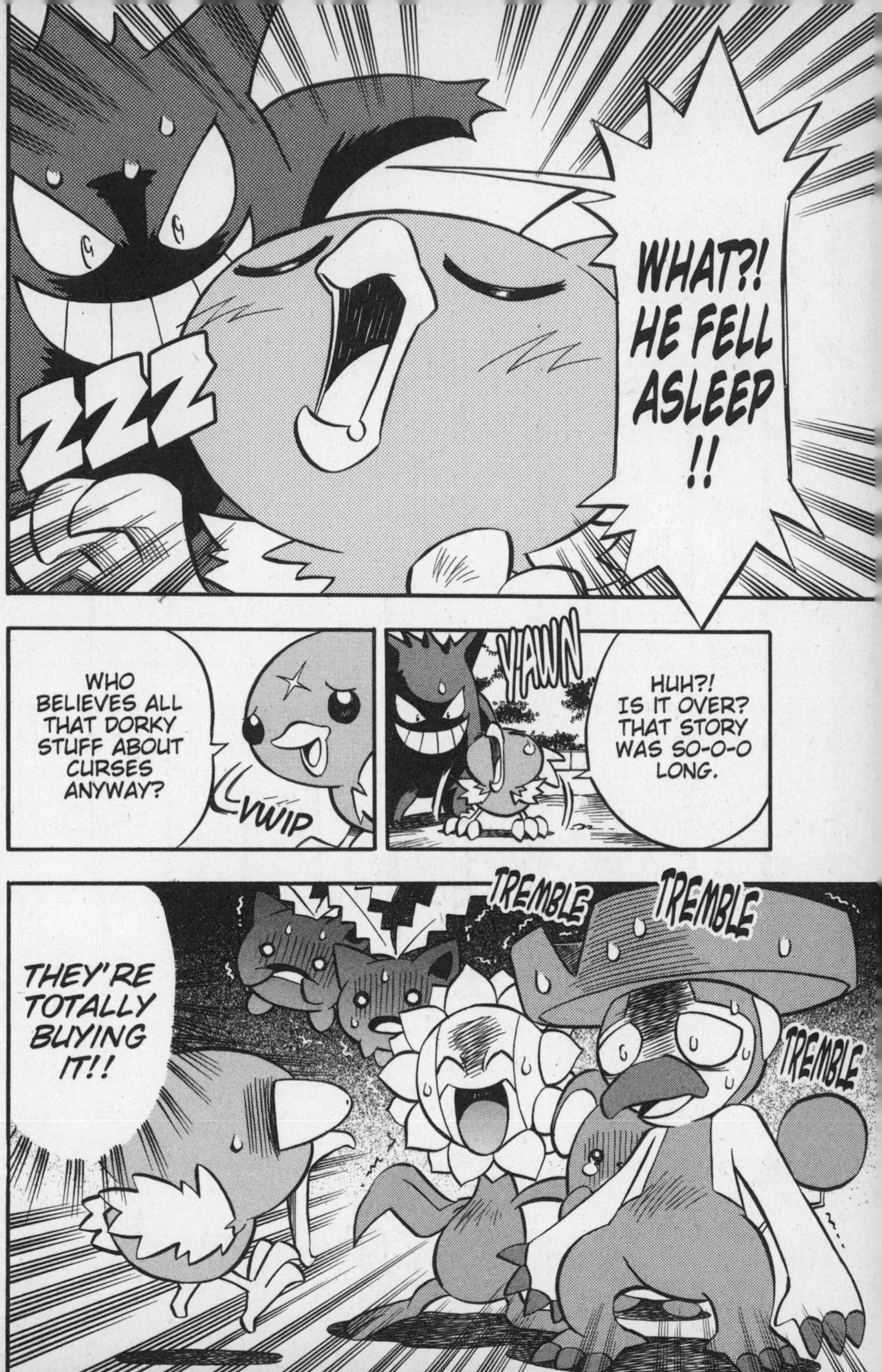
WHAT?! HE FELL ASLEEP !!
ZZZ
HUH?! IS IT OVER? THAT STORY WAS SO-O-O LONG.
YAWN
WHO BELIEVES ALL THAT DORKY STUFF ABOUT CURSES ANYWAY?
VWIP
TREMBLE
TREMBLE
TREMBLE
THEY'RE TOTALLY BUYING IT!!

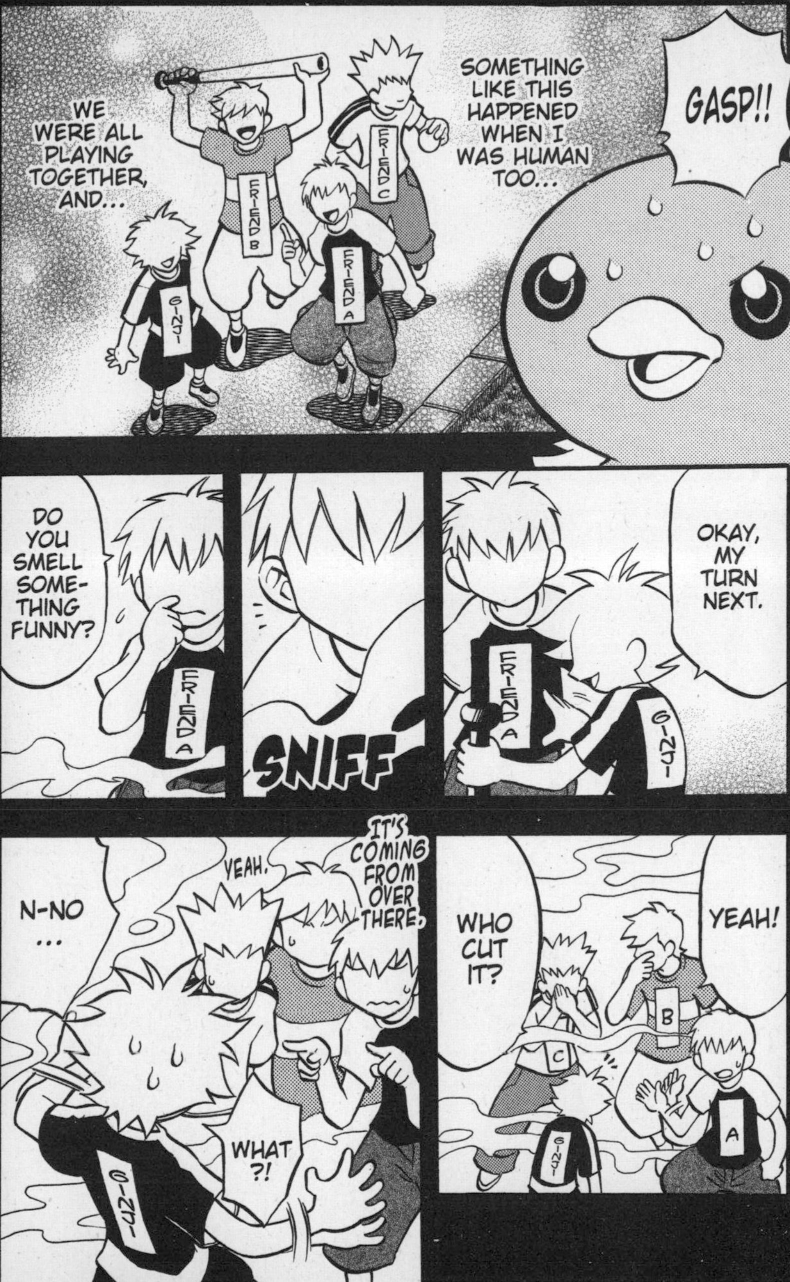
GASP!!
SOMETHING LIKE THIS HAPPENED WHEN I WAS HUMAN TOO...
WE WERE ALL PLAYING TOGETHER, AND...
FRIEND C
FRIEND B
FRIEND A
GINJI
OKAY, MY TURN NEXT.
FRIEND A
GINJI
SNIFF
DO YOU SMELL SOMETHING FUNNY?
FRIEND A
YEAH!
WHO CUT IT?
B
C
A
GINJI
IT'S COMING FROM OVER THERE.
YEAH.
N-NO ...
WHAT?!
GINJI

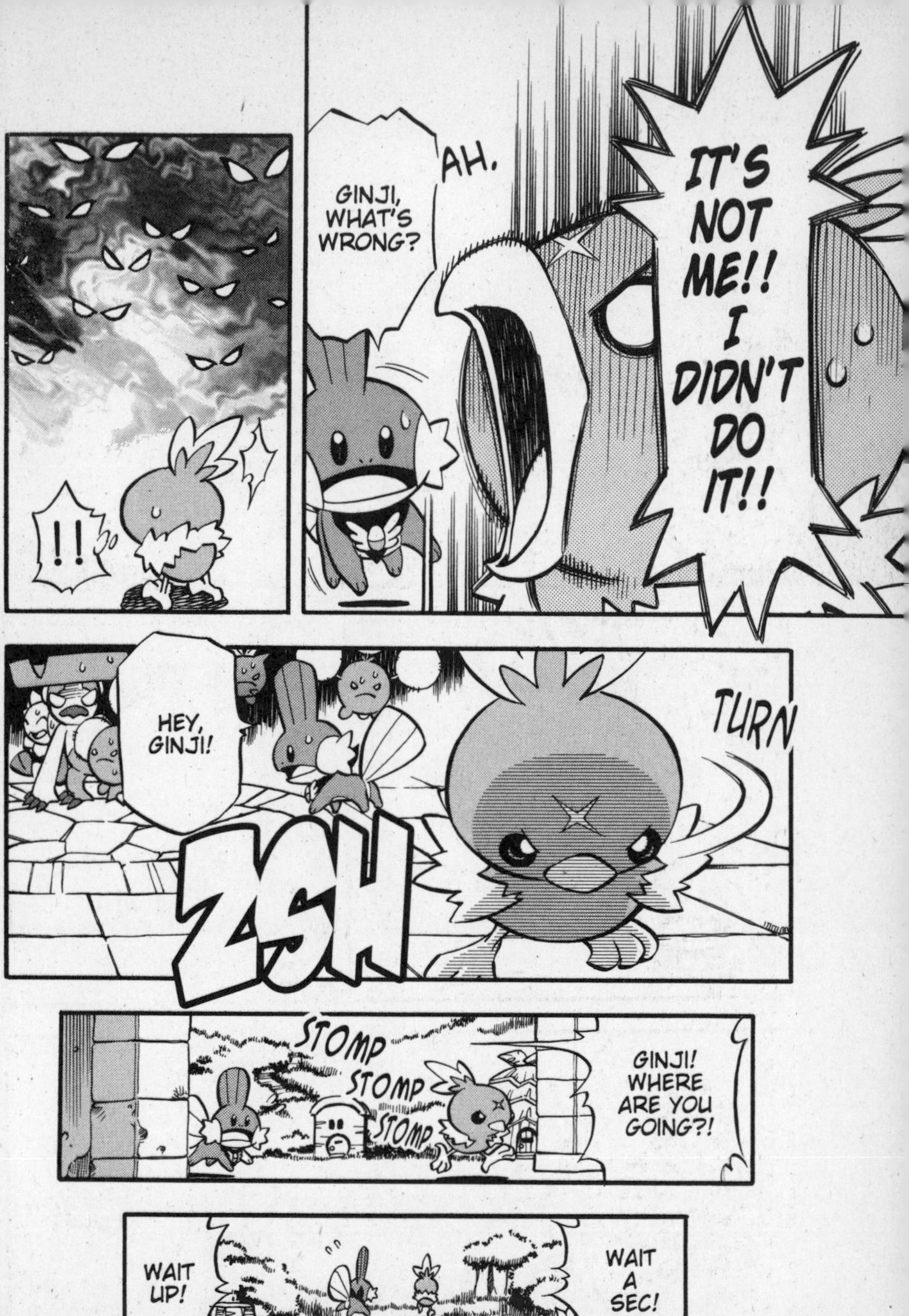
IT'S NOT ME!! I DIDN'T DO IT!!
AH.
GINJI, WHAT'S WRONG?
!!
TURN
HEY, GINJI!
ZSH
GINJI! WHERE ARE YOU GOING?!
STOMP
STOMP
STOMP
WAIT A SEC!
WAIT UP!

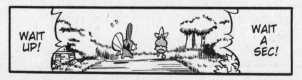

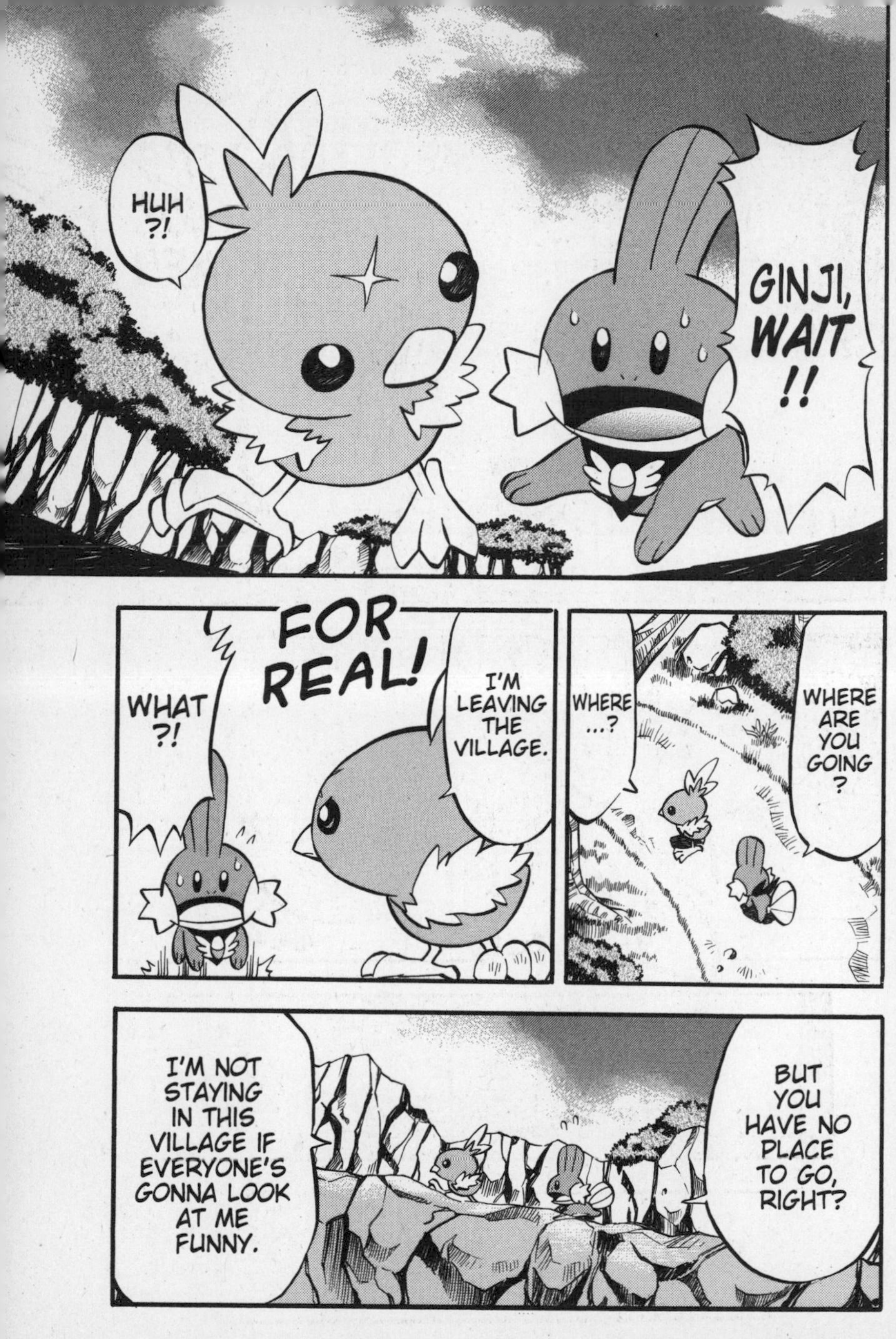
GINJI, WAIT!!
HUH?!
WHERE ARE YOU GOING?
WHERE...?
I'M LEAVING THE VILLAGE.
FOR REAL!
WHAT?!
BUT YOU HAVE NO PLACE TO GO, RIGHT?
I'M NOT STAYING IN THIS VILLAGE IF EVERYONE'S GONNA LOOK AT ME FUNNY.

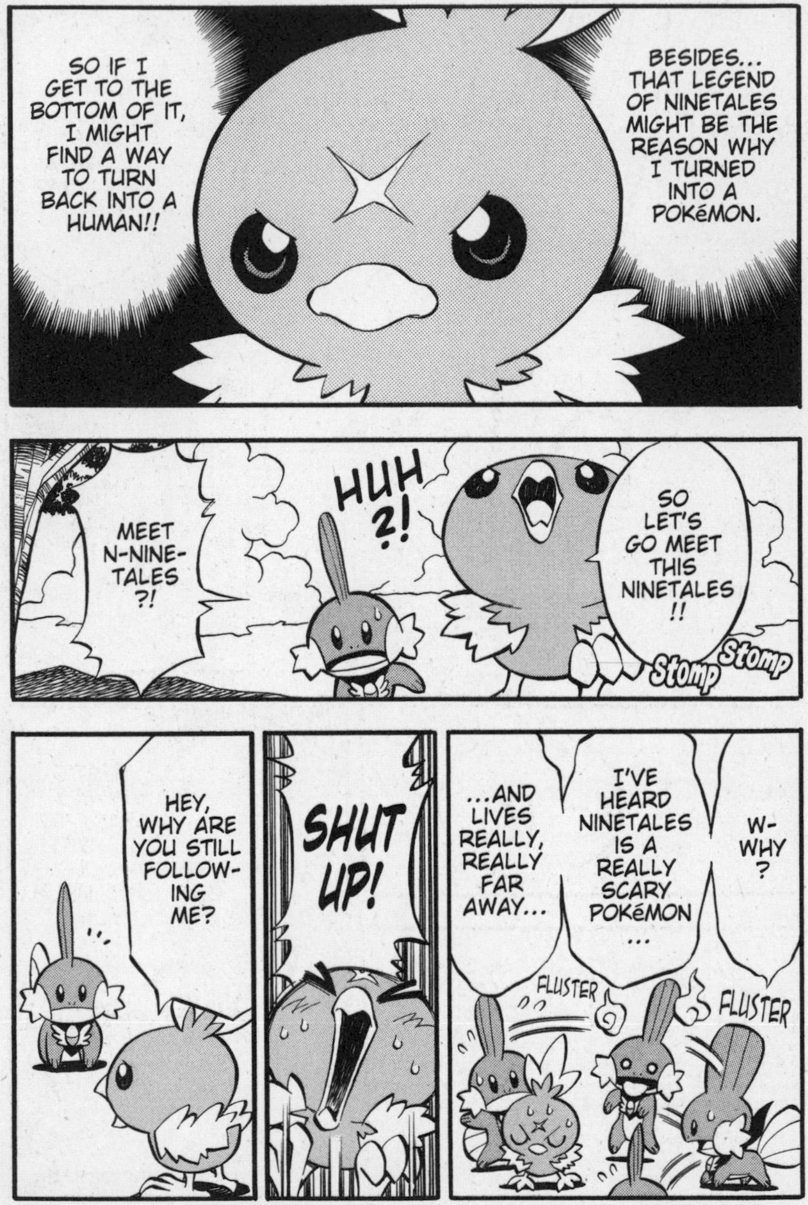
BESIDES... THAT LEGEND OF NINETALES MIGHT BE THE REASON WHY I TURNED INTO A POKéMON.
SO IF I GET TO THE BOTTOM OF IT, I MIGHT FIND A WAY TO TURN BACK INTO A HUMAN!!
SO LET'S GO MEET THIS NINETALES!!
Stomp
Stomp
HUH?!
MEET N-NINE-TALES?!
W-WHY?
I'VE HEARD NINETALES IS A REALLY SCARY POKéMON...
...AND LIVES REALLY, REALLY FAR AWAY...
FLUSTER
FLUSTER
SHUT UP!
HEY, WHY ARE YOU STILL FOLLOW-ING ME?
...

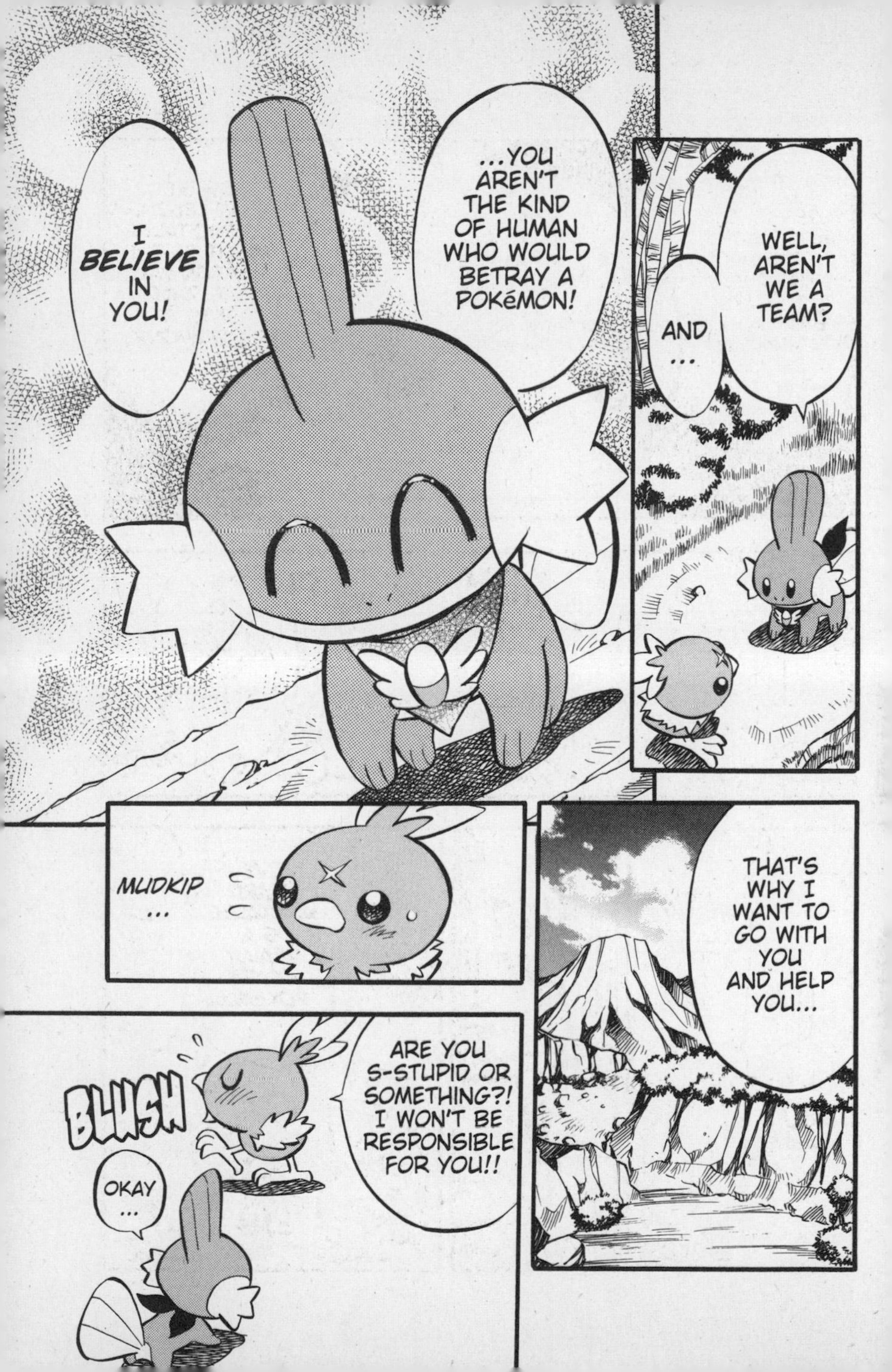
WELL, AREN'T WE A TEAM?
AND ...
...YOU AREN'T THE KIND OF HUMAN WHO WOULD BETRAY A POKéMON!
I BELIEVE IN YOU!
THAT'S WHY I WANT TO GO WITH YOU AND HELP YOU...
MUDKIP ...
ARE YOU S-STUPID OR SOMETHING?! I WON'T BE RESPONSIBLE FOR YOU!!
BLUSH
OKAY ...

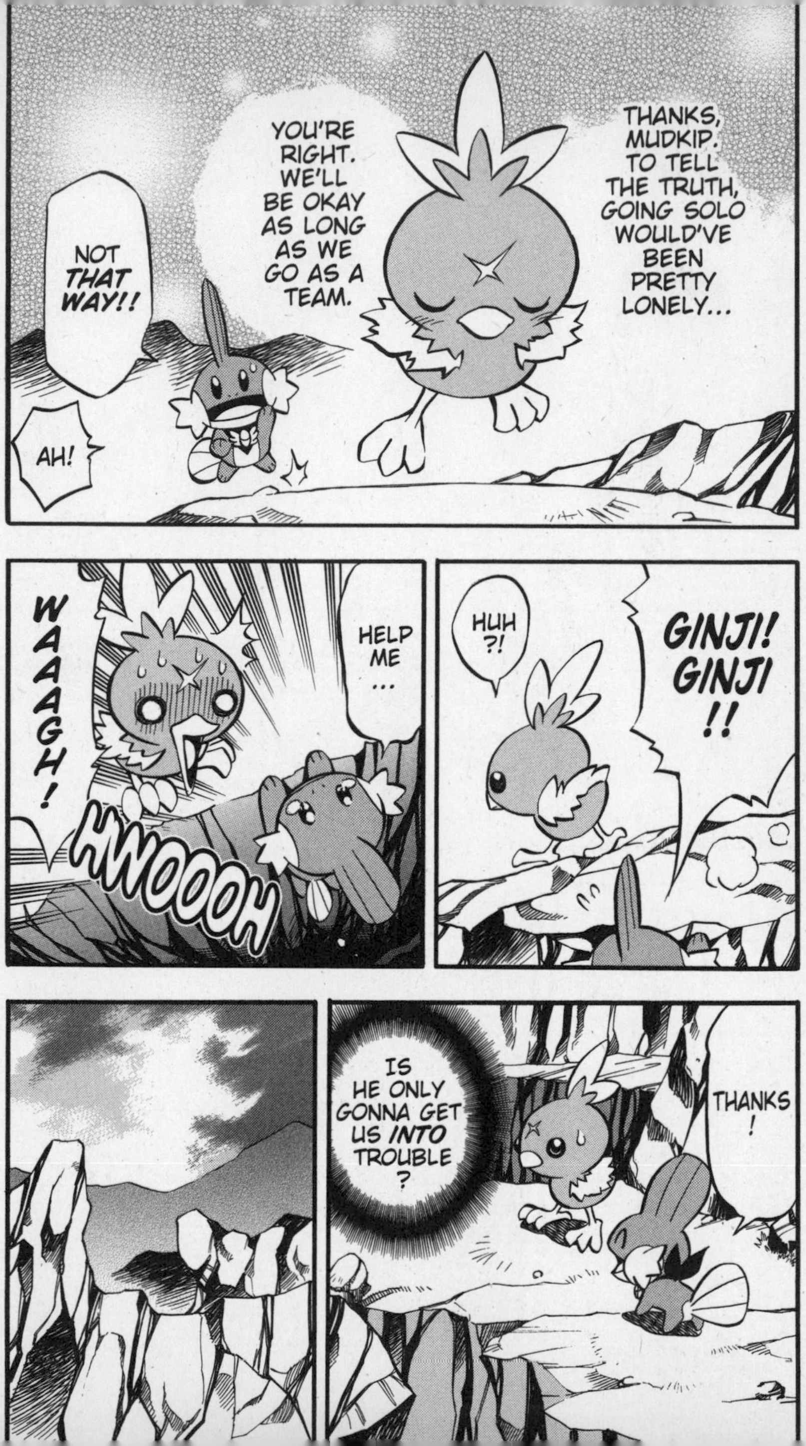
THANKS, MUDKIP. TO TELL THE TRUTH, GOING SOLO WOULD'VE BEEN PRETTY LONELY...
YOU'RE RIGHT. WE'LL BE OKAY AS LONG AS WE GO AS A TEAM.
NOT *THAT WAY!!*
AH!
GINJI! GINJI!!
HUH?!
HELP ME...
WAAAAGH!
HWOOOH
THANKS!
IS HE ONLY GONNA GET US *INTO* TROUBLE?

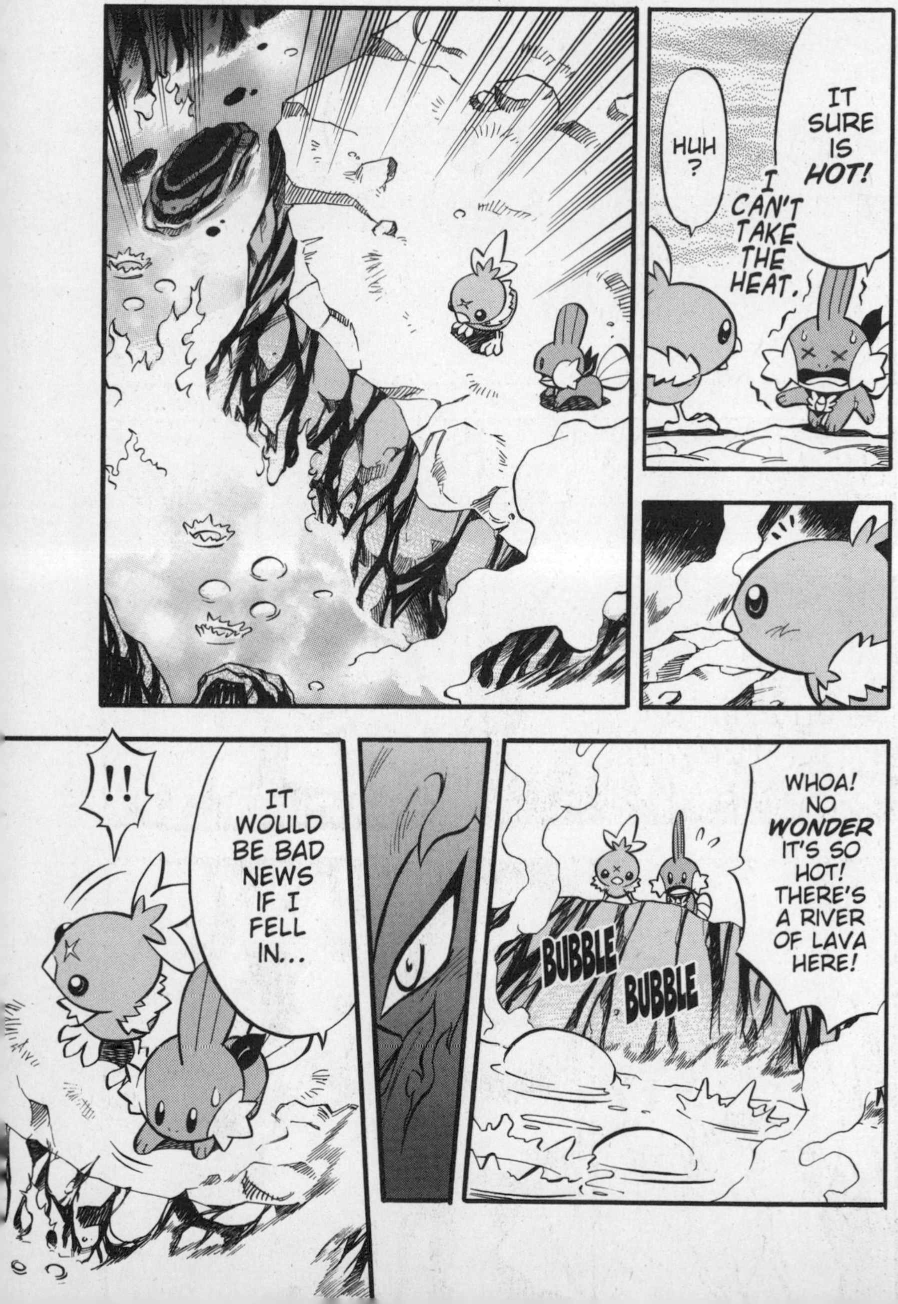
IT SURE IS HOT!
I CAN'T TAKE THE HEAT.
HUH?
WHOA! NO WONDER IT'S SO HOT! THERE'S A RIVER OF LAVA HERE!
BUBBLE
BUBBLE
IT WOULD BE BAD NEWS IF I FELL IN...
!!

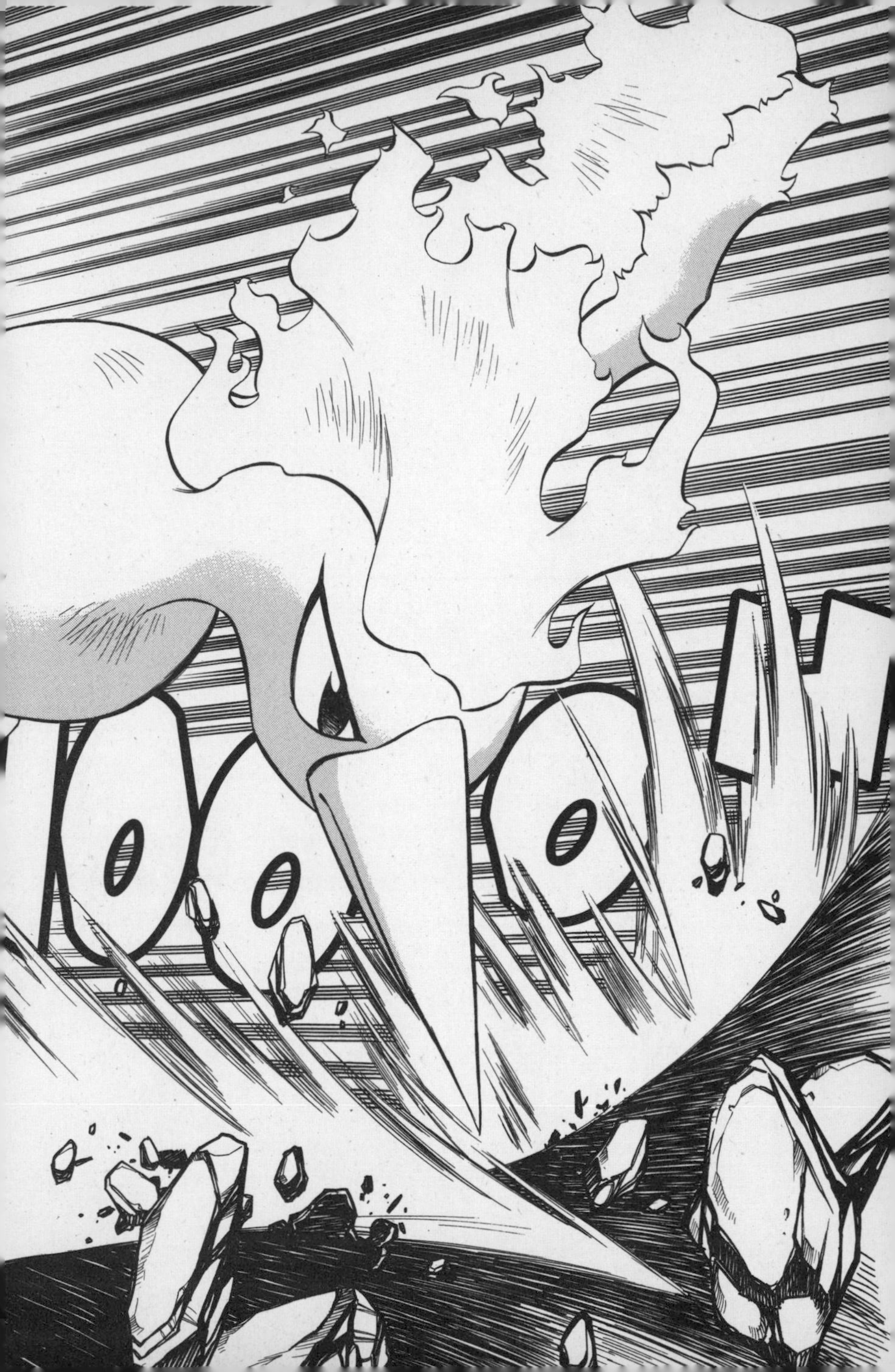

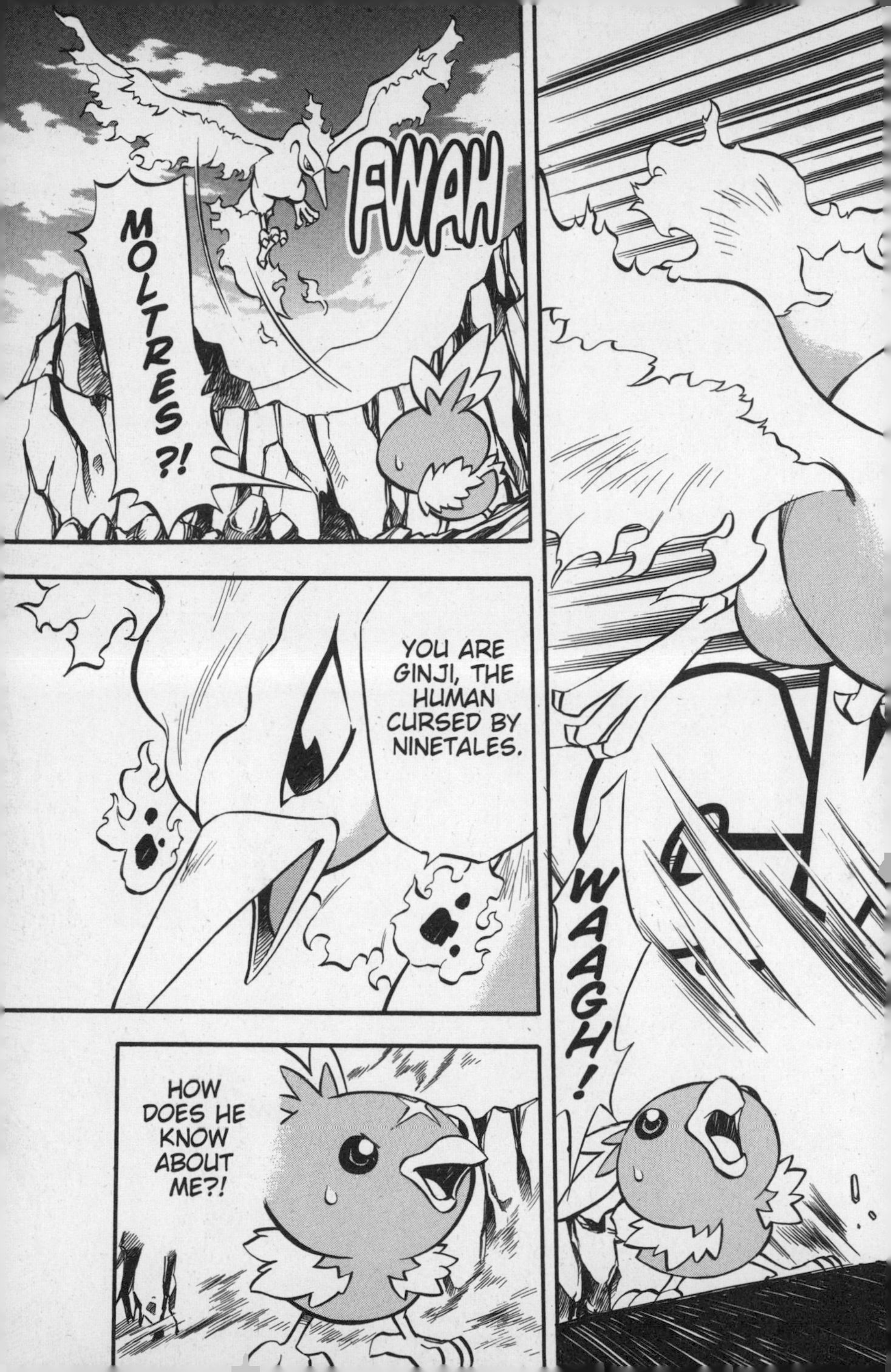
WAAGH!
!
FWAH
MOLTRES?!
YOU ARE GINJI, THE HUMAN CURSED BY NINETALES.
HOW DOES HE KNOW ABOUT ME?!

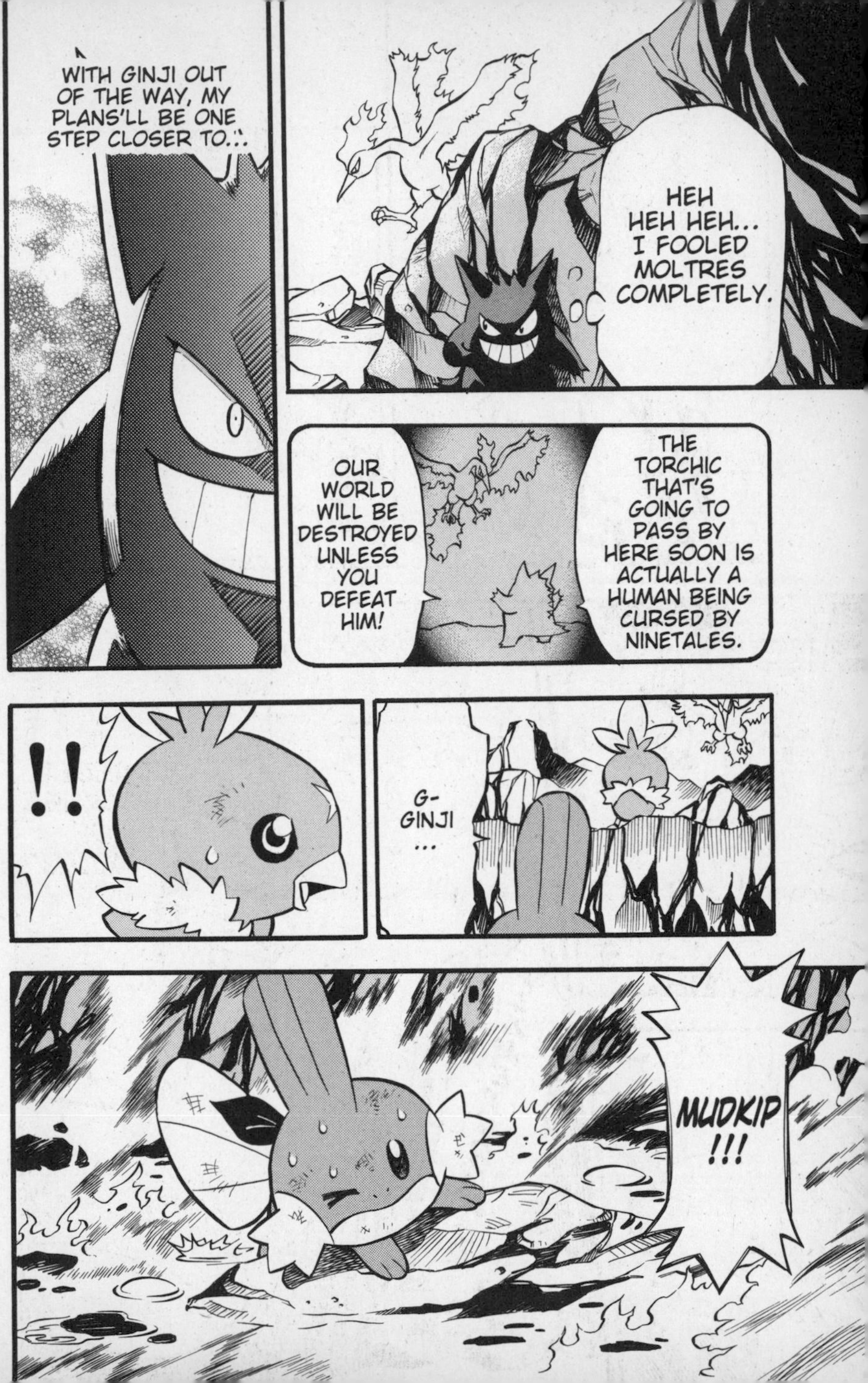
HEH HEH HEH... I FOOLED MOLTRES COMPLETELY.
THE TORCHIC THAT'S GOING TO PASS BY HERE SOON IS ACTUALLY A HUMAN BEING CURSED BY NINETALES.
OUR WORLD WILL BE DESTROYED UNLESS YOU DEFEAT HIM!
WITH GINJI OUT OF THE WAY, MY PLANS'LL BE ONE STEP CLOSER TO...
G-GINJI ...
!!
MUDKIP !!!

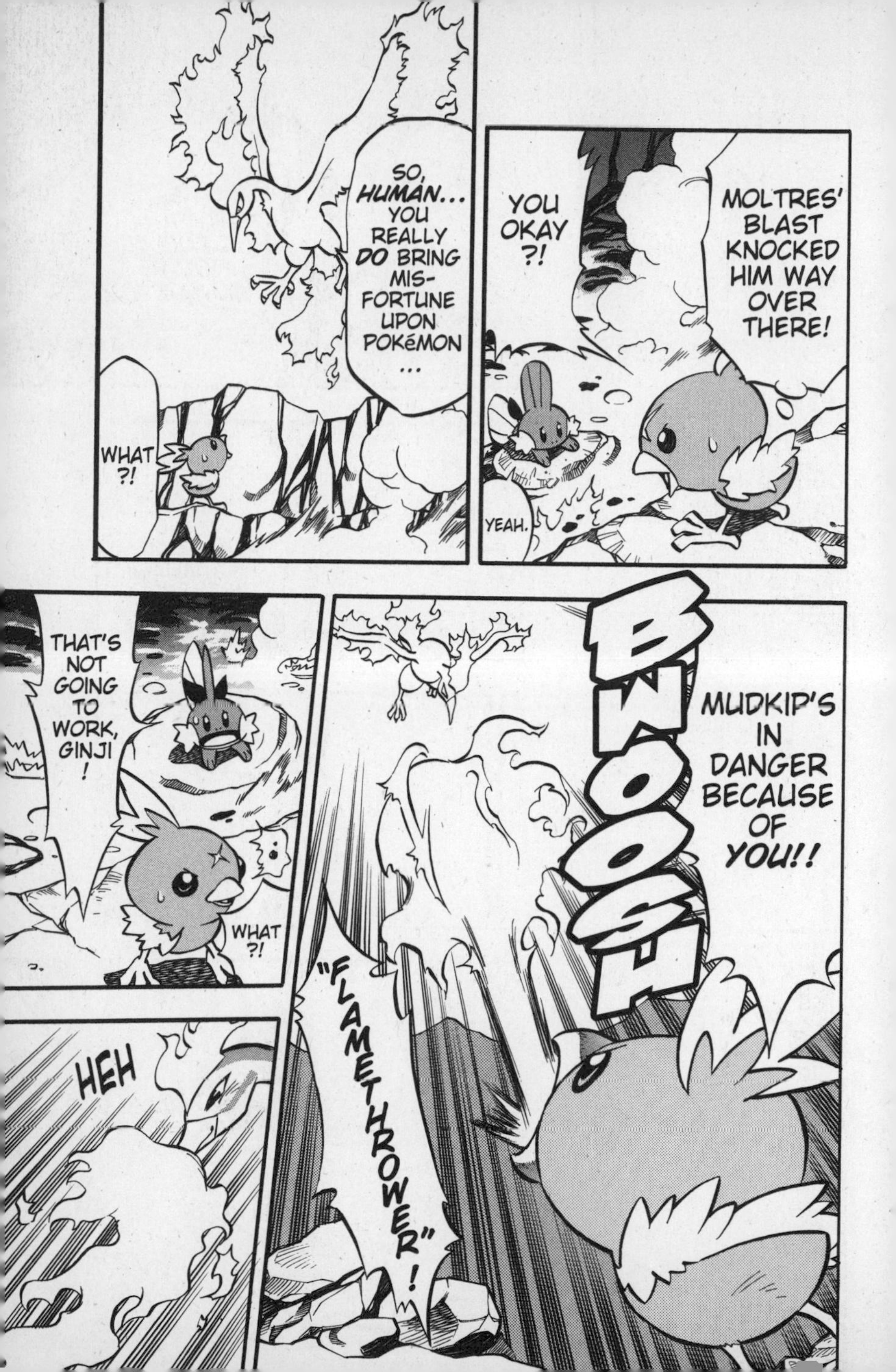
MOLTRES' BLAST KNOCKED HIM WAY OVER THERE!
YOU OKAY ?!
YEAH.
SO, *HUMAN*... YOU REALLY *DO* BRING MIS-FORTUNE UPON POKéMON ...
WHAT ?!
BWOOSH
MUDKIP'S IN DANGER BECAUSE OF *YOU!!*
"FLAMETHROWER"!
THAT'S NOT GOING TO WORK, GINJI !
WHAT ?!
HEH

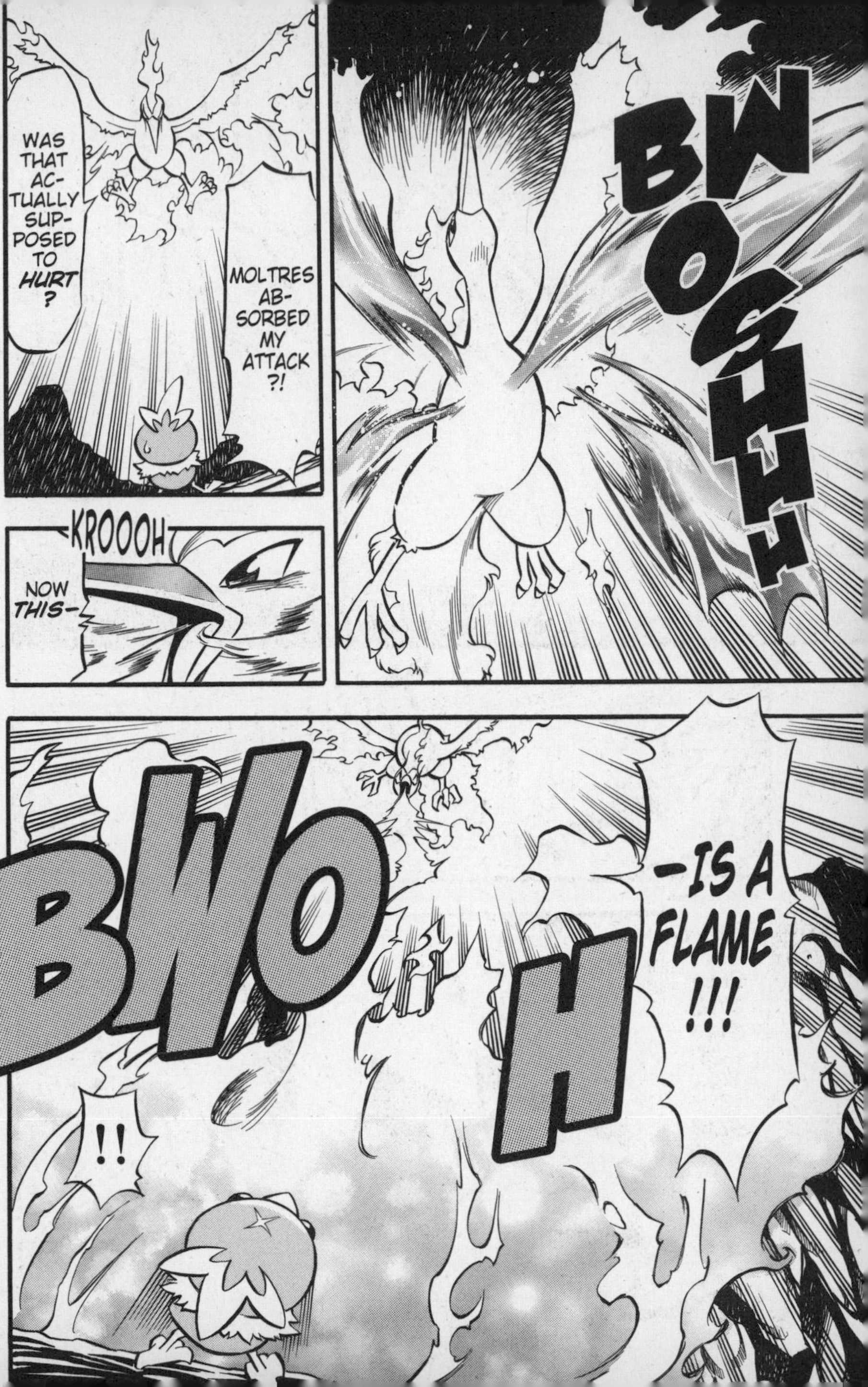
BWOSHHH
MOLTRES ABSORBED MY ATTACK ?!
WAS THAT ACTUALLY SUPPOSED TO *HURT* ?
KROOOH
NOW *THIS*-
-IS A FLAME !!!
BWO
H
!!

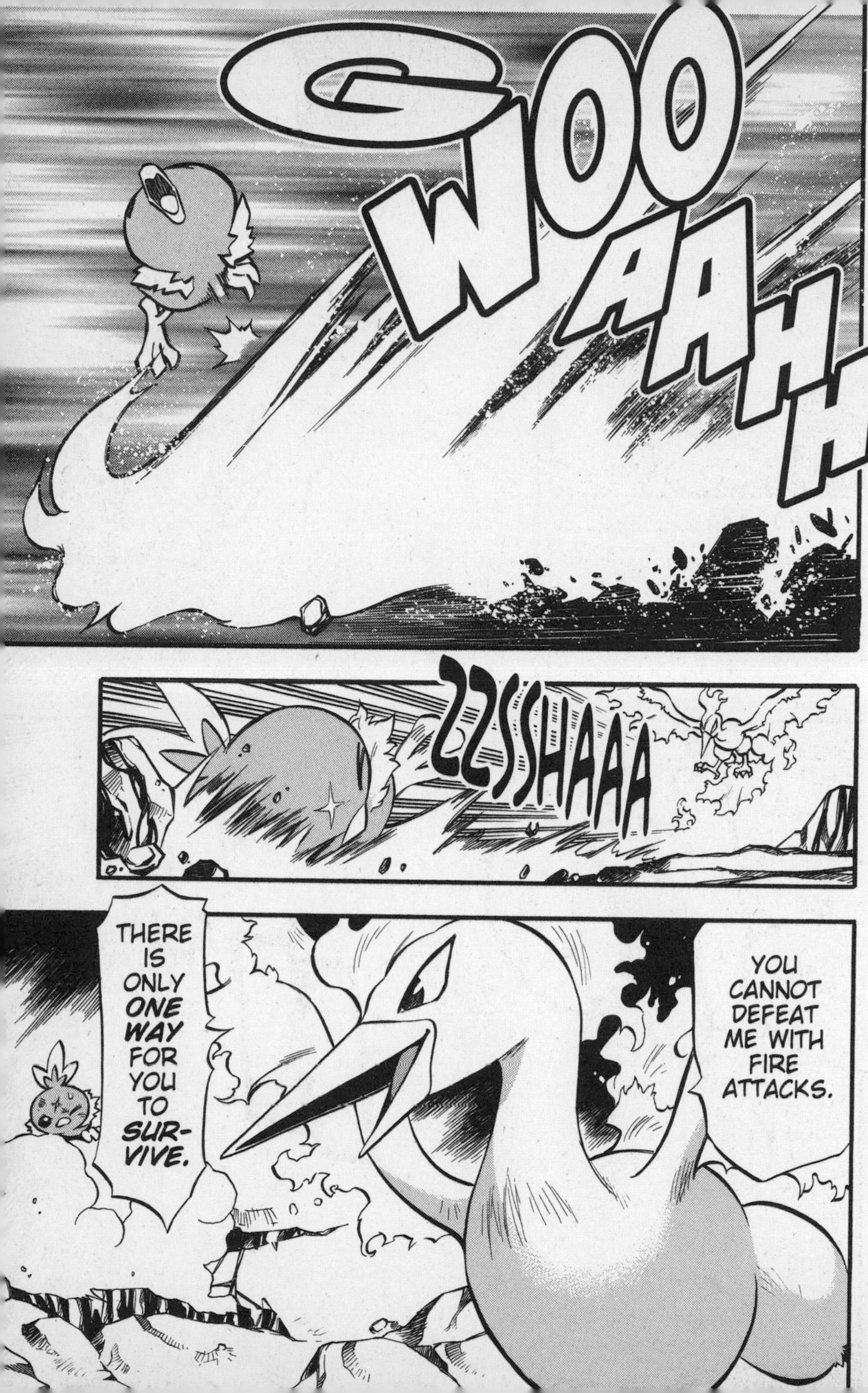
GOOWAAHH
ZZSSHAAA
YOU CANNOT DEFEAT ME WITH FIRE ATTACKS.
THERE IS ONLY ONE WAY FOR YOU TO SURVIVE.

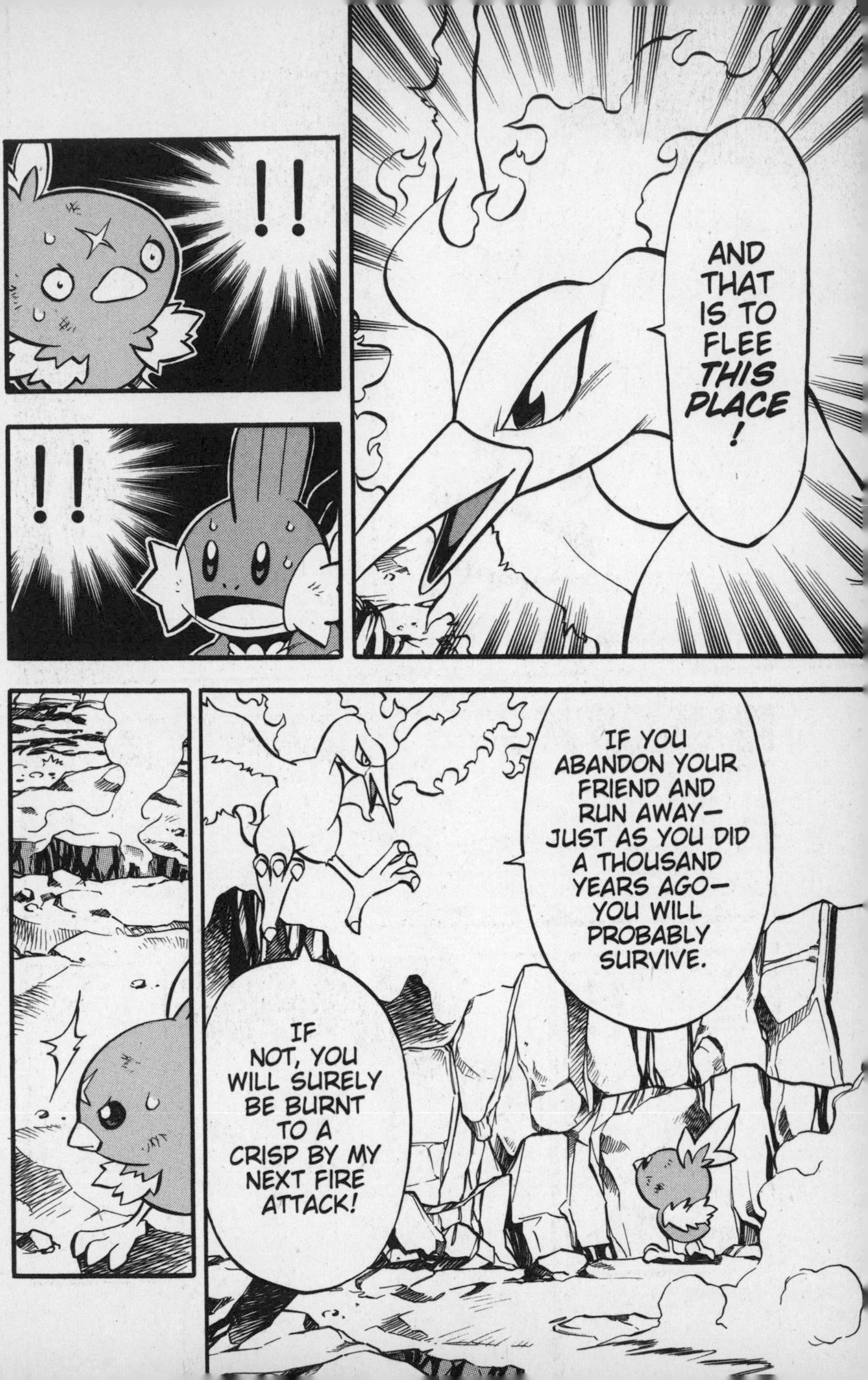
AND THAT IS TO FLEE THIS PLACE!
!!
!!
IF YOU ABANDON YOUR FRIEND AND RUN AWAY—JUST AS YOU DID A THOUSAND YEARS AGO—YOU WILL PROBABLY SURVIVE.
IF NOT, YOU WILL SURELY BE BURNT TO A CRISP BY MY NEXT FIRE ATTACK!

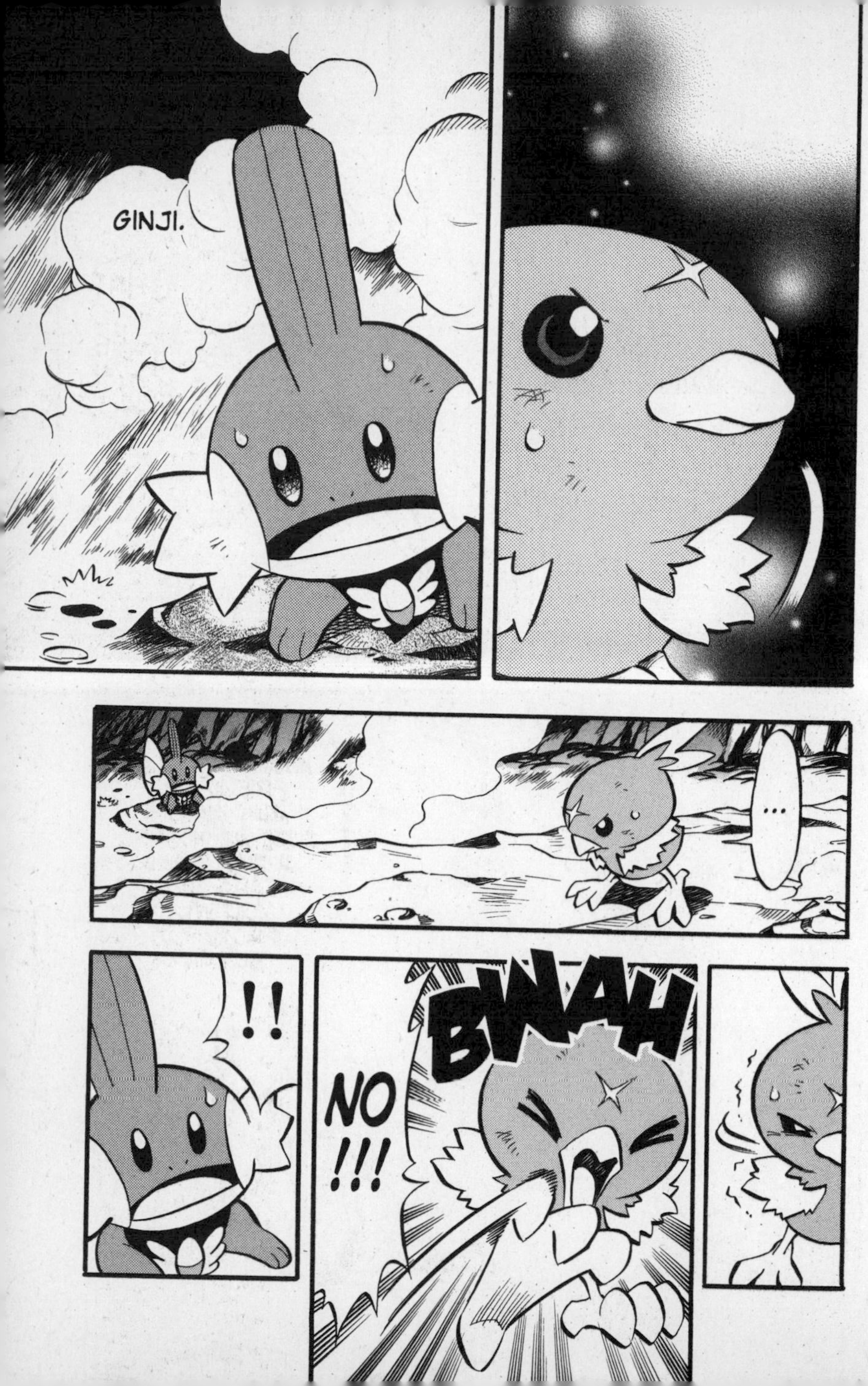
GINJI.
...
BWAH
NO !!!
!!

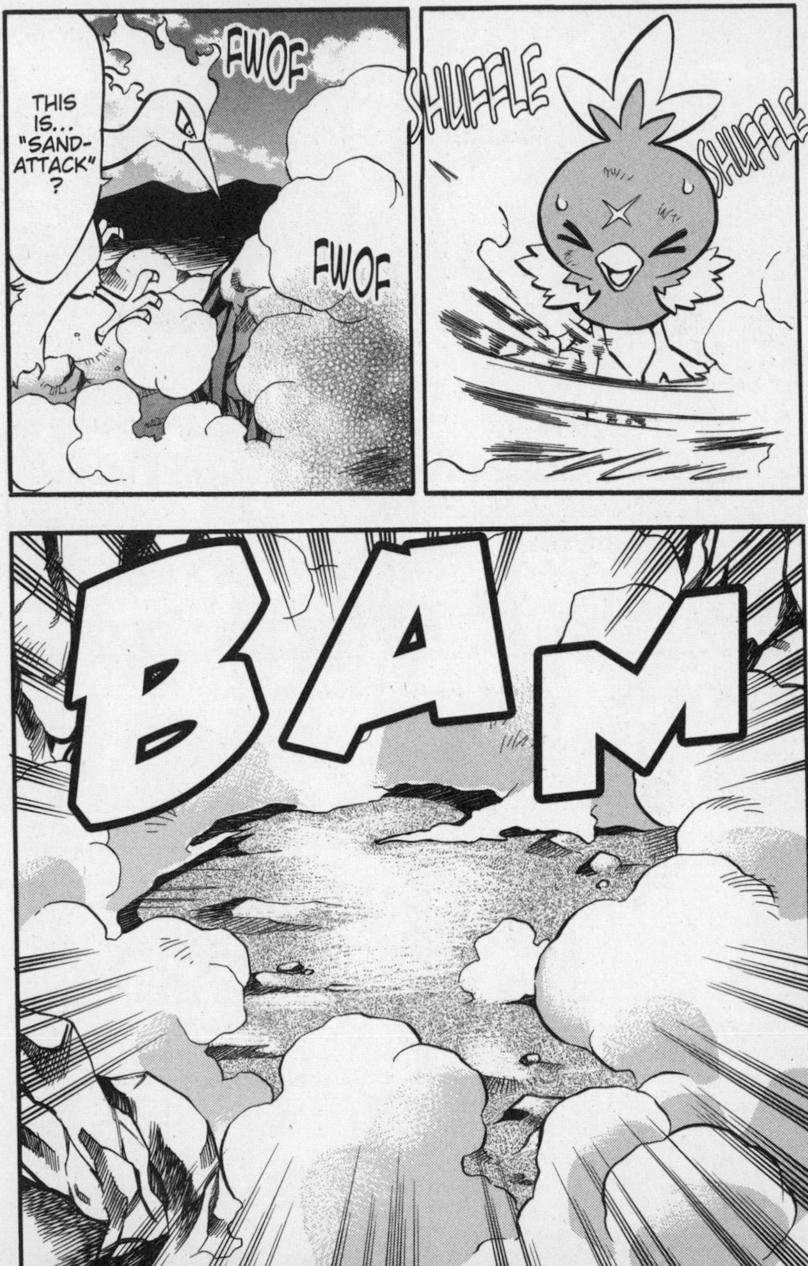
SHUFFLE
SHUFFLE
FWOF
THIS IS... "SAND-ATTACK"?
FWOF
BAM

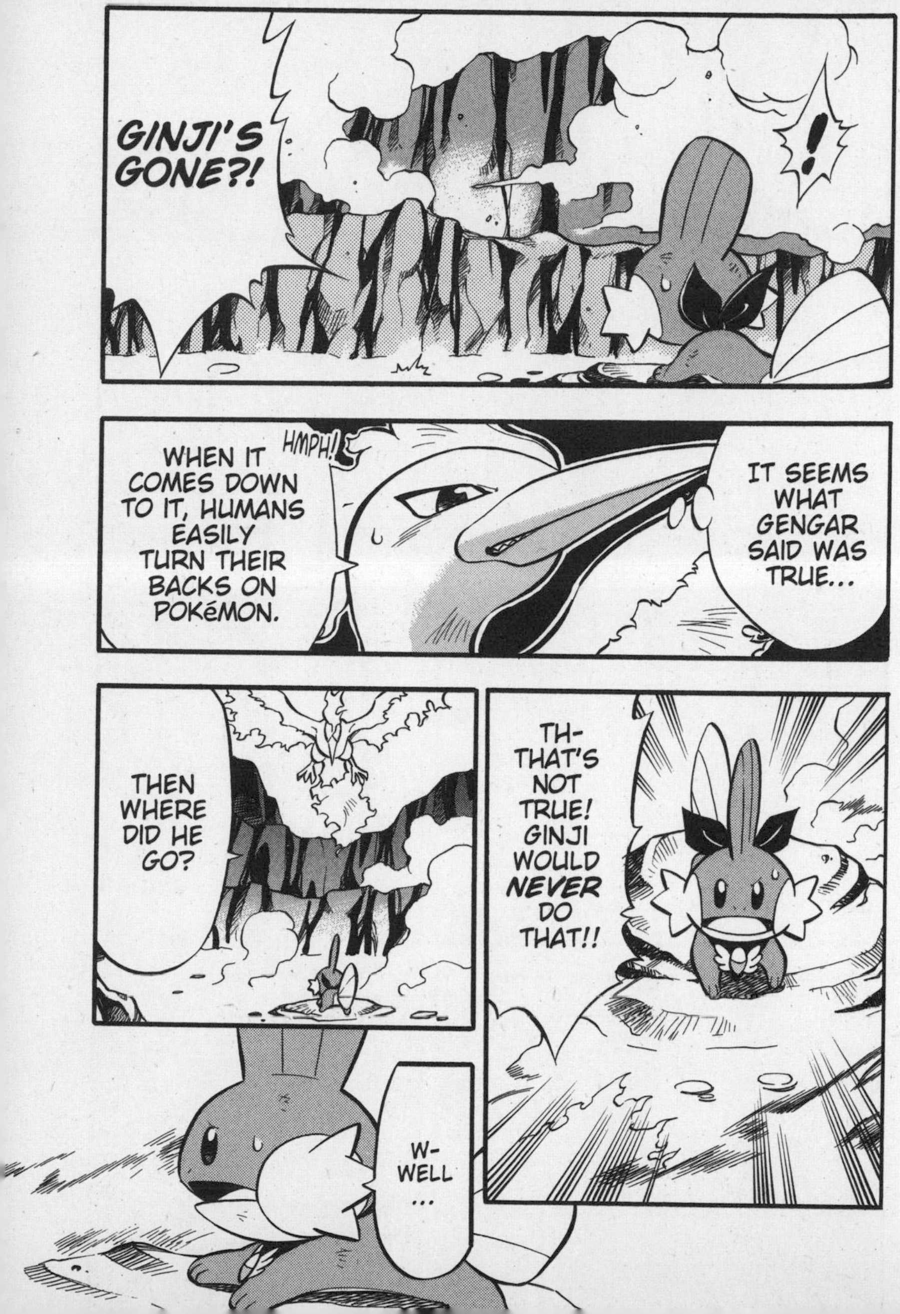
GINJI'S GONE?!
!
WHEN IT COMES DOWN TO IT, HUMANS EASILY TURN THEIR BACKS ON POKéMON.
HMPH!
IT SEEMS WHAT GENGAR SAID WAS TRUE...
THEN WHERE DID HE GO?
TH-THAT'S NOT TRUE! GINJI WOULD NEVER DO THAT!!
W-WELL...

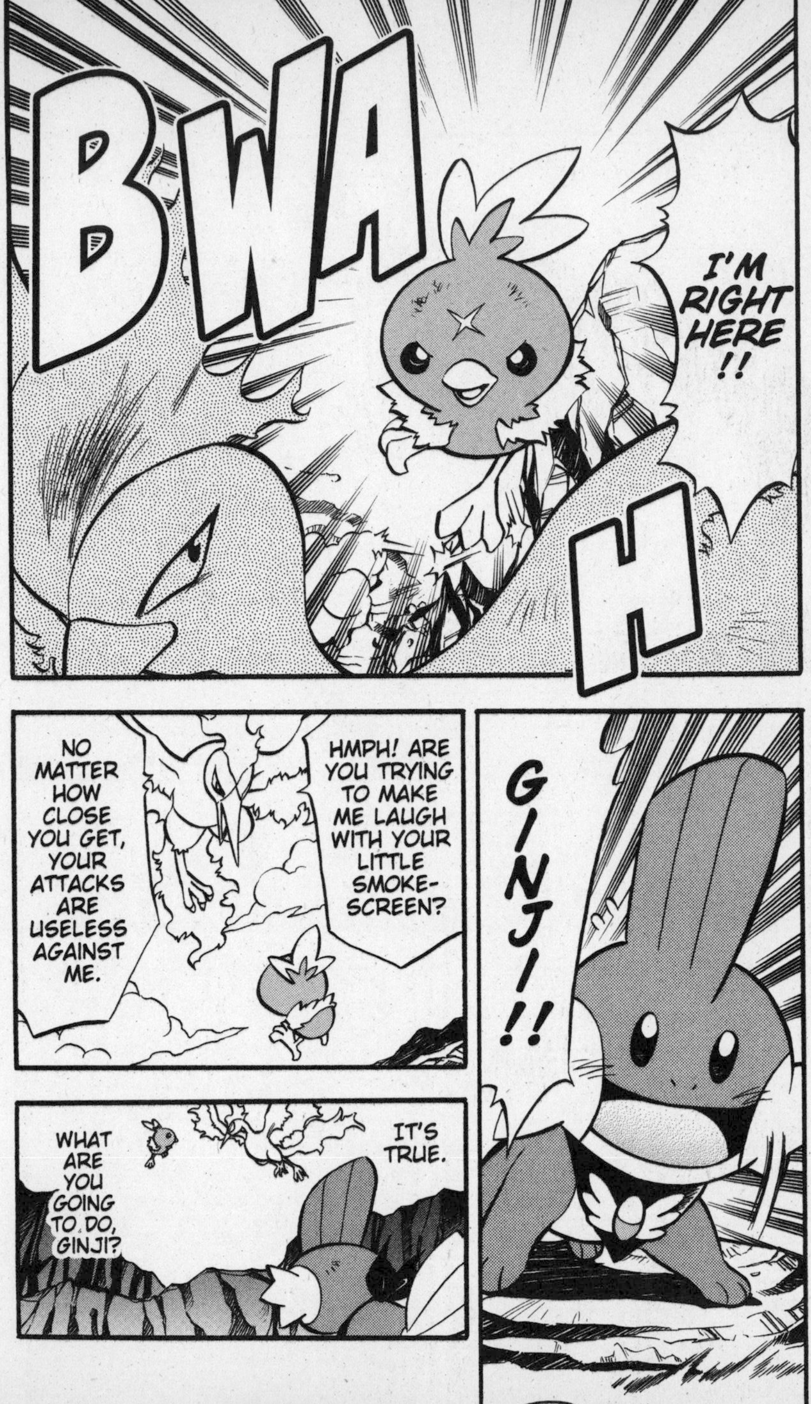
BWAH
I'M RIGHT HERE!!
GINJI!!
HMPH! ARE YOU TRYING TO MAKE ME LAUGH WITH YOUR LITTLE SMOKE-SCREEN?
NO MATTER HOW CLOSE YOU GET, YOUR ATTACKS ARE USELESS AGAINST ME.
IT'S TRUE.
WHAT ARE YOU GOING TO DO, GINJI?

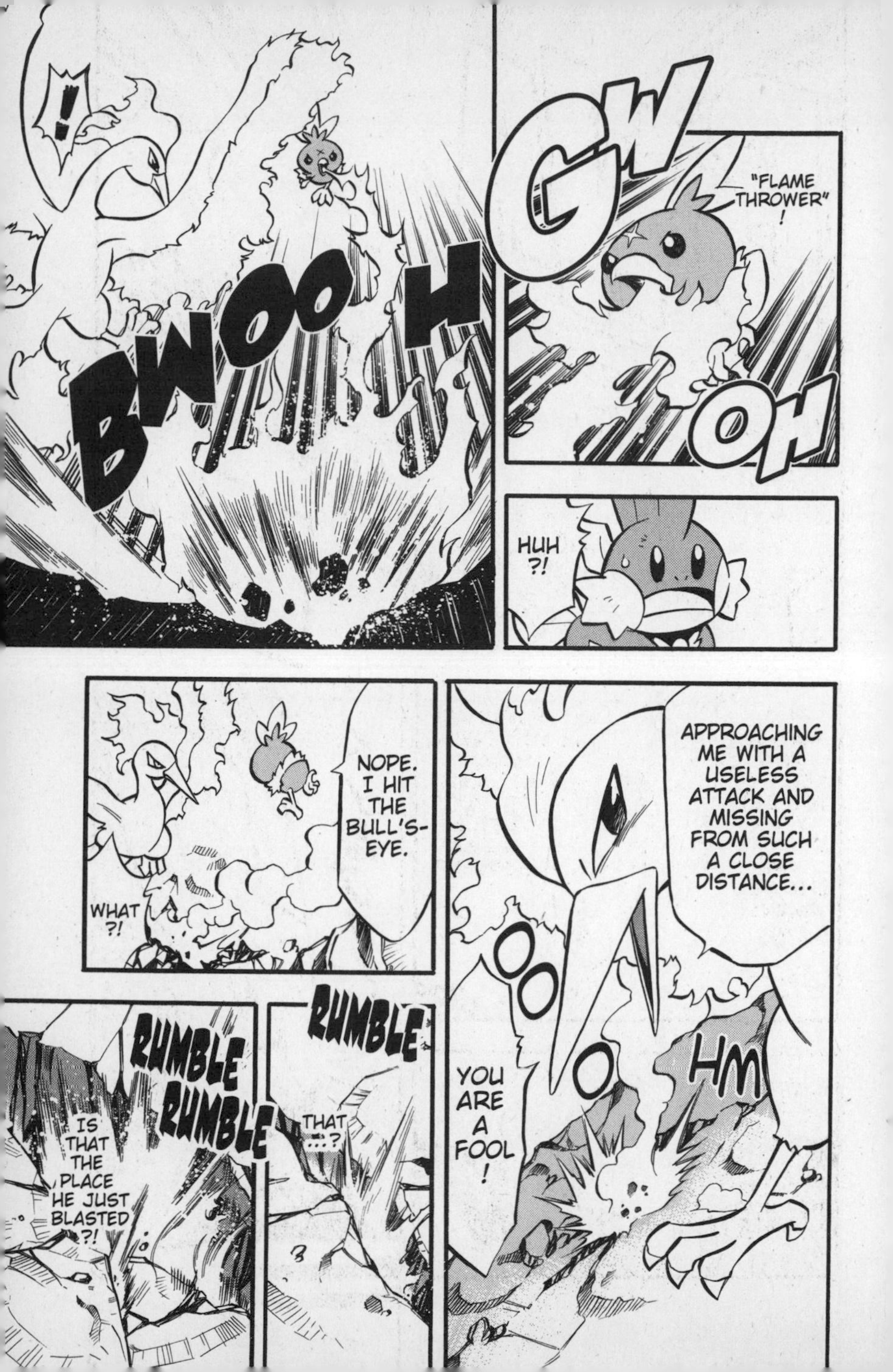
GW
"FLAME THROWER" !
OH
HUH ?!
!
BWOOH
APPROACHING ME WITH A USELESS ATTACK AND MISSING FROM SUCH A CLOSE DISTANCE...
OOOHM
YOU ARE A FOOL !
NOPE. I HIT THE BULL'S-EYE.
WHAT ?!
RUMBLE
THAT ...?
RUMBLE RUMBLE
IS THAT THE PLACE HE JUST BLASTED ?!

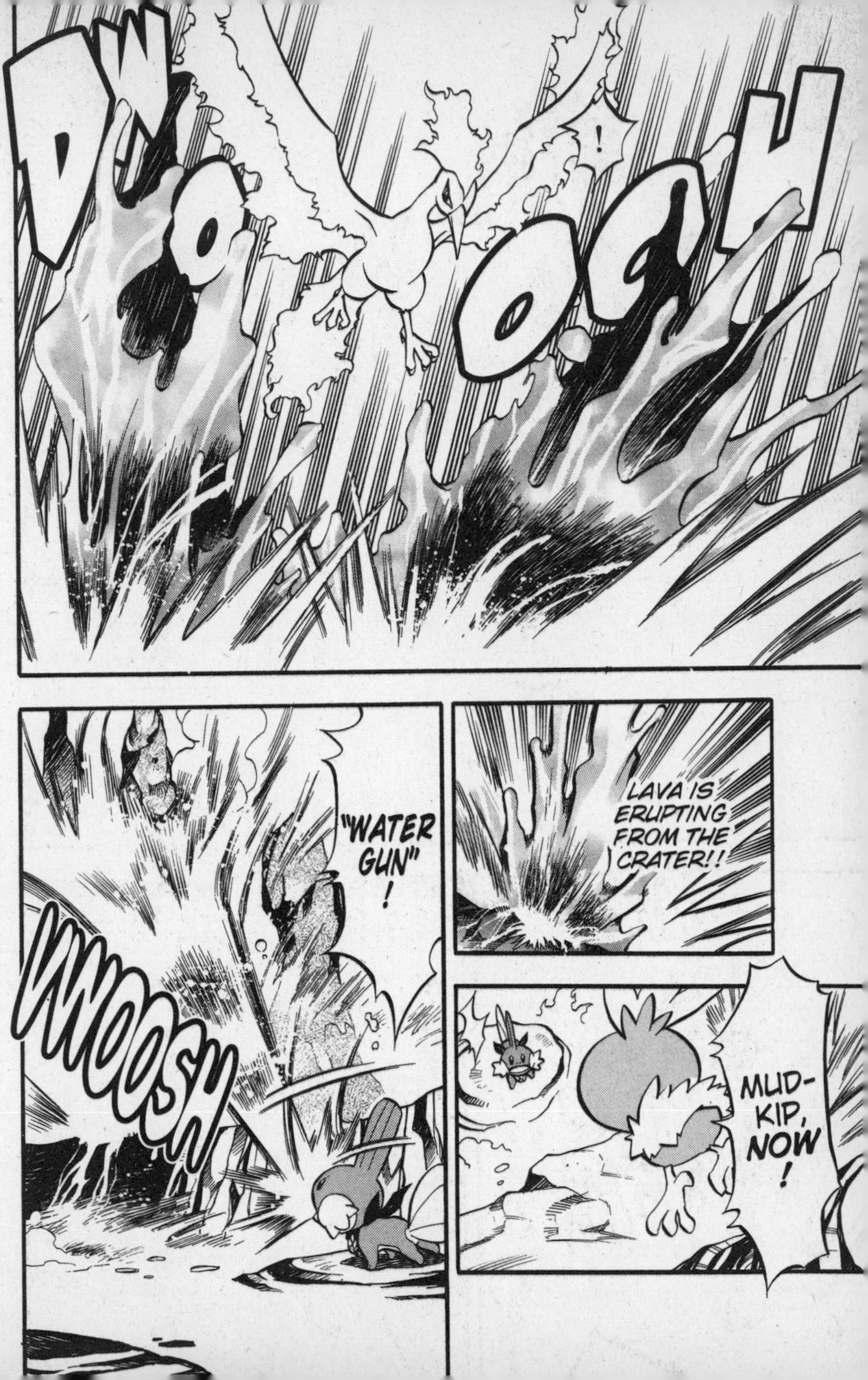
DWOOSH
!
LAVA IS ERUPTING FROM THE CRATER!!
MUD-KIP, NOW!
"WATER GUN"!
WHOOSH

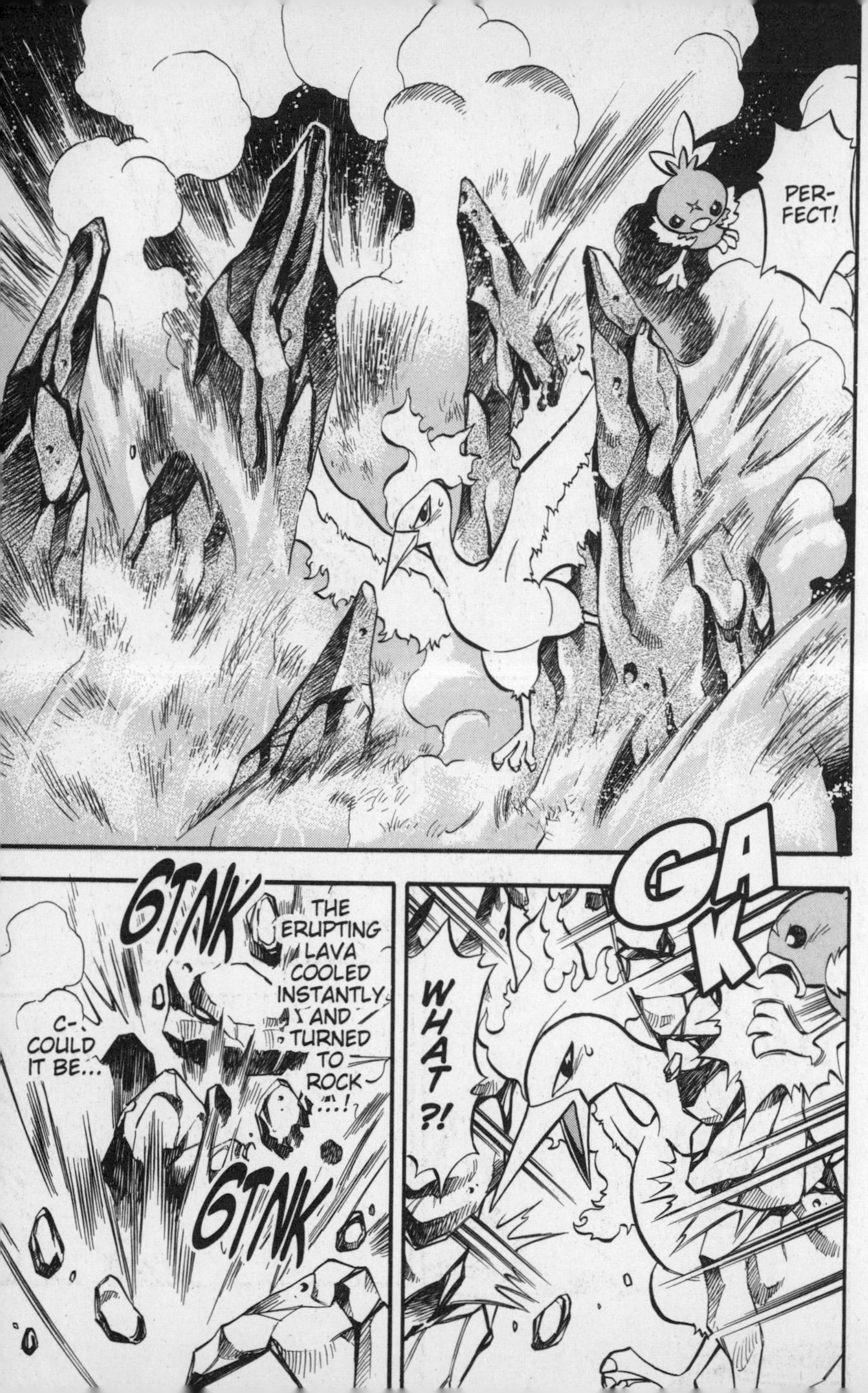
PER-
FECT!
GAK
WHAT?!
GTNK
THE ERUPTING LAVA COOLED INSTANTLY AND TURNED TO ROCK...!
C-COULD IT BE...
GTNK

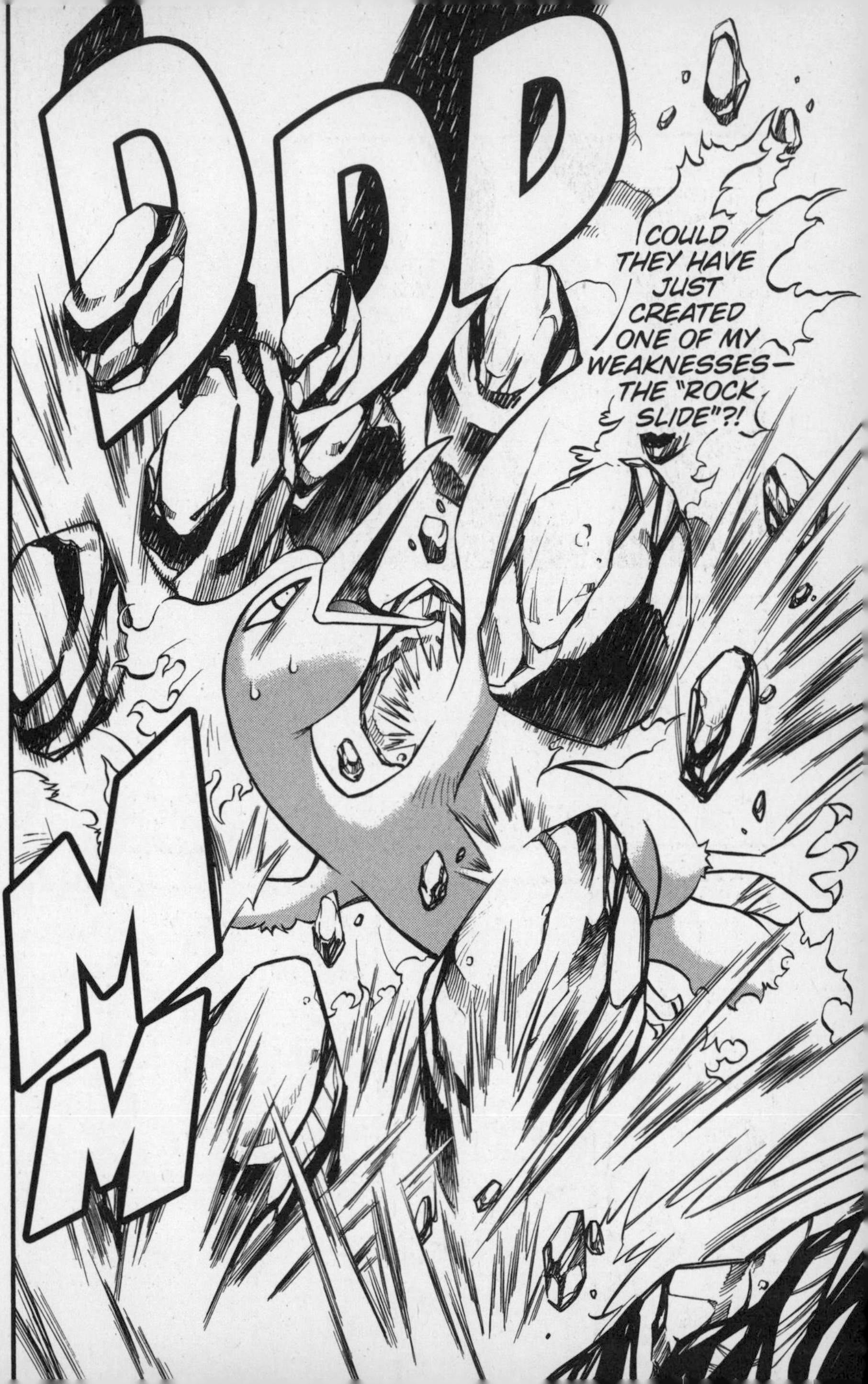
COULD THEY HAVE JUST CREATED ONE OF MY WEAKNESSES— THE "ROCK SLIDE"?!
DDDMMM

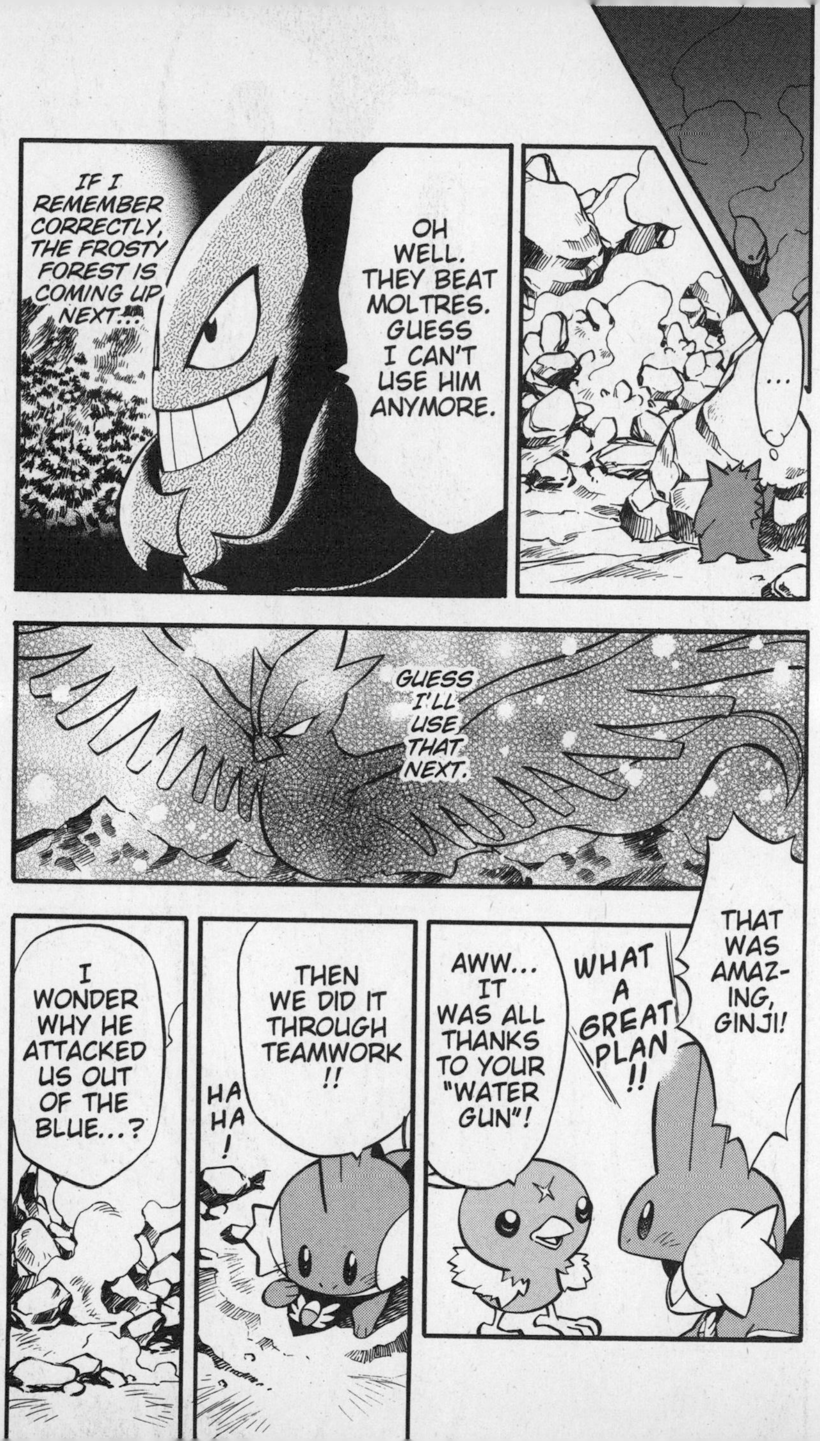
...
OH WELL. THEY BEAT MOLTRES. GUESS I CAN'T USE HIM ANYMORE.
IF I REMEMBER CORRECTLY, THE FROSTY FOREST IS COMING UP NEXT...
GUESS I'LL USE THAT NEXT.
THAT WAS AMAZ-ING, GINJI!
WHAT A GREAT PLAN!!
AWW... IT WAS ALL THANKS TO YOUR "WATER GUN"!
THEN WE DID IT THROUGH TEAMWORK!!
HA HA!
I WONDER WHY HE ATTACKED US OUT OF THE BLUE...?

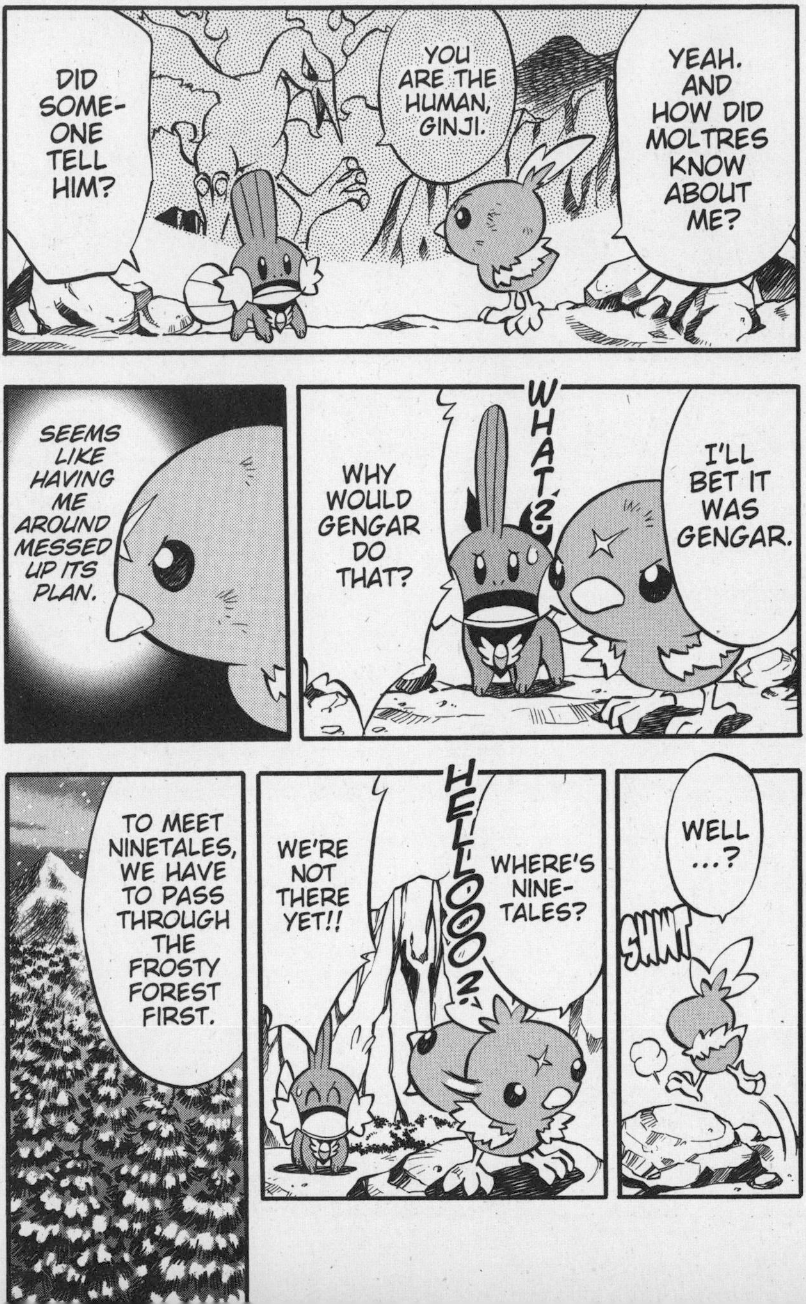
YEAH. AND HOW DID MOLTRES KNOW ABOUT ME?
YOU ARE THE HUMAN, GINJI.
DID SOME-ONE TELL HIM?
I'LL BET IT WAS GENGAR.
WHAT?!
WHY WOULD GENGAR DO THAT?
SEEMS LIKE HAVING ME AROUND MESSED UP ITS PLAN.
WELL ...?
SHNT
WHERE'S NINE-TALES?
HELLOOOO?!
WE'RE NOT THERE YET!!
TO MEET NINETALES, WE HAVE TO PASS THROUGH THE FROSTY FOREST FIRST.

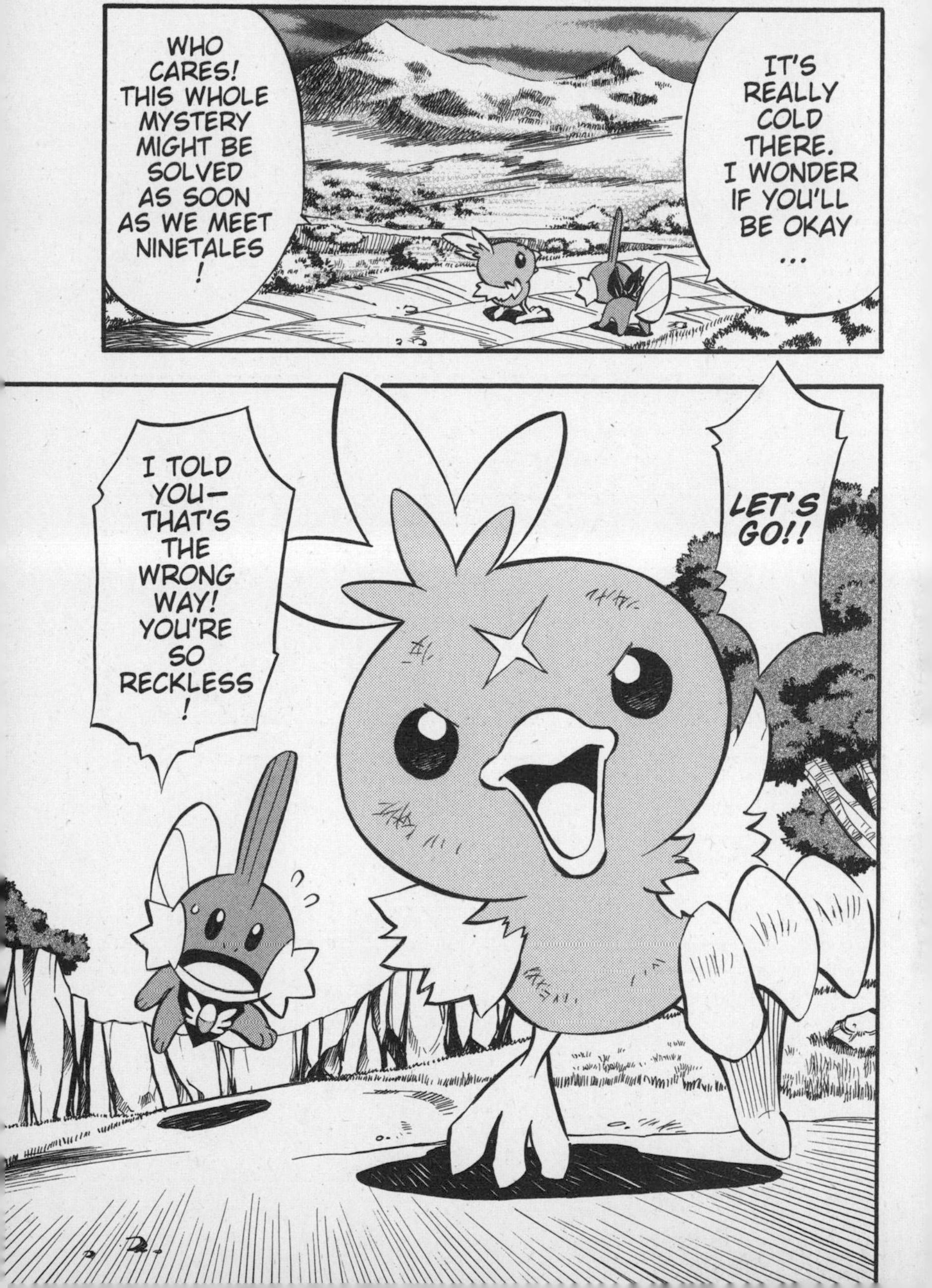
IT'S REALLY COLD THERE. I WONDER IF YOU'LL BE OKAY ...
WHO CARES! THIS WHOLE MYSTERY MIGHT BE SOLVED AS SOON AS WE MEET NINETALES!
LET'S GO!!
I TOLD YOU—THAT'S THE WRONG WAY! YOU'RE SO RECKLESS!

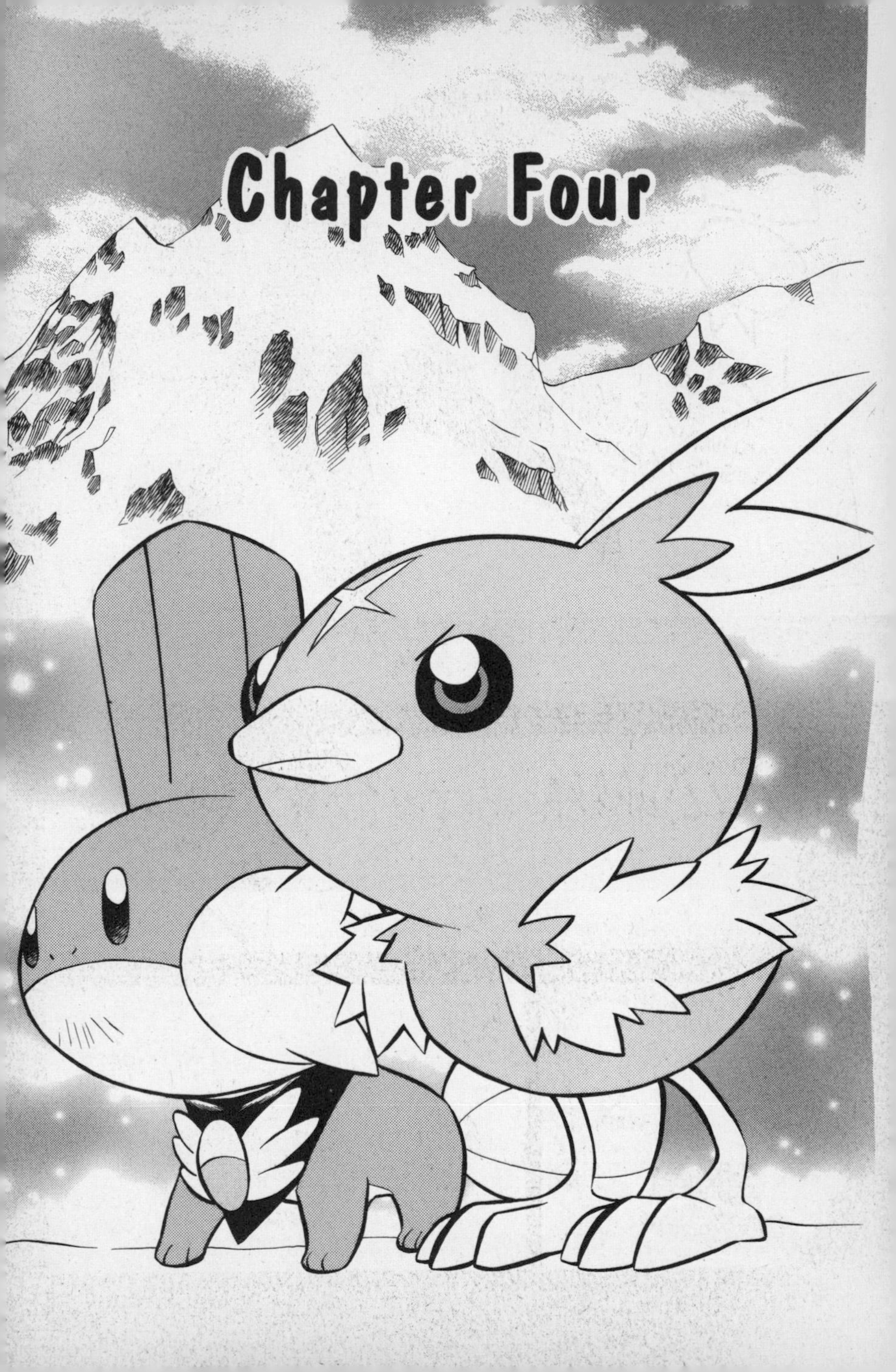
Chapter Four

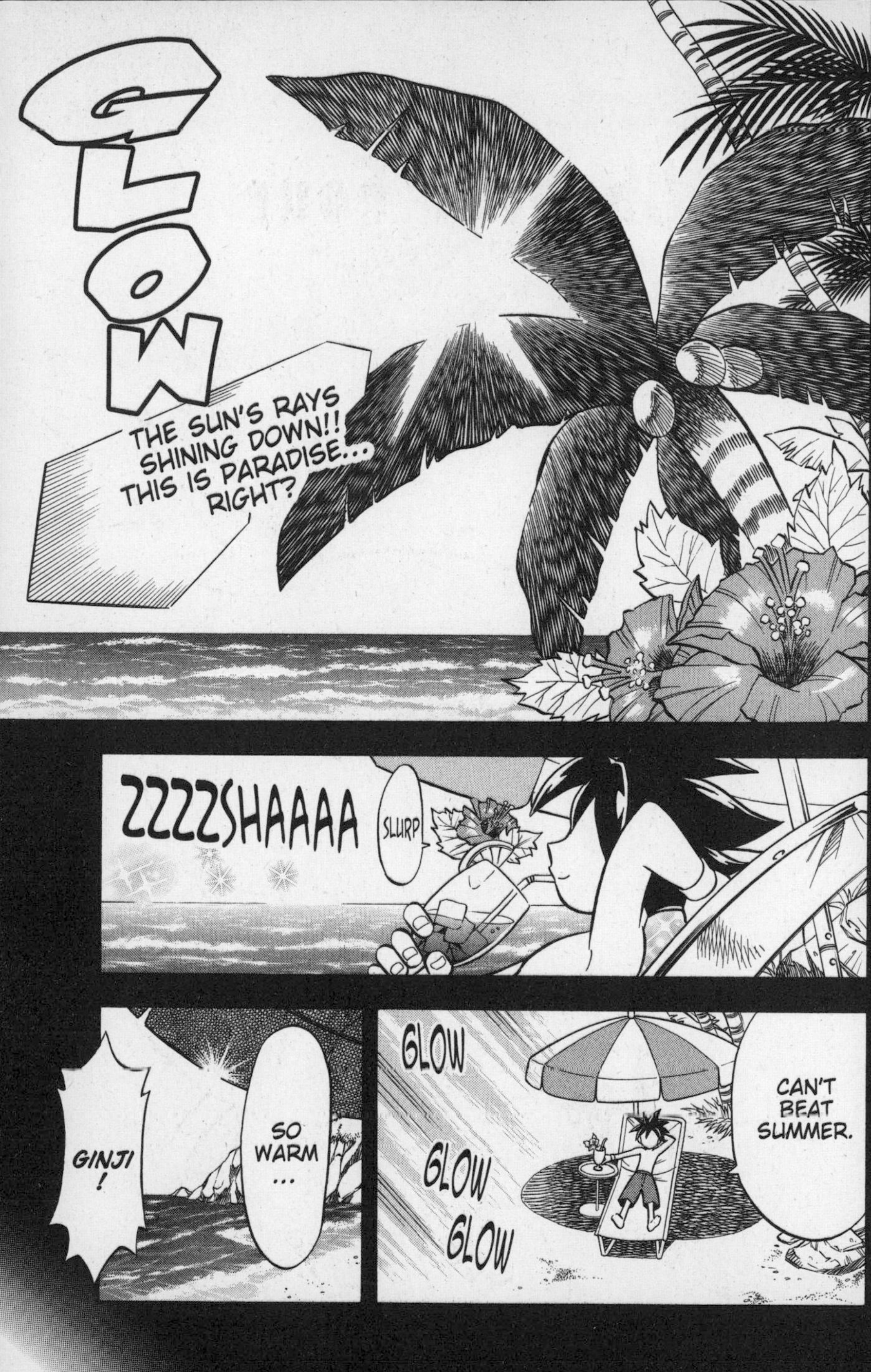
GLOW
THE SUN'S RAYS SHINING DOWN!! THIS IS PARADISE... RIGHT?
ZZZZSHAAAA
SLURP
CAN'T BEAT SUMMER.
GLOW
GLOW
GLOW
SO WARM...
GINJI!

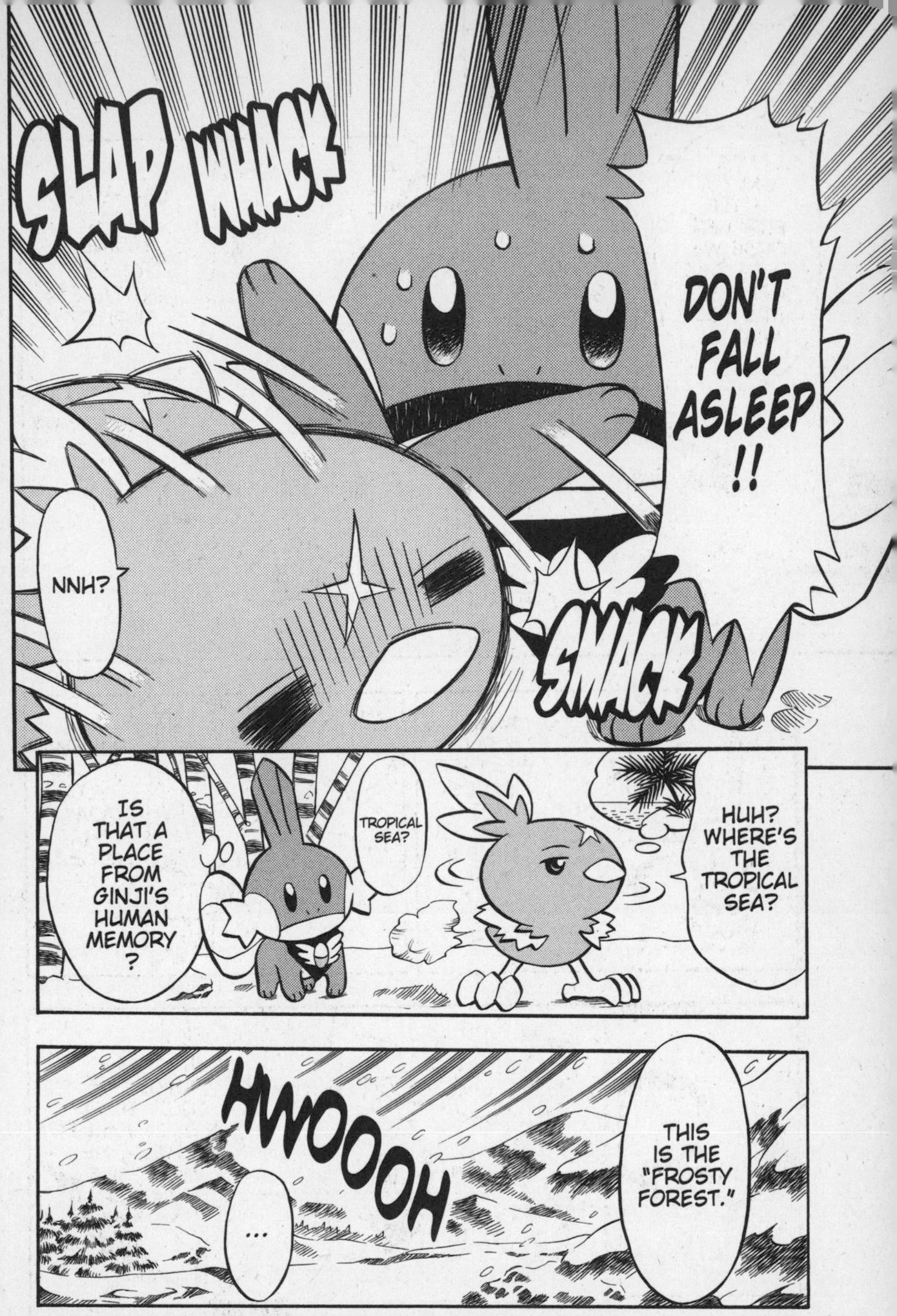
DON'T FALL ASLEEP!!
WHACK
SLAP
SMACK
NNH?
HUH? WHERE'S THE TROPICAL SEA?
TROPICAL SEA?
IS THAT A PLACE FROM GINJI'S HUMAN MEMORY?
THIS IS THE "FROSTY FOREST."
HWOOOOH
...

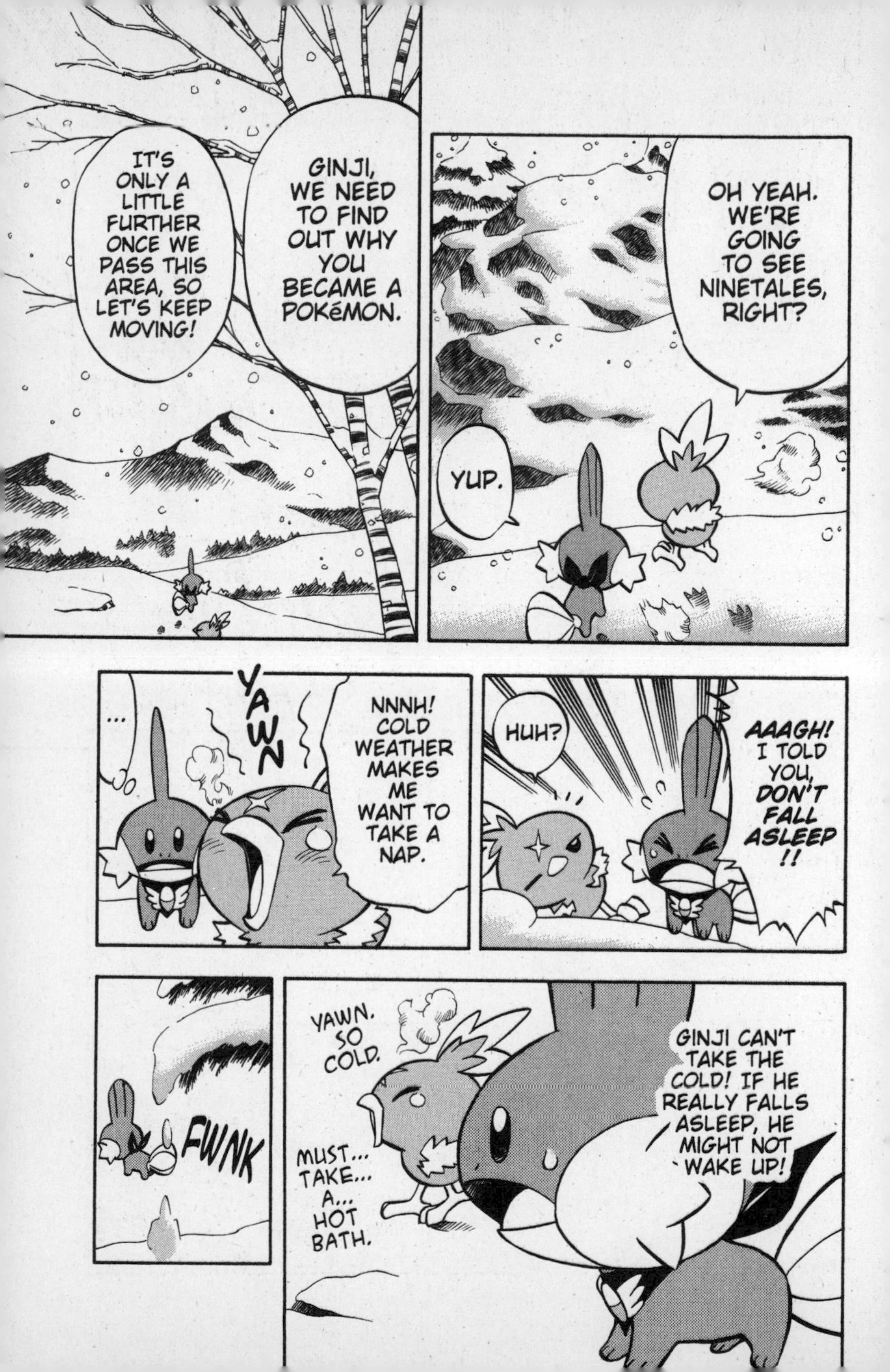
IT'S ONLY A LITTLE FURTHER ONCE WE PASS THIS AREA, SO LET'S KEEP MOVING!
GINJI, WE NEED TO FIND OUT WHY YOU BECAME A POKéMON.
OH YEAH. WE'RE GOING TO SEE NINETALES, RIGHT?
YUP.
...
YAWN
NNNH! COLD WEATHER MAKES ME WANT TO TAKE A NAP.
HUH?
AAAGH! I TOLD YOU, DON'T FALL ASLEEP!!
FWNK
YAWN. SO COLD.
MUST... TAKE... A... HOT BATH.
GINJI CAN'T TAKE THE COLD! IF HE REALLY FALLS ASLEEP, HE MIGHT NOT WAKE UP!

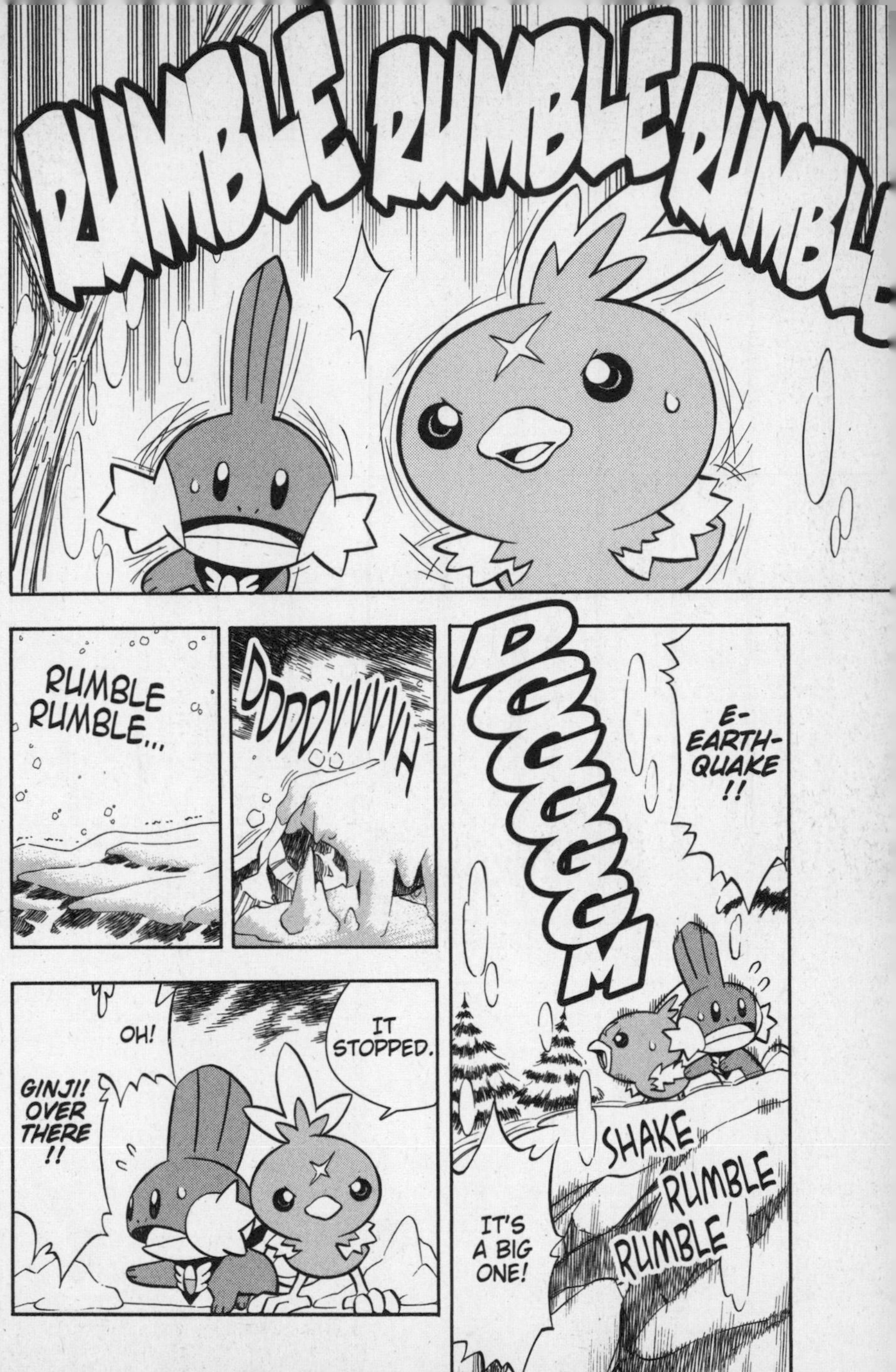
RUMBLE RUMBLE RUMBL
DOOOOOM
E-EARTHQUAKE!!
SHAKE RUMBLE RUMBLE
IT'S A BIG ONE!
DDDDVVVVVH
RUMBLE RUMBLE...
IT STOPPED.
OH!
GINJI! OVER THERE!!

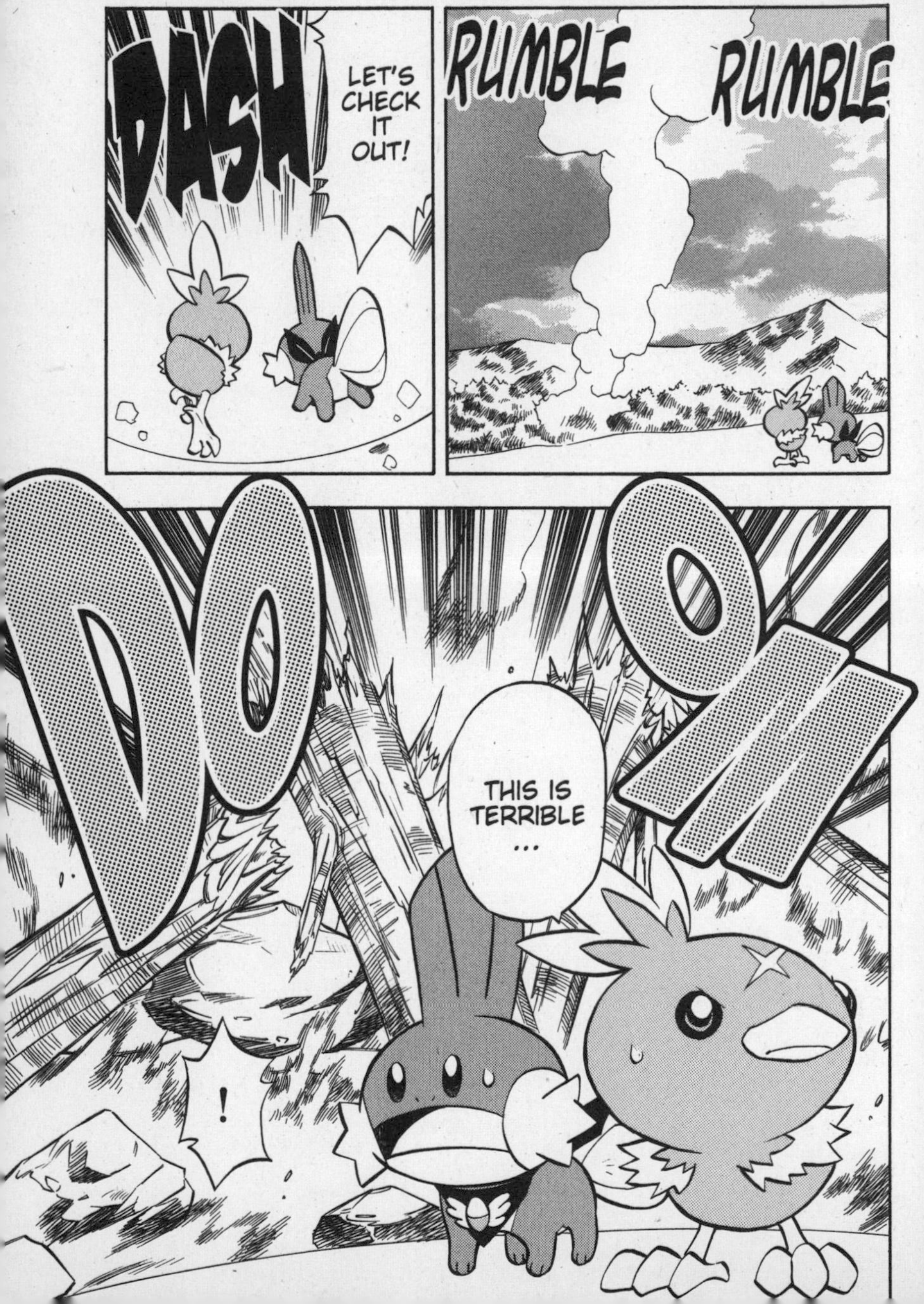
RUMBLE
RUMBLE
DASH
LET'S CHECK IT OUT!
DOOM
THIS IS TERRIBLE ...
!

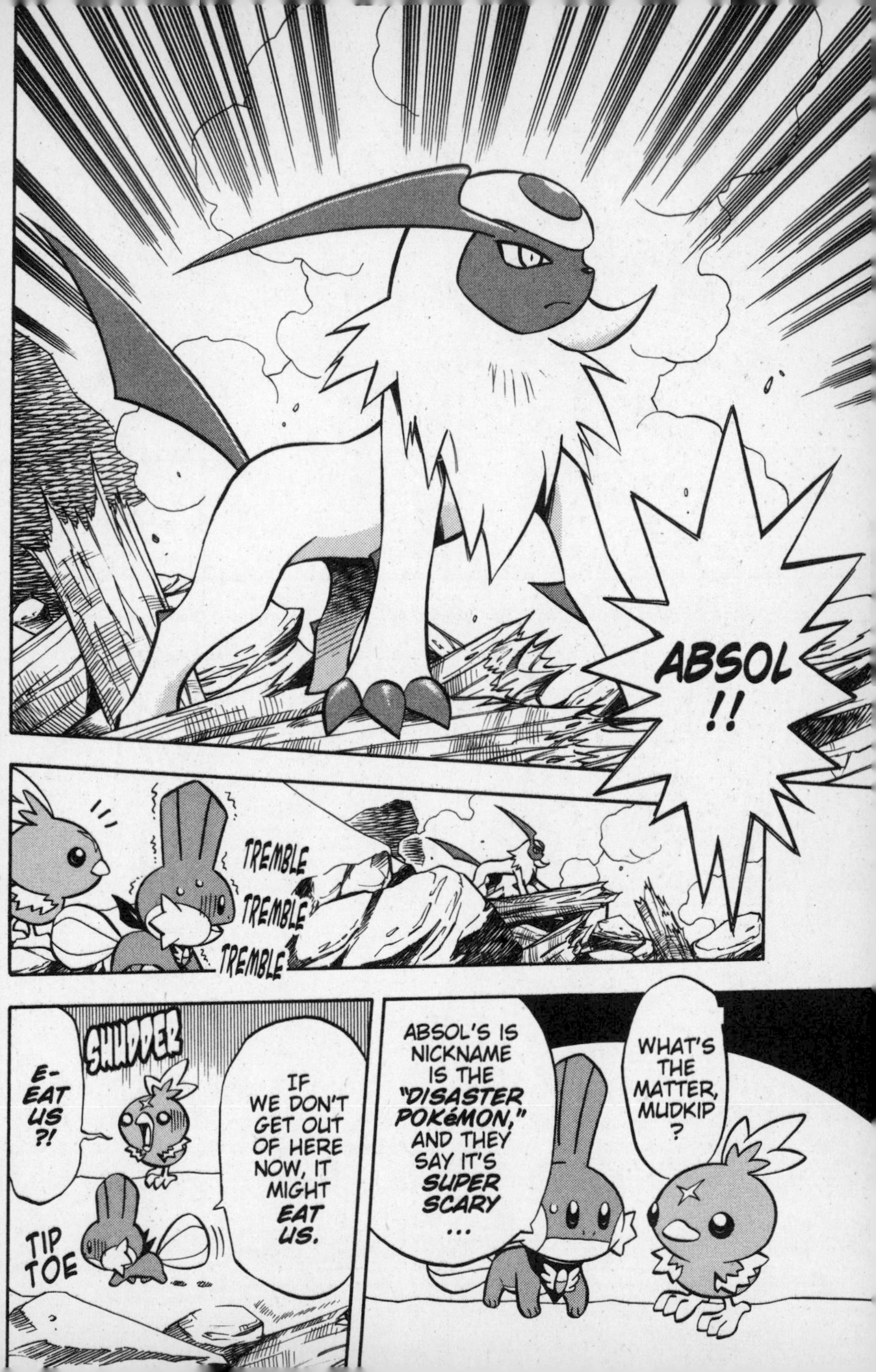
ABSOL!!
TREMBLE
TREMBLE
TREMBLE
WHAT'S THE MATTER, MUDKIP?
ABSOL'S IS NICKNAME IS THE "DISASTER POKéMON," AND THEY SAY IT'S SUPER SCARY...
SHUDDER
IF WE DON'T GET OUT OF HERE NOW, IT MIGHT EAT US.
E-EAT US?!
TIP TOE

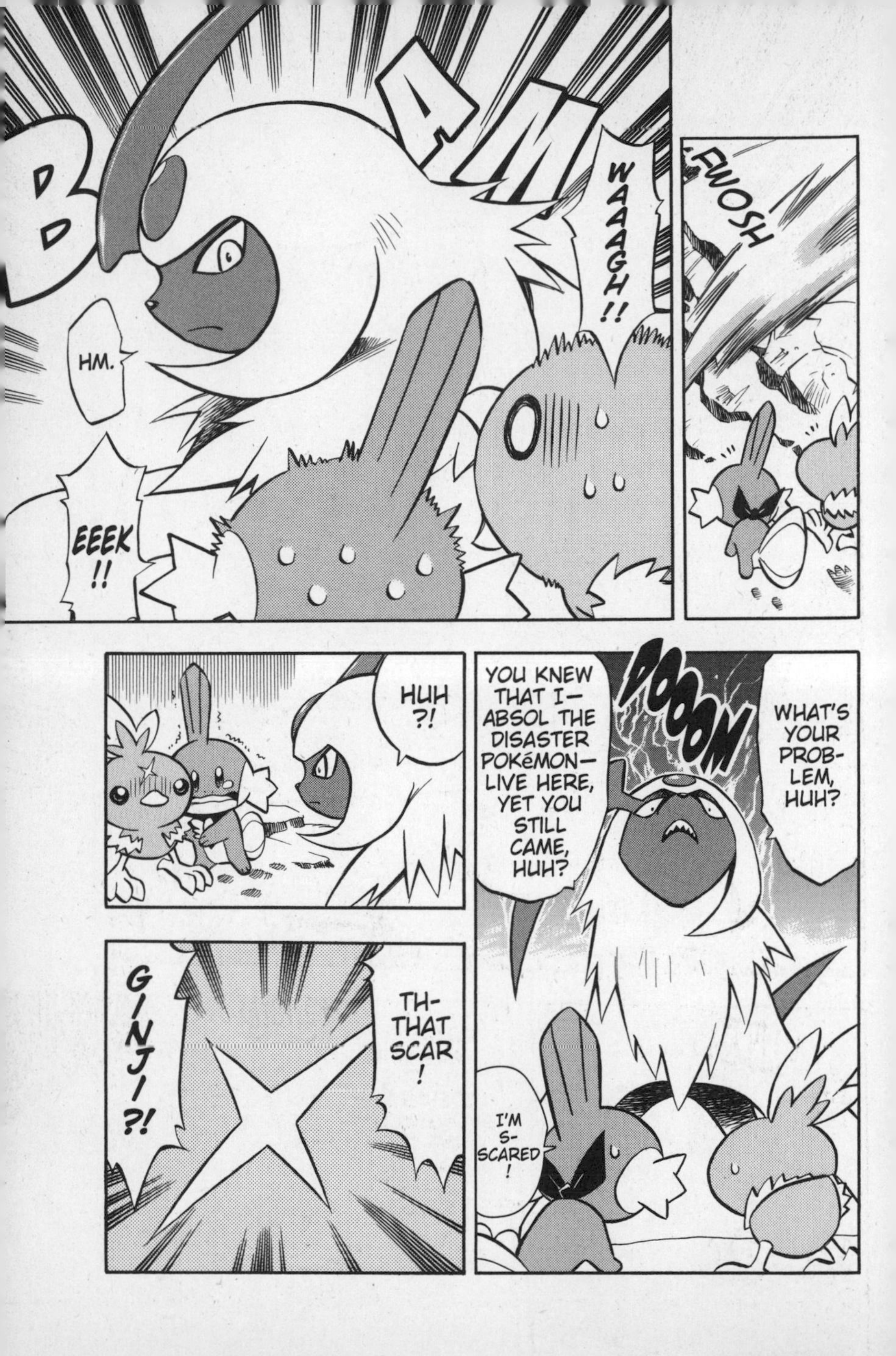
FWOSH
WAAAGH!!
HM.
EEEK!!
WHAT'S YOUR PROB-LEM, HUH?
DOOOM
YOU KNEW THAT I—ABSOL THE DISASTER POKéMON—LIVE HERE, YET YOU STILL CAME, HUH?
I'M S-SCARED!
HUH?!
TH-THAT SCAR!
GINJI?!

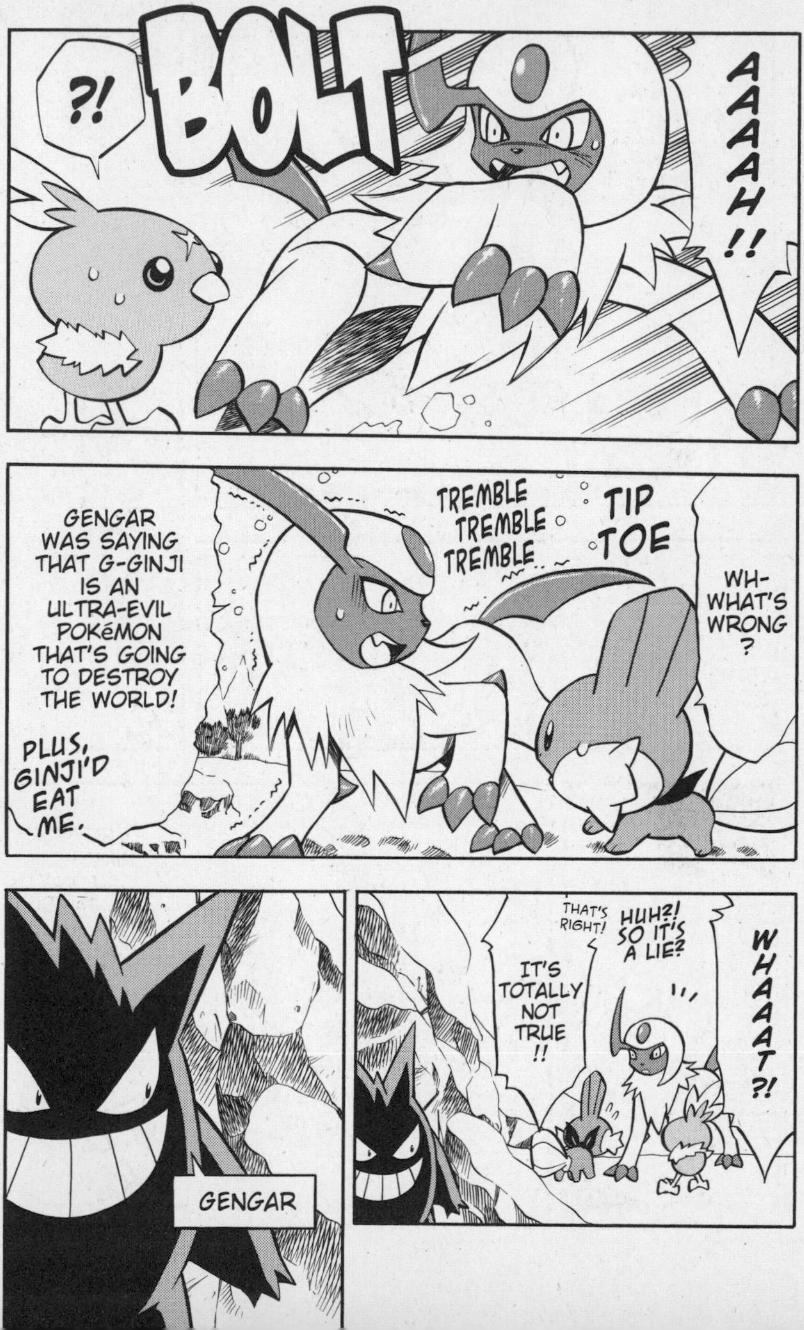
AAAAAH!!
BOLT
?!
WH-WHAT'S WRONG?
TIP TOE
TREMBLE TREMBLE TREMBLE
GENGAR WAS SAYING THAT G-GINJI IS AN ULTRA-EVIL POKéMON THAT'S GOING TO DESTROY THE WORLD!
PLUS, GINJI'D EAT ME.
WHAAAAT?!
HUH?! SO IT'S A LIE?
THAT'S RIGHT!
IT'S TOTALLY NOT TRUE!!
GENGAR

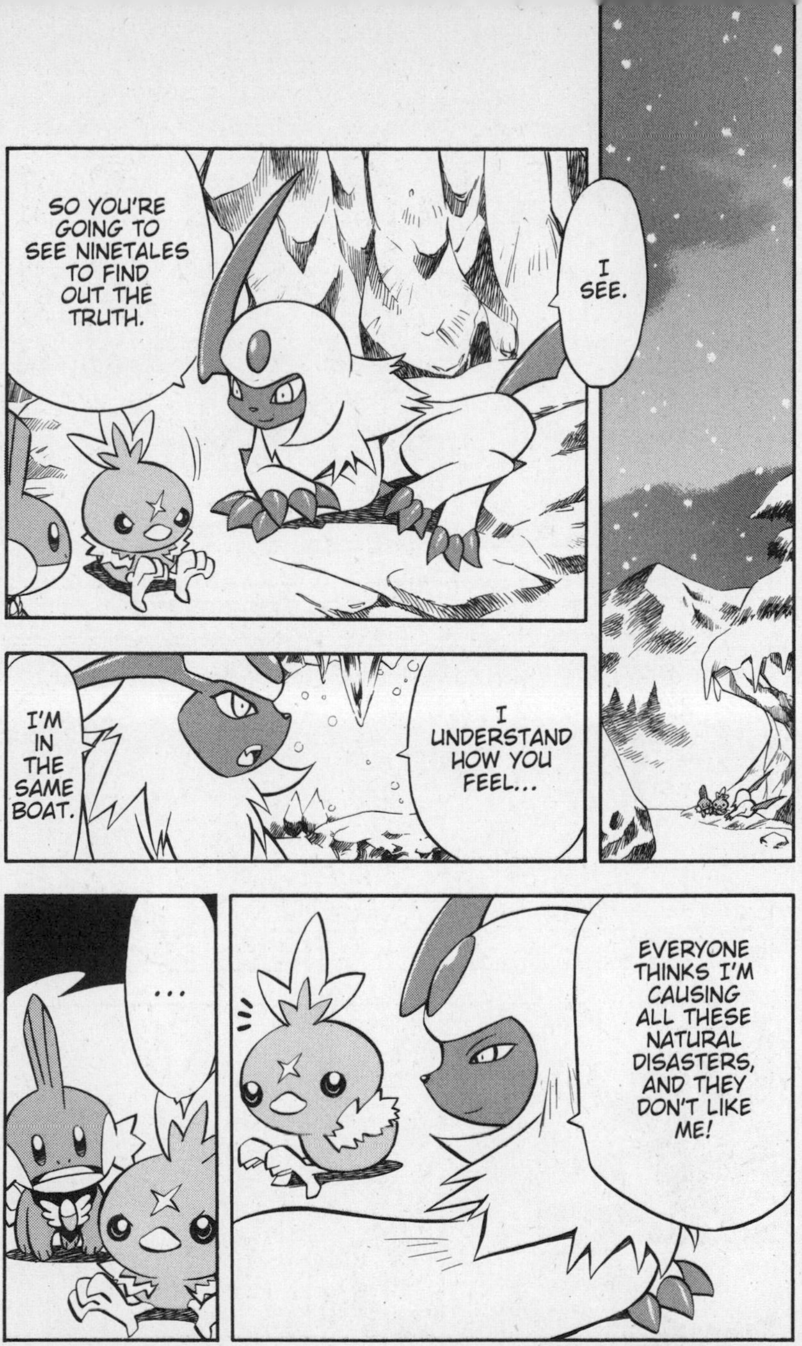
I SEE.
SO YOU'RE GOING TO SEE NINETALES TO FIND OUT THE TRUTH.
I UNDERSTAND HOW YOU FEEL...
I'M IN THE SAME BOAT.
EVERYONE THINKS I'M CAUSING ALL THESE NATURAL DISASTERS, AND THEY DON'T LIKE ME!
...

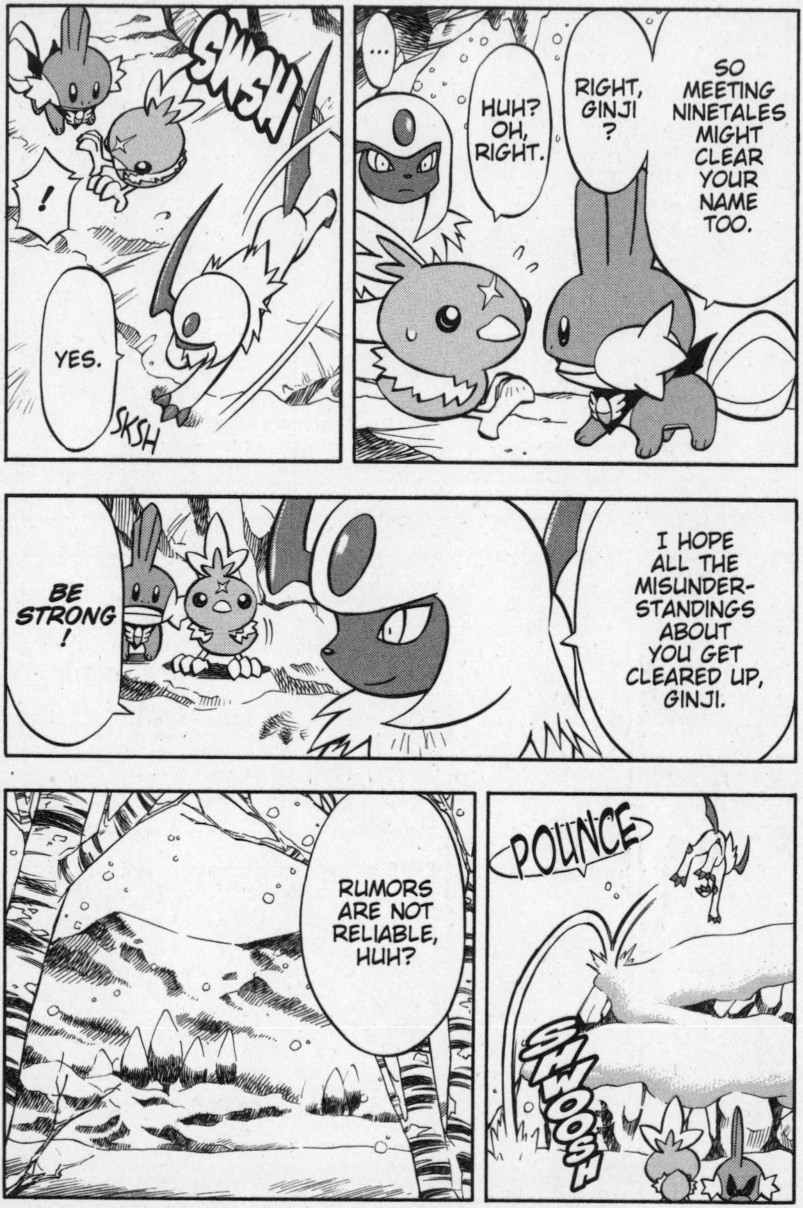

SO MEETING NINETALES MIGHT CLEAR YOUR NAME TOO.
RIGHT, GINJI ?
HUH? OH, RIGHT.
...
SWSH
!
YES.
SKSH
I HOPE ALL THE MISUNDER-STANDINGS ABOUT YOU GET CLEARED UP, GINJI.
BE STRONG !
POUNCE
SHWOOSH
RUMORS ARE NOT RELIABLE, HUH?

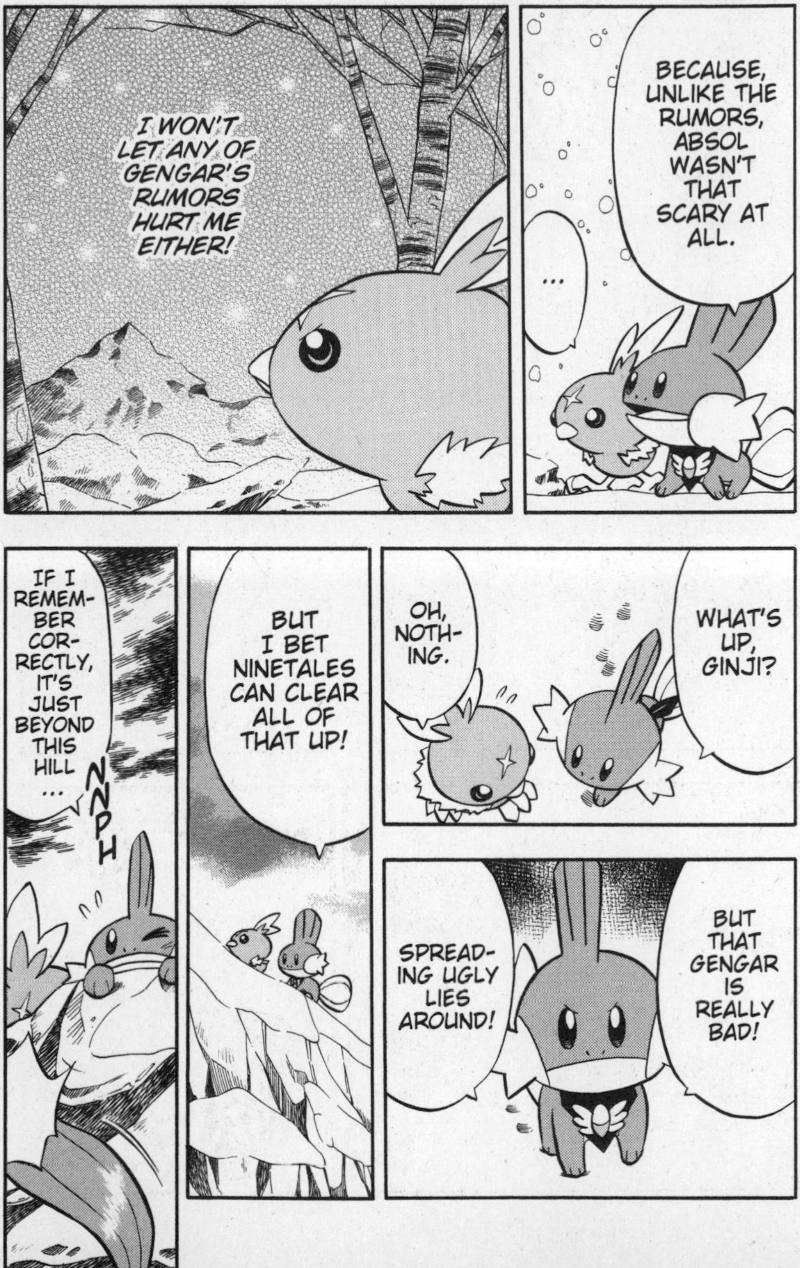
BECAUSE, UNLIKE THE RUMORS, ABSOL WASN'T THAT SCARY AT ALL.
...
I WON'T LET ANY OF GENGAR'S RUMORS HURT ME EITHER!
WHAT'S UP, GINJI?
OH, NOTHING.
BUT THAT GENGAR IS REALLY BAD!
SPREADING UGLY LIES AROUND!
BUT I BET NINETALES CAN CLEAR ALL OF THAT UP!
IF I REMEMBER CORRECTLY, IT'S JUST BEYOND THIS HILL...
NNPH

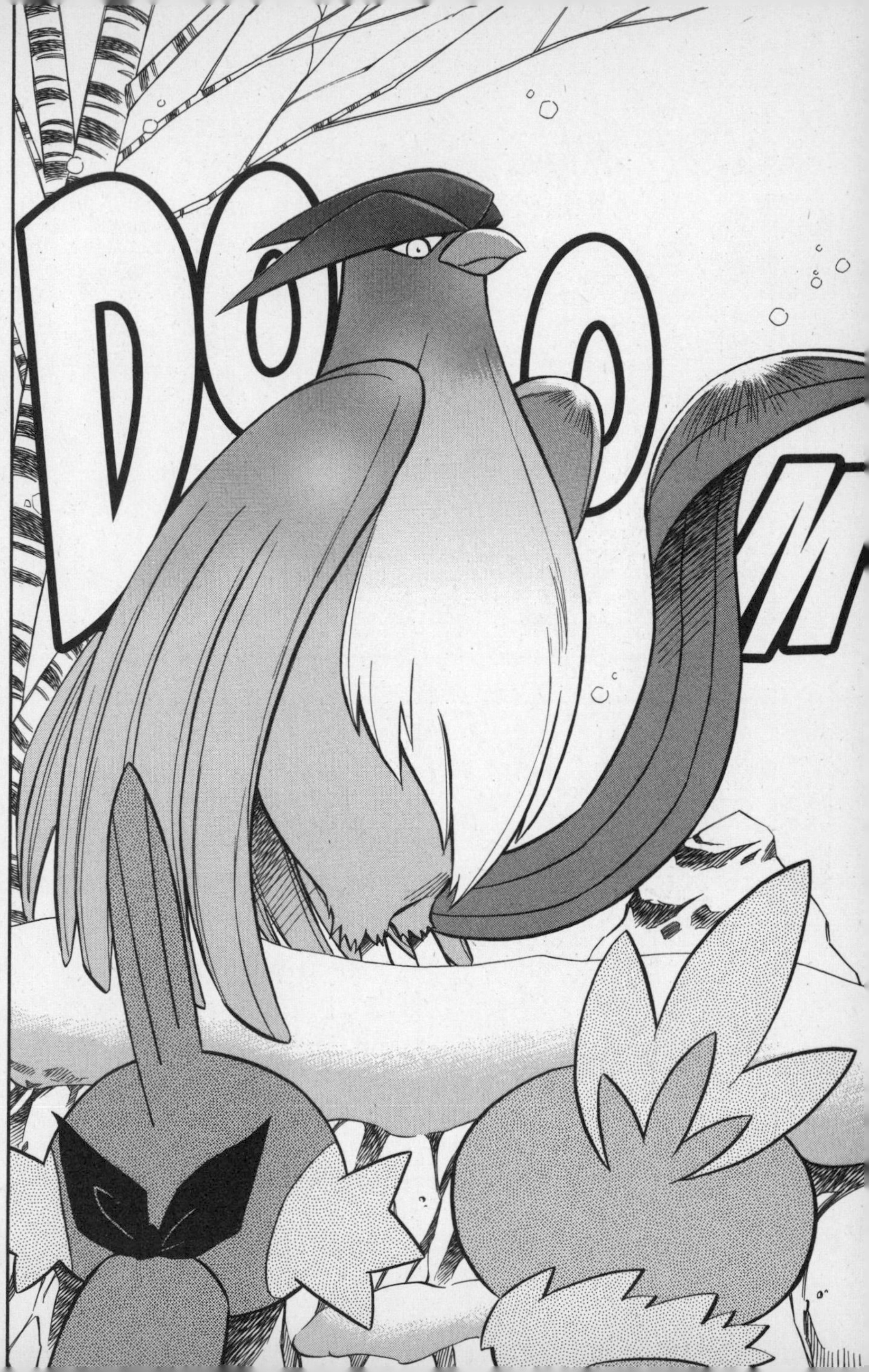
DOOM

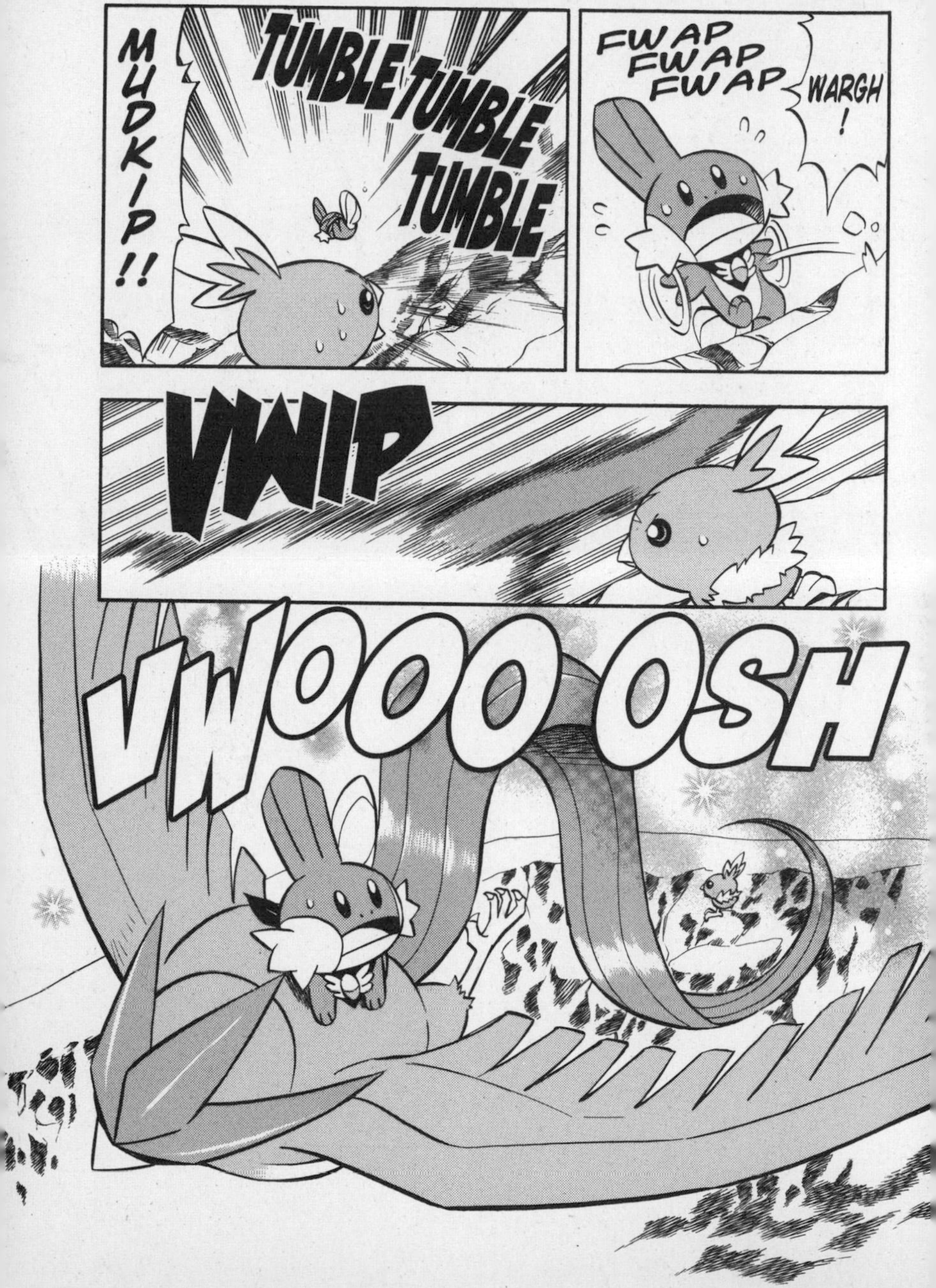
FWAP FWAP FWAP
WARGH!
TUMBLE TUMBLE TUMBLE
MUDKIP!!
VWIP
VWOOO OSH

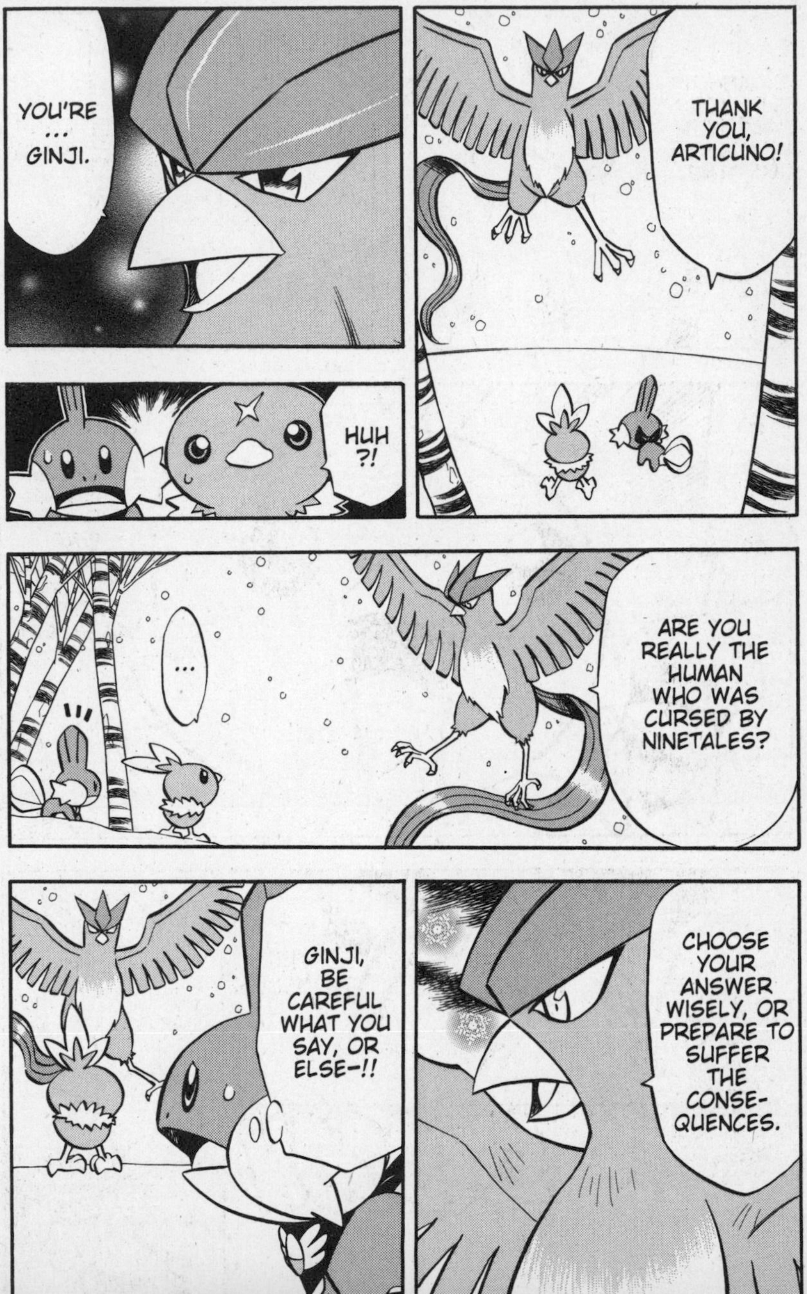
THANK YOU, ARTICUNO!
YOU'RE ... GINJI.
HUH ?!
ARE YOU REALLY THE HUMAN WHO WAS CURSED BY NINETALES?
...
CHOOSE YOUR ANSWER WISELY, OR PREPARE TO SUFFER THE CONSE-QUENCES.
GINJI, BE CAREFUL WHAT YOU SAY, OR ELSE-!!

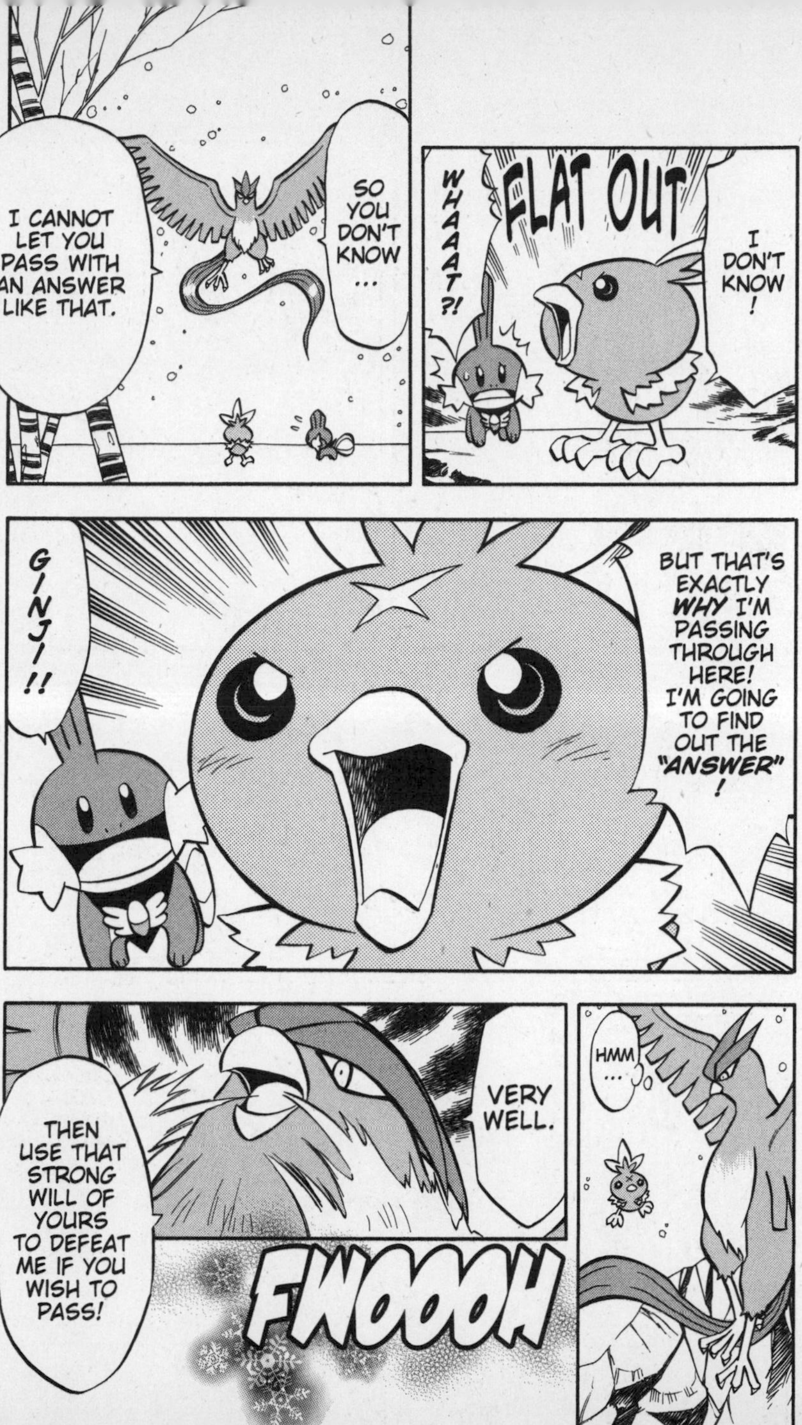
I DON'T KNOW!
FLAT OUT
WHAAAAT?!
SO YOU DON'T KNOW...
I CANNOT LET YOU PASS WITH AN ANSWER LIKE THAT.
BUT THAT'S EXACTLY **WHY** I'M PASSING THROUGH HERE! I'M GOING TO FIND OUT THE ***"ANSWER"***!
GINJI!!
HMM...
VERY WELL.
THEN USE THAT STRONG WILL OF YOURS TO DEFEAT ME IF YOU WISH TO PASS!
FWOOOOH

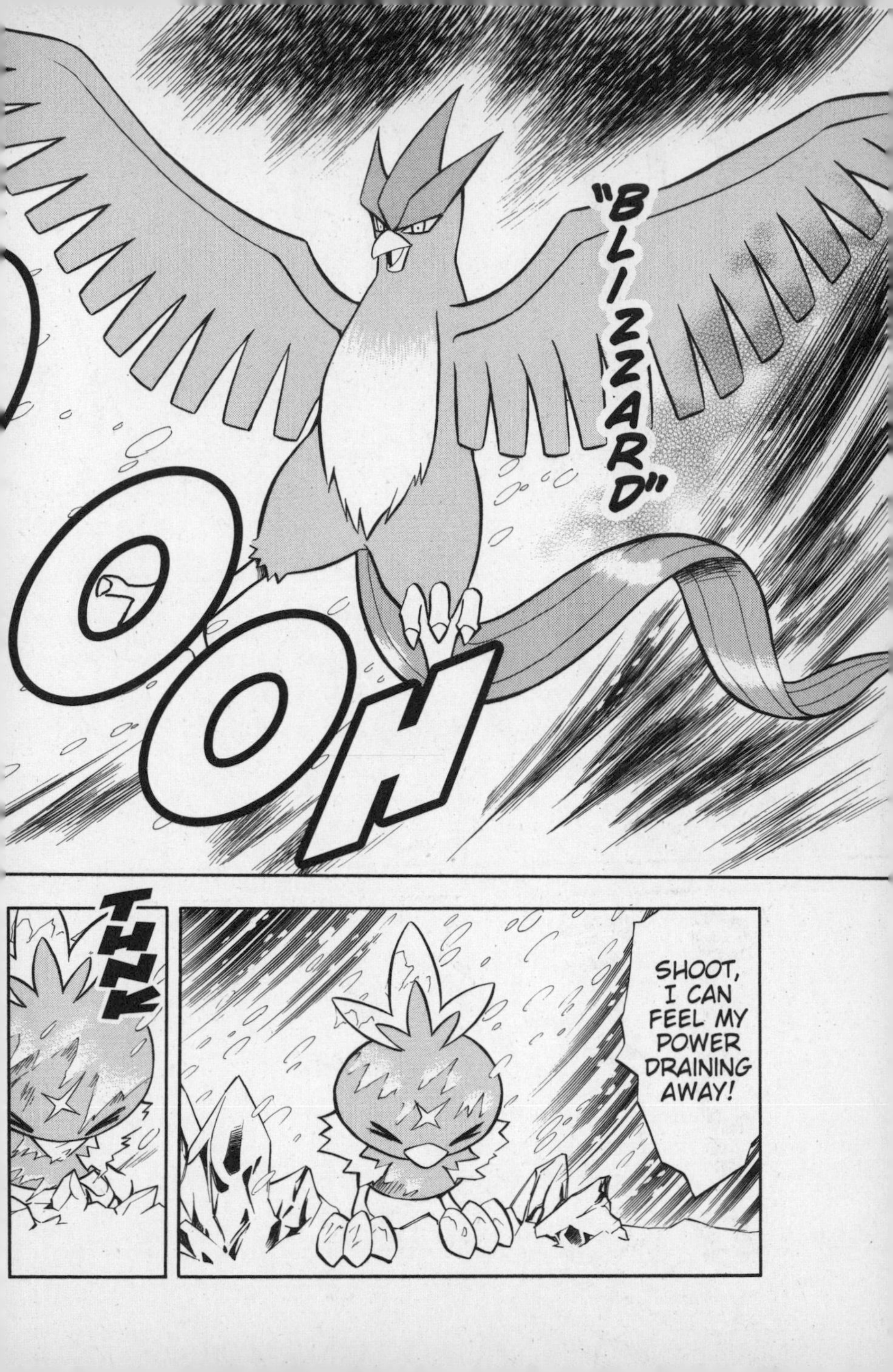
"BLIZZARD"
OOOH
SHOOT, I CAN FEEL MY POWER DRAINING AWAY!
THNK

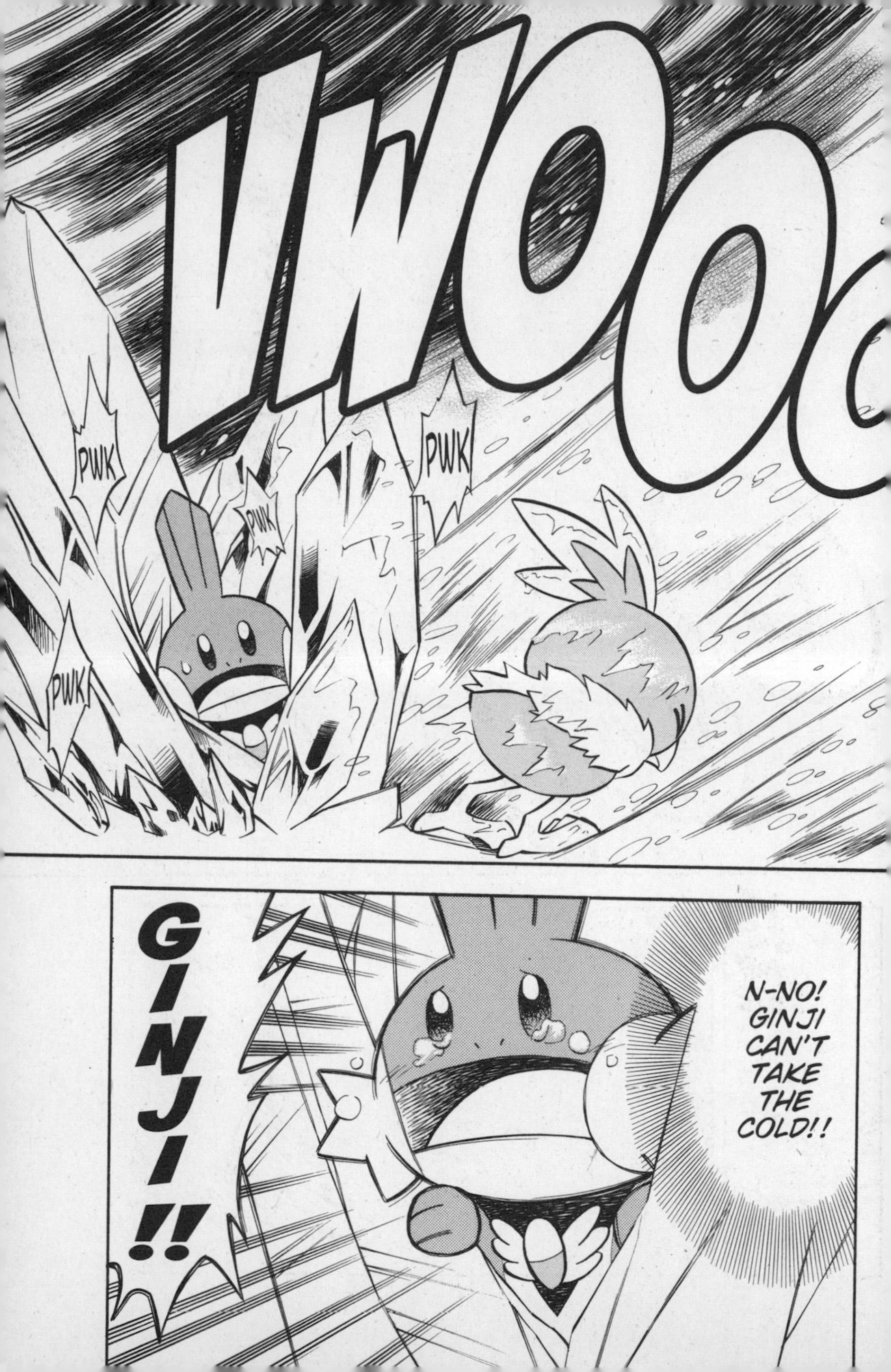
WHOOO
PWK
PWK
PWK
PWK
N-NO! GINJI CAN'T TAKE THE COLD!!
GINJI!!

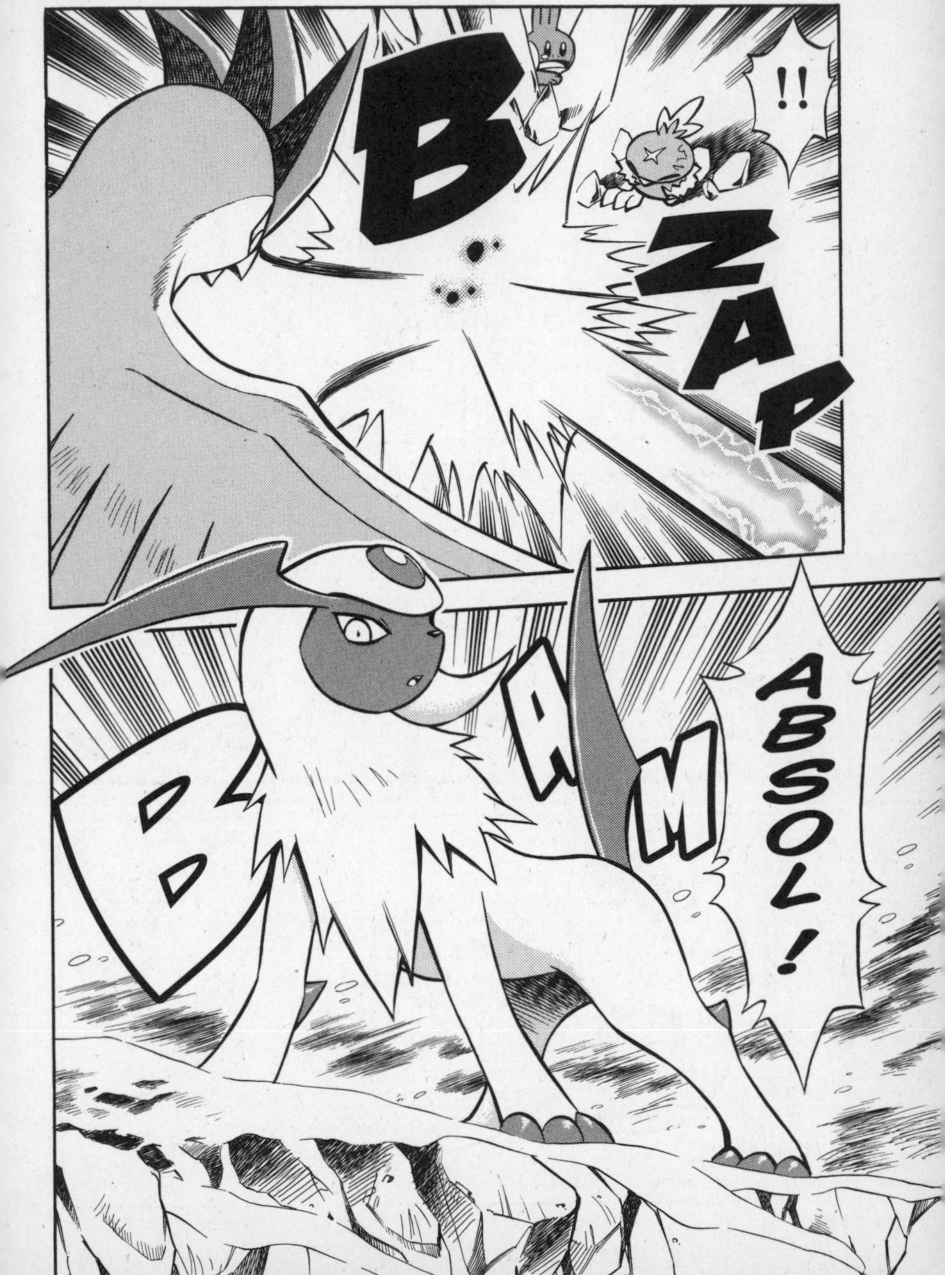
!!
BZAP
ABSOL!
BAM

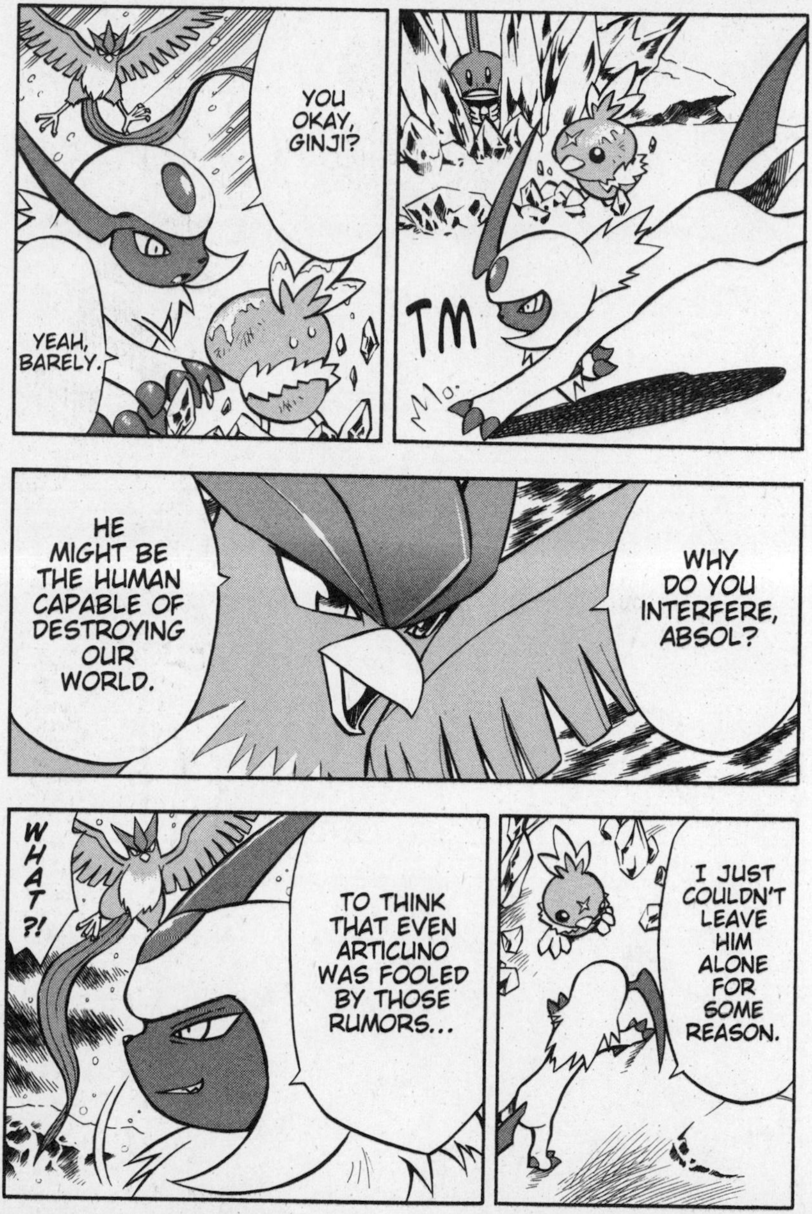
TM
YOU OKAY, GINJI?
YEAH, BARELY.
WHY DO YOU INTERFERE, ABSOL?
HE MIGHT BE THE HUMAN CAPABLE OF DESTROYING OUR WORLD.
I JUST COULDN'T LEAVE HIM ALONE FOR SOME REASON.
TO THINK THAT EVEN ARTICUNO WAS FOOLED BY THOSE RUMORS...
WHAT?!

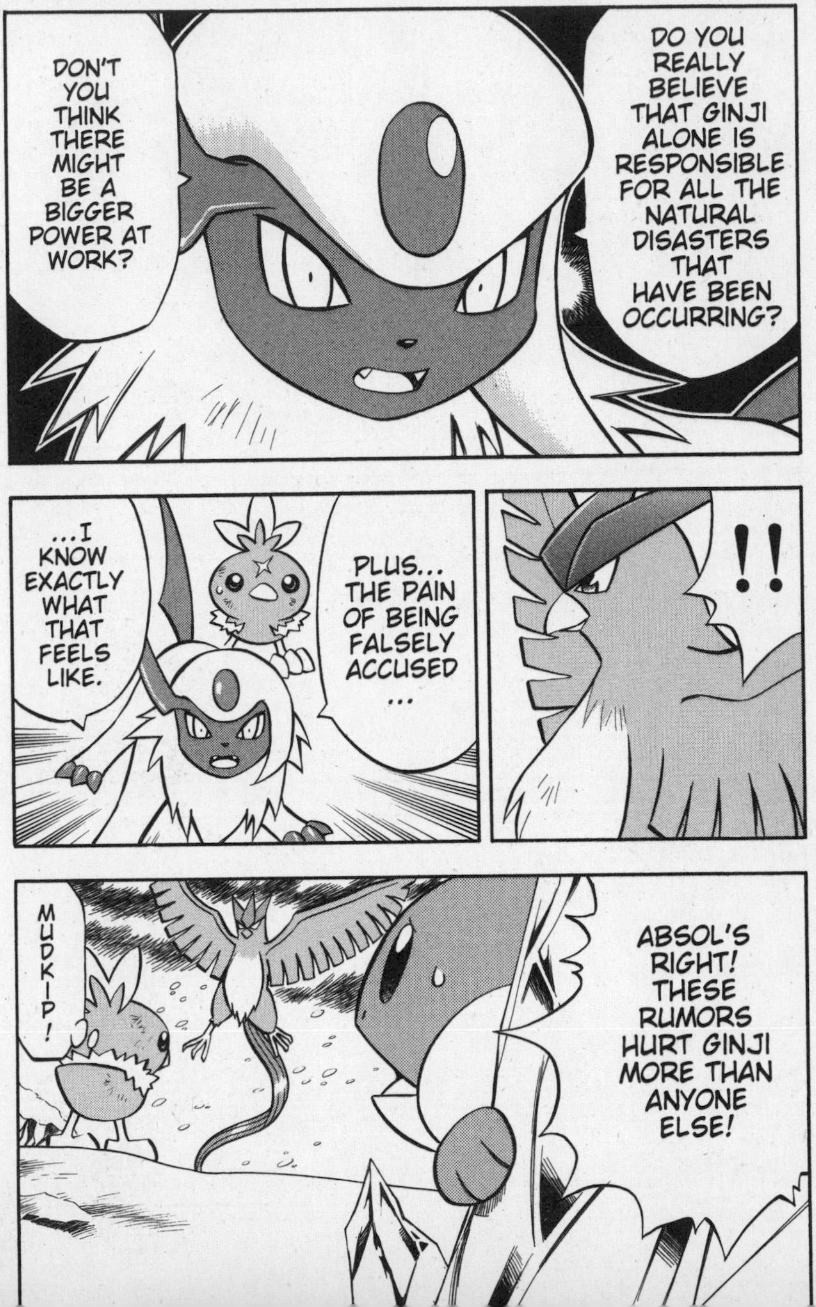
DO YOU REALLY BELIEVE THAT GINJI ALONE IS RESPONSIBLE FOR ALL THE NATURAL DISASTERS THAT HAVE BEEN OCCURRING?
DON'T YOU THINK THERE MIGHT BE A BIGGER POWER AT WORK?
!!
PLUS... THE PAIN OF BEING FALSELY ACCUSED ...
...I KNOW EXACTLY WHAT THAT FEELS LIKE.
ABSOL'S RIGHT! THESE RUMORS HURT GINJI MORE THAN ANYONE ELSE!
MUDKIP!

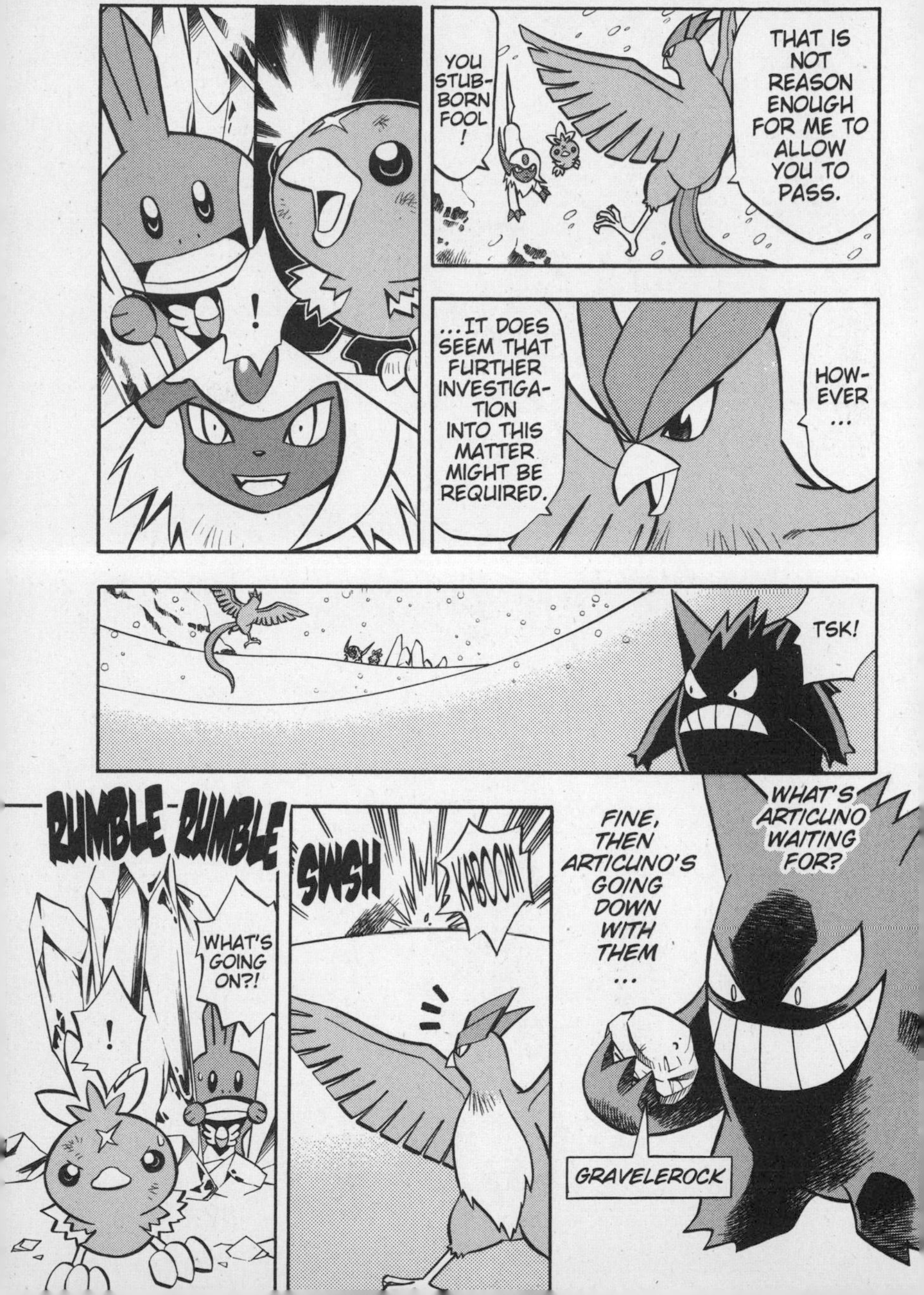
THAT IS NOT REASON ENOUGH FOR ME TO ALLOW YOU TO PASS.
YOU STUB-BORN FOOL!
HOW-EVER...
...IT DOES SEEM THAT FURTHER INVESTIGA-TION INTO THIS MATTER MIGHT BE REQUIRED.
!
TSK!
WHAT'S ARTICUNO WAITING FOR?
FINE, THEN ARTICUNO'S GOING DOWN WITH THEM...
GRAVELEROCK
KABOOM
SWISH
RUMBLE RUMBLE
WHAT'S GOING ON?!
!

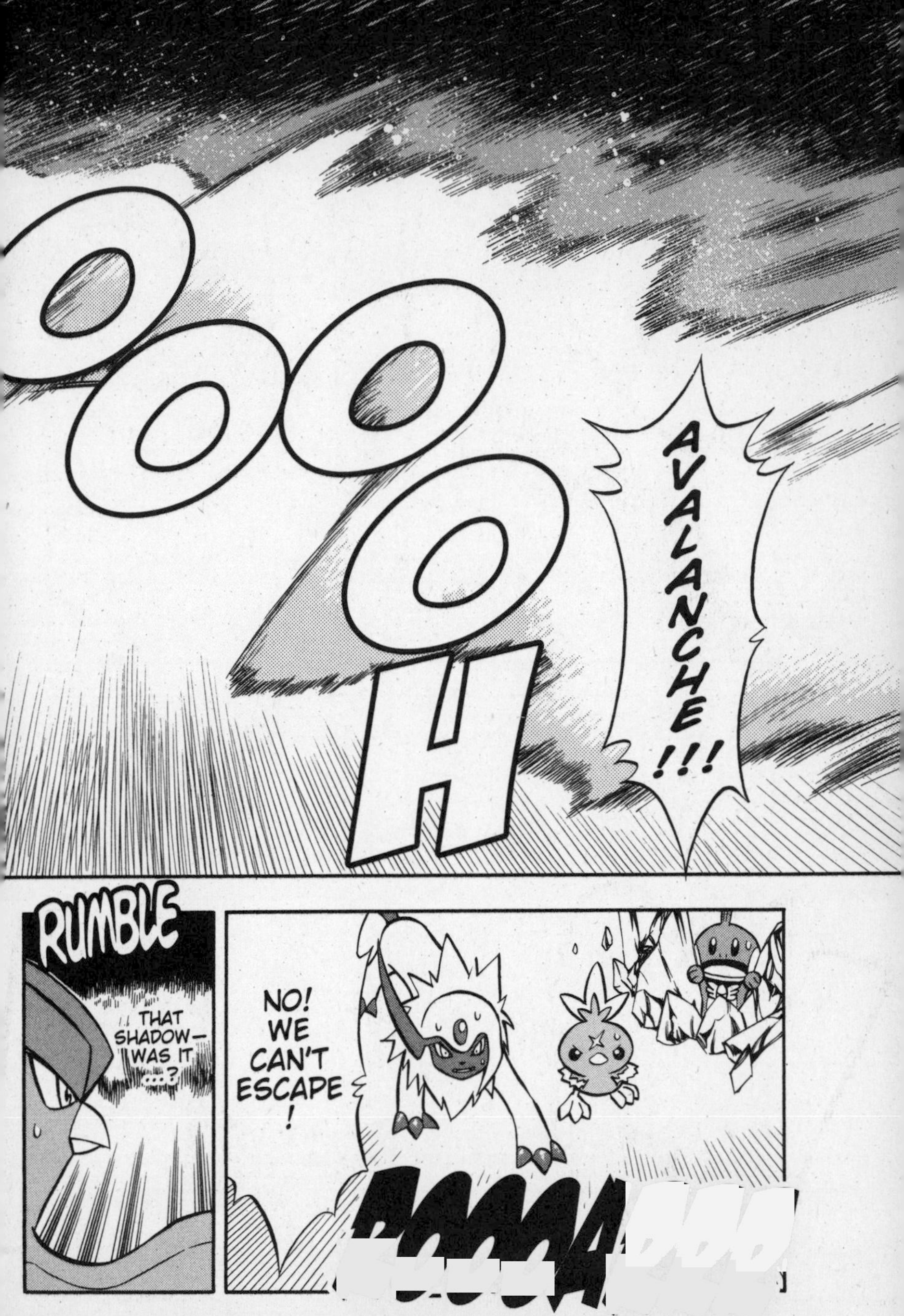
AVALANCHE!!!
OOOOH
NO! WE CAN'T ESCAPE!
RUMBLE
...THAT SHADOW—WAS IT ...?

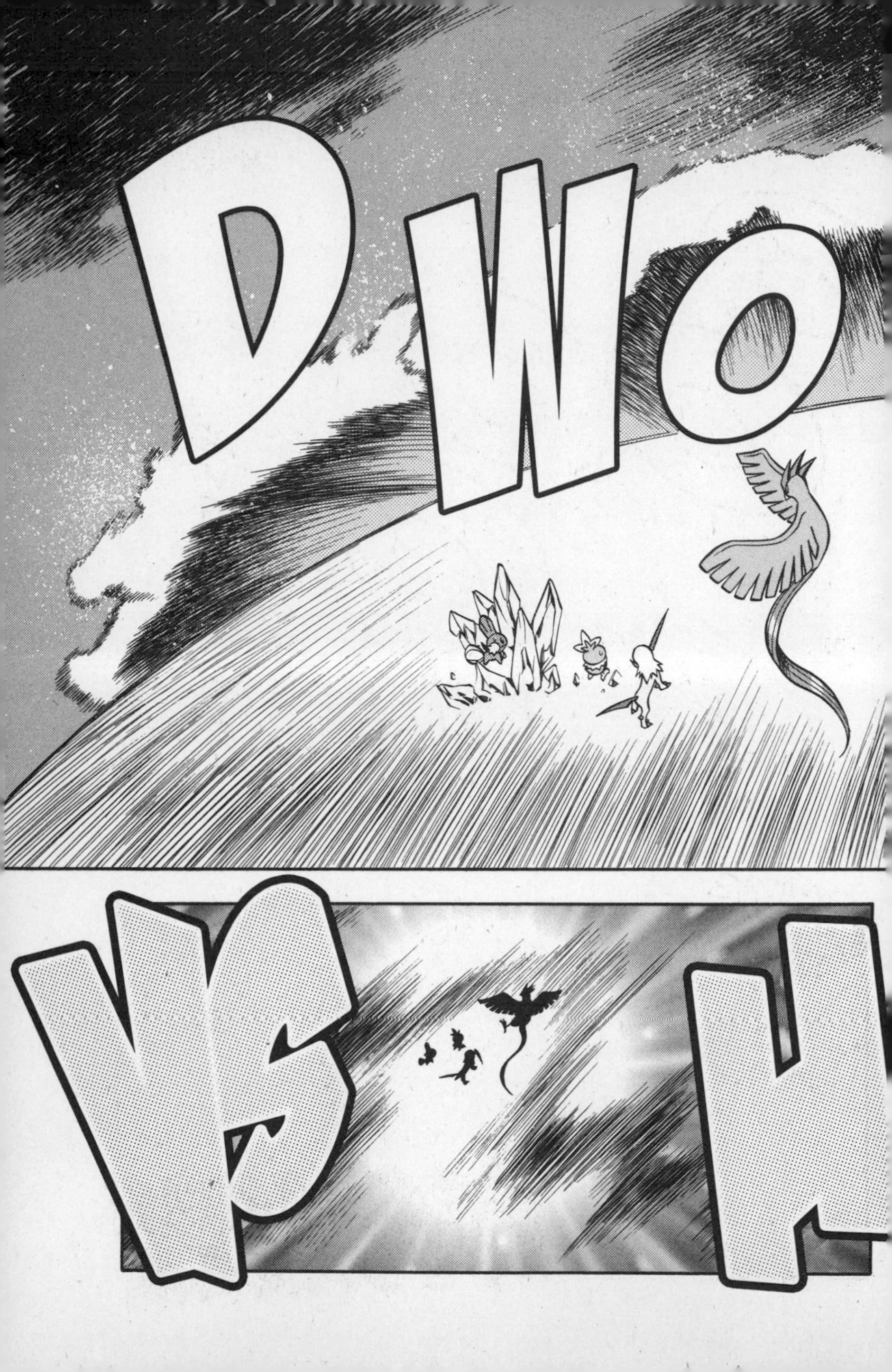
DWO
VSH

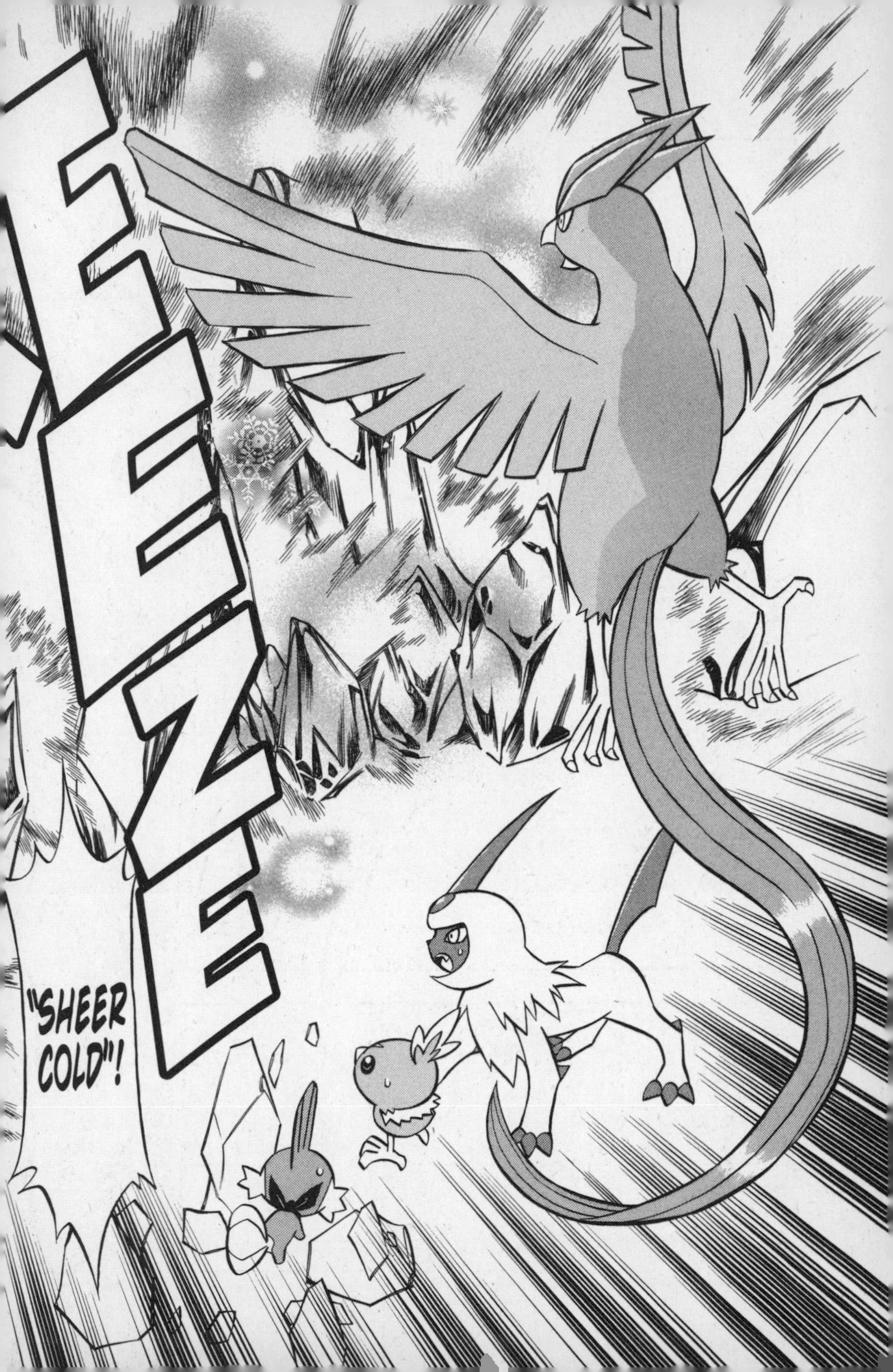
"SHEER COLD"!

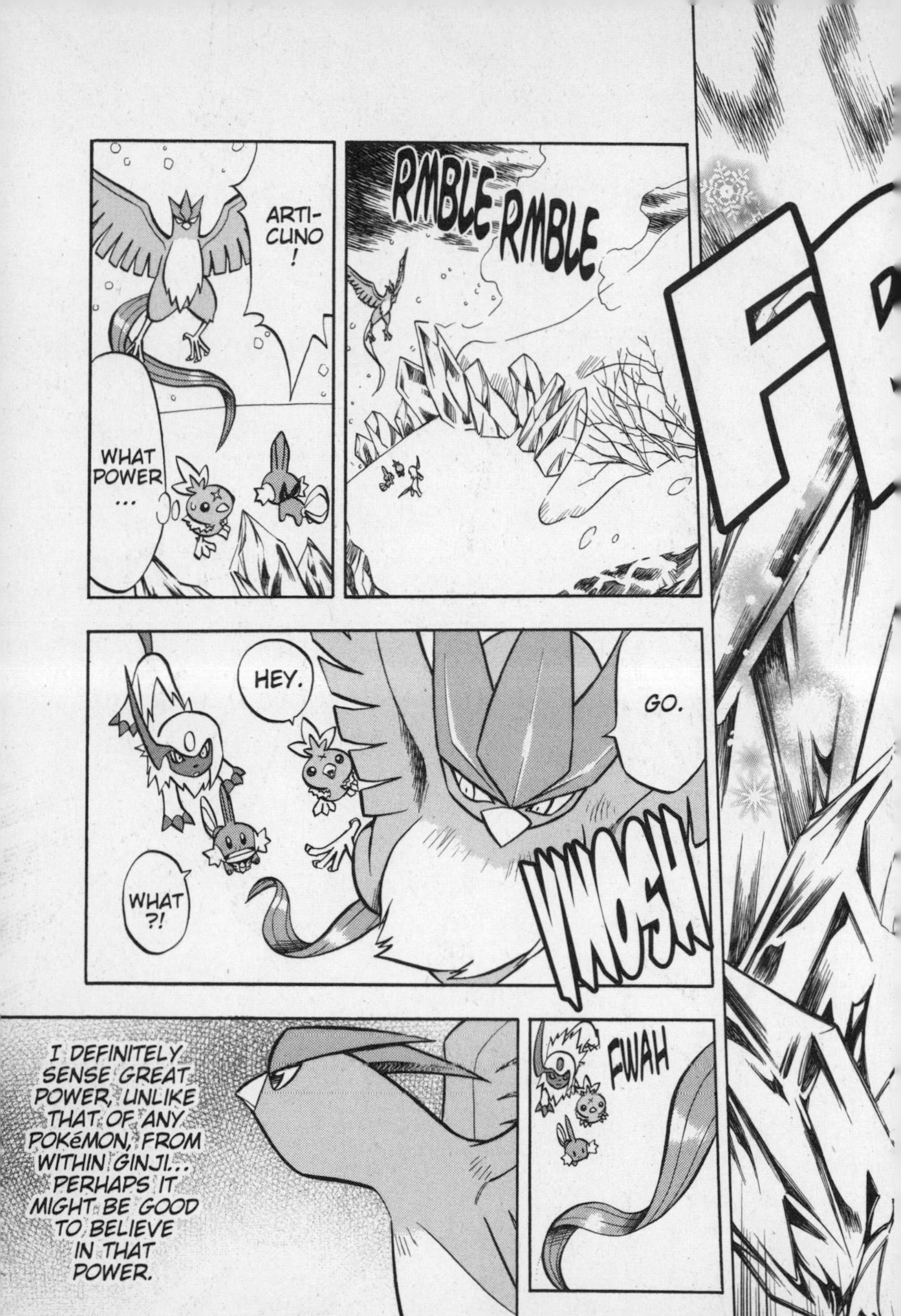
RMBLE RMBLE
ARTI-CUNO!
WHAT POWER...
GO.
HEY.
WHAT?!
WHOSH!
FWAH
I DEFINITELY SENSE GREAT POWER, UNLIKE THAT OF ANY POKéMON, FROM WITHIN GINJI... PERHAPS IT MIGHT BE GOOD TO BELIEVE IN THAT POWER.

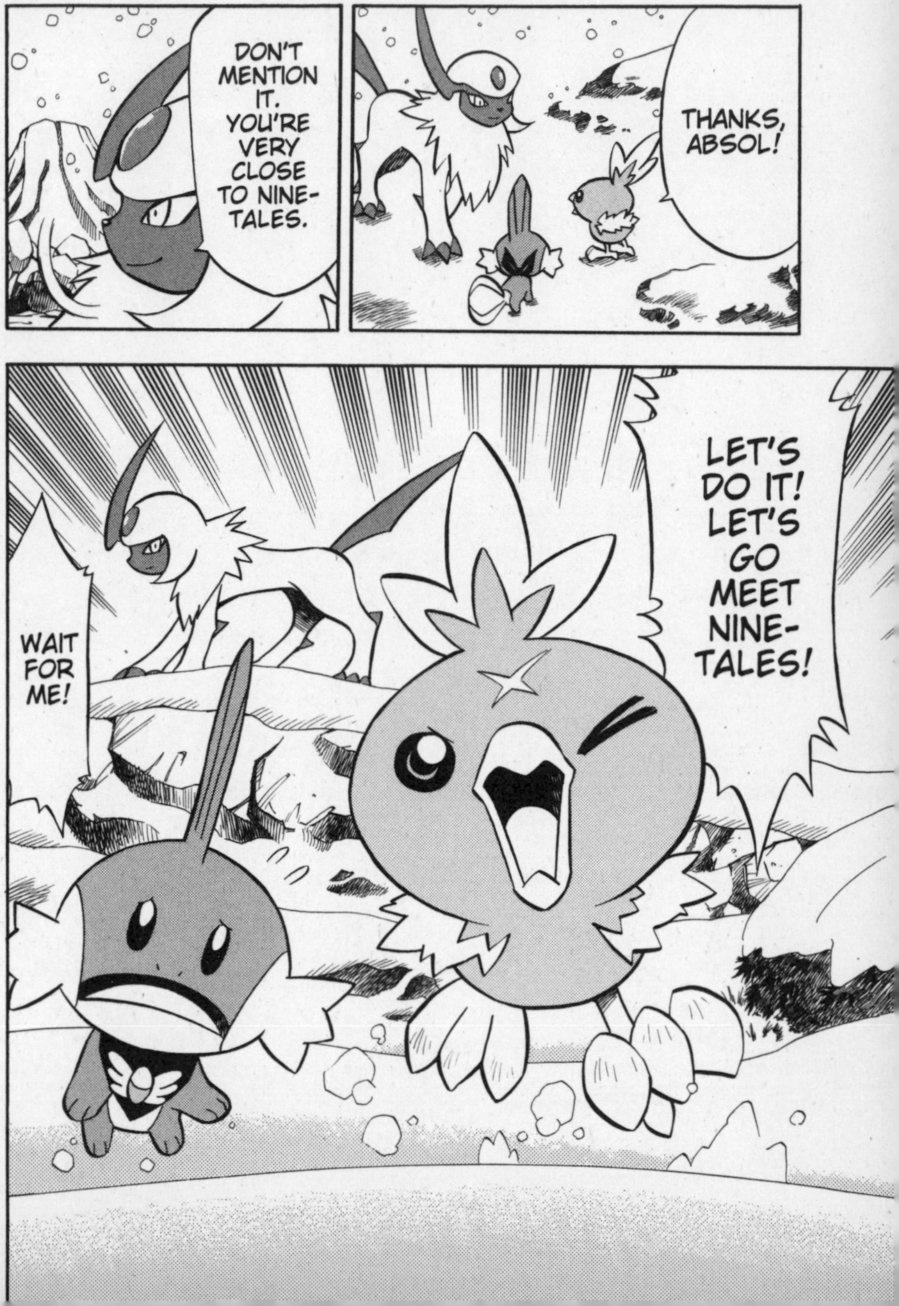
THANKS, ABSOL!
DON'T MENTION IT. YOU'RE VERY CLOSE TO NINE-TALES.
LET'S DO IT! LET'S GO MEET NINE-TALES!
WAIT FOR ME!

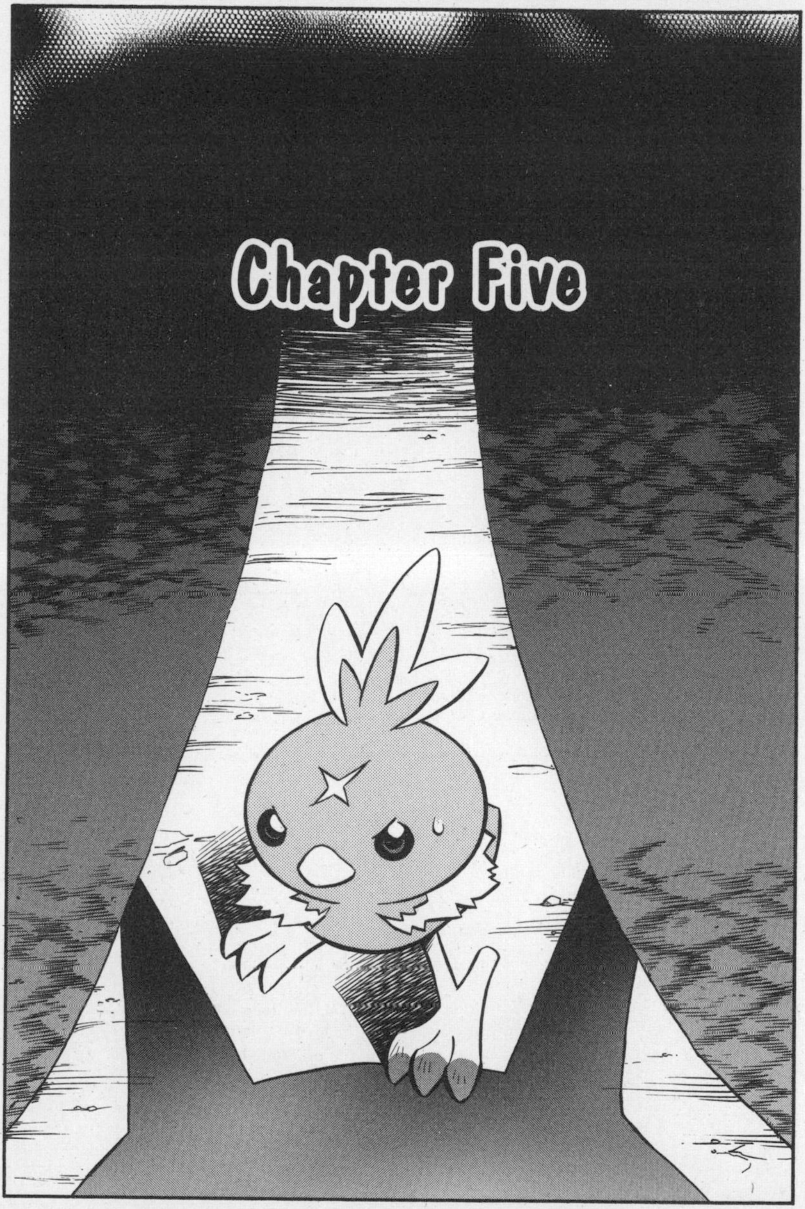
Chapter Five

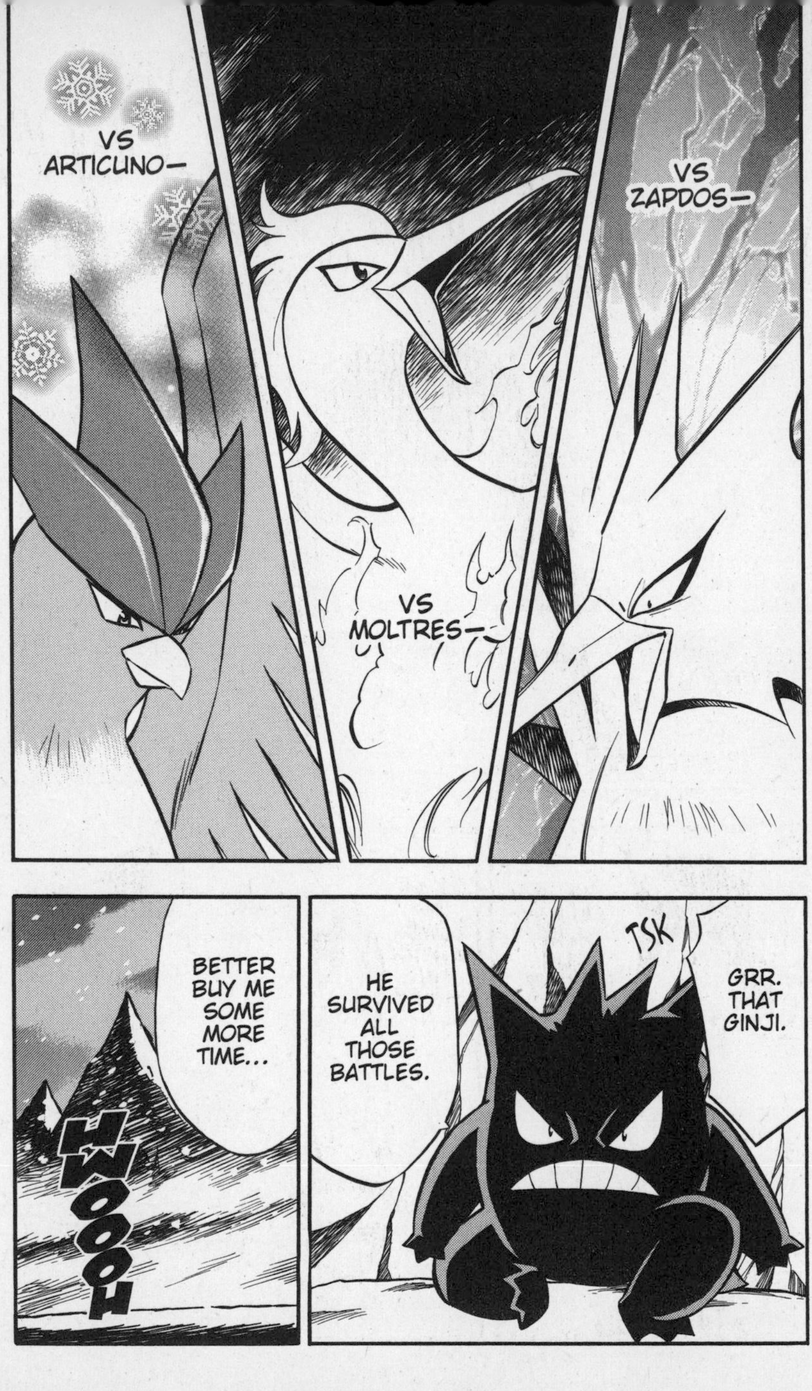
VS ZAPDOS—
VS MOLTRES—
VS ARTICUNO—
TSK
GRR. THAT GINJI.
HE SURVIVED ALL THOSE BATTLES.
BETTER BUY ME SOME MORE TIME...
HWOOOOH

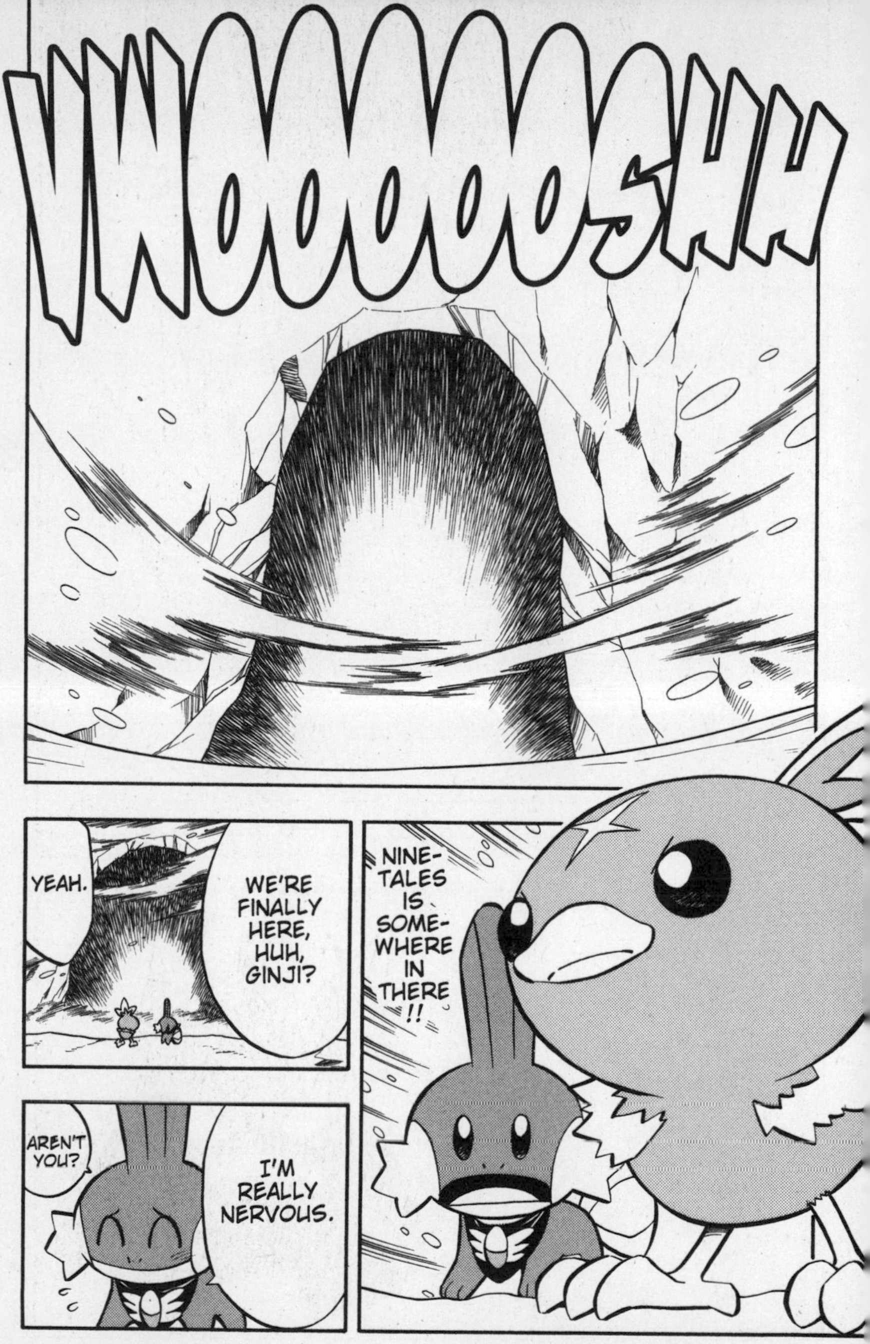
VWOOOOOSHH
NINE-TALES IS SOMEWHERE IN THERE!!
WE'RE FINALLY HERE, HUH, GINJI?
YEAH.
I'M REALLY NERVOUS.
AREN'T YOU?

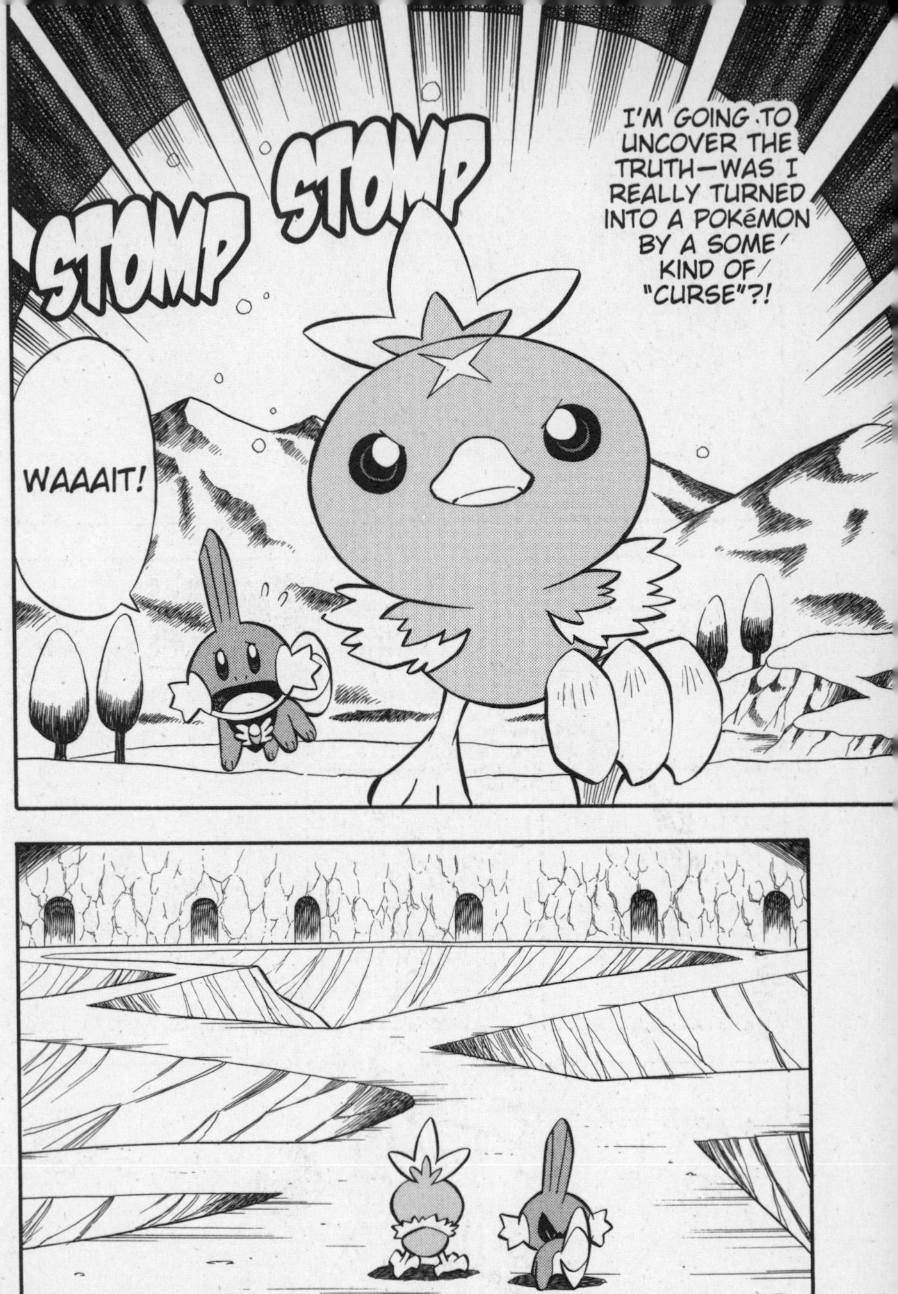
I'M GOING TO UNCOVER THE TRUTH—WAS I REALLY TURNED INTO A POKéMON BY A SOME KIND OF "CURSE"?!
STOMP STOMP
WAAAIT!

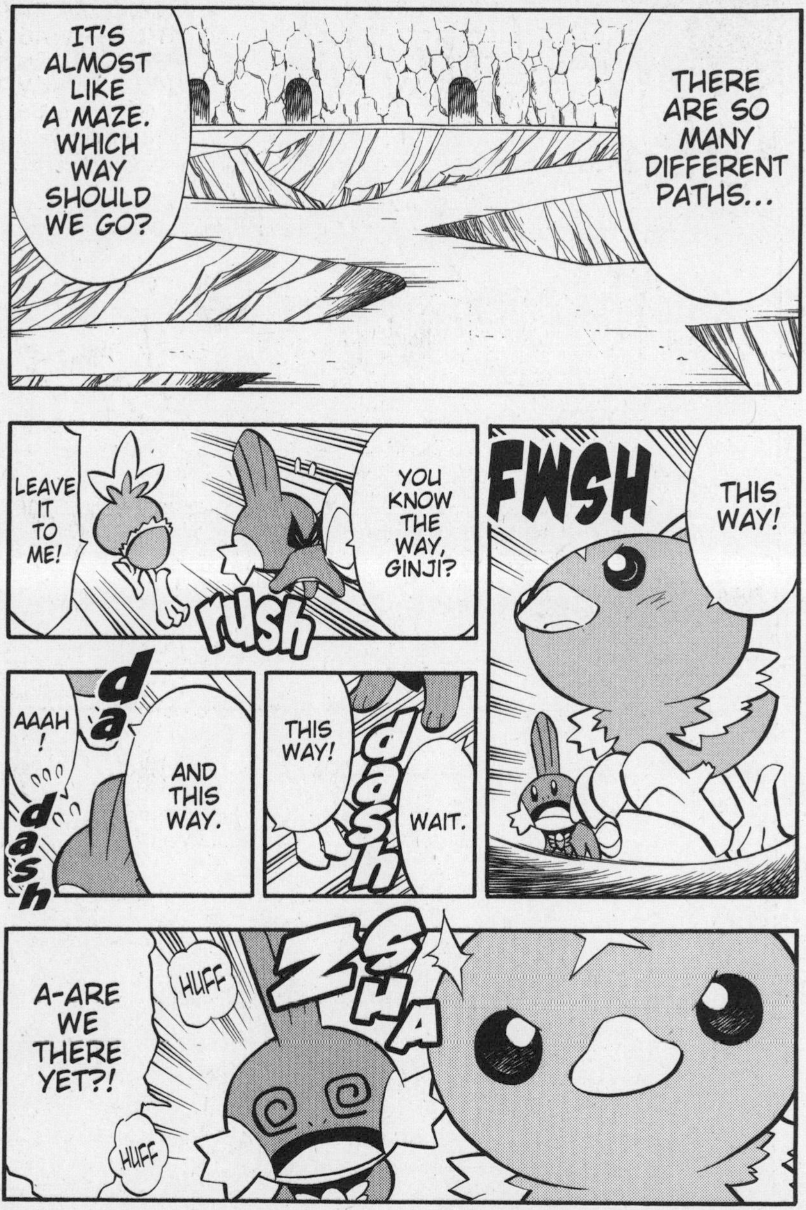
THERE ARE SO MANY DIFFERENT PATHS...
IT'S ALMOST LIKE A MAZE. WHICH WAY SHOULD WE GO?
YOU KNOW THE WAY, GINJI?
LEAVE IT TO ME!
rush
FWSH
THIS WAY!
WAIT.
dash
THIS WAY!
AND THIS WAY.
da
AAAH!
dash
ZSHA
HUFF
HUFF
A-ARE WE THERE YET?!

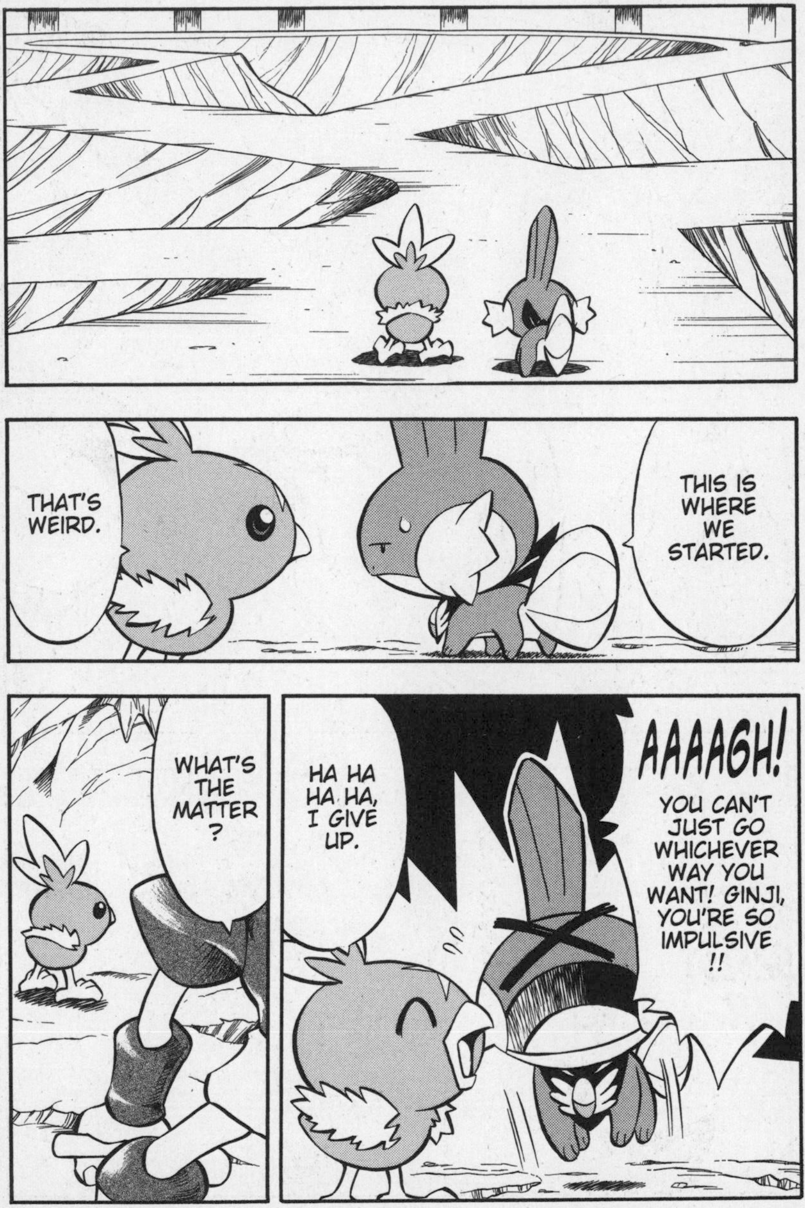
THIS IS WHERE WE STARTED.
THAT'S WEIRD.
AAAAGH!
YOU CAN'T JUST GO WHICHEVER WAY YOU WANT! GINJI, YOU'RE SO IMPULSIVE !!
HA HA HA HA, I GIVE UP.
WHAT'S THE MATTER ?

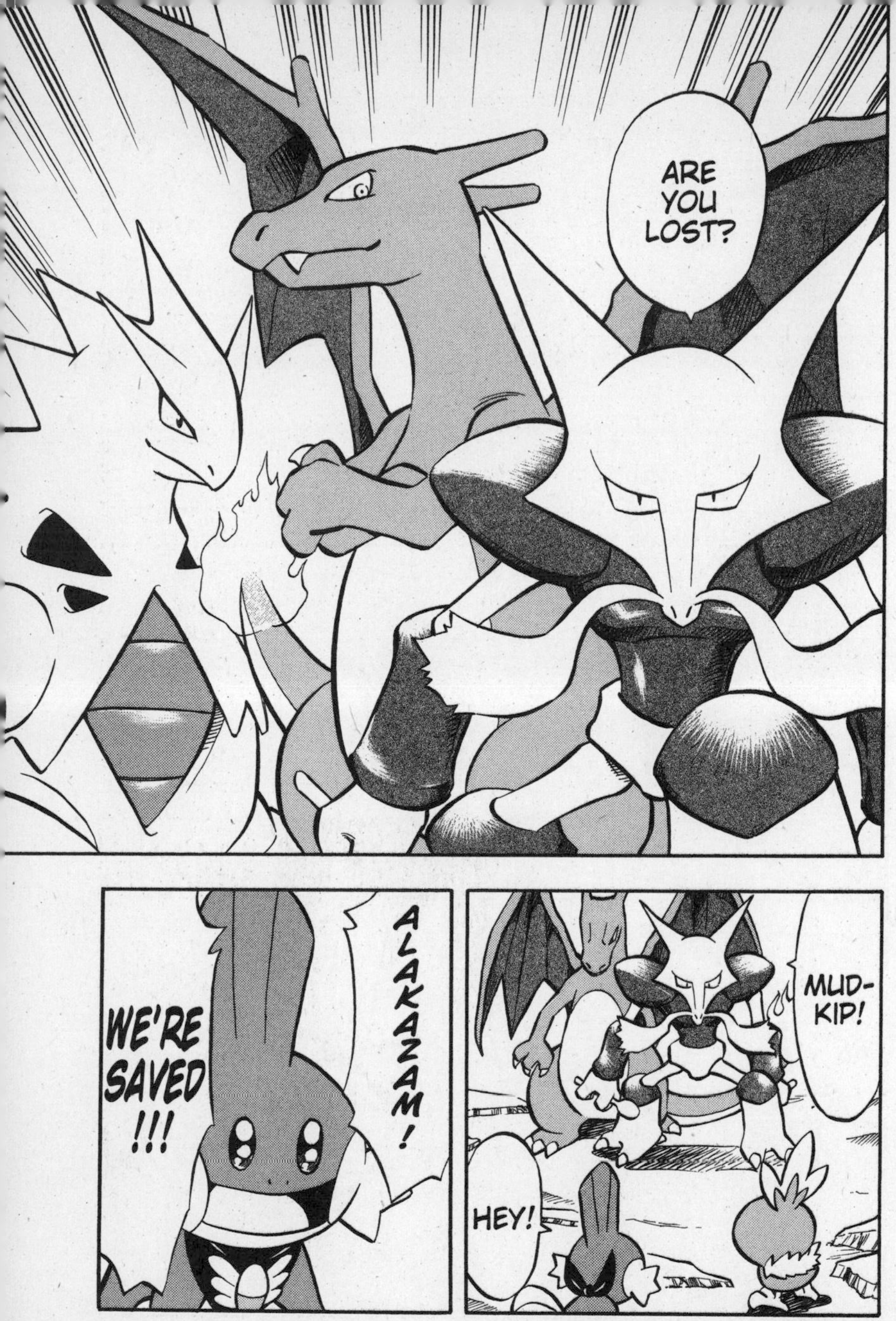
ARE YOU LOST?
MUD-KIP!
HEY!
ALAKAZAM!
WE'RE SAVED!!!

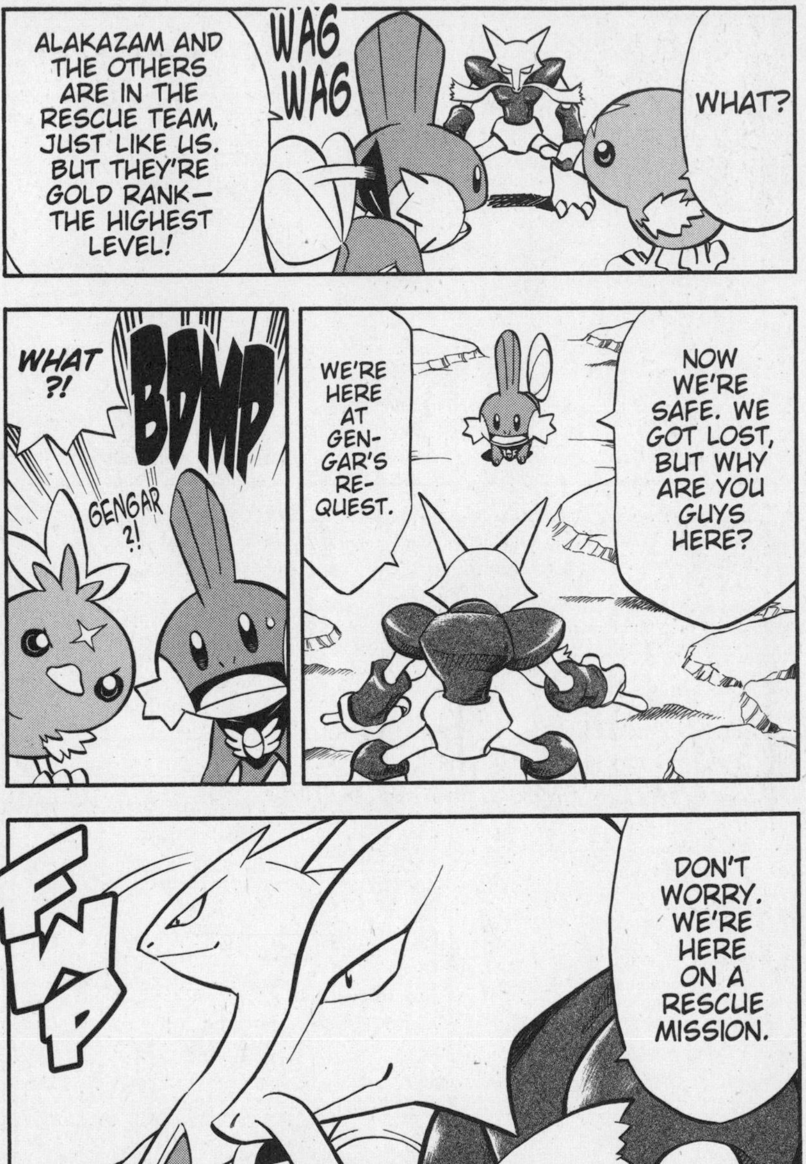
WHAT?
WAG WAG
ALAKAZAM AND THE OTHERS ARE IN THE RESCUE TEAM, JUST LIKE US. BUT THEY'RE GOLD RANK—THE HIGHEST LEVEL!
NOW WE'RE SAFE. WE GOT LOST, BUT WHY ARE YOU GUYS HERE?
WE'RE HERE AT GEN-GAR'S RE-QUEST.
BDMP
WHAT?!
GENGAR?!
DON'T WORRY. WE'RE HERE ON A RESCUE MISSION.
FWAP

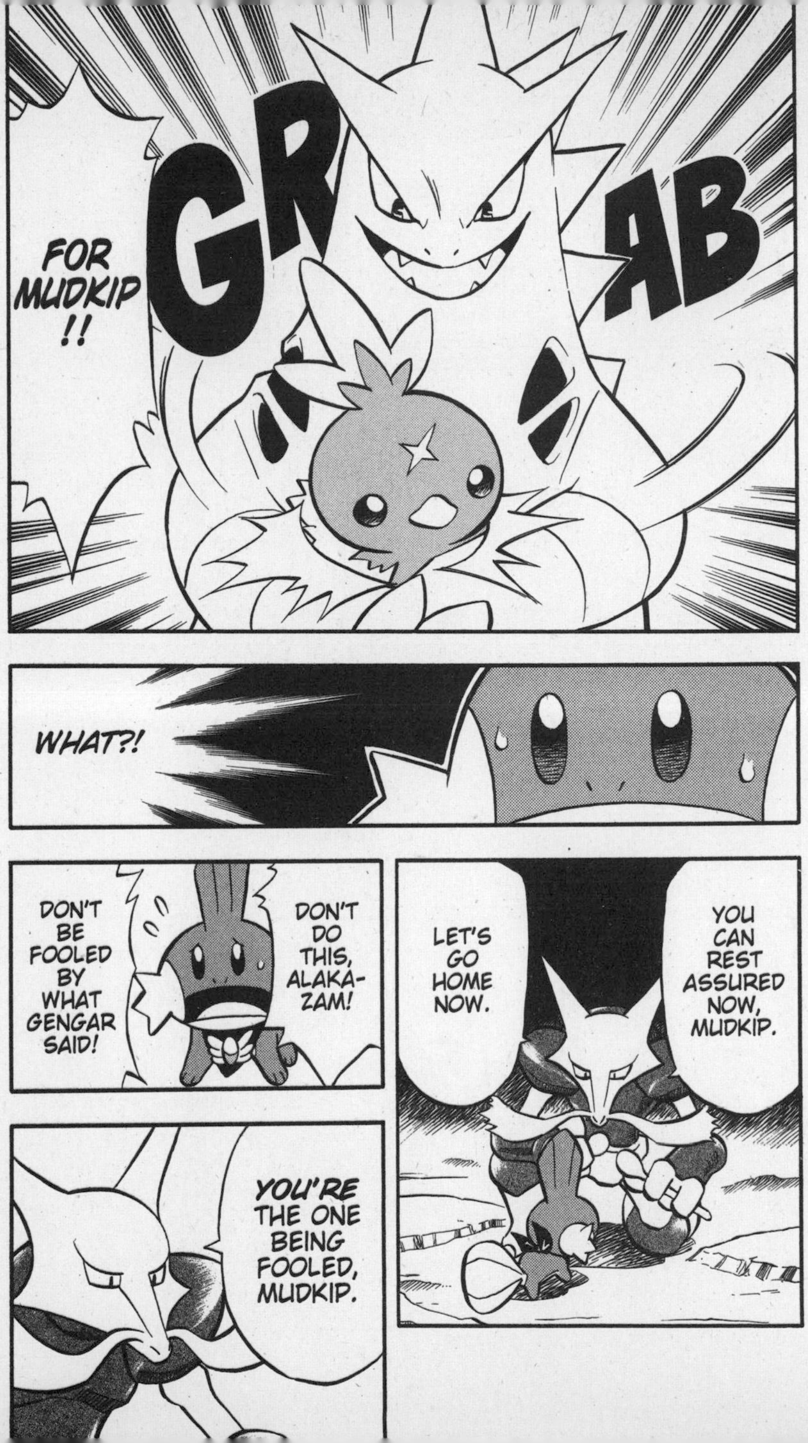
GRAB
FOR MUDKIP!!
WHAT?!
YOU CAN REST ASSURED NOW, MUDKIP.
LET'S GO HOME NOW.
DON'T DO THIS, ALAKAZAM!
DON'T BE FOOLED BY WHAT GENGAR SAID!
YOU'RE THE ONE BEING FOOLED, MUDKIP.

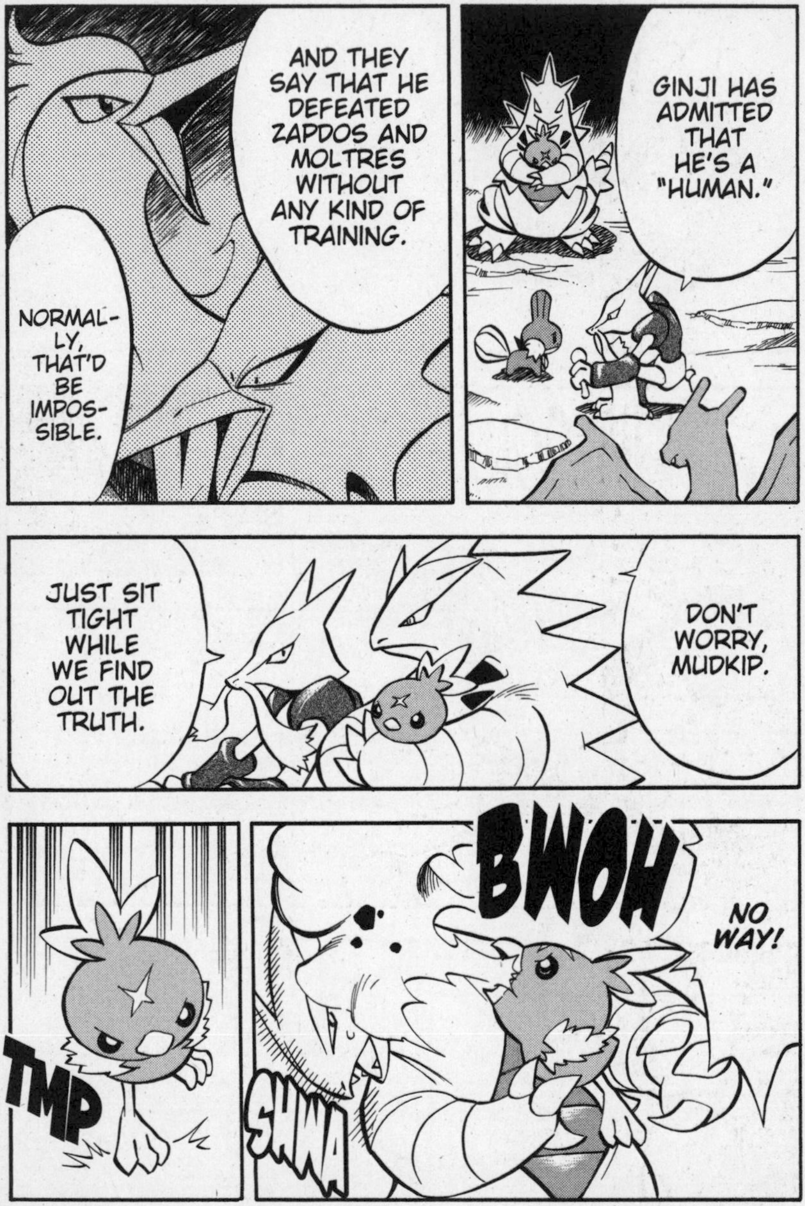
GINJI HAS ADMITTED THAT HE'S A "HUMAN."
AND THEY SAY THAT HE DEFEATED ZAPDOS AND MOLTRES WITHOUT ANY KIND OF TRAINING.
NORMALLY, THAT'D BE IMPOSSIBLE.
DON'T WORRY, MUDKIP.
JUST SIT TIGHT WHILE WE FIND OUT THE TRUTH.
BWOH
NO WAY!
SHWA
TMP

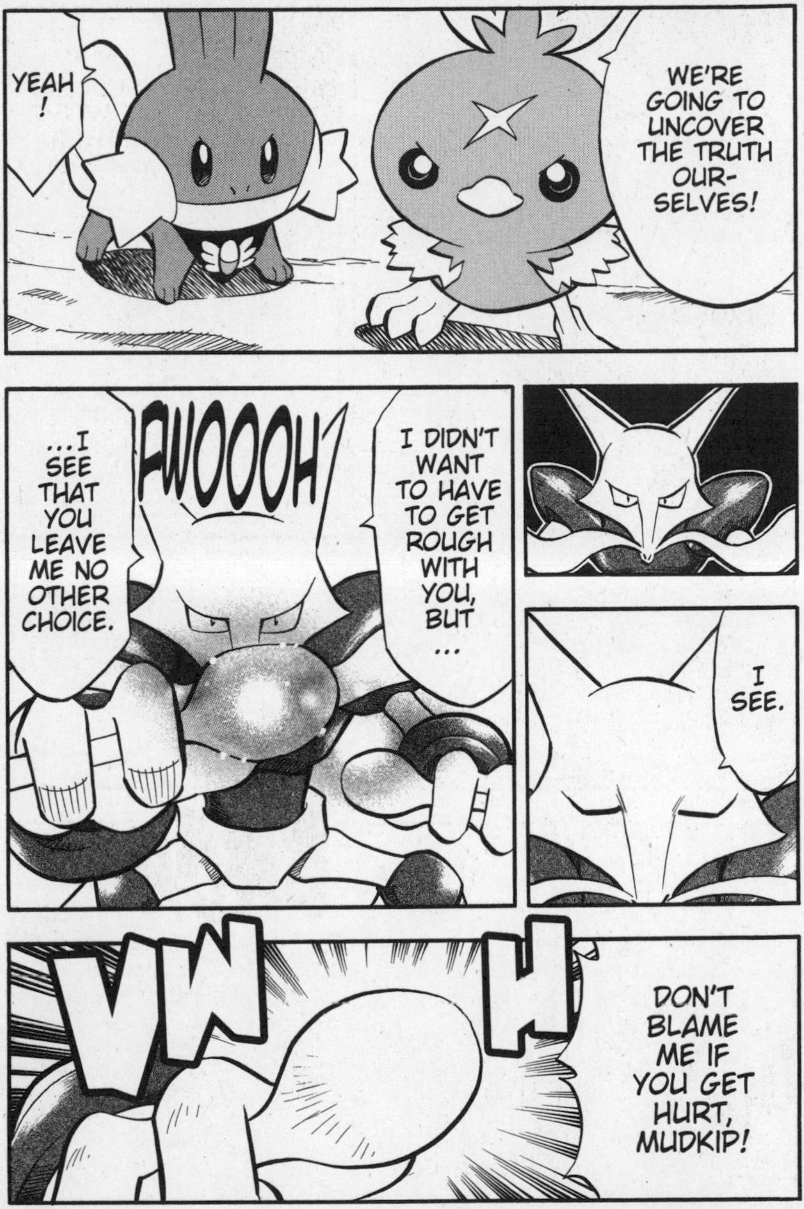

WE'RE GOING TO UNCOVER THE TRUTH OUR-SELVES!
YEAH!
I SEE.
I DIDN'T WANT TO HAVE TO GET ROUGH WITH YOU, BUT ...
FWOOOH
...I SEE THAT YOU LEAVE ME NO OTHER CHOICE.
DON'T BLAME ME IF YOU GET HURT, MUDKIP!
VW H

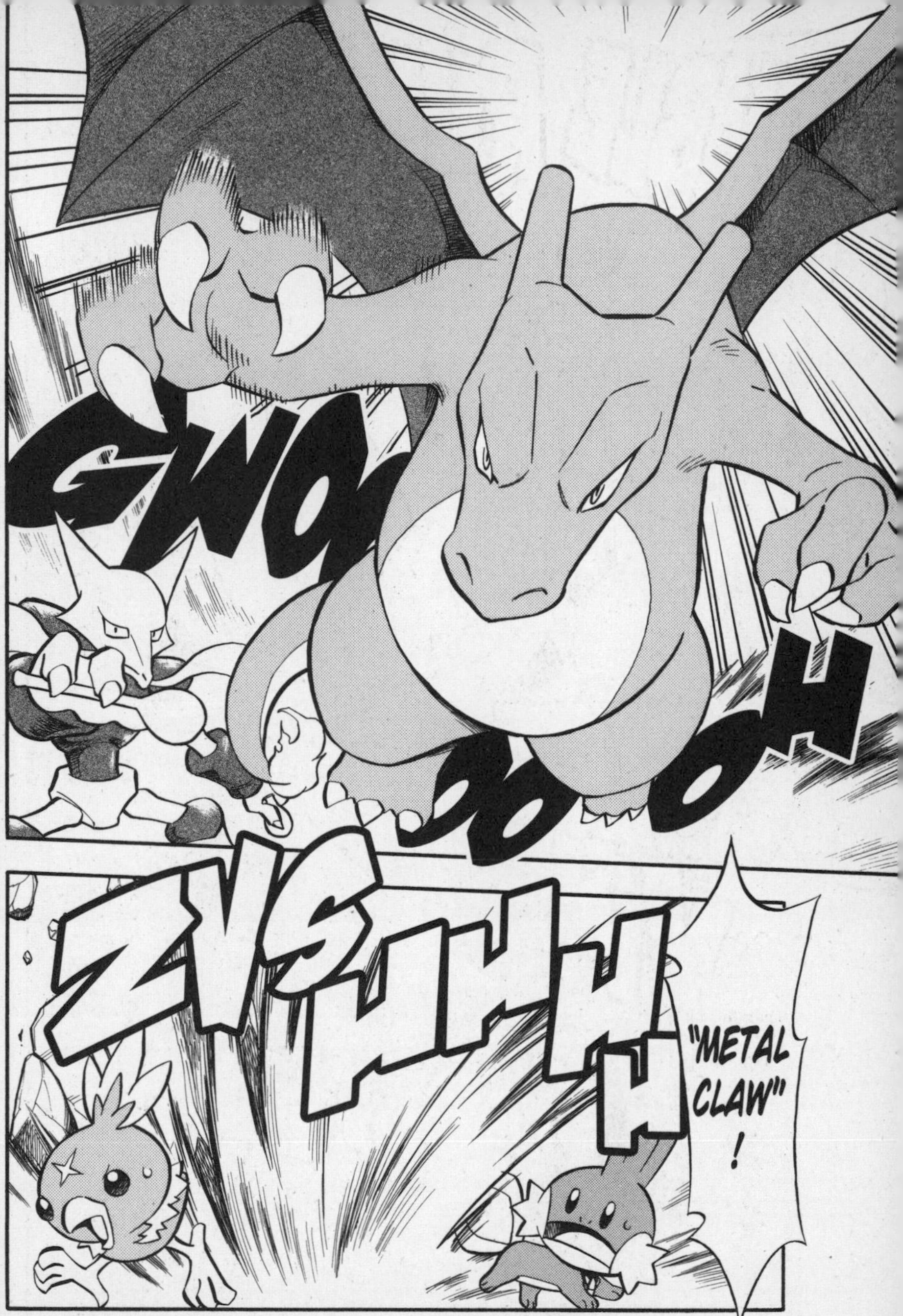
GWOOOOH
"METAL CLAW"!
ZVSHHHH

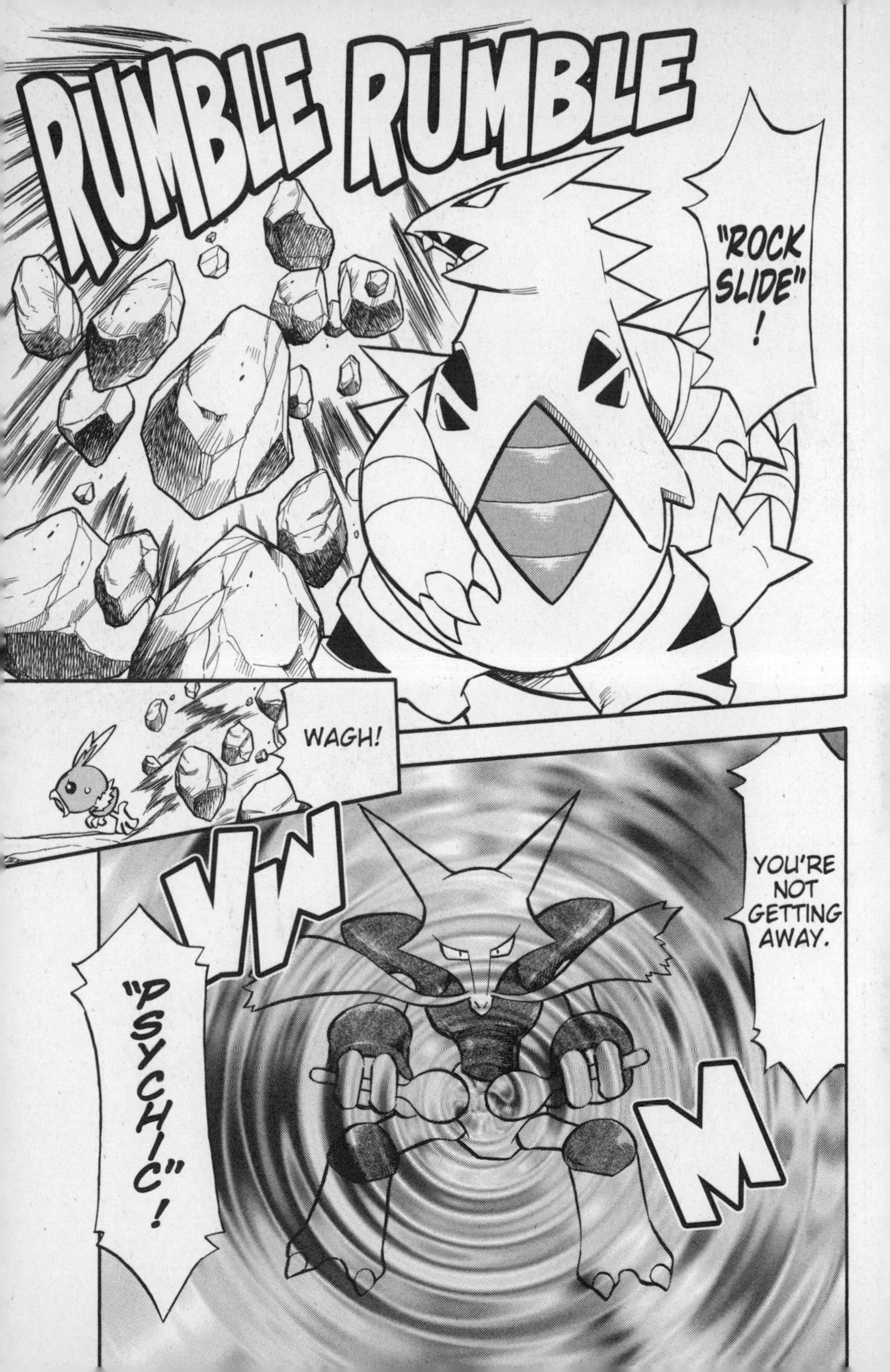
RUMBLE RUMBLE
"ROCK SLIDE"!
WAGH!
YOU'RE NOT GETTING AWAY.
VWM
"PSYCHIC"!

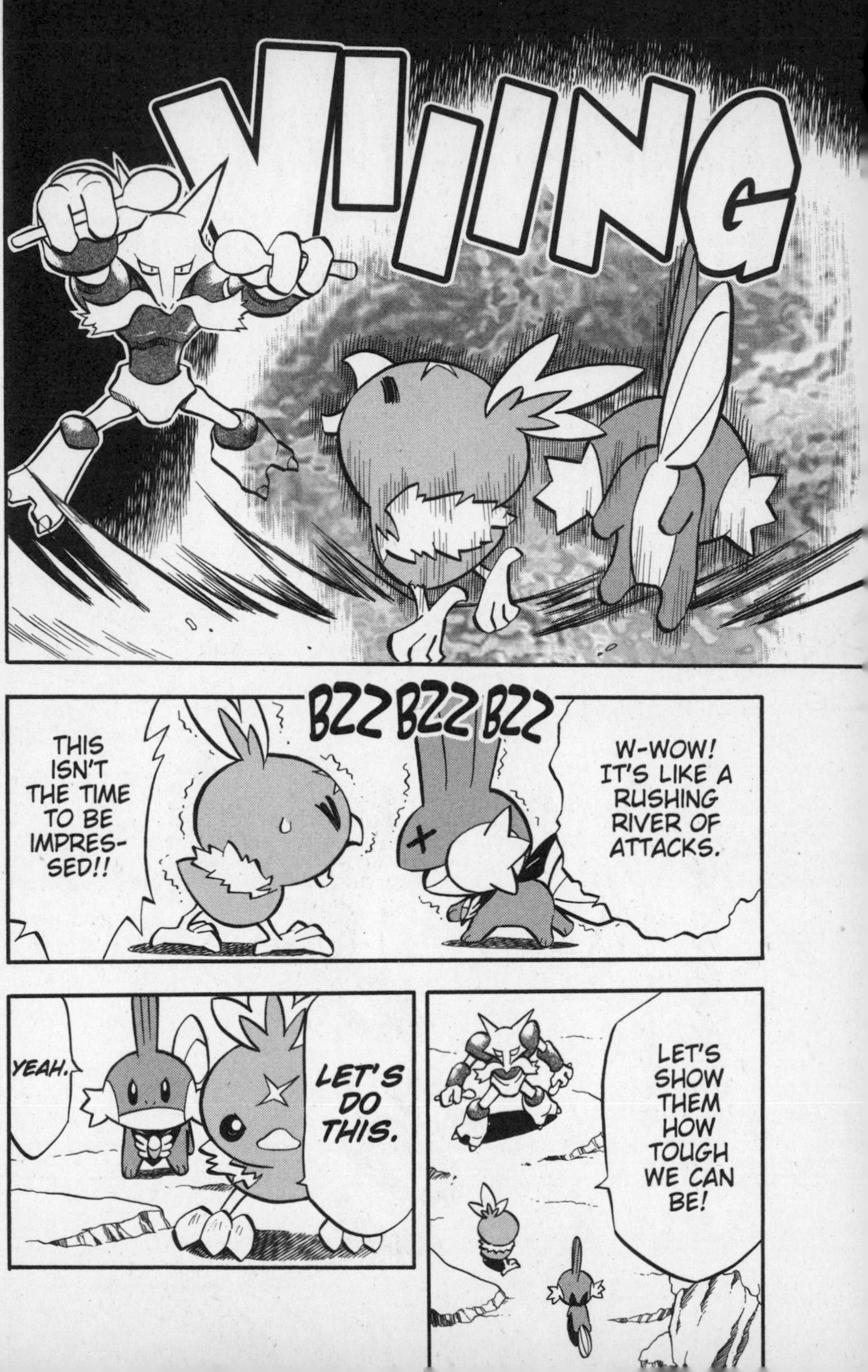
VIIING
W-WOW! IT'S LIKE A RUSHING RIVER OF ATTACKS.
BZZ BZZ BZZ
THIS ISN'T THE TIME TO BE IMPRES-SED!!
LET'S SHOW THEM HOW TOUGH WE CAN BE!
LET'S DO THIS.
YEAH.

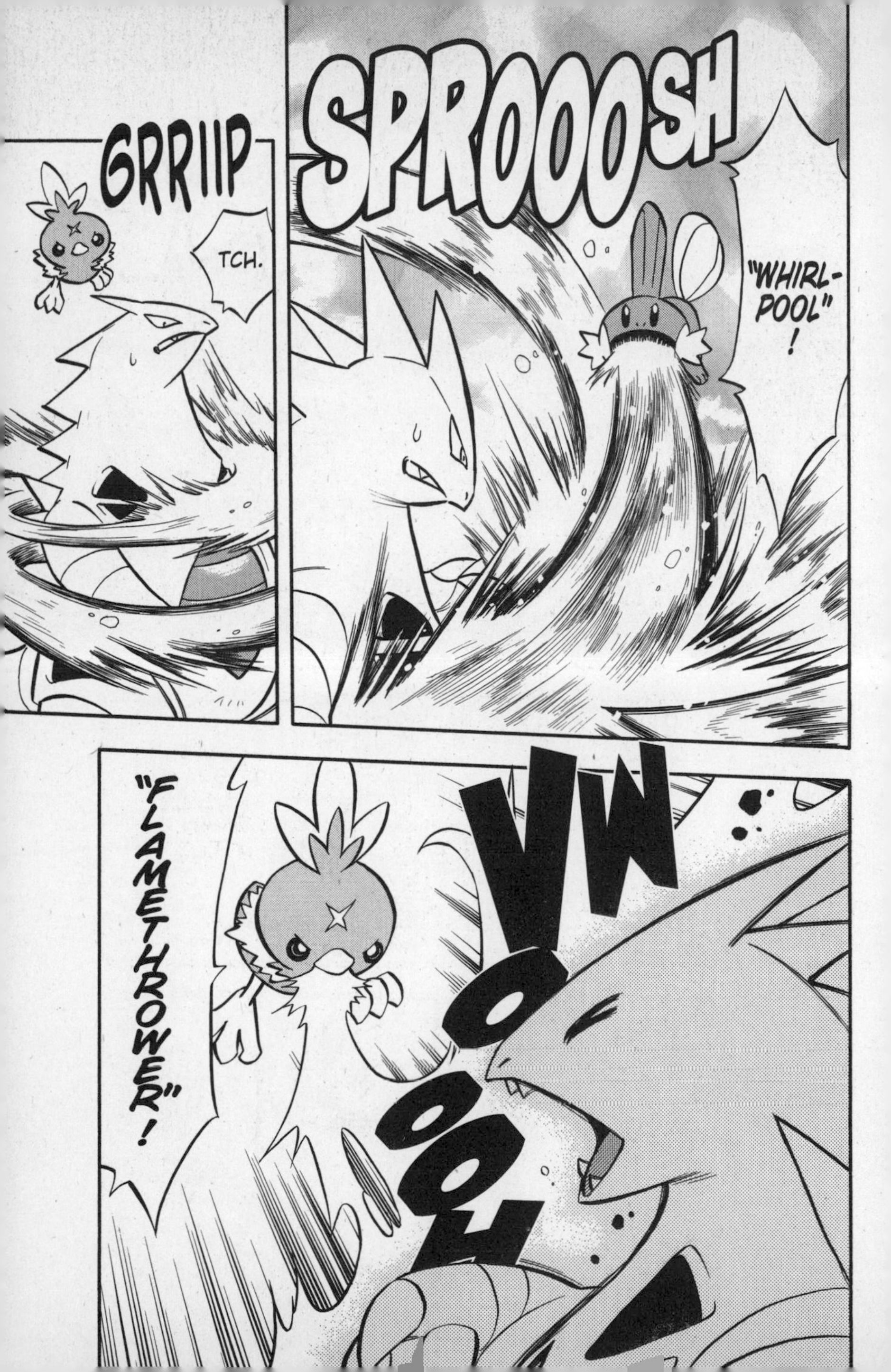
SPROOOSH
"WHIRL-POOL"!
GRRIIP
TCH.
VWOOOSH
"FLAMETHROWER"!

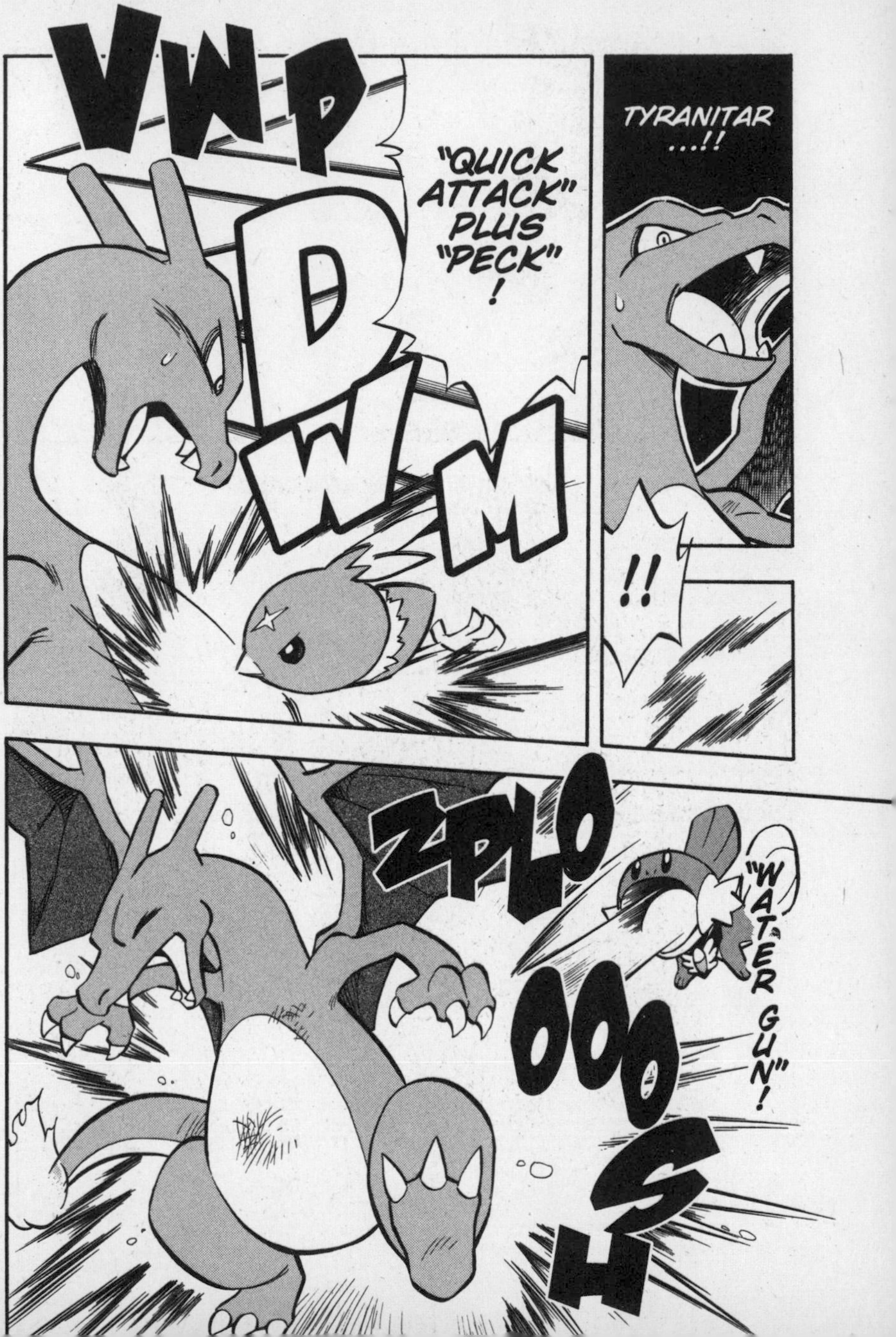
TYRANITAR ...!!
!!
VWP
DWM
"QUICK ATTACK" PLUS "PECK"!
"WATER GUN"!
ZPLOOOOSH

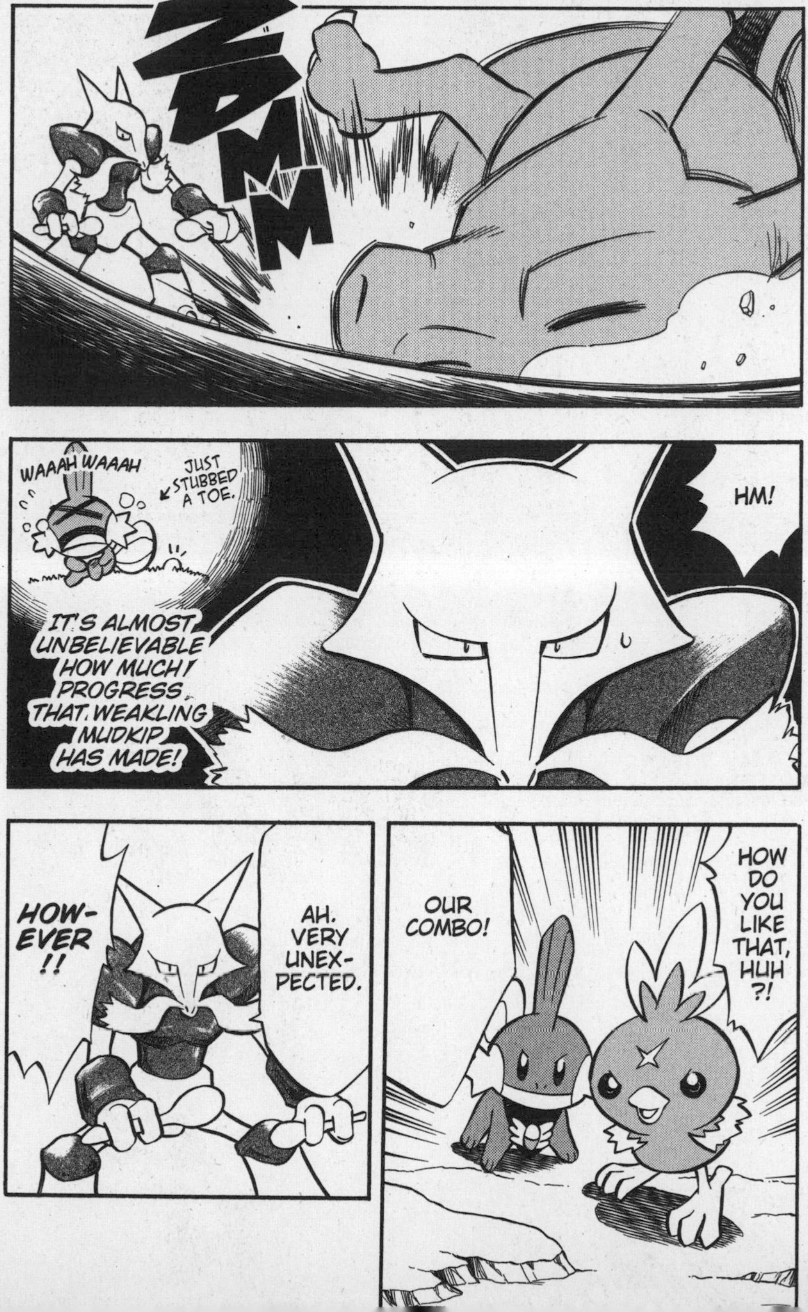
ZDMMM
HM!
JUST STUBBED A TOE.
WAAAH WAAAH
IT'S ALMOST UNBELIEVABLE HOW MUCH PROGRESS THAT WEAKLING MUDKIP HAS MADE!
HOW DO YOU LIKE THAT, HUH?!
OUR COMBO!
AH. VERY UNEXPECTED.
HOW-EVER!!

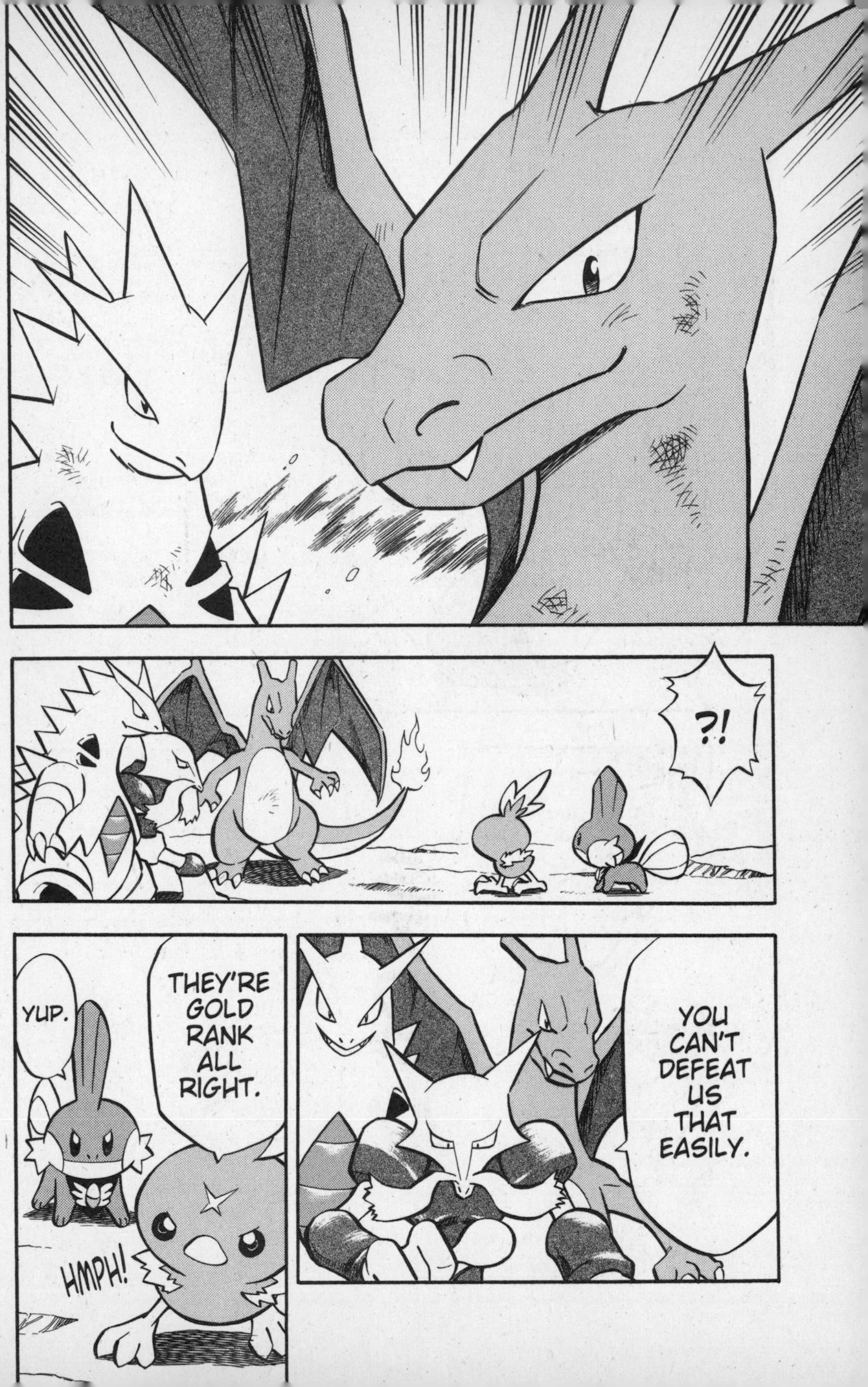
?!
YOU CAN'T DEFEAT US THAT EASILY.
THEY'RE GOLD RANK ALL RIGHT.
YUP.
HMPH!

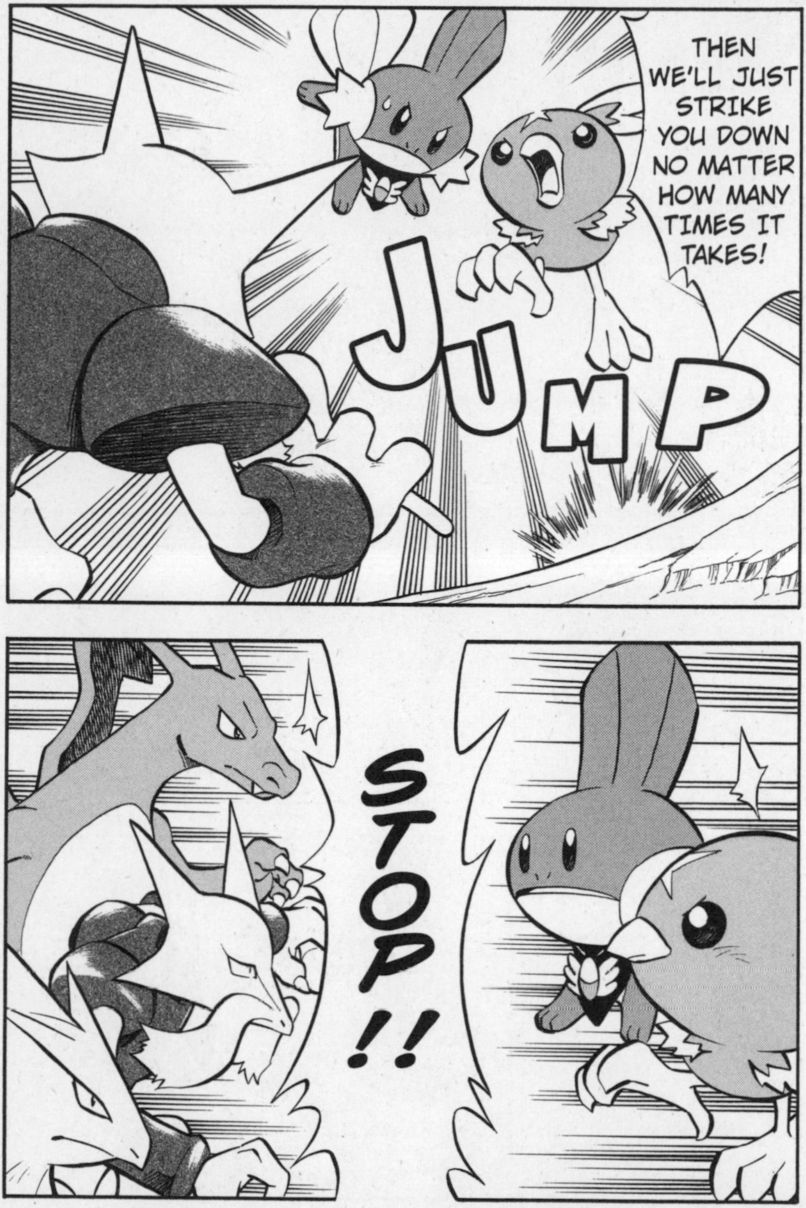
THEN WE'LL JUST STRIKE YOU DOWN NO MATTER HOW MANY TIMES IT TAKES!
JUMP
STOP!!

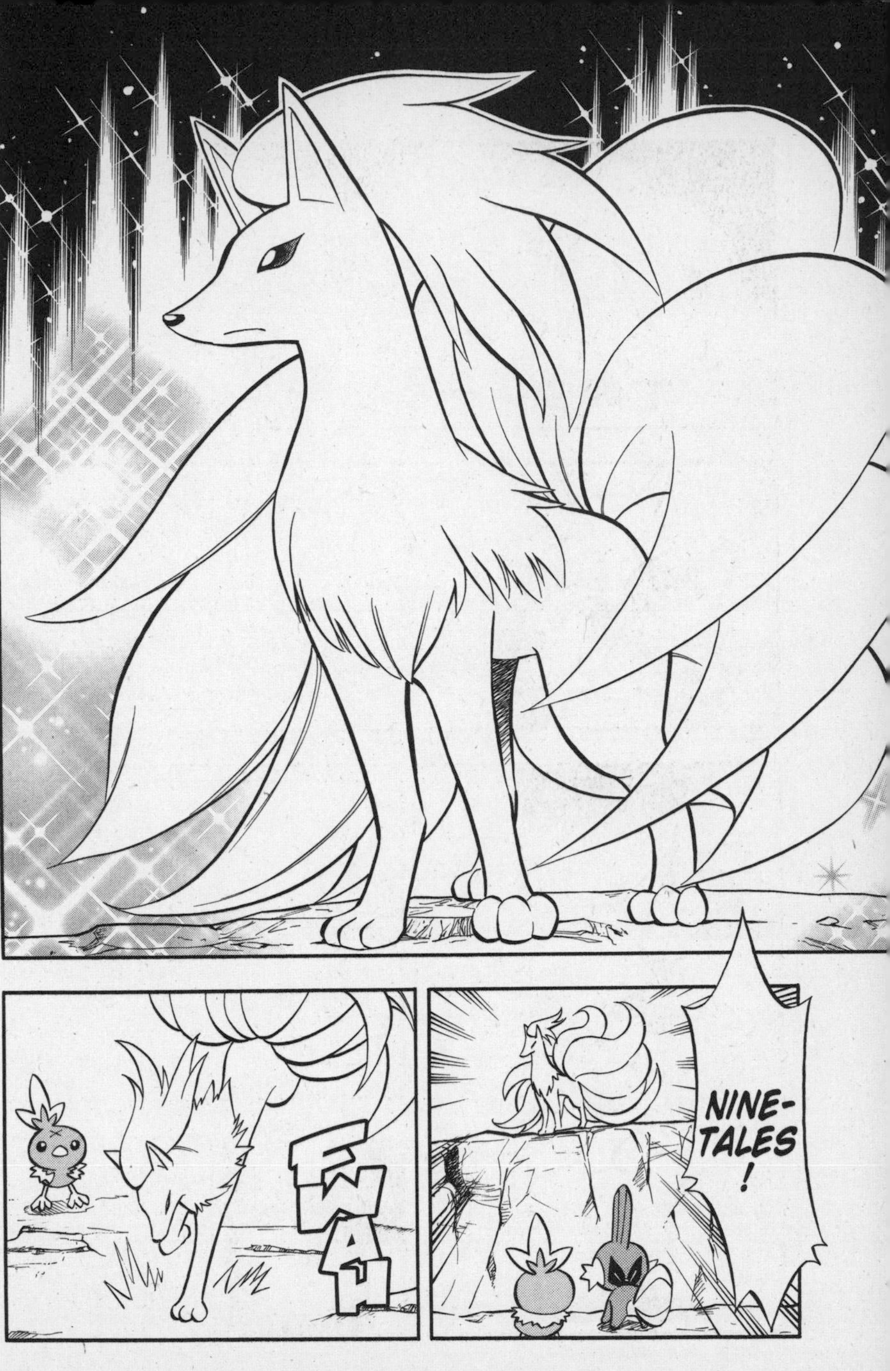
NINE-TALES!
FWAH

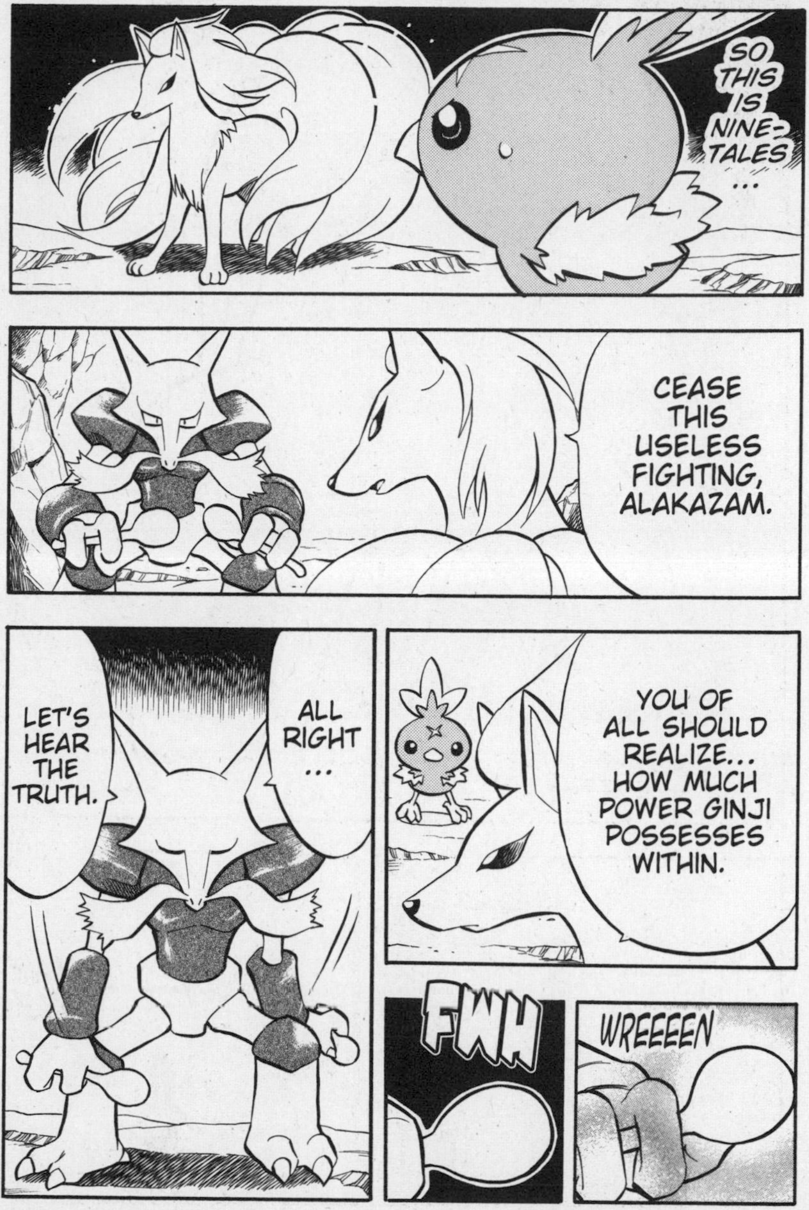
SO THIS IS NINE-TALES...
CEASE THIS USELESS FIGHTING, ALAKAZAM.
YOU OF ALL SHOULD REALIZE... HOW MUCH POWER GINJI POSSESSES WITHIN.
WREEEEN
FWH
ALL RIGHT...
LET'S HEAR THE TRUTH.

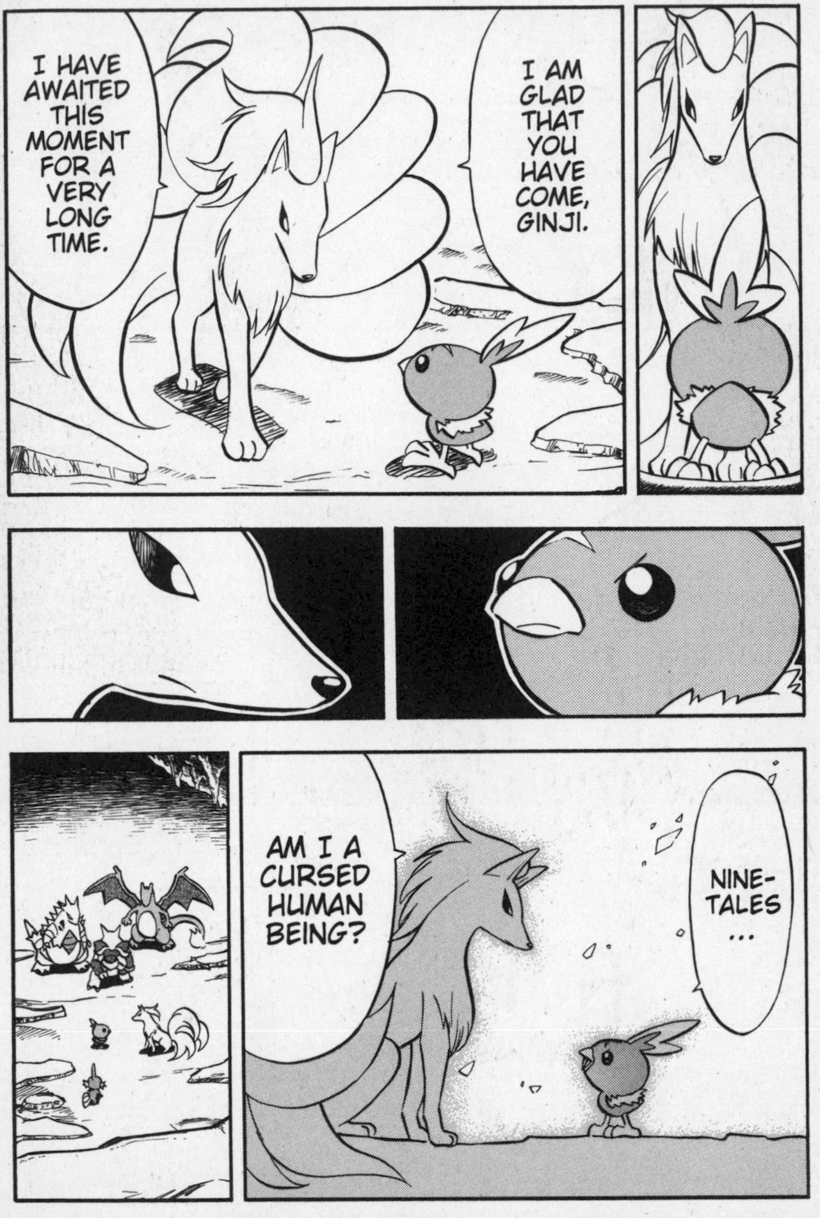
I AM GLAD THAT YOU HAVE COME, GINJI.
I HAVE AWAITED THIS MOMENT FOR A VERY LONG TIME.
NINE-TALES...
AM I A CURSED HUMAN BEING?

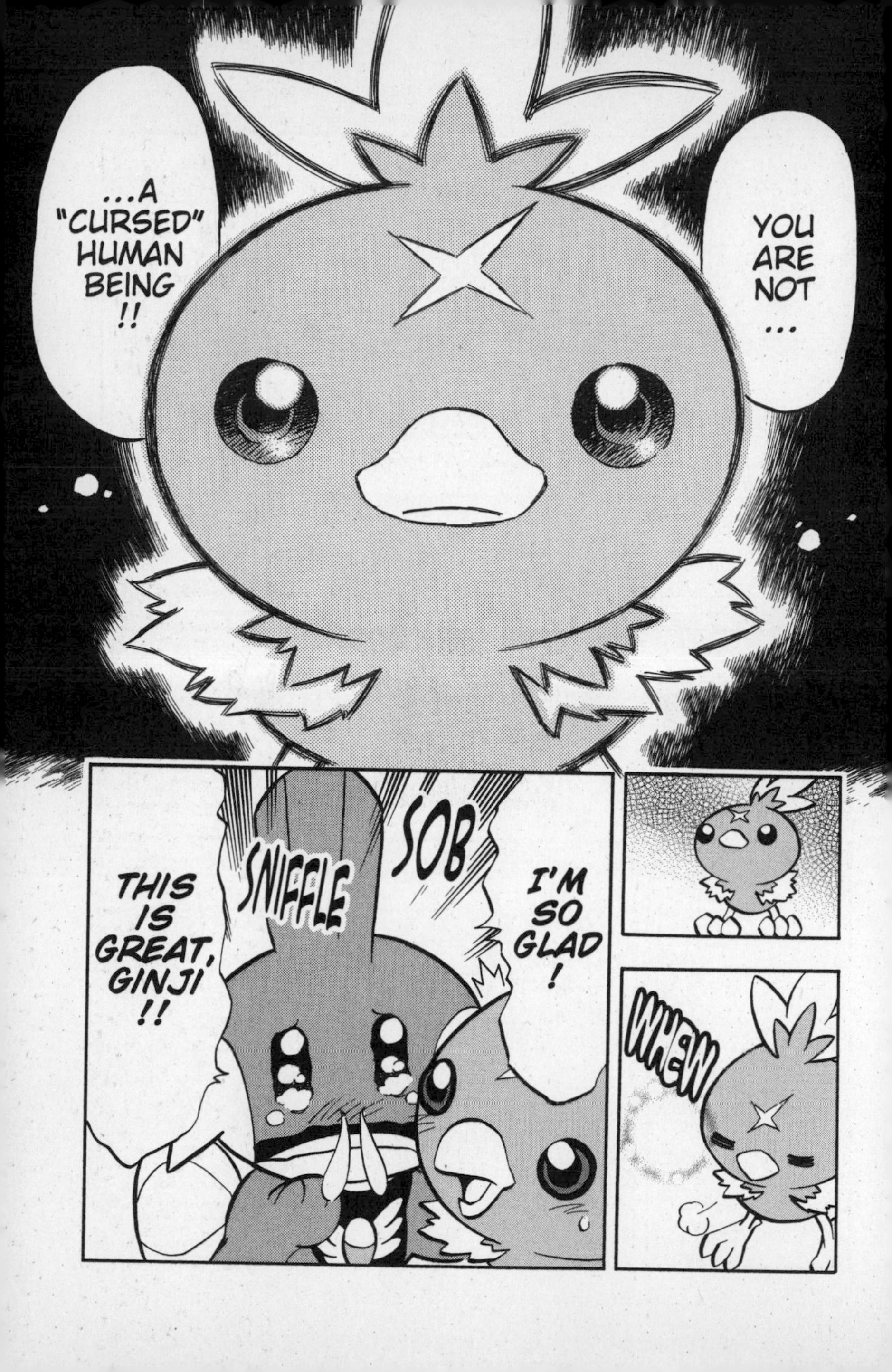
YOU ARE NOT ...
...A "CURSED" HUMAN BEING !!
WHEW
SOB
I'M SO GLAD !
SNIFFLE
THIS IS GREAT, GINJI !!

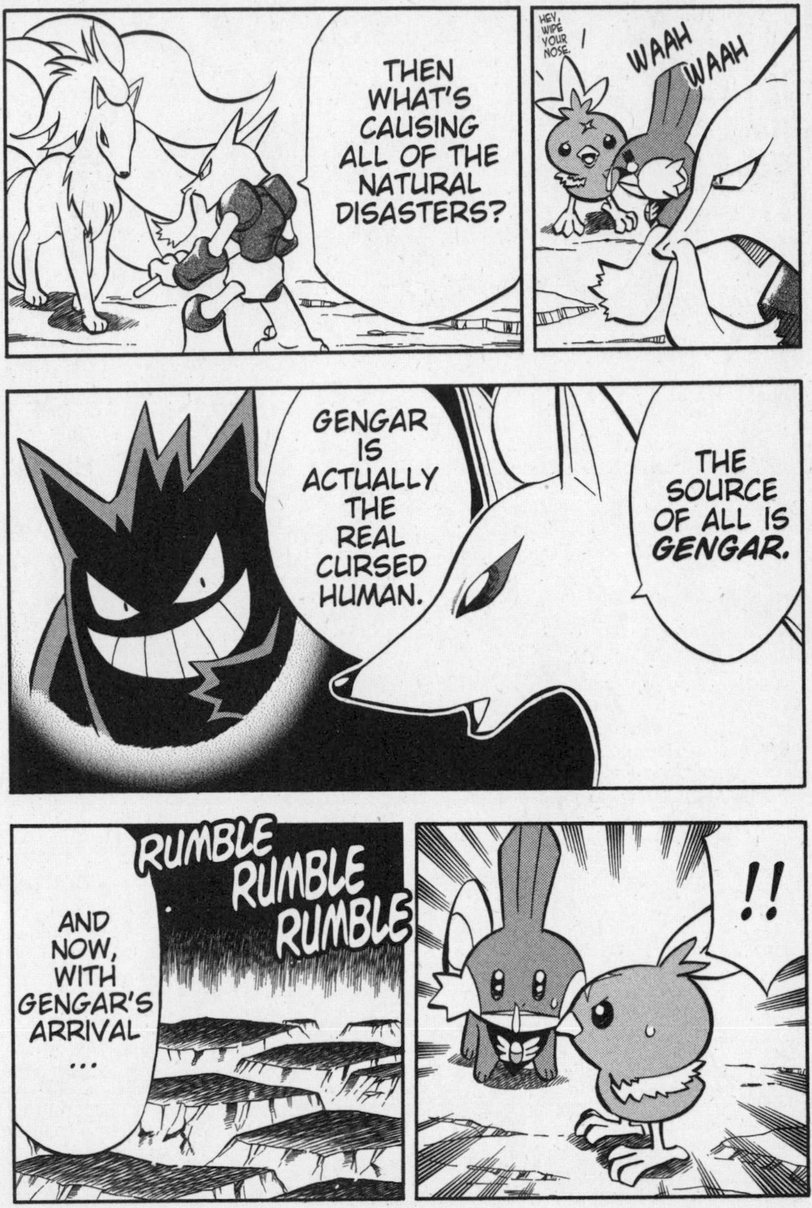
HEY, WIPE YOUR NOSE.
WAAH WAAH
THEN WHAT'S CAUSING ALL OF THE NATURAL DISASTERS?
THE SOURCE OF ALL IS GENGAR.
GENGAR IS ACTUALLY THE REAL CURSED HUMAN.
!!
RUMBLE RUMBLE RUMBLE
AND NOW, WITH GENGAR'S ARRIVAL ...

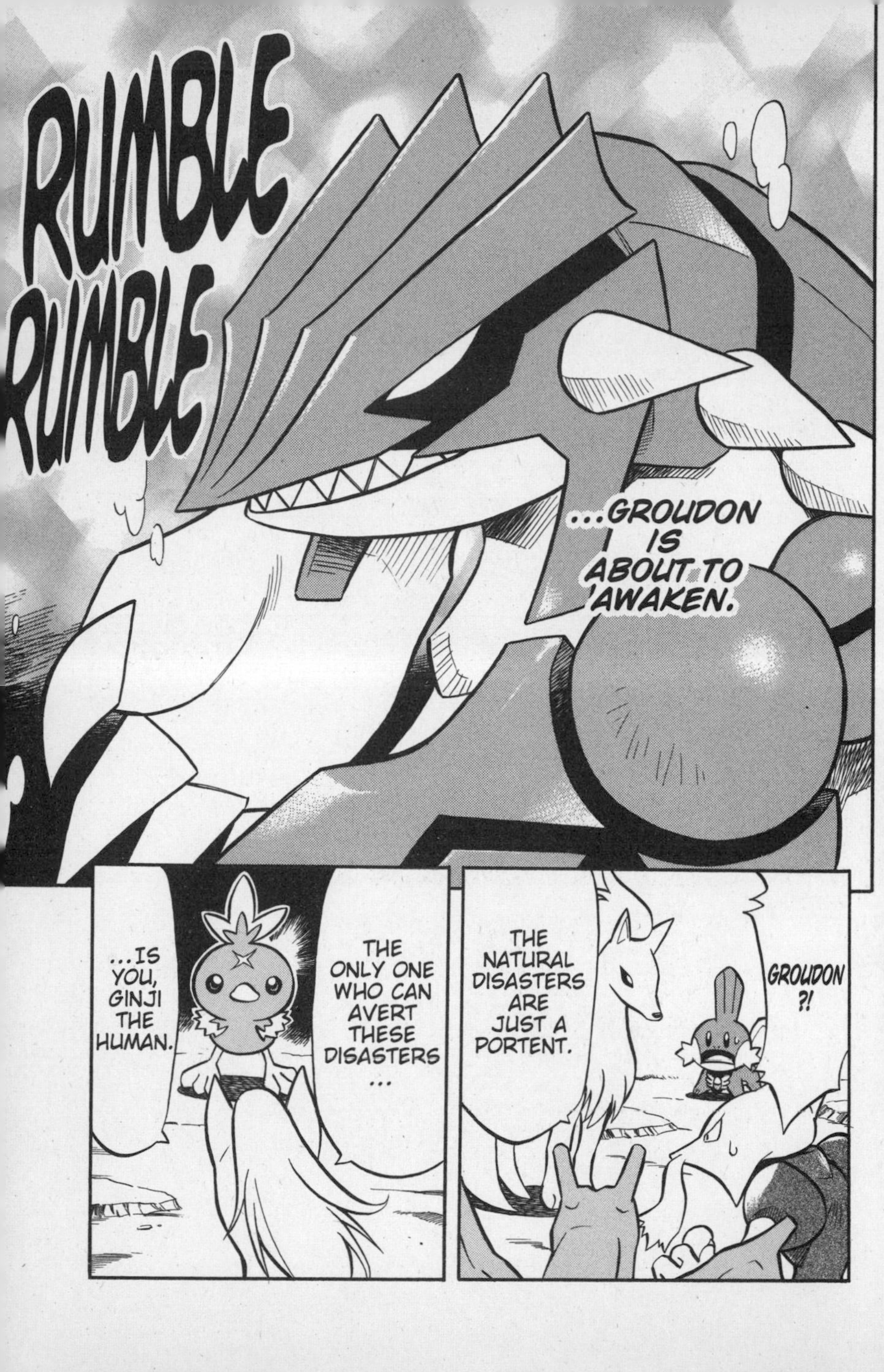
RUMBLE RUMBLE
...GROUDON IS ABOUT TO AWAKEN.
GROUDON?!
THE NATURAL DISASTERS ARE JUST A PORTENT.
THE ONLY ONE WHO CAN AVERT THESE DISASTERS...
...IS YOU, GINJI THE HUMAN.

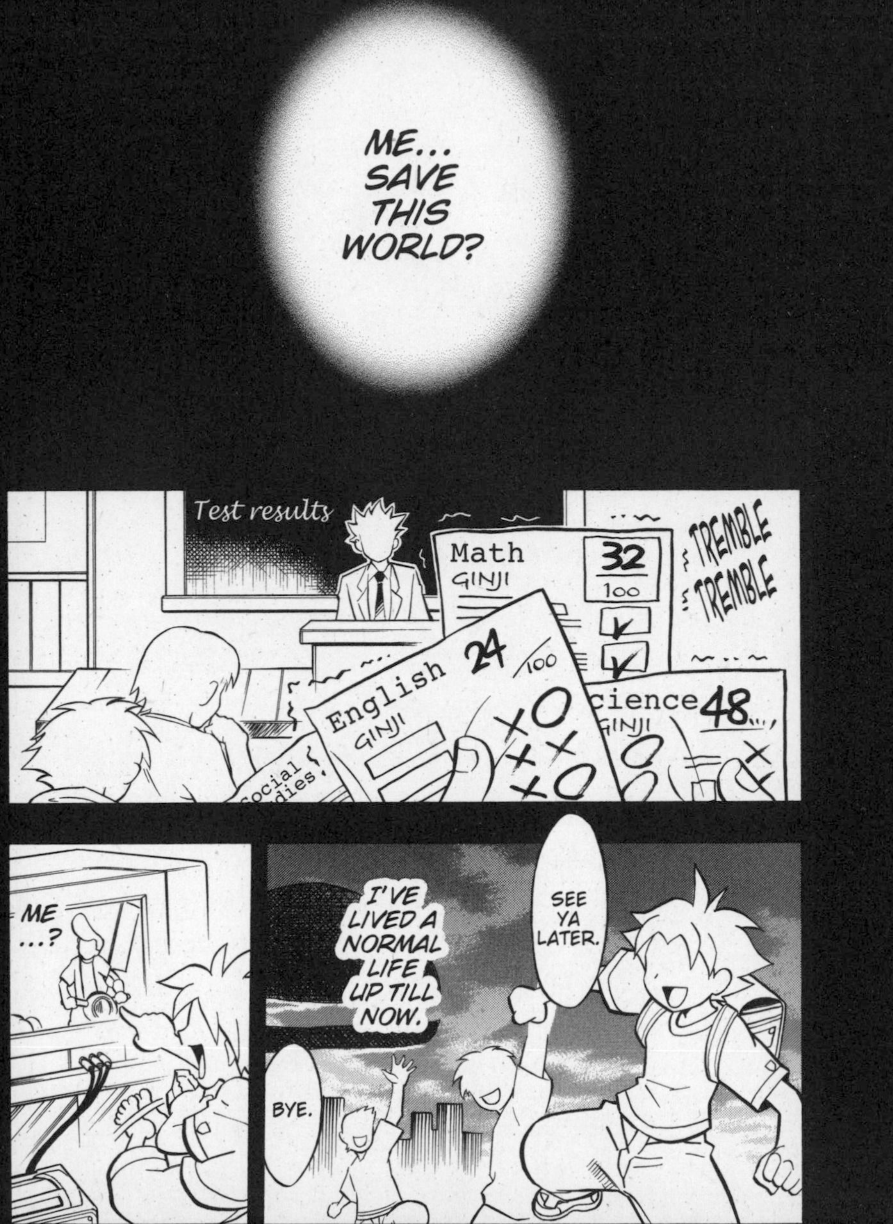
ME... SAVE THIS WORLD?
Test results
TREMBLE TREMBLE
Math GINJI 32 100
English GINJI 24 100
48
SEE YA LATER.
I'VE LIVED A NORMAL LIFE UP TILL NOW.
BYE.
ME ...?

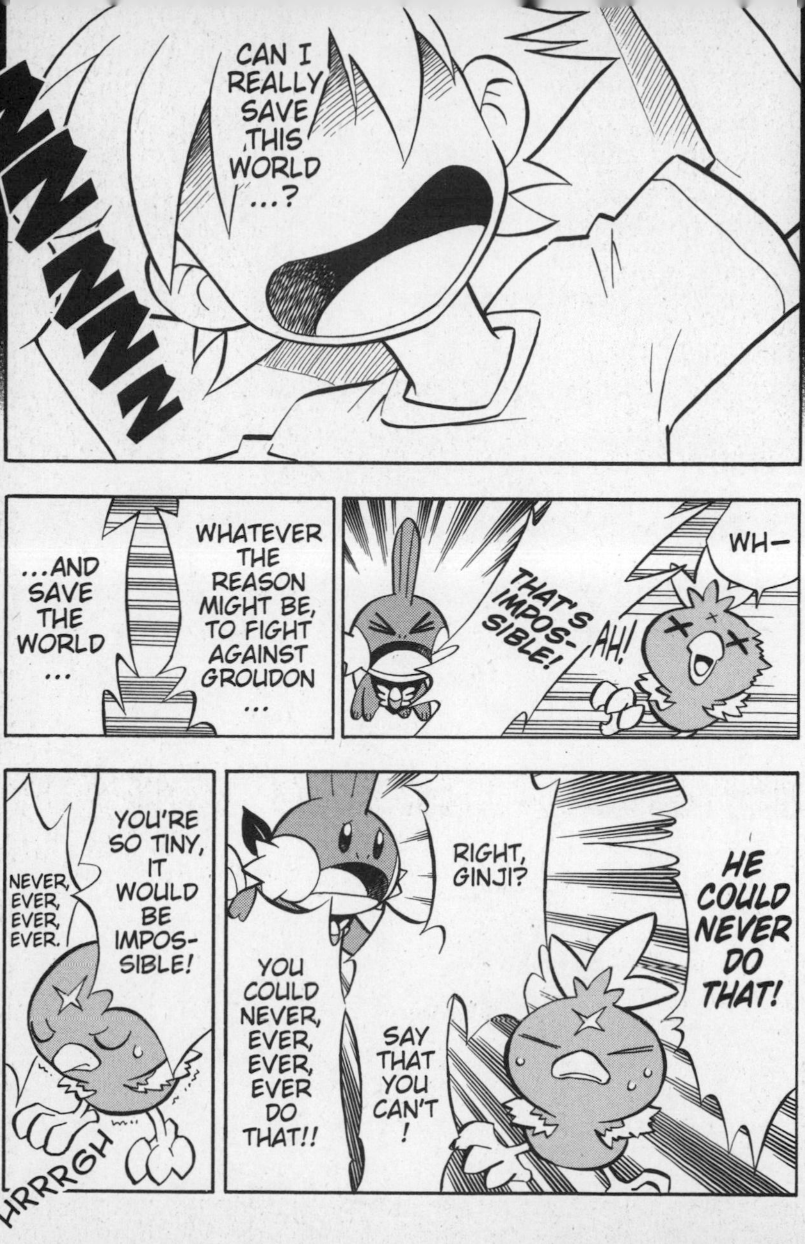
CAN I REALLY SAVE THIS WORLD ...?
NNNNNN
WH—
AH!
THAT'S IMPOS-SIBLE!
WHATEVER THE REASON MIGHT BE, TO FIGHT AGAINST GROUDON ...
...AND SAVE THE WORLD ...
HE COULD NEVER DO THAT!
RIGHT, GINJI?
SAY THAT YOU CAN'T!
YOU COULD NEVER, EVER, EVER, EVER DO THAT!!
YOU'RE SO TINY, IT WOULD BE IMPOS-SIBLE!
NEVER, EVER, EVER, EVER.
HRRRGH

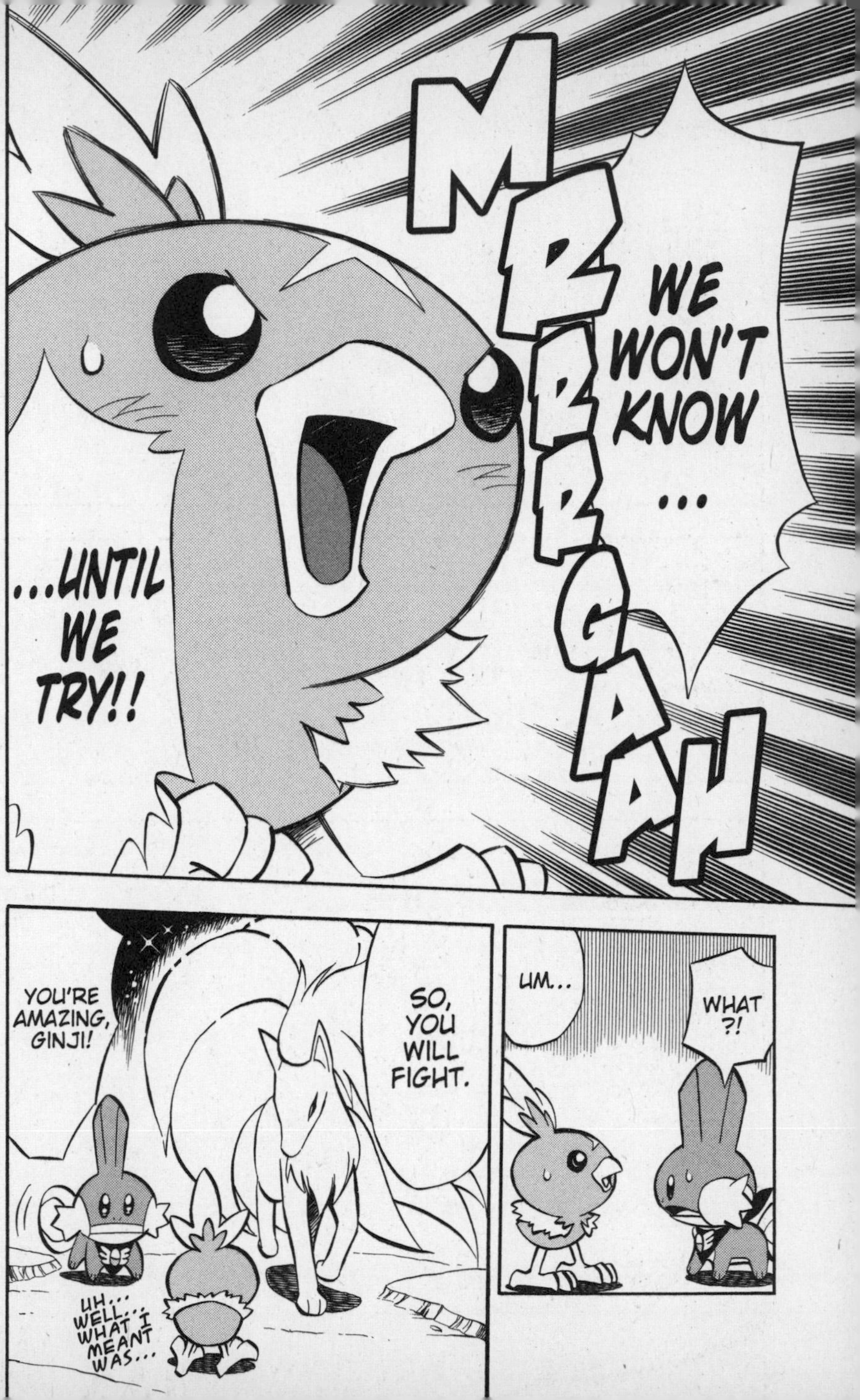
MRRRGAAH
WE WON'T KNOW ...
...UNTIL WE TRY!!
WHAT?!
UM...
SO, YOU WILL FIGHT.
YOU'RE AMAZING, GINJI!
UH... WELL... WHAT I MEANT WAS...

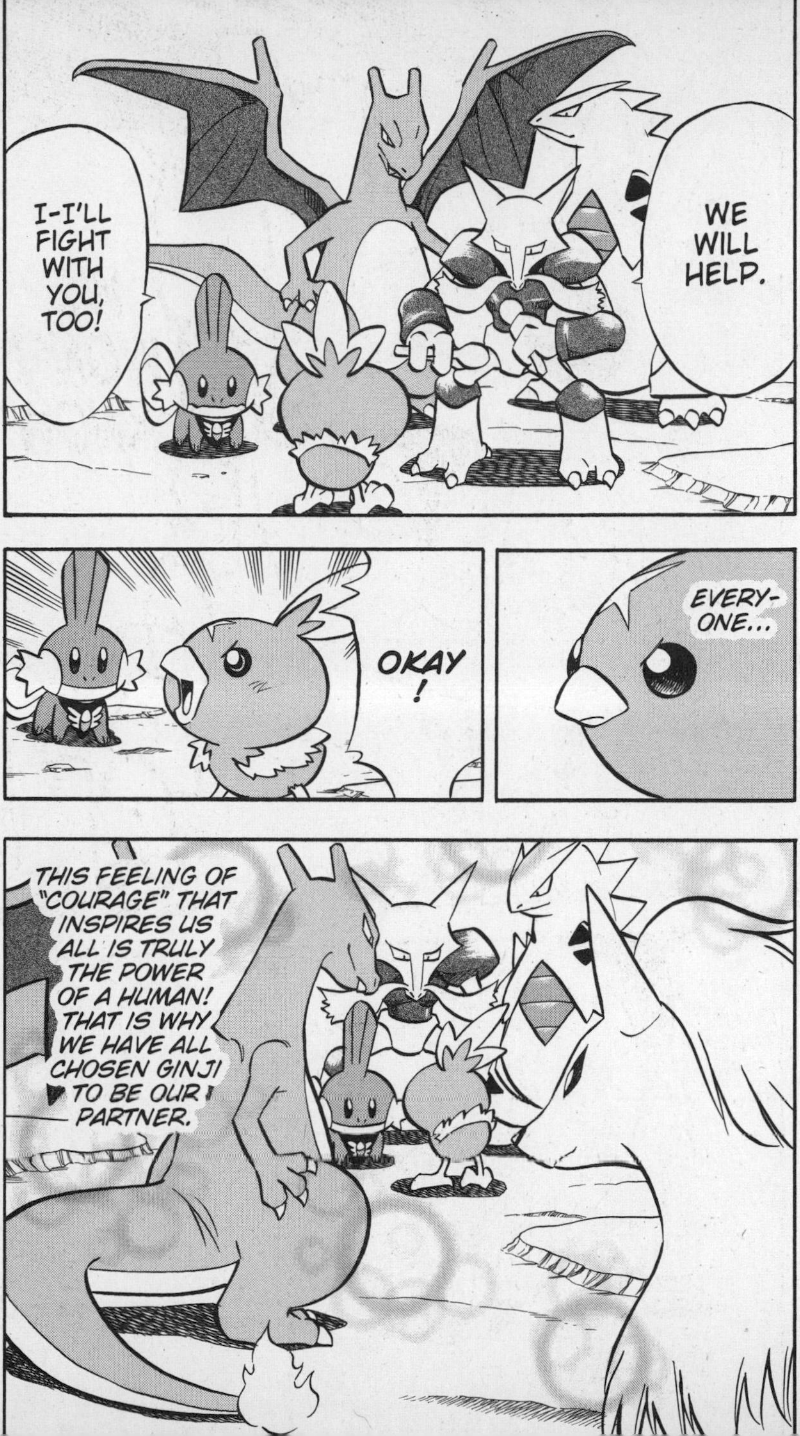
WE WILL HELP.
I-I'LL FIGHT WITH YOU, TOO!
EVERY-ONE...
OKAY!
THIS FEELING OF "COURAGE" THAT INSPIRES US ALL IS TRULY THE POWER OF A HUMAN! THAT IS WHY WE HAVE ALL CHOSEN GINJI TO BE OUR PARTNER.

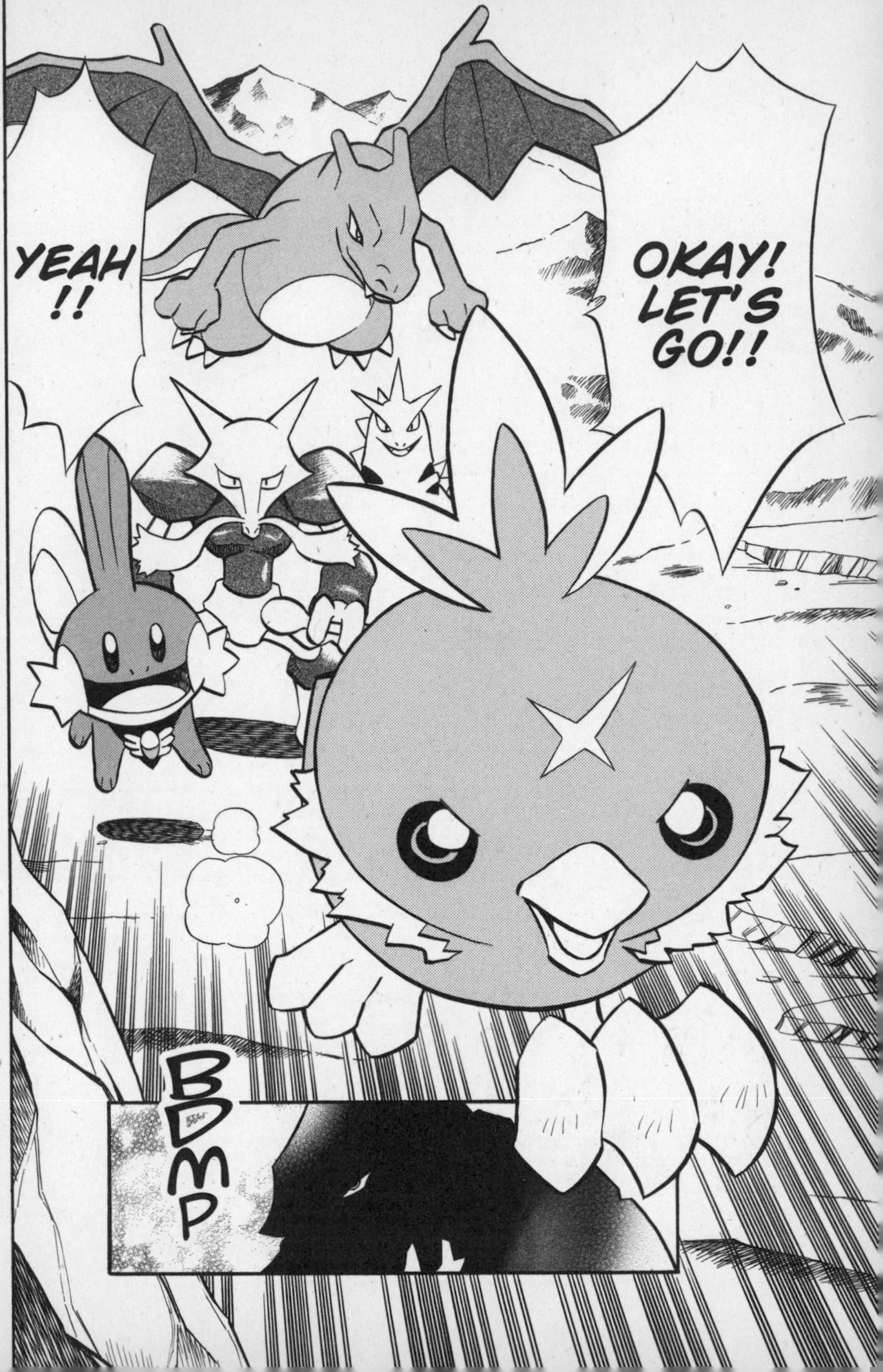
OKAY! LET'S GO!!
YEAH!!
BDMP

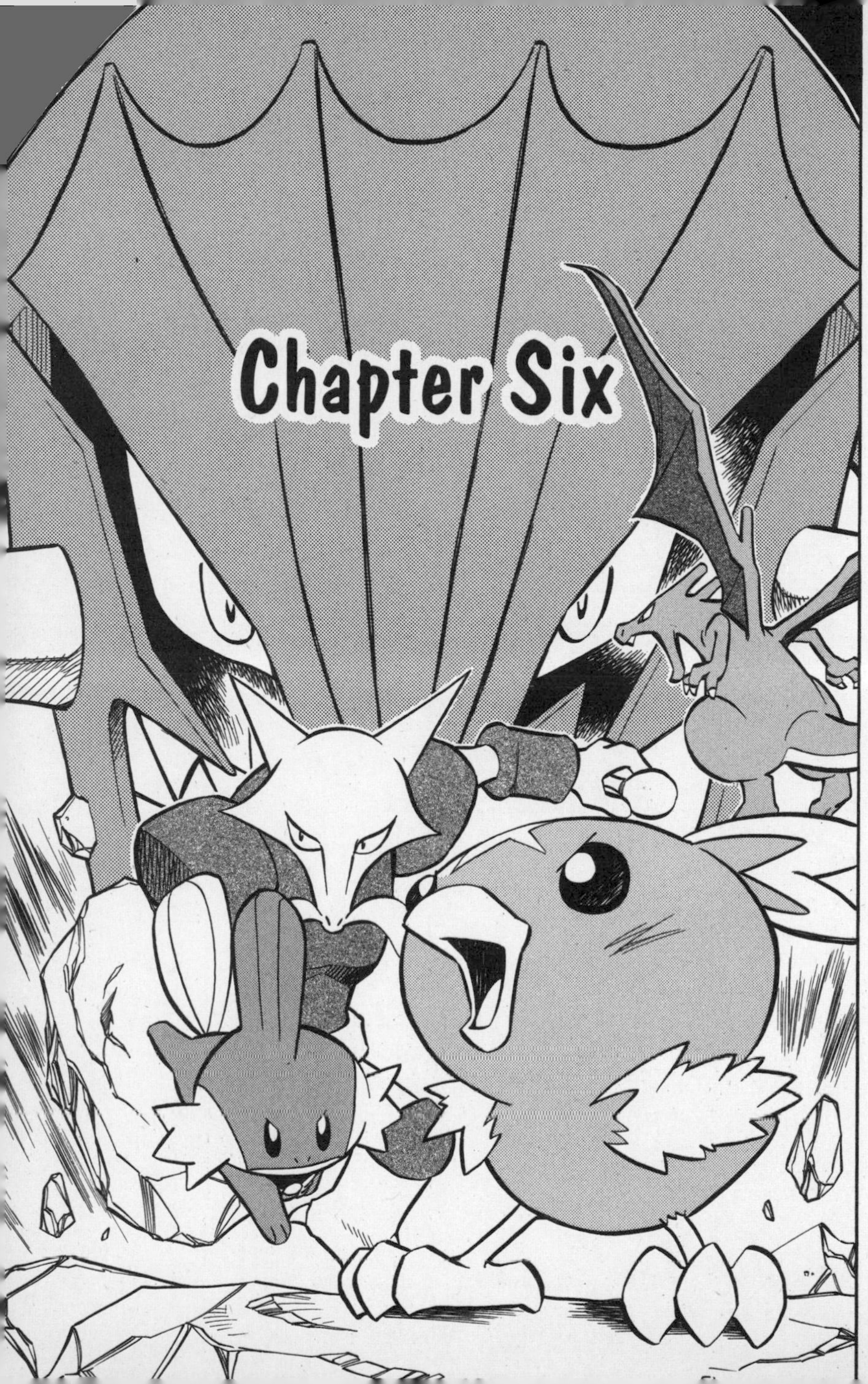
Chapter Six

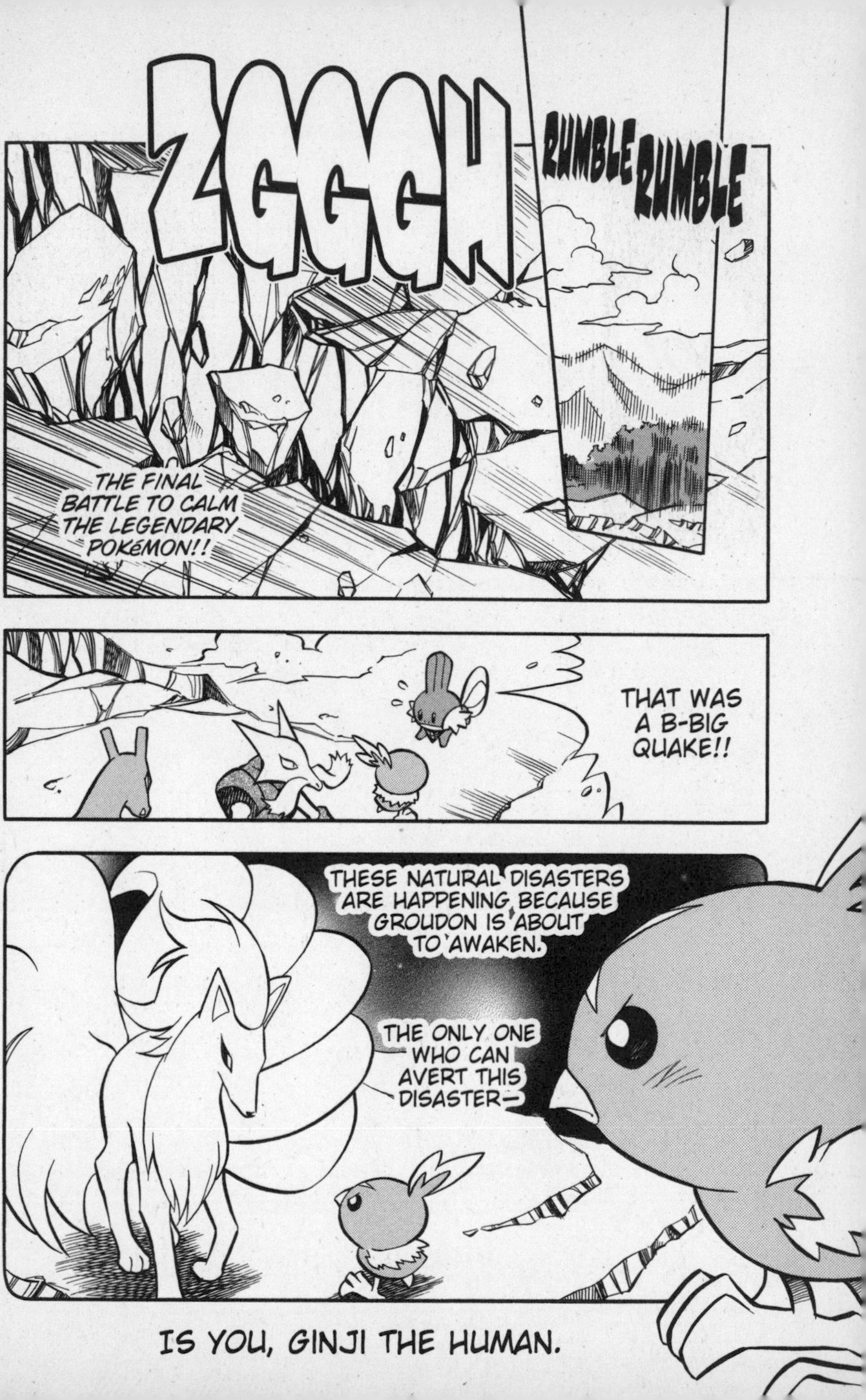
RUMBLE RUMBLE
ZGGGH
THE FINAL BATTLE TO CALM THE LEGENDARY POKéMON!!
THAT WAS A B-BIG QUAKE!!
THESE NATURAL DISASTERS ARE HAPPENING BECAUSE GROUDON IS ABOUT TO AWAKEN.
THE ONLY ONE WHO CAN AVERT THIS DISASTER—
IS YOU, GINJI THE HUMAN.

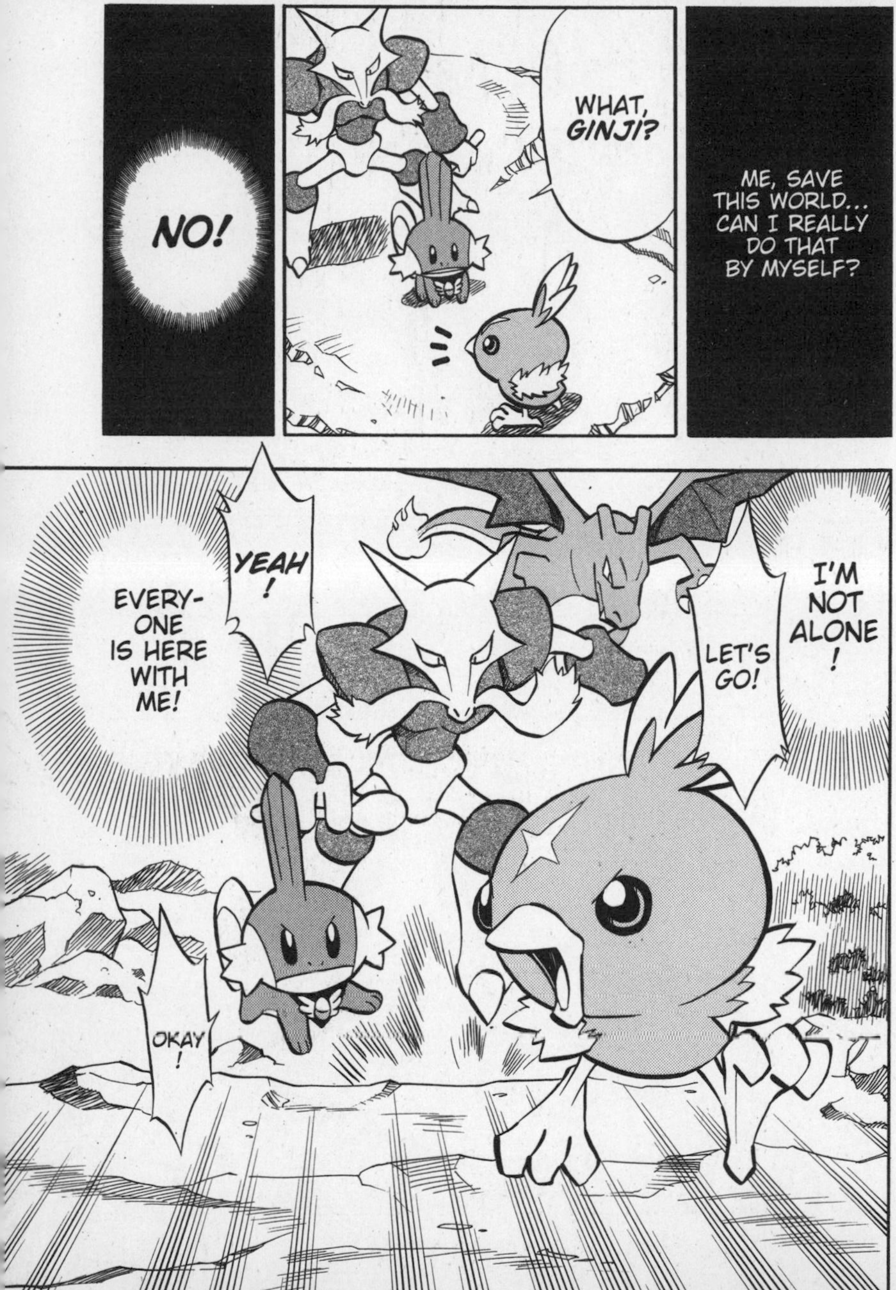
ME, SAVE THIS WORLD... CAN I REALLY DO THAT BY MYSELF?
WHAT, GINJI?
NO!
I'M NOT ALONE!
LET'S GO!
YEAH!
EVERY-ONE IS HERE WITH ME!
OKAY!

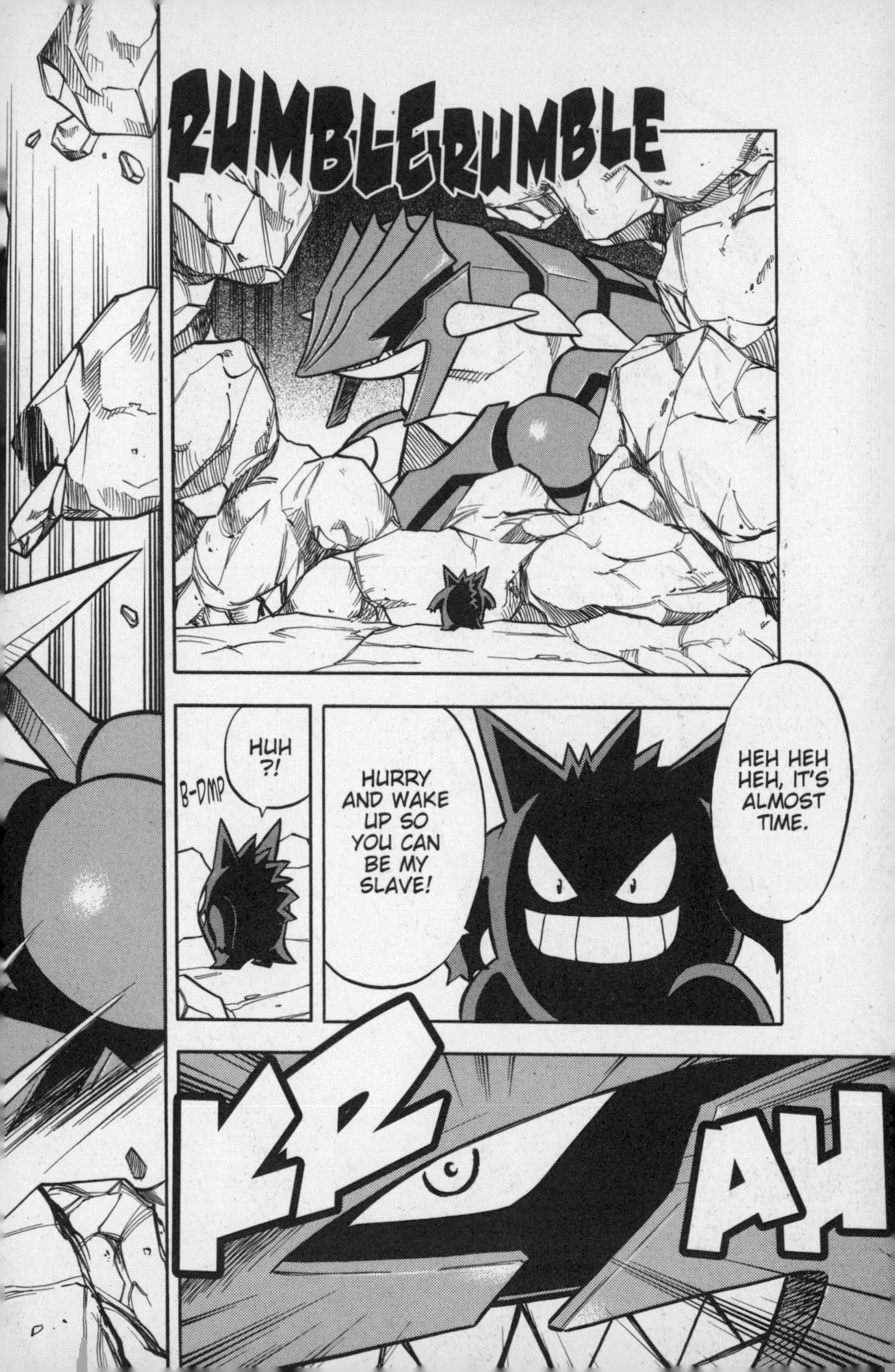
RUMBLE RUMBLE
HEH HEH HEH, IT'S ALMOST TIME.
HURRY AND WAKE UP SO YOU CAN BE MY SLAVE!
HUH ?!
B-DMP
KR
AH

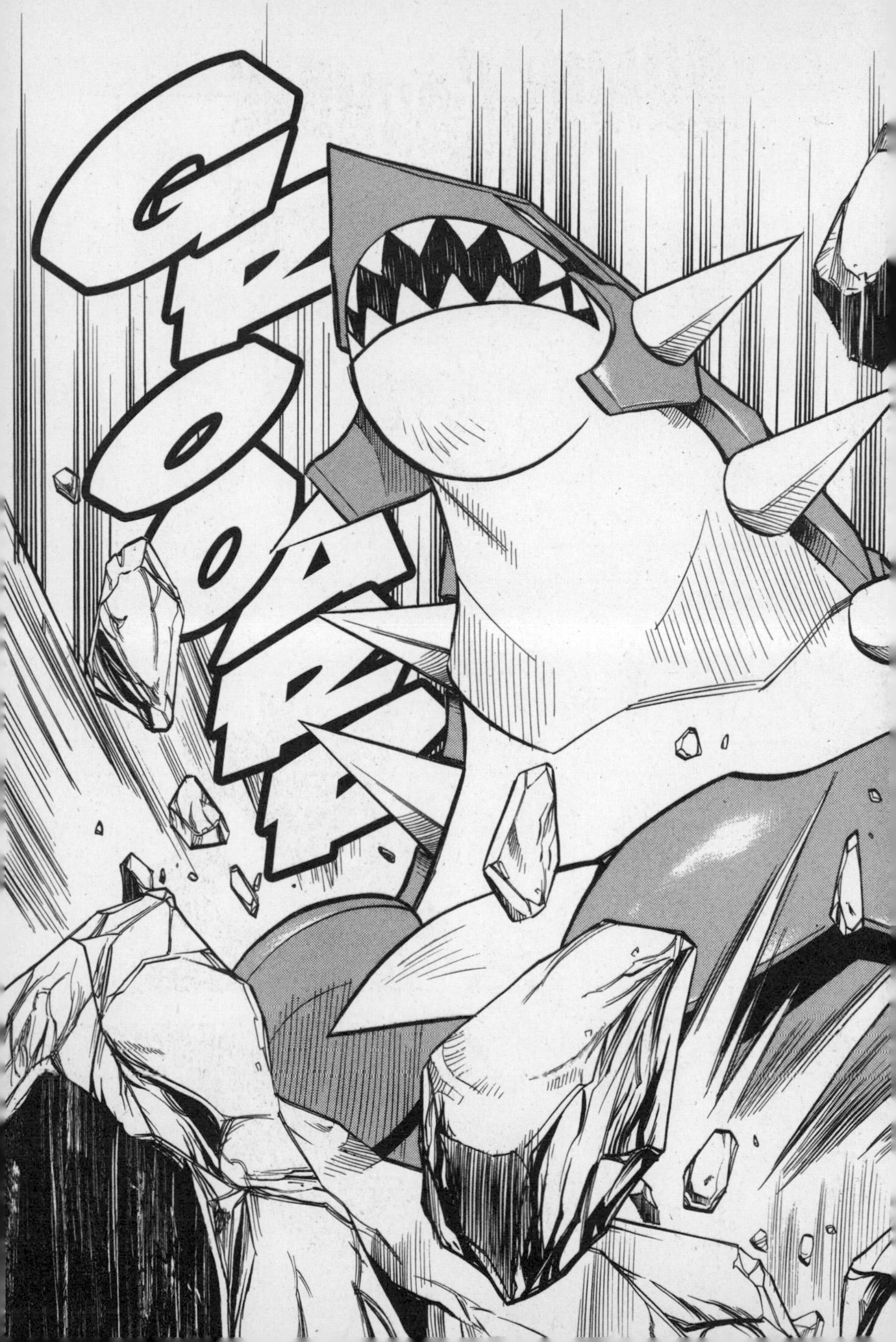
GROORRR

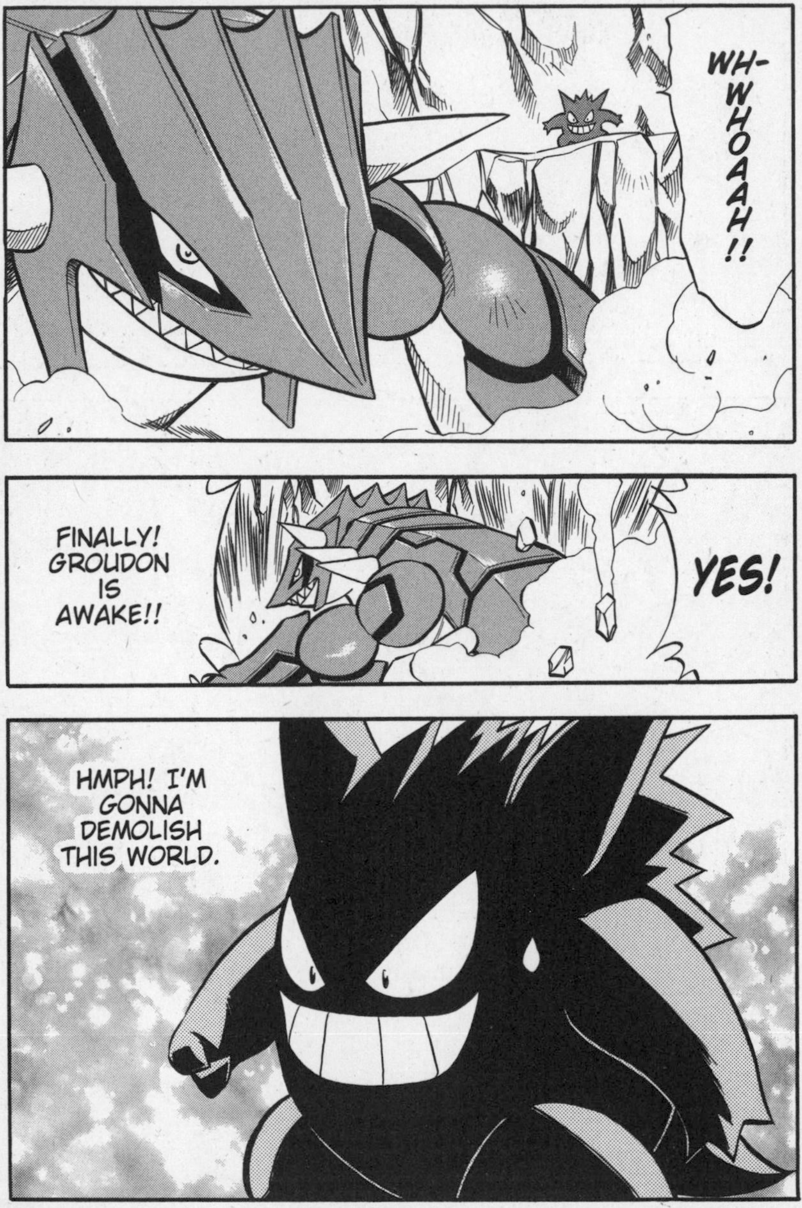
WH-WHOAAAH!!
YES!
FINALLY! GROUDON IS AWAKE!!
HMPH! I'M GONNA DEMOLISH THIS WORLD.

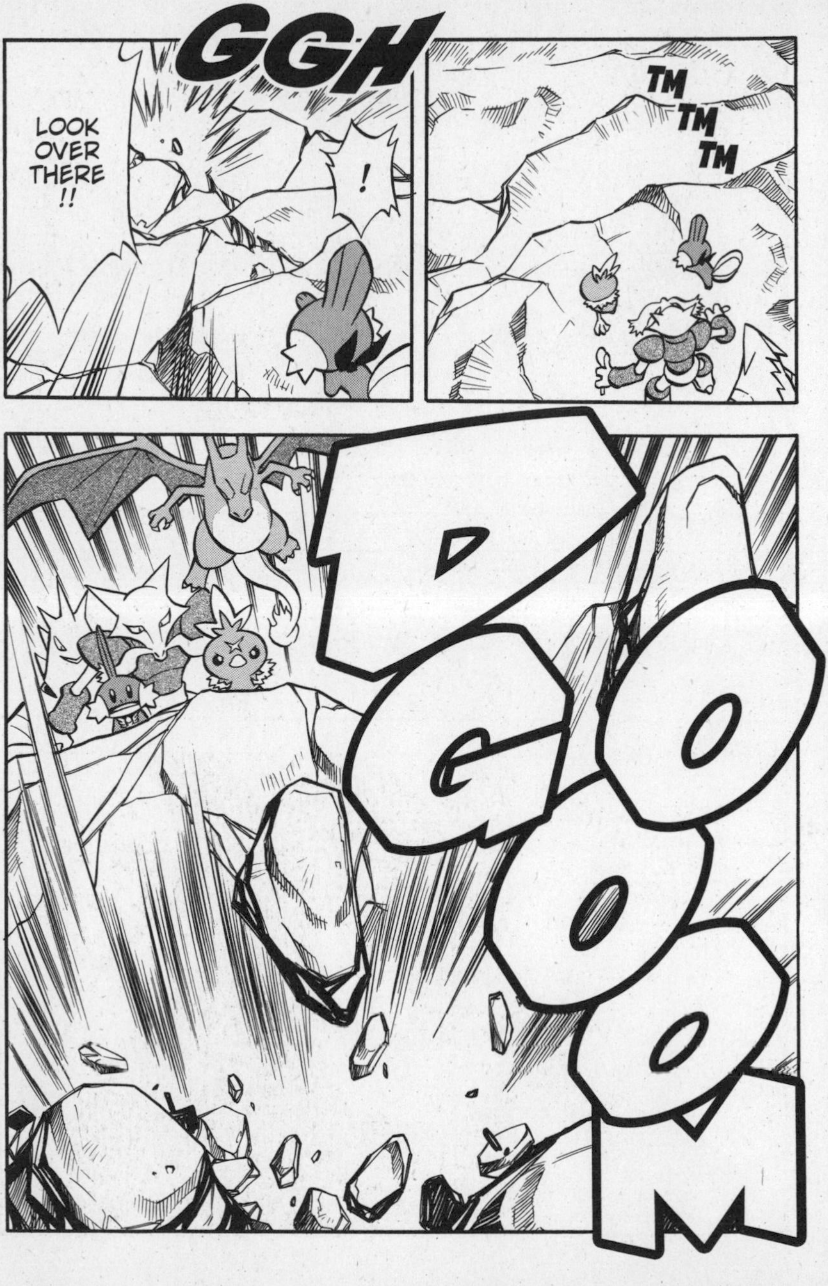
TM TM TM
GGH
LOOK OVER THERE !!
!
DGOOOM

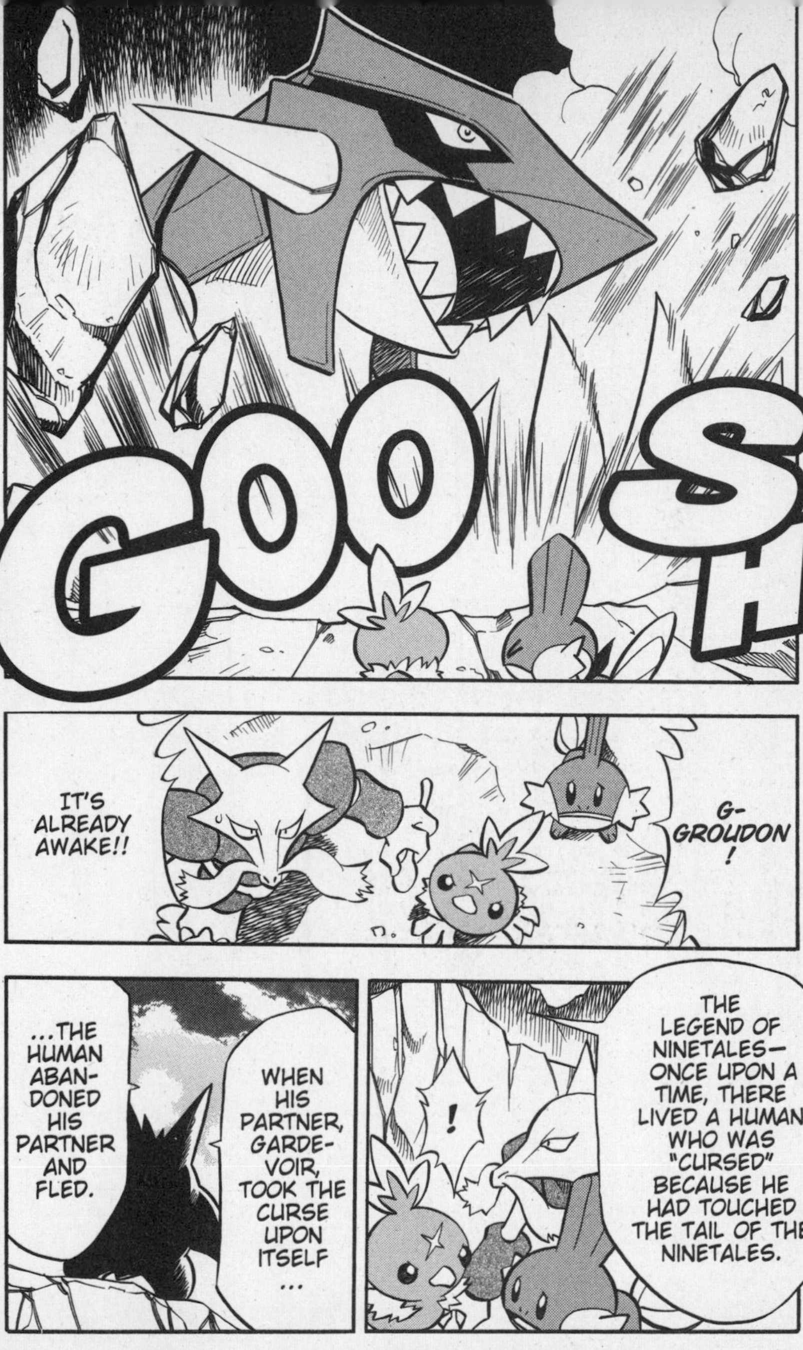
GOO-SH
G-GROUDON!
IT'S ALREADY AWAKE!!
THE LEGEND OF NINETALES—ONCE UPON A TIME, THERE LIVED A HUMAN WHO WAS "CURSED" BECAUSE HE HAD TOUCHED THE TAIL OF THE NINETALES.
!
WHEN HIS PARTNER, GARDEVOIR, TOOK THE CURSE UPON ITSELF...
...THE HUMAN ABANDONED HIS PARTNER AND FLED.

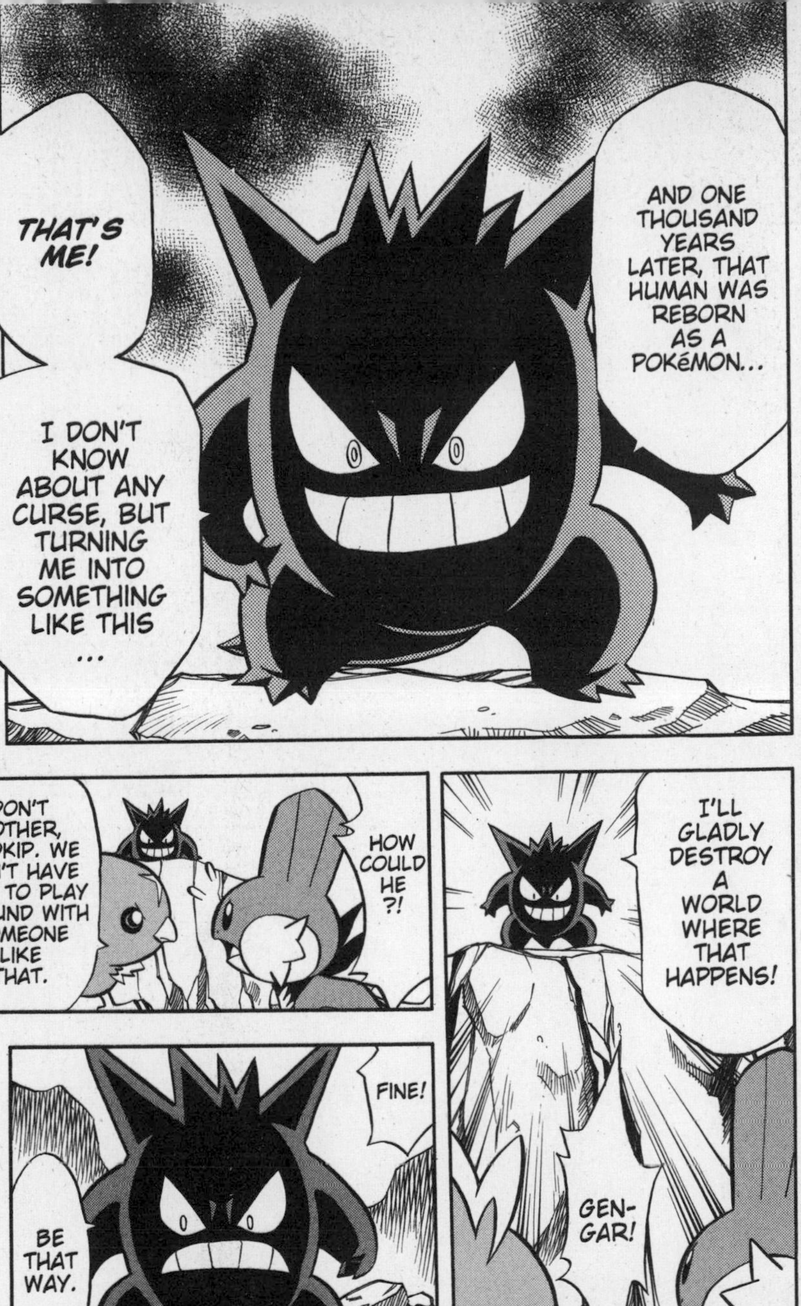

AND ONE THOUSAND YEARS LATER, THAT HUMAN WAS REBORN AS A POKéMON...
THAT'S ME!
I DON'T KNOW ABOUT ANY CURSE, BUT TURNING ME INTO SOMETHING LIKE THIS ...
I'LL GLADLY DESTROY A WORLD WHERE THAT HAPPENS!
GEN-GAR!
HOW COULD HE ?!
DON'T BOTHER, MUDKIP. WE DON'T HAVE TIME TO PLAY AROUND WITH SOMEONE LIKE THAT.
FINE!
BE THAT WAY.

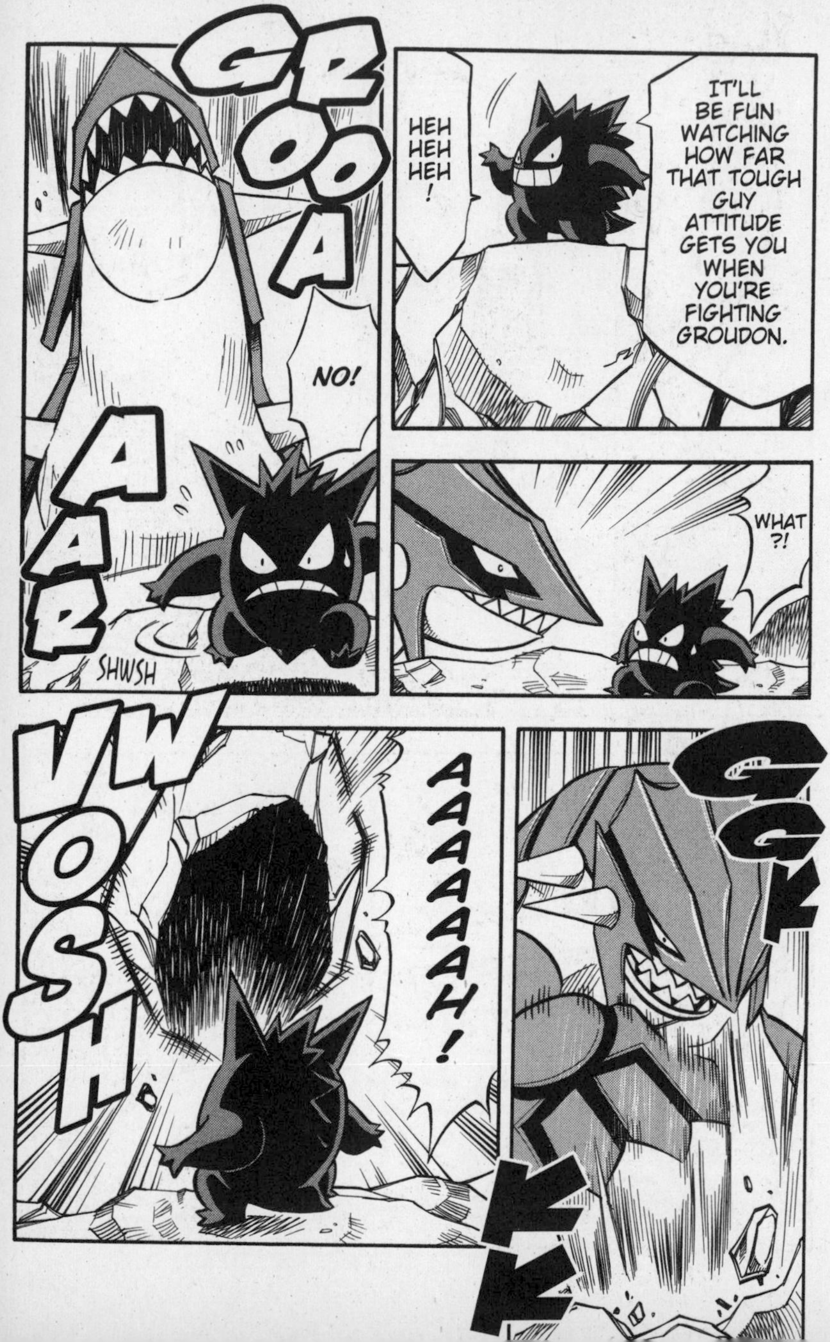
IT'LL BE FUN WATCHING HOW FAR THAT TOUGH GUY ATTITUDE GETS YOU WHEN YOU'RE FIGHTING GROUDON.
HEH HEH HEH!
WHAT?!
GROOA
NO!
AAAR
SHWSH
GGK
KKK
AAAAAAH!
VWOSH

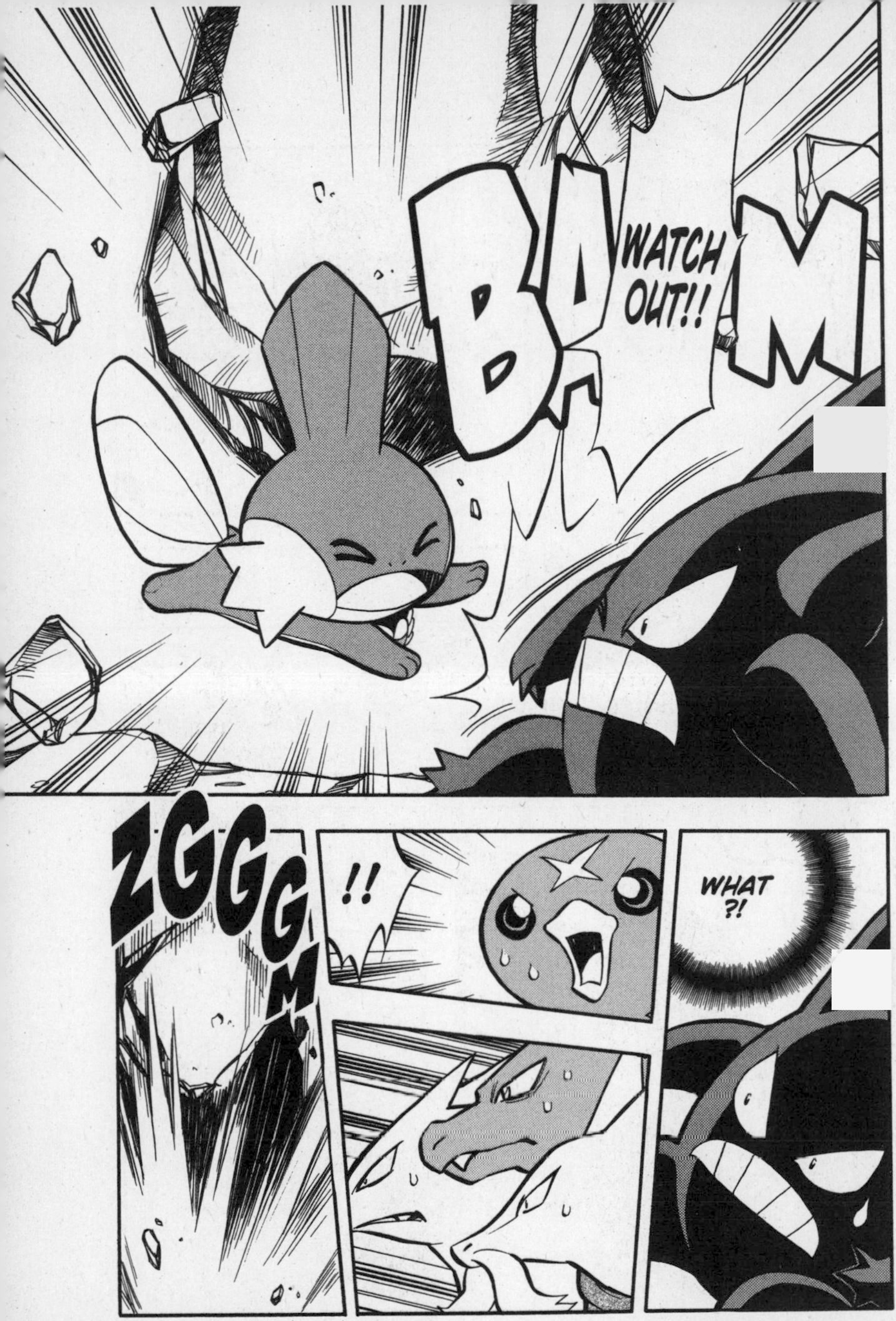
BAM
WATCH OUT!!
WHAT ?!
!!
ZGGGM

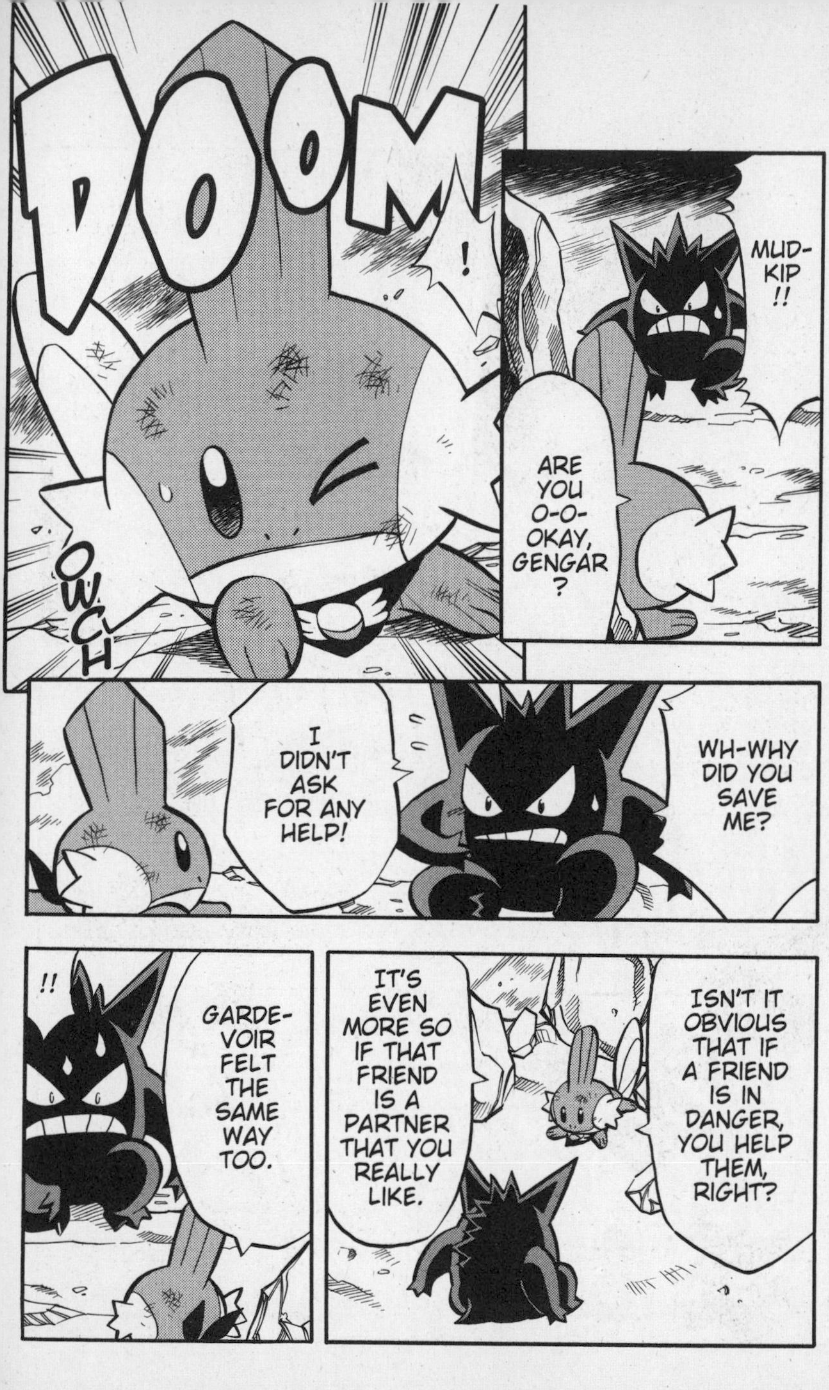
MUD-KIP !!
ARE YOU O-O-OKAY, GENGAR ?
DOOM
!
OWCH
WH-WHY DID YOU SAVE ME?
I DIDN'T ASK FOR ANY HELP!
ISN'T IT OBVIOUS THAT IF A FRIEND IS IN DANGER, YOU HELP THEM, RIGHT?
IT'S EVEN MORE SO IF THAT FRIEND IS A PARTNER THAT YOU REALLY LIKE.
!!
GARDE-VOIR FELT THE SAME WAY TOO.

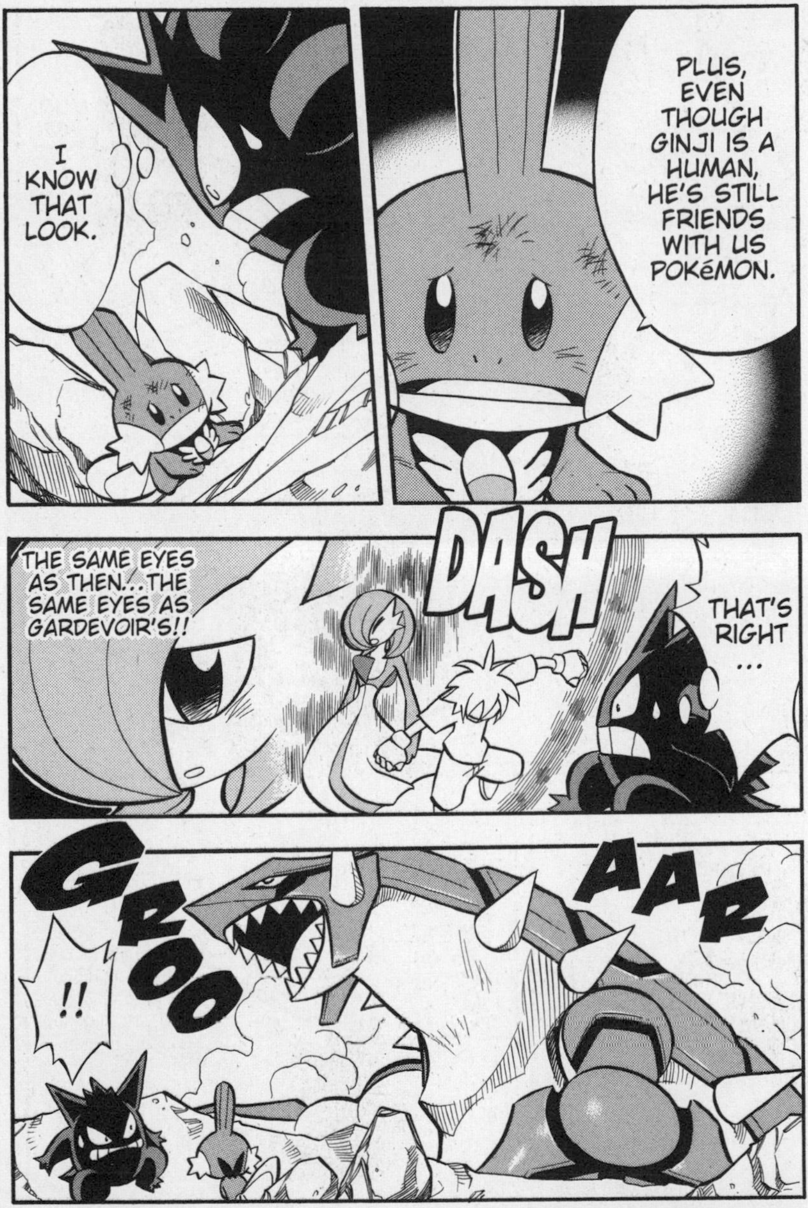

PLUS, EVEN THOUGH GINJI IS A HUMAN, HE'S STILL FRIENDS WITH US POKéMON.
I KNOW THAT LOOK.
DASH
THAT'S RIGHT ...
THE SAME EYES AS THEN... THE SAME EYES AS GARDEVOIR'S!!
GROOOAAR
!!

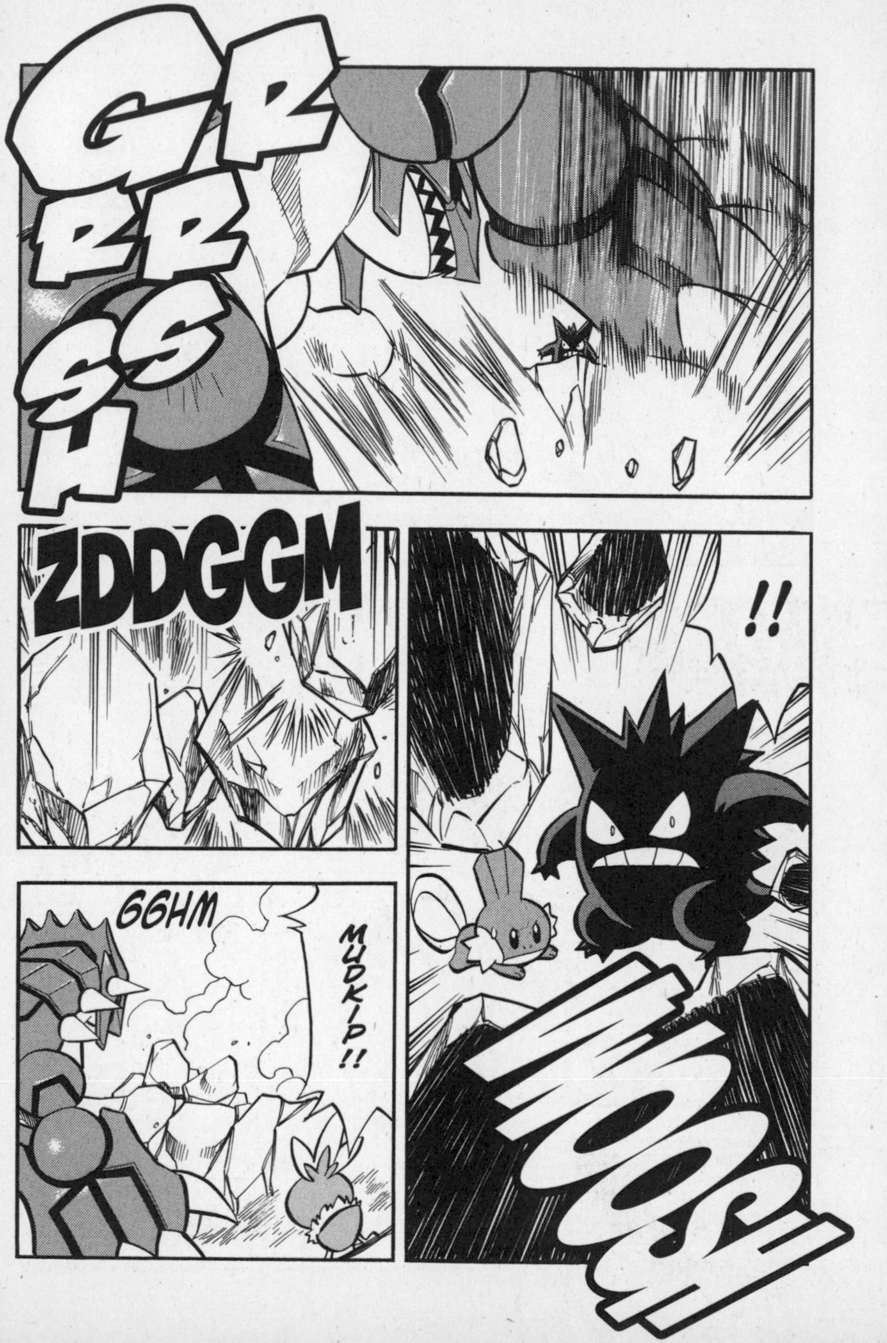
GRRRSSH
!!
WHOOSH!
ZDDGGM
GGHM
MUDKIP!!

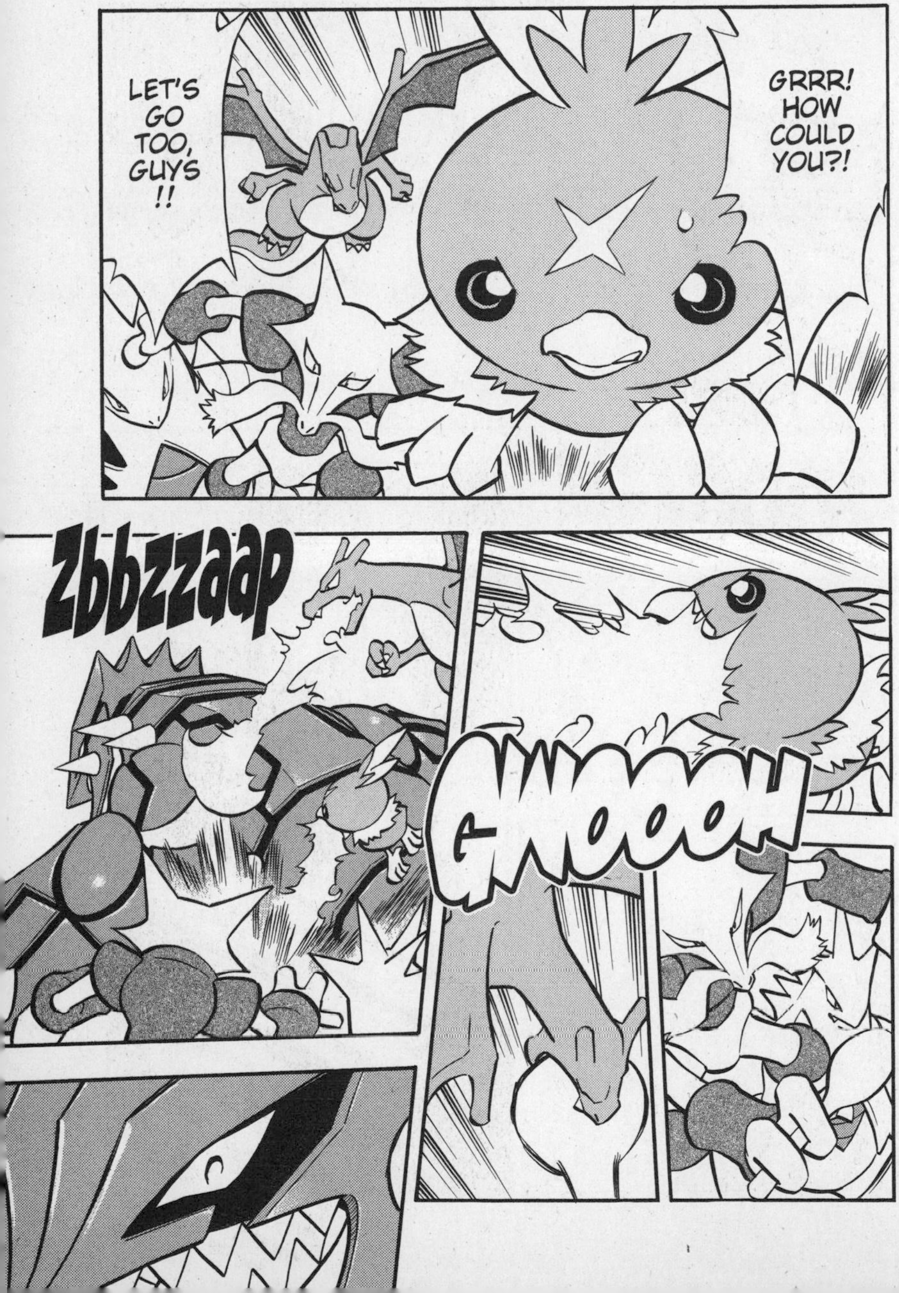
GRRR! HOW COULD YOU?!
LET'S GO TOO, GUYS!!
GWOOOH
Zbbzzaap

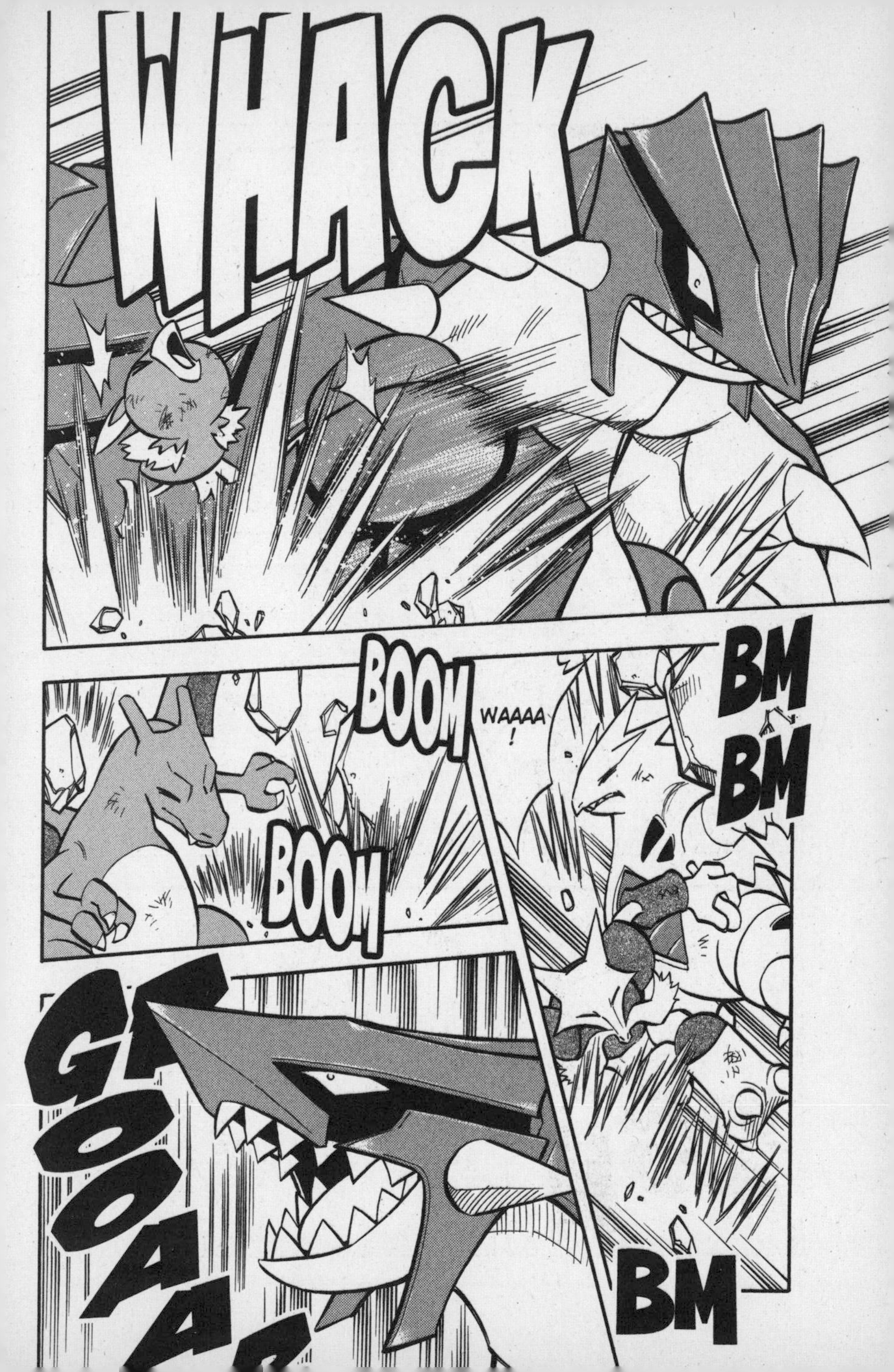
WHACK
BM
BM
WAAAA!
BM
BOOM
BOOM
GAOOAA

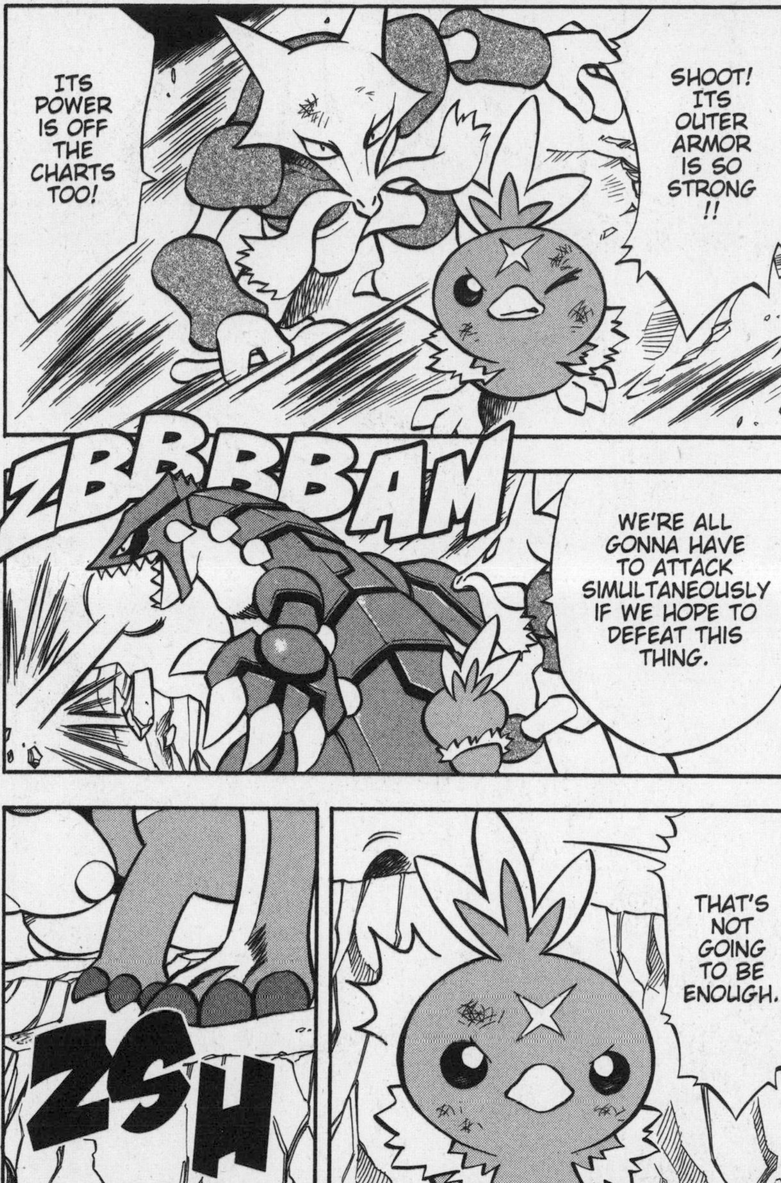
SHOOT! ITS OUTER ARMOR IS SO STRONG!!
ITS POWER IS OFF THE CHARTS TOO!
WE'RE ALL GONNA HAVE TO ATTACK SIMULTANEOUSLY IF WE HOPE TO DEFEAT THIS THING.
ZBBBAM
THAT'S NOT GOING TO BE ENOUGH.
ZSH

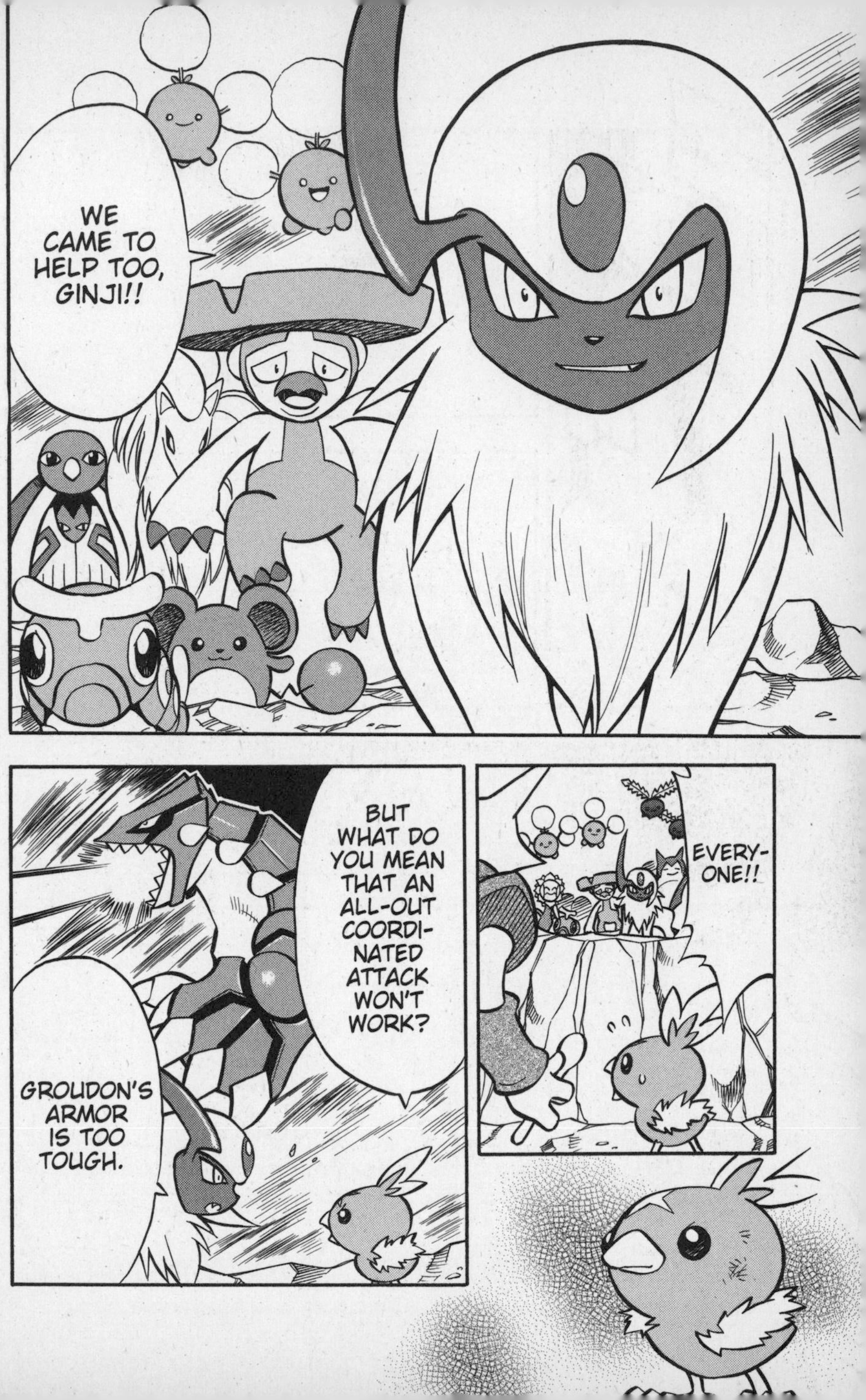
WE CAME TO HELP TOO, GINJI!!
EVERY-ONE!!
BUT WHAT DO YOU MEAN THAT AN ALL-OUT COORDI-NATED ATTACK WON'T WORK?
GROUDON'S ARMOR IS TOO TOUGH.

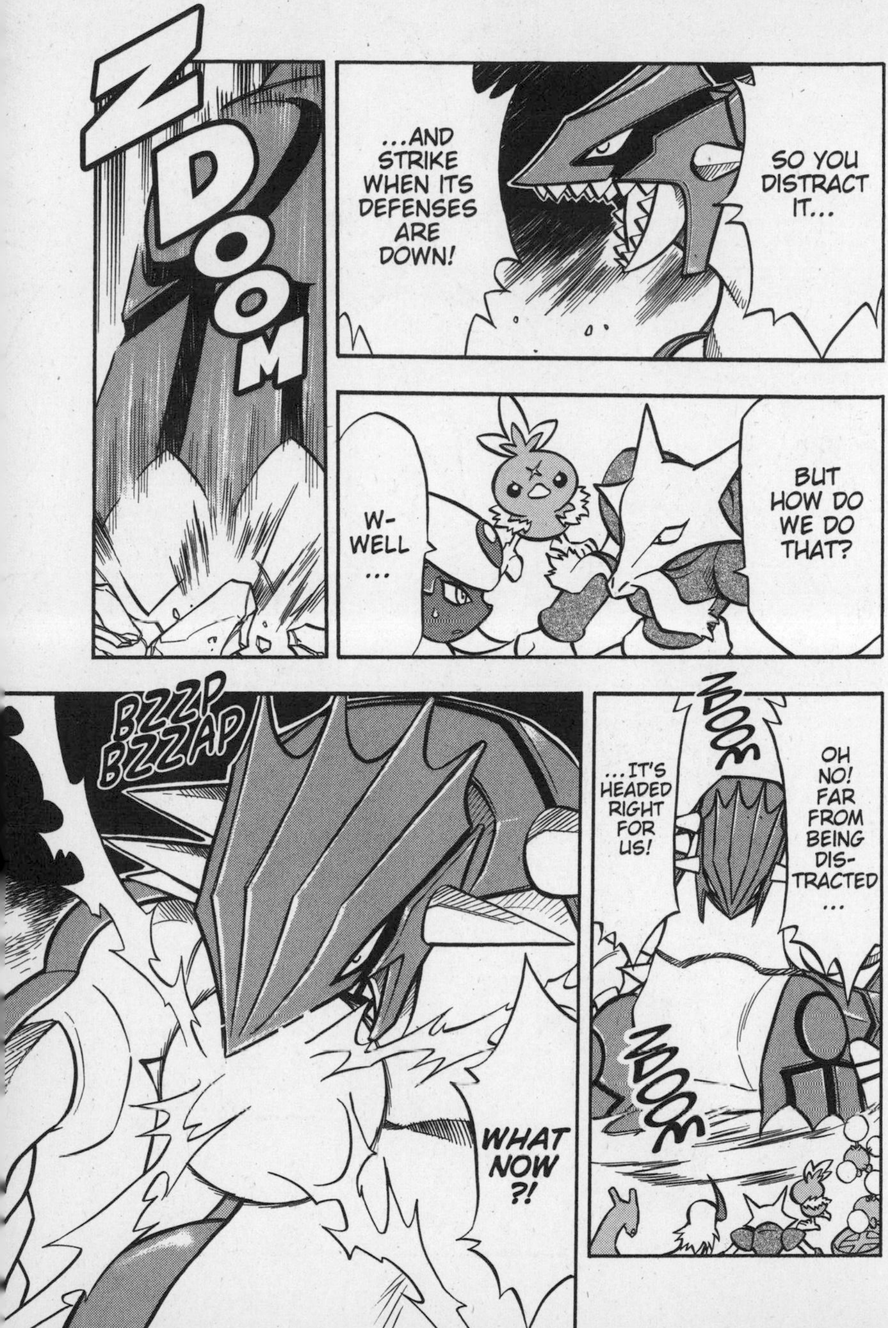
SO YOU DISTRACT IT...
...AND STRIKE WHEN ITS DEFENSES ARE DOWN!
BUT HOW DO WE DO THAT?
W-WELL...
ZDOOM
OH NO! FAR FROM BEING DIS-TRACTED...
...IT'S HEADED RIGHT FOR US!
ZDOOM
ZDOOM
BZZZP BZZZAP
WHAT NOW?!

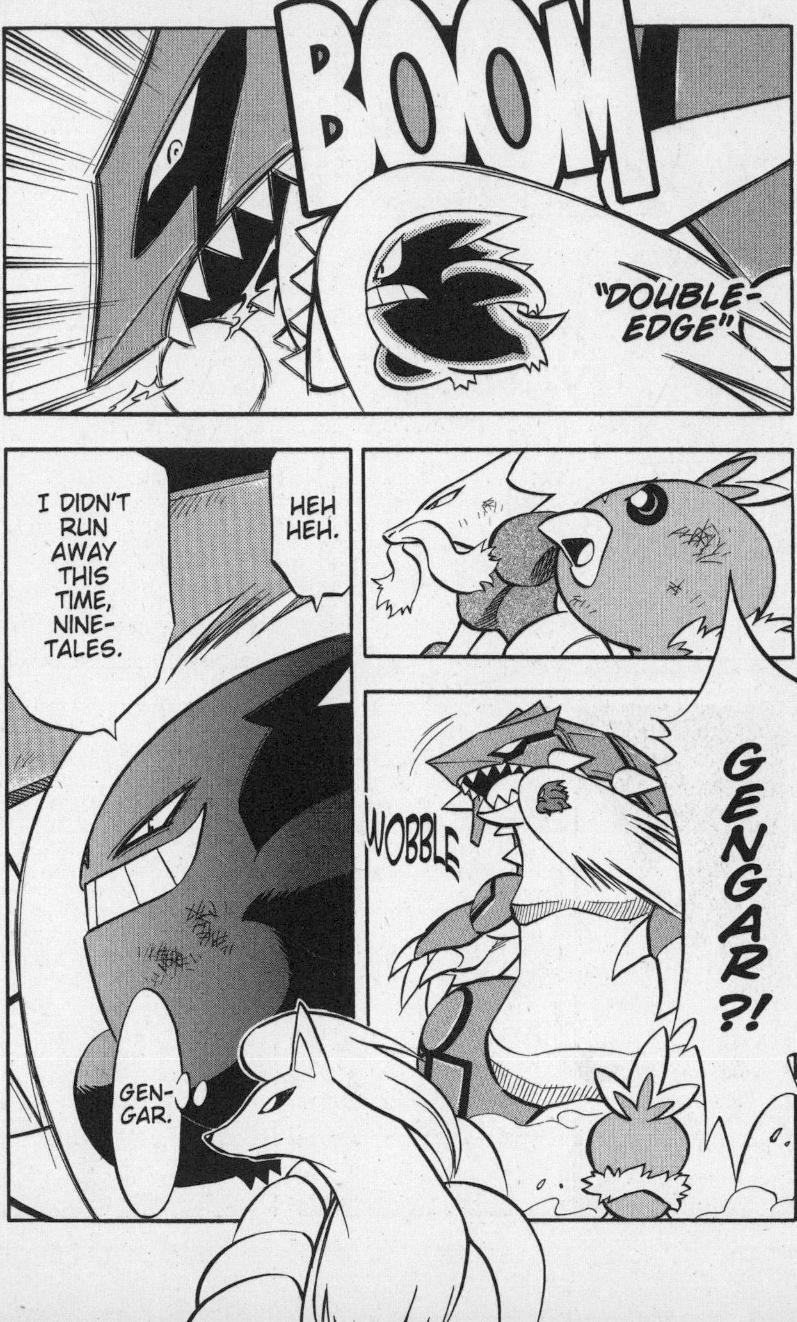
BOOM
"DOUBLE-EDGE"
GENGAR?!
WOBBLE
HEH HEH.
I DIDN'T RUN AWAY THIS TIME, NINE-TALES.
GEN-GAR.

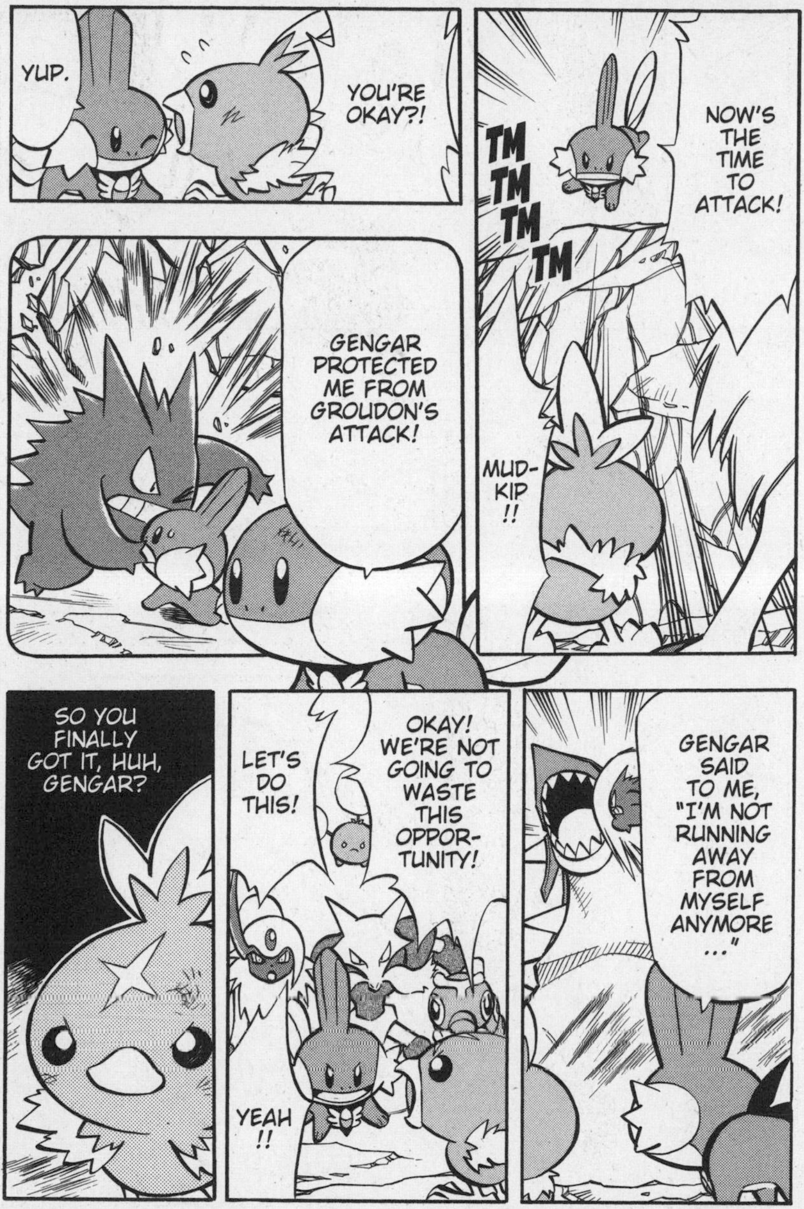
NOW'S THE TIME TO ATTACK!
TM TM TM TM
MUD-KIP!!
YOU'RE OKAY?!
YUP.
GENGAR PROTECTED ME FROM GROUDON'S ATTACK!
GENGAR SAID TO ME, "I'M NOT RUNNING AWAY FROM MYSELF ANYMORE..."
OKAY! WE'RE NOT GOING TO WASTE THIS OPPOR-TUNITY!
LET'S DO THIS!
YEAH!!
SO YOU FINALLY GOT IT, HUH, GENGAR?

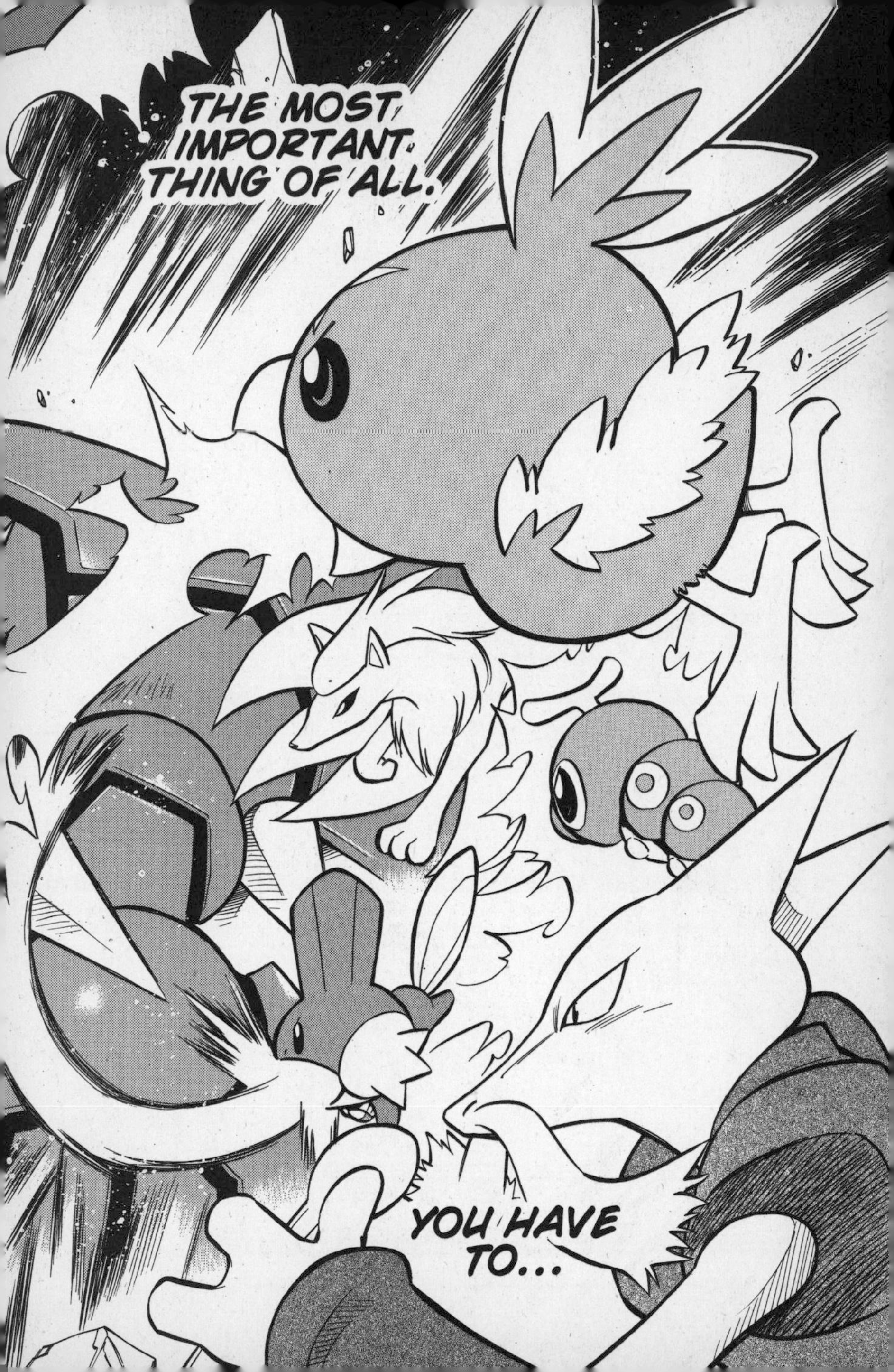
THE MOST IMPORTANT THING OF ALL.
YOU HAVE TO...

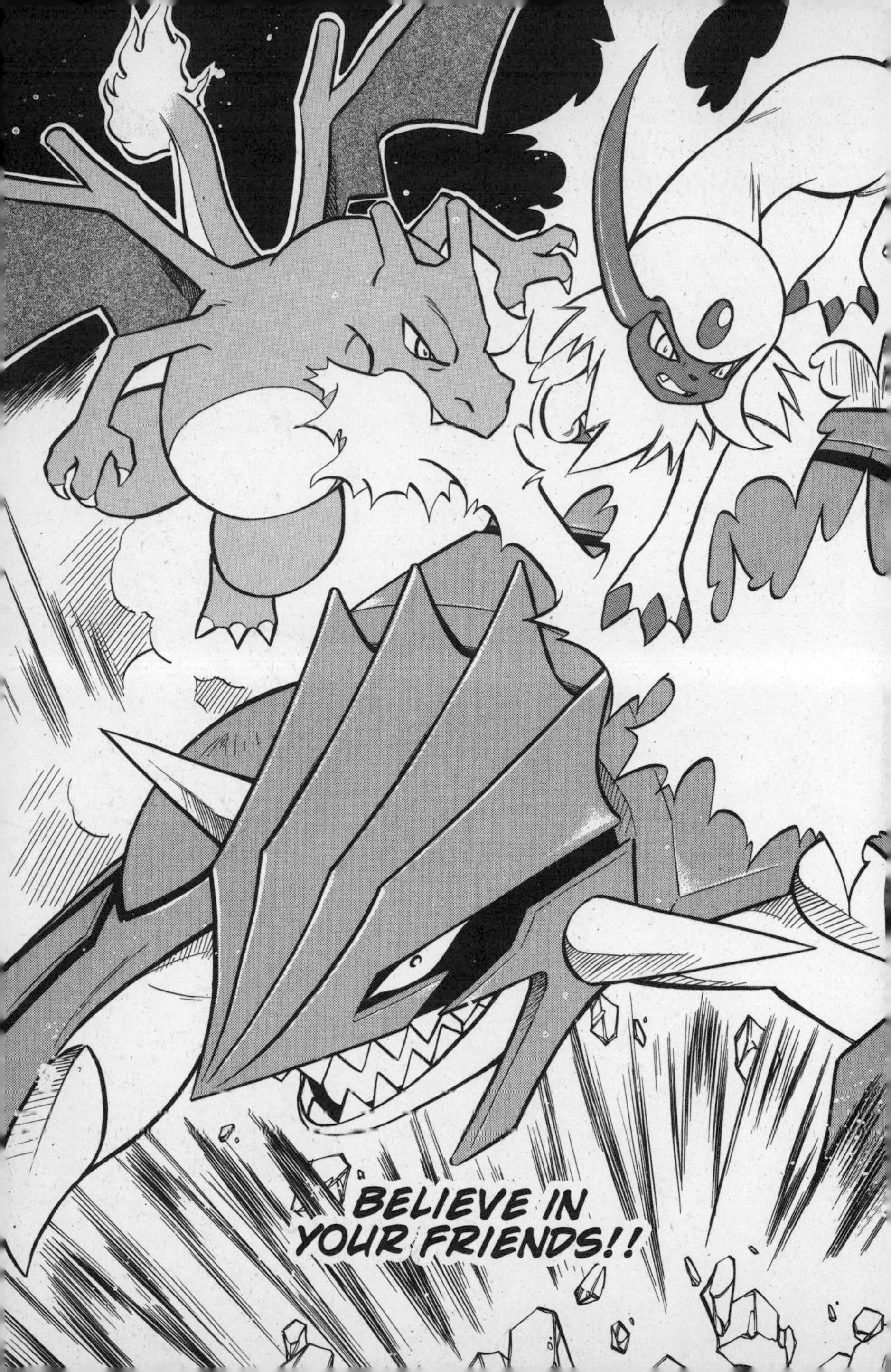
BELIEVE IN YOUR FRIENDS!!

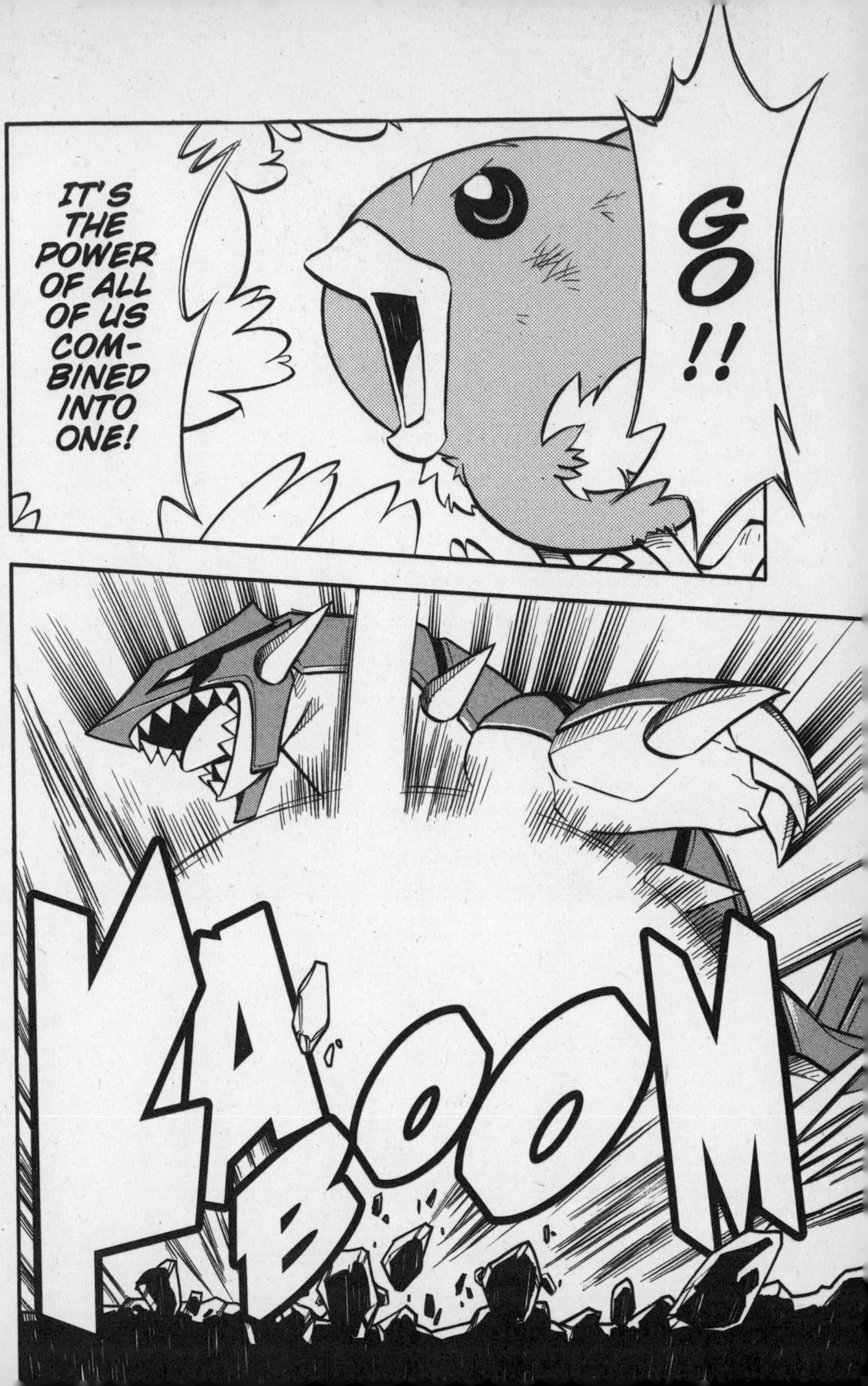
GO!!
IT'S THE POWER OF ALL OF US COMBINED INTO ONE!
KA-BOOM

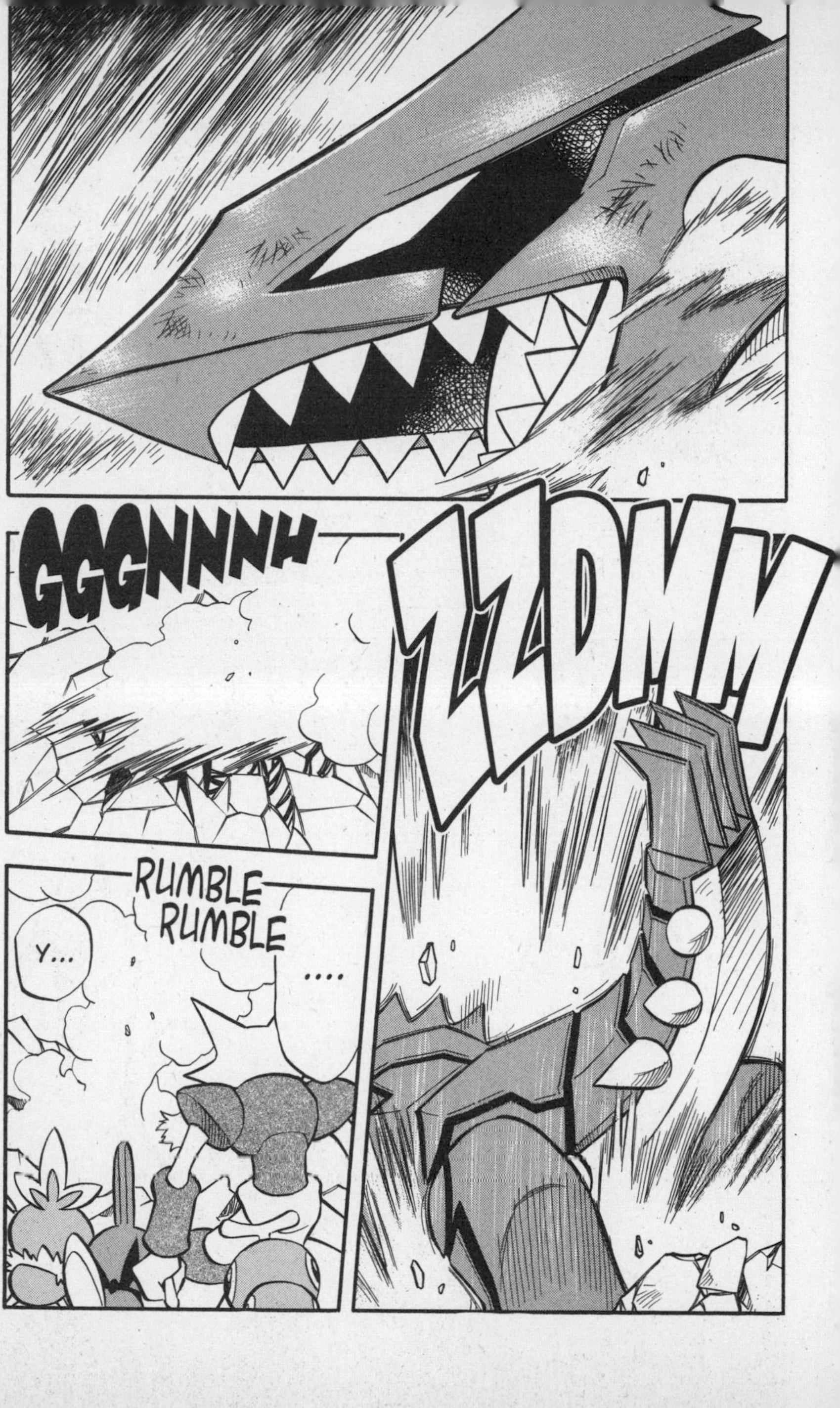
ZZDMM
GGGNNNH
RUMBLE RUMBLE
....
Y...

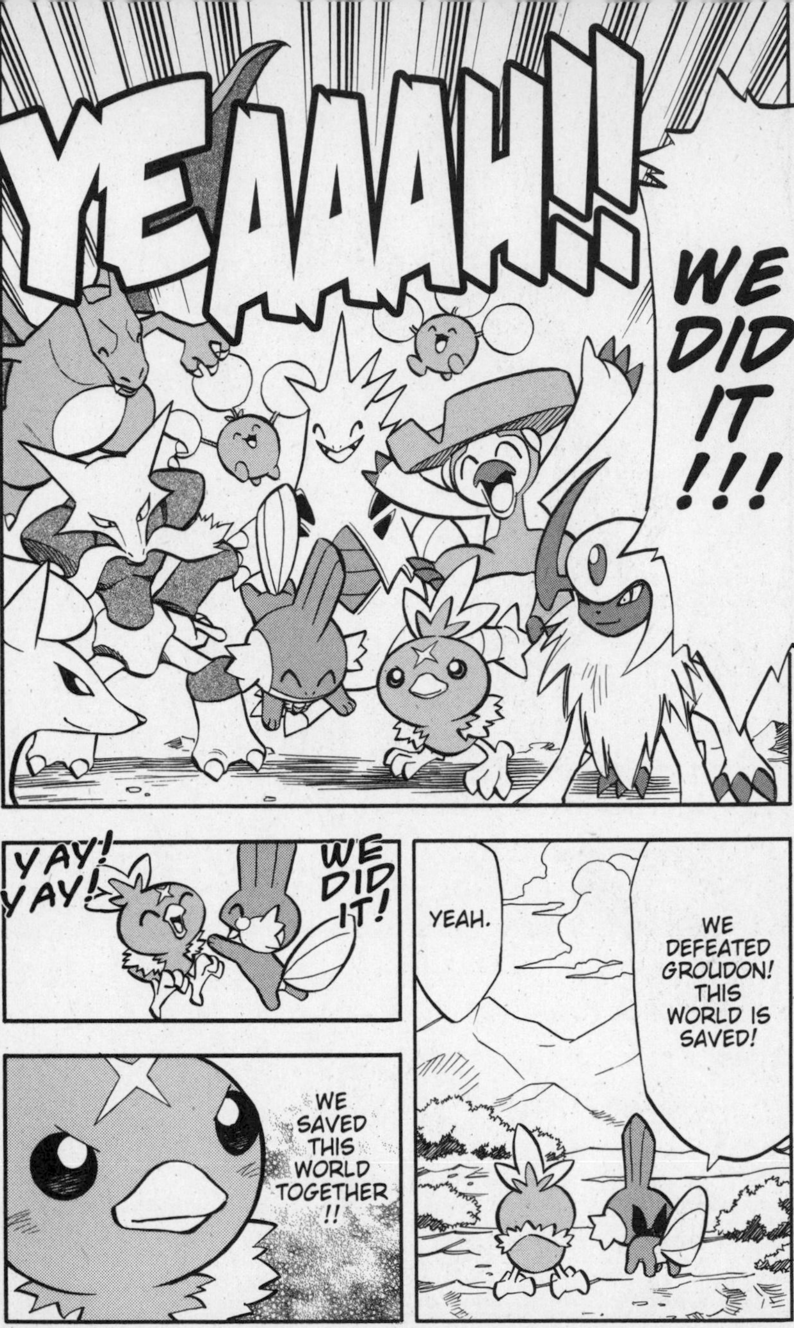
YEAAAH!!
WE DID IT!!!
WE DEFEATED GROUDON! THIS WORLD IS SAVED!
YEAH.
WE DID IT!
YAY! YAY!
WE SAVED THIS WORLD TOGETHER!!

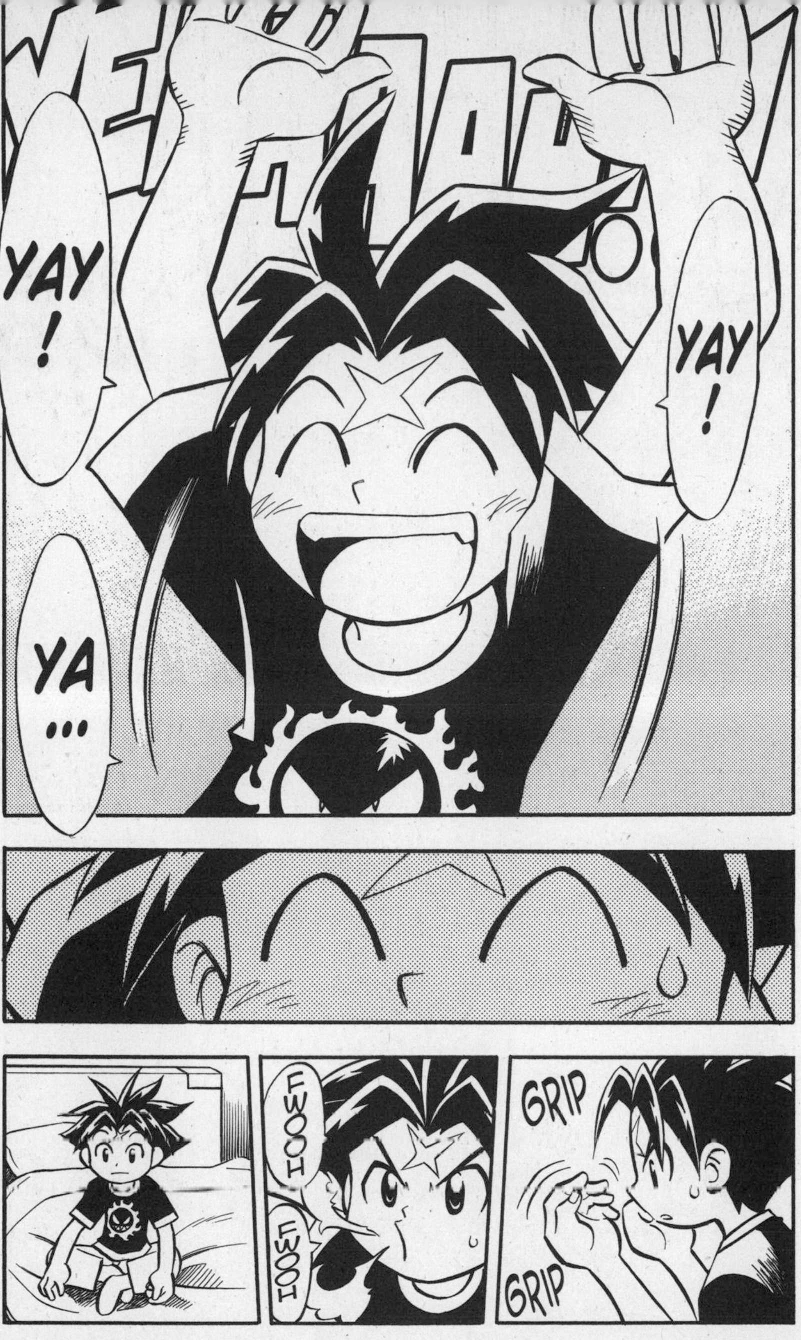
YAY!
YAY!
YA...
GRIP
GRIP
FWOOH
FWOOH

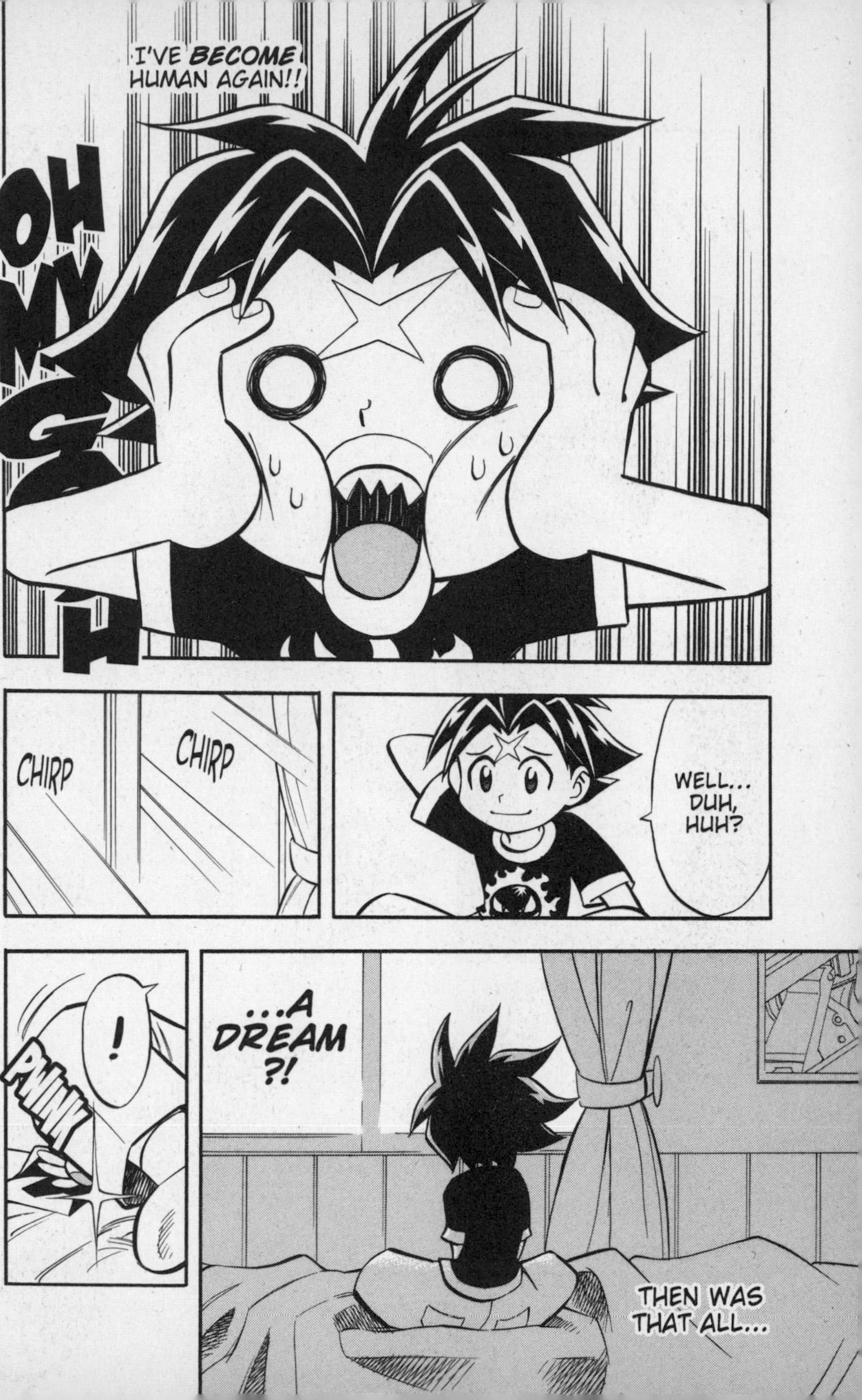
I'VE BECOME HUMAN AGAIN!!
OH MY GOSH
WELL... DUH, HUH?
CHIRP
CHIRP
THEN WAS THAT ALL...
...A DREAM ?!
!
PWINK

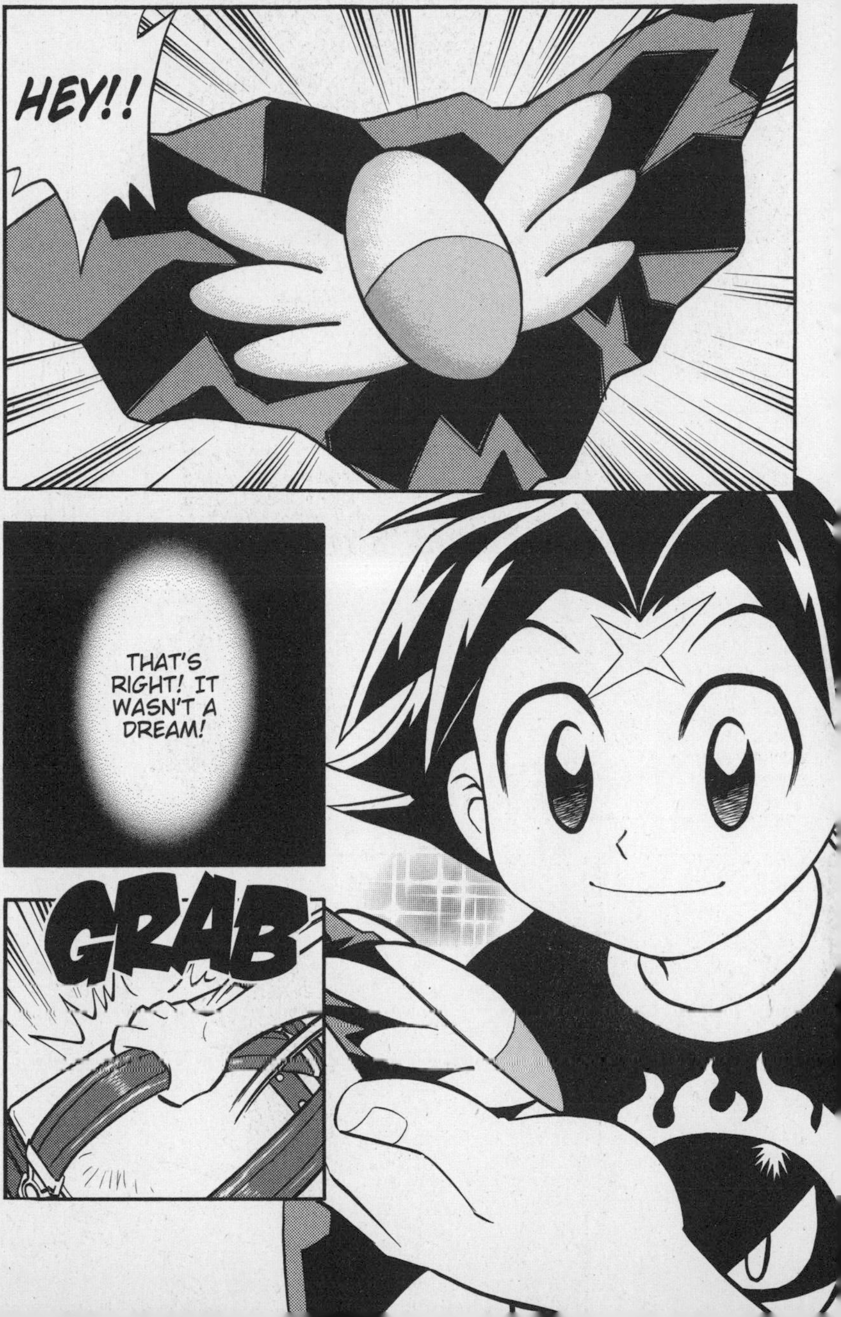
HEY!!
THAT'S RIGHT! IT WASN'T A DREAM!
GRAB

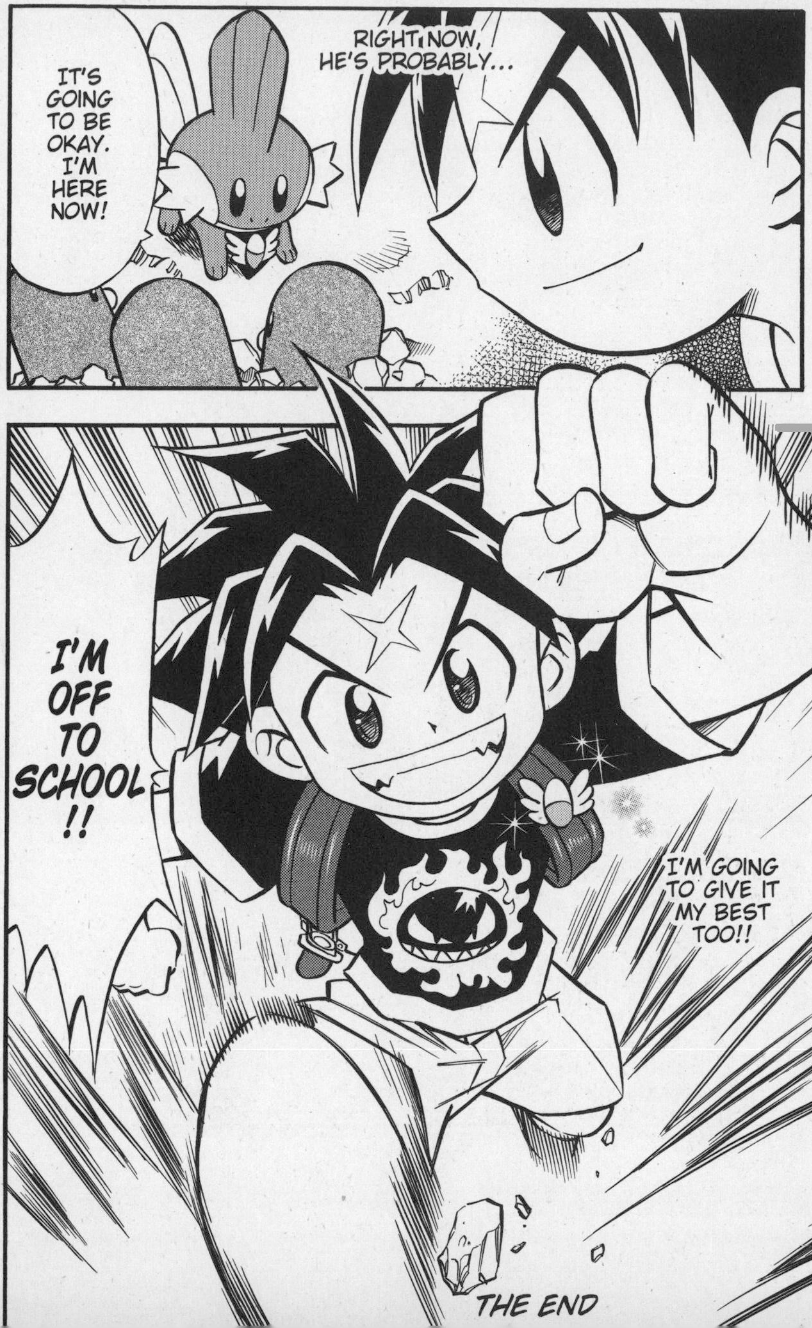
RIGHT NOW, HE'S PROBABLY...
IT'S GOING TO BE OKAY. I'M HERE NOW!
I'M OFF TO SCHOOL!!
I'M GOING TO GIVE IT MY BEST TOO!!
THE END

Story and Art by MAKOTO MIZOBUCHI

Translation/Kaori Inoue
Touch-up Art & Lettering/Rina Mapa
Design/Sam Elzway
Editor/Kit Fox

Editor in Chief, Books/Alvin Lu
Editor in Chief, Magazines/Marc Weidenbaum
VP of Publishing Licensing/Rika Inouye
VP of Sales/Gonzalo Ferreyra
Sr. VP of Marketing/Liza Coppola
Publisher/Hyoe Narita

Published by VIZ Media, LLC
P.O. Box 77010
San Francisco, CA 94107

VIZ Kids Edition
10 9 8 7 6 5 4 3 2
First printing, March 2007
Second printing, March 2007

store.viz.com

www.viz.com

PARENTAL ADVISORY
POKÉMON MYSTERY DUNGEON
is rated A and is suitable for
readers of all ages.

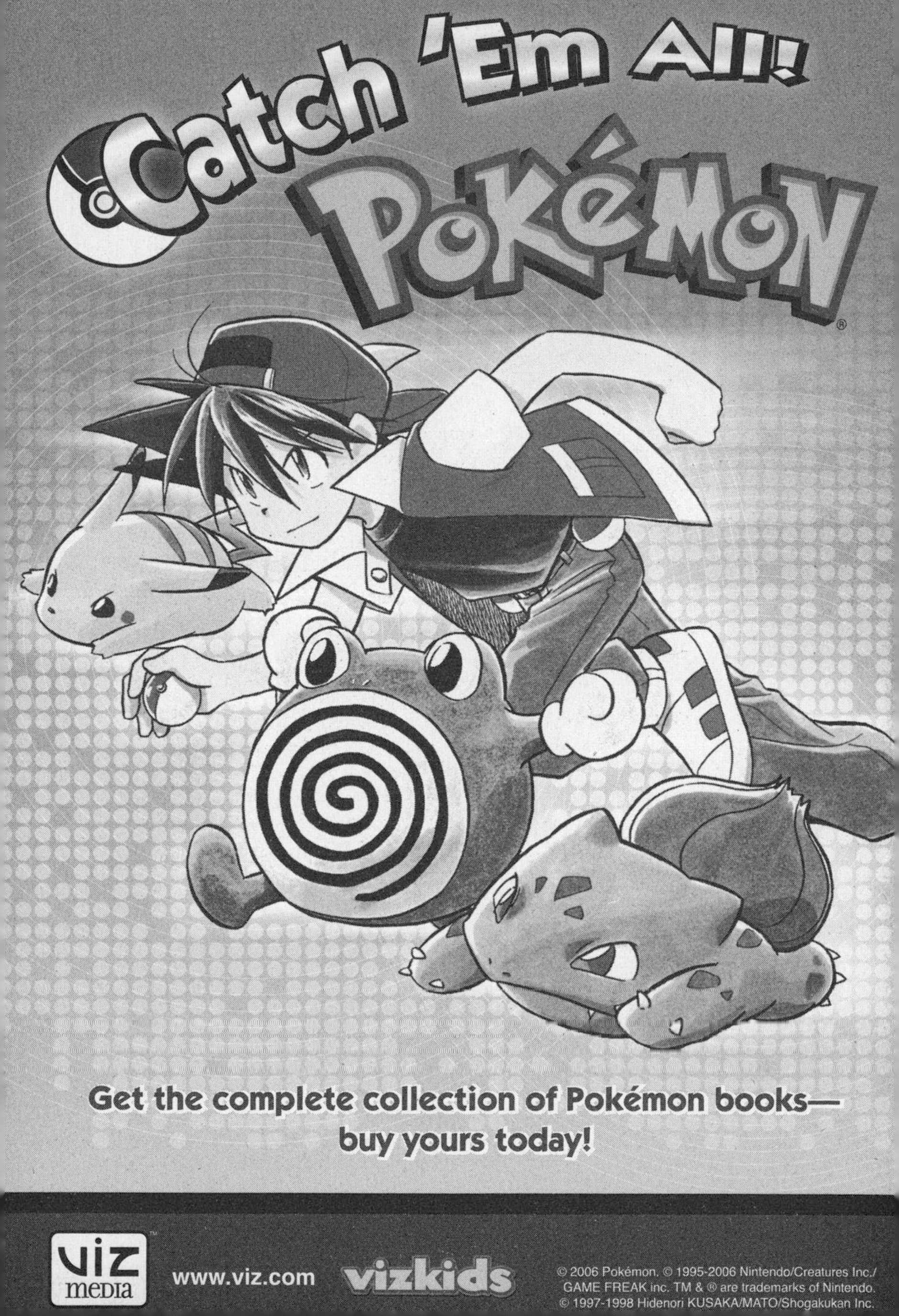
Catch 'Em All!
Pokémon®

POKéMON STORY BOOKS

Follow the manga adventures of Red and Yellow!

Two complete Pikachu short stories in one full color manga!

POKéMON

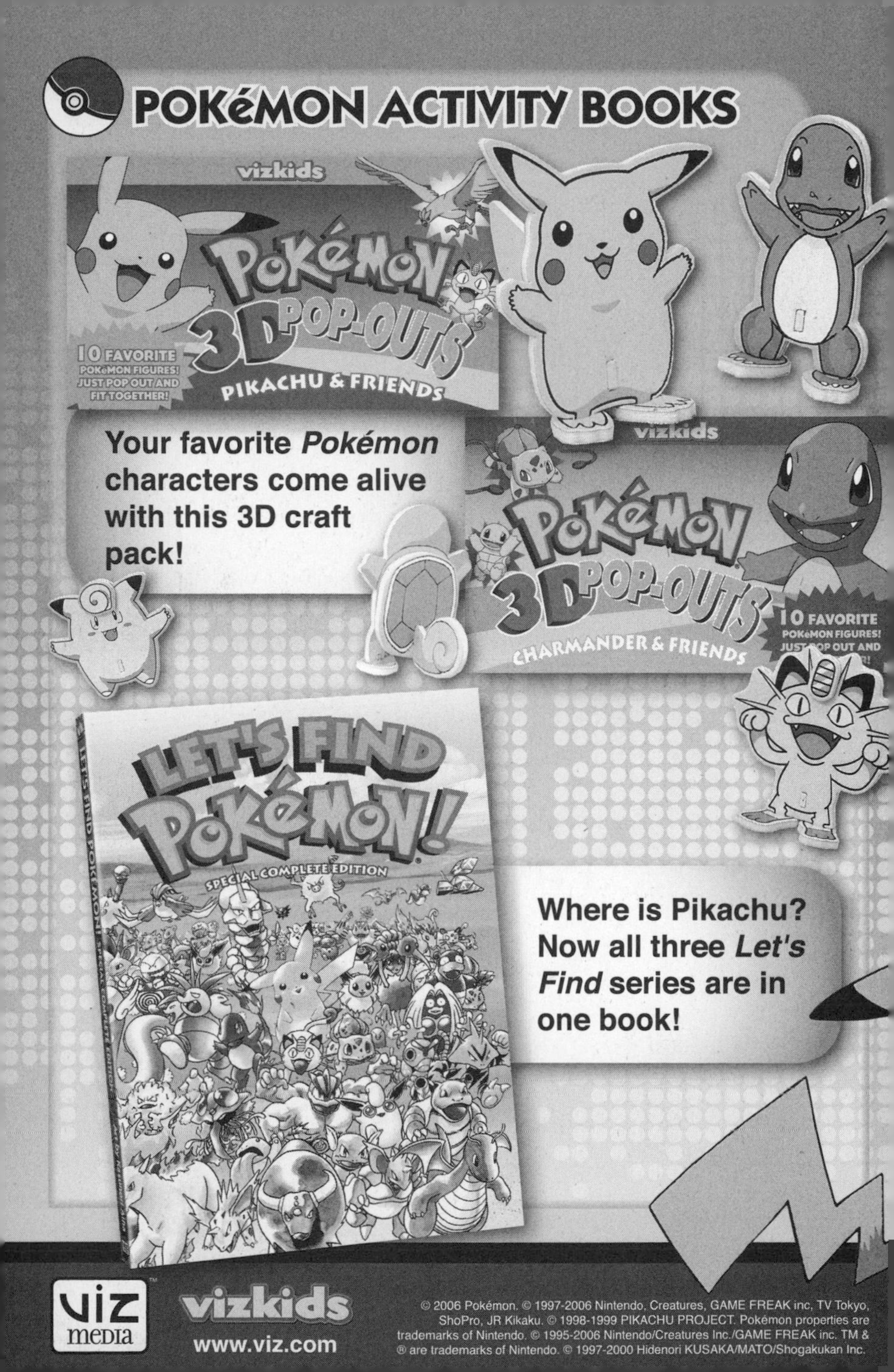
POKéMON ACTIVITY BOOKS
vizkids
POKéMON 3D POP-OUTS
PIKACHU & FRIENDS
10 FAVORITE POKéMON FIGURES! JUST POP OUT AND FIT TOGETHER!
Your favorite *Pokémon* characters come alive with this 3D craft pack!
vizkids
POKéMON 3D POP-OUTS
CHARMANDER & FRIENDS
10 FAVORITE POKéMON FIGURES!
LET'S FIND POKéMON!
SPECIAL COMPLETE EDITION
Where is Pikachu? Now all three *Let's Find* series are in one book!
VIZ MEDIA
vizkids
www.viz.com
© 2006 Pokémon. © 1997-2006 Nintendo, Creatures, GAME FREAK inc, TV Tokyo, ShoPro, JR Kikaku. © 1998-1999 PIKACHU PROJECT. Pokémon properties are trademarks of Nintendo. © 1995-2006 Nintendo/Creatures Inc./GAME FREAK inc. TM & ® are trademarks of Nintendo. © 1997-2000 Hidenori KUSAKA/MATO/Shogakukan Inc.

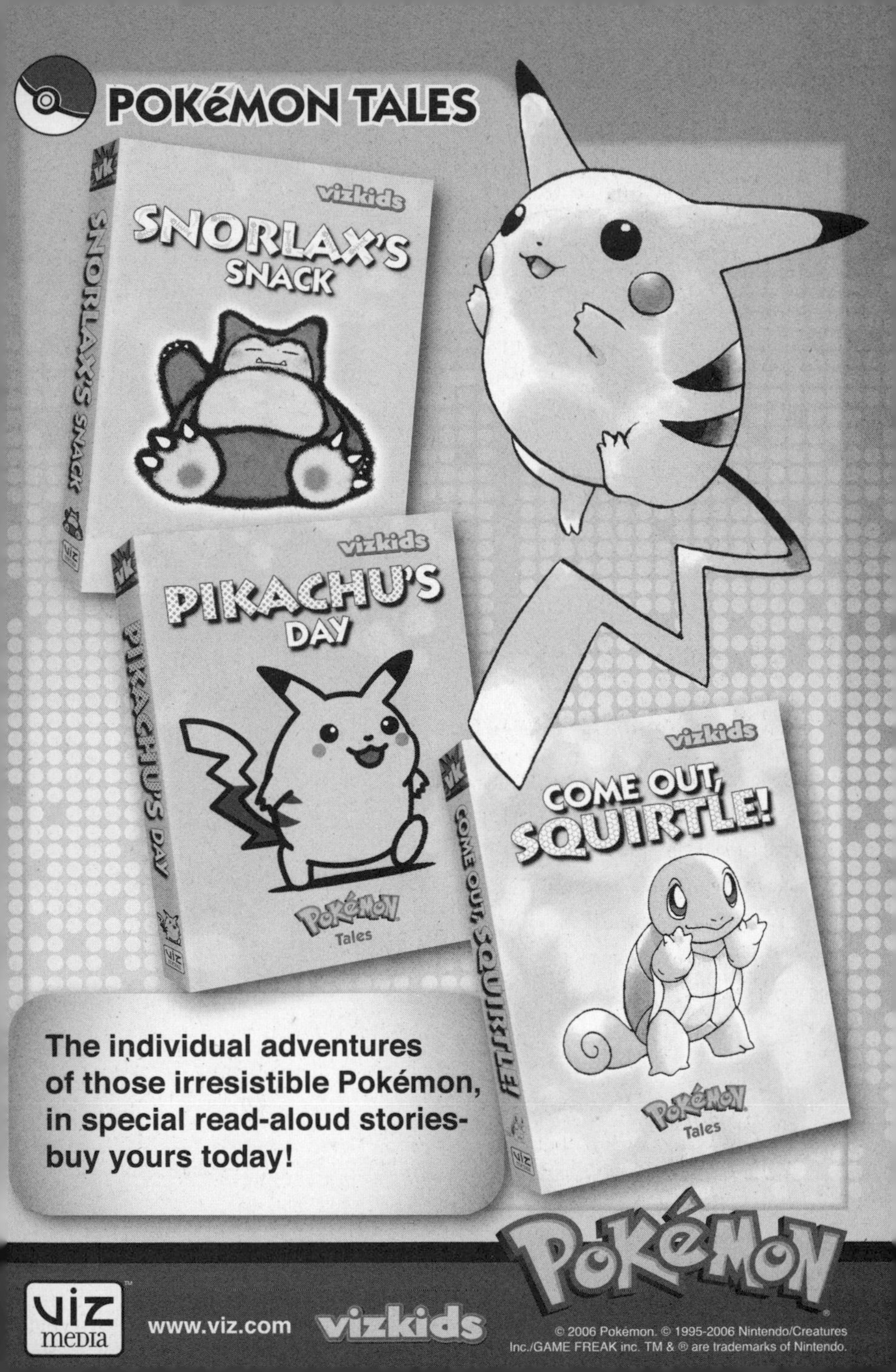
POKéMON TALES
vizkids
SNORLAX'S SNACK
vizkids
PIKACHU'S DAY
Pokémon Tales
vizkids
COME OUT, SQUIRTLE!
Pokémon Tales
The individual adventures of those irresistible Pokémon, in special read-aloud stories-buy yours today!
Pokémon
viz media
www.viz.com
vizkids
© 2006 Pokémon. © 1995-2006 Nintendo/Creatures Inc./GAME FREAK inc. TM & ® are trademarks of Nintendo.

POWER UP Your Collections!

In the year 200X, everyone is connected to the Cyber Network and the world is a virtual utopia. But computer hacking, viruses, and high-tech crime are on the rise, creating chaos in DenTech City. Can a kid named Lan and his NetNavi MegaMan stop the madness before it destroys the world?

Manga only $7.99!

DVD only $14.98!

Manga and anime now available —buy yours today at store.viz.com!

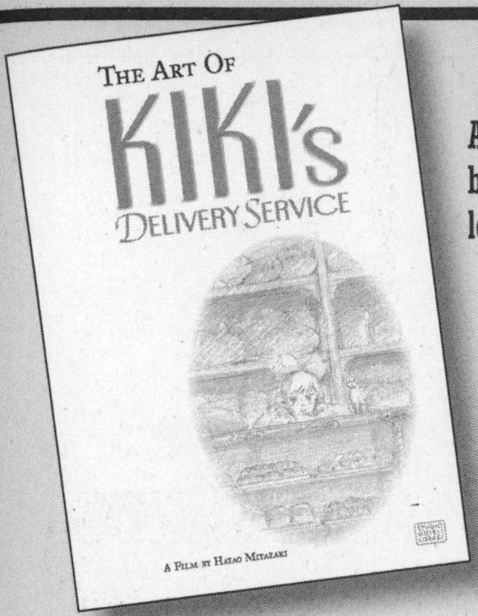
The Art Of
Kiki's
Delivery Service
A Film by Hayao Miyazaki

A lavishly illustrated hardbound book with a behind-the-scenes look at the film!

Hardcover $29.99!

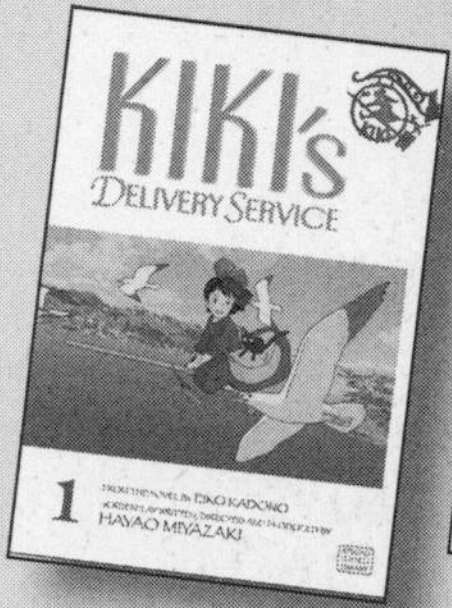
Kiki's
Delivery Service
1
Hayao Miyazaki

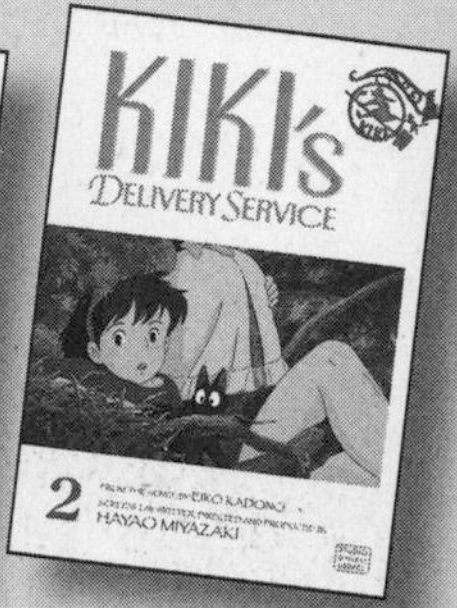
Kiki's
Delivery Service
2
Hayao Miyazaki

Relive Kiki's adventure with these full-color comics

Only $9.99!

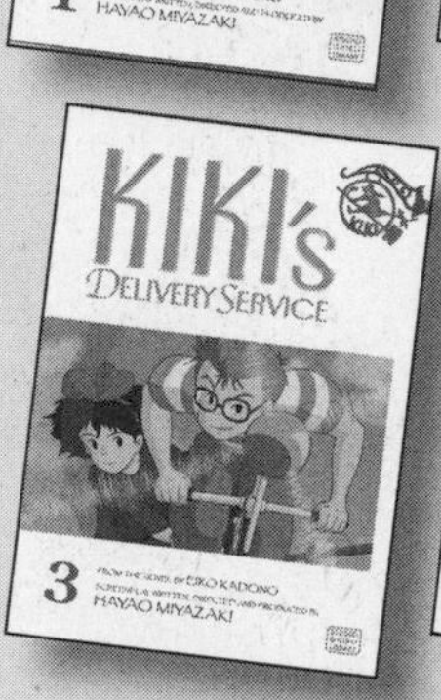
Kiki's
Delivery Service
3
Hayao Miyazaki

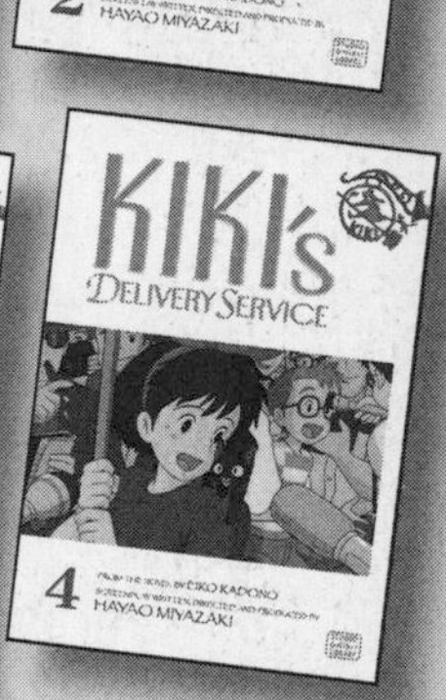
Kiki's
Delivery Service
4
Hayao Miyazaki

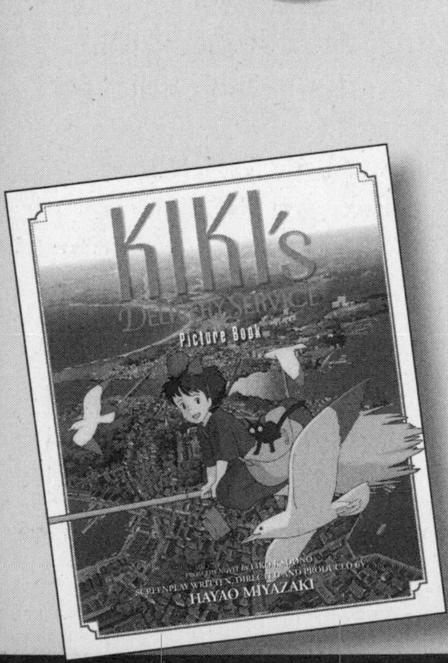
Kiki's
Delivery Service
Picture Book
Hayao Miyazaki

A hardbound book featuring actual artwork from the animated movie

Hardcover $14.99

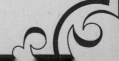